PRAISE FOR *THE UNQ*

'A tale of rich complexity... intrica[...]
revealed' – **Luke McCallin, author** [...]

'Stunning, both for its beautiful writing and for the visceral brutality and terror of its subject matter, *The Unquiet Dead* reads more like fine literature than standard crime novel. This book is an experience, not just a novel, and deserves a close reading' – *The Crime Review*

'*The Unquiet Dead* is a powerful and haunting story'
– *Guardian*

'A debut to remember and one that even those who eschew the genre will devour in one breathtaking sitting' – *LA Times*

PRAISE FOR *AMONG THE RUINS*

'A fast-paced, heart-racing mystery with incredible details of Iran and its political upheaval as the backdrop' – *RT Book Reviews*

'A lyrically written look into a country many think of as war-torn and bleak reveals many sides to the place and its people' – *Kirkus*

'Deeply political without becoming pedantic, Khan's crime novel offers a fictionalized yet very real look at a region that is steeped in both beauty and misery' – *Library Journal Starred Review*

PRAISE FOR *THE LANGUAGE OF SECRETS*

'Thought-provoking, intelligent plot' – *Daily Mail*

'A superb follow-up to the first novel in the series, perfectly balancing lyrical prose with intense thriller pacing for a brilliantly handled,

'Khan deli[...] [...]nented by
strong [...] *Press*

Also by Ausma Zehanat Khan
The Unquiet Dead
The Language of Secrets
A Death in Sarajevo (novella)
Among the Ruins

The Khorasan Archives Fantasy Series
The Bloodprint
The Black Khan

NO
PLACE
OF
REFUGE

An Esa Khattak and Rachel Getty Mystery

AUSMA ZEHANAT KHAN

NO EXIT PRESS

First published in the UK in 2019 by
No Exit Press, an imprint of Oldcastle Books Ltd,
Harpenden, UK.

noexit.co.uk

Previously published in the USA as *A Dangerous Crossing*

ISBN
978-0-85730-199-4 (print)
978-0-85730-200-7 (epub)

Typeset in 10.9pt Minion Pro
by Avocet Typeset, Somerton, Somerset, TA11 6RT
Printed and bound in Great Britain by Clays Ltd, Elcograf S.p.A.

Want to hear more from No Exit Press?
Sign up for our newsletter at noexit.co.uk/newsletter

To Elizabeth,
for everything,
from the beginning to now

Going is not going,
Nor staying, staying,
Bejan Matur, 'Lament'

Prologue

Eftalou Beach
Lesvos, Greece

Ali watched from the beach as Audrey made her way down the hill. She crossed under the sign that passed for welcome on Afghan Hill. It was a lacklustre attempt at a rainbow, the words 'Safe Passage' painted in several languages. In French, they were wished 'Bon Voyage,' in German 'Gute Reise.' The language of most use was the Afghan language, Dari, and the words 'Khuda Hafiz' translated more closely to 'May God Be Your Protector.' Afghan Hill on Lesvos was named for the refugees who'd traveled the route from Afghanistan. They slept in the muddy groves on the hill, their shelters pierced by rain. They didn't complain: they knew God was watching over them. It was how they'd gotten this far.

Ali had been following Audrey Clare since her arrival on Lesvos four months ago; she was a case worker from Canada, assisting Syrian refugees through the work of her NGO. He liked her because she didn't make false promises – she was blunt with the kids who were old enough to take it, boys like him who were almost men. She had a sincerity that made him think if he ended up somewhere safe, he wanted it to be Canada.

Audrey was smart too; she'd picked up a few phrases in Dari. When she came across kids roaming through the camps, she warned them with a smile that made him think of a fairy. Her small frame masked a grim determination. He knew this because he'd made himself indispensable: he acted as Audrey's translator.

9

Her NGO was called Woman to Woman, and its headquarters was at Kara Tepe, with a smaller office on Chios. She divided her time between Lesvos and Chios; once a week she made the trek out to Moria. The refugee compound inside Moria was separated from the sprawl on Afghan Hill by concrete barriers. It had formerly been a prison. Now only members of recognized NGOs were permitted entry into Moria. Audrey moved between the camps without fuss: Moria, Kara Tepe, Pikpa, Souda. Her NGO worked mainly with women. Ali qualified for her help only because of Israa. At the age of seventeen, he was the least significant of the refugees on the hill, in the boats out at sea, or stalled in the endless registration lines. The closest he'd get to refuge was the other side of Afghan Hill.

He wasn't planning on staying in the camps. Kara Tepe wasn't deliverance; it was a necessary evil, a pit stop on a journey abounding in necessary evils. No one stayed on Lesvos unless the sea was too dangerous to cross. They came to the islands with the goal of making it to Continental Europe. On Lesvos, they were given papers, blankets, and a good meal in the food tent that doubled as a dance hall. They may have been victims of circumstance, but they hadn't forgotten how to celebrate transient moments of joy.

Audrey Clare understood this. She'd brought music to Kara Tepe. She'd brought coloring books and crayons and gallons of hot chocolate, and a rare fluency in bureaucratic language. She knew the transit routes better than anyone else he'd met. She also knew Fortress Europe had barred its gates – there was no way onward now. Even if the gates were flung open, Ali couldn't leave. He had to wait with Sami and Aya, until he found Israa again.

Audrey was wise enough to know this. She was helping him look for Israa, asking questions of everyone she met: bakers, villagers, fishermen, ambulance drivers, policemen, representatives of the Hellenic Rescue Team, UN officials, members of the Italian Coast Guard, the loosely coordinated volunteers who came from Northern Europe.

She was meeting the boats at his side, and she kept her own list of names.

She'd told him to stay put; he was doing his best to listen.

He stamped his feet, waiting for Audrey to reach him. His jacket wasn't warm enough for the cold, and he'd yielded his blanket to Aya, Israa's sister. He'd grabbed another one from a tent when no one was looking, but as soon as he did this, he felt ashamed, remembering the volunteer from Denmark who'd slept in a chair so Aya could use her blanket and take her spot on the couch.

The Danish girl, Freja, was little short of an angel. She'd called them a tent full of miracles, a word most people didn't use.

If he reached Canada, he'd write to Freja to thank her. He kept a notebook full of the volunteers' information. He did this not just for himself, but for the members of his family who might one day make the journey out of Syria: some were trapped in ISIS territory, others under the barrage of Assad's bombs. If his cousins made it out, he hoped Freja would remember him and show them the same kindness she'd shown him.

Audrey found him with Sami, waiting for the boat on the waves to spot the rescue team. Vinny was already in the water. The figure deep in the waves was Illario, who always took point on the boats. Peter and Hans were farther up the beach, using flashlights to guide the boat to shore.

Audrey caught at his hand, demanding his attention. From the anxious knitting of her eyebrows, he knew she had something to tell him.

'Did you find her?' He was frightened to know the answer.

She held up her satellite phone. 'The Interpol agent I told you about is waiting for us at Kara Tepe. She needs to talk to you.'

Ali swung back to the sea. The boat was fifty feet out, riding the silver-blue of the waves, too far to see the faces of passengers.

'Israa might be on the boat.'

Audrey didn't agree, but he wasn't going to argue. 'You go ahead. I'll meet you at Kara Tepe once I've checked the boat. The others might need help.'

Audrey tried to convince him. 'This is really important.'

He nodded over at Sami. 'Go with her. You get started, I'm coming.' She was reluctant to leave without him, but she knew him well enough to know he couldn't be pulled away. Each new boat brought with it the hope that Israa had survived. He couldn't leave the beach until he knew beyond doubt.

Sami followed Audrey up the road. He wasn't agile like Ali; the movement of his limbs was tentative, as if his bones had been newly rearranged.

'Hurry,' Audrey called back.

Another boat, another dead end. The road that ran along the beach was deserted, and all the time the sky was changing, its velvety shadows deepening, the half-moon lost behind the clouds. Ali was tired after his efforts, but he was anxious to hear Audrey's news. Then he'd find the tent he shared with his friends, and with the old man and his grandchildren. The children's mother had drowned on the crossing, their father had been killed in Syria. The shelter they shared was crowded, but it was safe and clean, and warmer than the tents on Afghan Hill. He'd made friends with the boys who camped out on the hill – he wasn't about to complain.

He was almost at Kara Tepe when he heard the sharp report of the shots. Two gunshots in a row.

He began to run. There was noise and movement ahead, coming from Audrey's shelter. He reached it before anyone else did, flinging open the door.

There were bodies on the ground: one woman, one man.

He looked the bodies over, blinking back tears, moving quickly. They had fallen on their backs, side by side, the gunshot wounds oozing blood. There was nothing he could do to save them, so he did what he had to do.

The flap at the back fluttered. A scream sounded outside. The camp was dark, just beginning to react to the noise. He caught a flash of Audrey's yellow coat as the clouds passed overhead. She stumbled down the path behind the camp, her gumboots slipping in the mud.

People began to stir, but no one left their shelters. They were in survival mode, unable to think of others. The volunteers would respond, but he didn't know how long that might take.

Audrey was headed to the water. If he ducked back the way he'd come, there was a shortcut to the main road. He passed people rushing up the road. Peter, Shukri, Vincenzo – his partners on the beach. He evaded their questions – Audrey was in trouble. He shouted at them to head to Woman to Woman, then he cut across the hill, using the switchback.

He was running on instinct; he couldn't see in the dark. The trees threw up veiled shadows, their branches dancing wildly under a star-strewn sky.

He caught a glimpse of Audrey's coat in the light, and the breathless sound of her sob. She tore off her coat. Some instinct told him not to call to her.

At a gap in the switchback, a shadow moved away from the hills. It closed the distance between Ali and Audrey, a metallic gleam glinting off the object in its hand. Whoever had fired the gunshots was chasing Audrey with a gun.

Her pursuer was letting her run, herding her to the road.

His breath tight in his chest, Ali's chase became a sprint. She was pulling out of reach, but she came to a halt at a sound from the road.

The hill and track were deserted. She sprang off the track to flag a car. Ali tried to make it out. It made its slow approach with its lights off.

The driver jumped out. Ali hurled himself down the hill, breaking through the cover of the trees. Pebbles scattered to his left. He stopped mid-descent, trying to pinpoint the source.

Where was Audrey's pursuer?

A heavy hand clipped his head. His head down, he fell to his knees.

The shadow leapt past him to the road. He heard the sounds of a scuffle, echoed by a startled cry. A door slammed with a heavy thud. Tires scraped the road. The vehicle reversed and sped away.

Ali searched the cool, blue landscape of the beach. The shadow had disappeared.

Audrey Clare was gone.

1

Ottawa, Canada

RACHEL GETTY HAD NEVER EXPECTED to find herself at a state dinner at Rideau Hall, the governor general's residence. Even though she was at the tail end of the dinner, mingling with other guests, she found herself bemused, silenced by the splendor of the hall and by the amiability of the prime minister.

They'd left the long white dinner table with its golden candelabra and thickets of crystal glasses for an alcove under ivory arches, the whole scene illuminated by cascading chandeliers. It was pomp and circumstance on a scale familiar to most Canadians, gracious yet subdued.

That didn't stop Rachel from feeling overwhelmed, as she peered, tongue-tied, into the affable face of the strikingly young prime minister. Trying not to draw attention to herself, she smoothed her hands down the length of her black evening dress, cut simply, and had Rachel known it, showcasing her athletic figure to great effect. She wore a pair of dangling earrings given to her by her brother, Zachary, and had even taken the trouble to style her lackluster hair into a smooth chignon.

Earlier, during the photo opportunity portion of this unexpected evening, she and her boss, Inspector Esa Khattak, had posed for a photograph with the prime minister and his wife.

Rachel's sense of being out of her depth was diminished by the matter-of-fact welcome extended by both the prime minister and his wife, whose Quebecois accent fell charmingly on Rachel's ear.

A few moments later, Rachel found herself in the alcove with Khattak and the prime minister. The two men were discussing the current status of Community Policing, the division of law enforcement Rachel and Khattak worked for. Despite a period of trial, Community Policing was back on its feet. A recent parliamentary inquiry into a war criminal's death had exonerated Khattak of wrongdoing, and of late, CPS had been subjected to better press than usual. Khattak was back on the job with accolades in his file.

Rachel suspected this had more to do with a government contact they had assisted on a recent case in Iran than with any change to Khattak's approach to police work. His administrative leave was over, and the budget of their section had been enlarged – they had brought back two of their original team members.

Across the glittering table in the dining hall, Rachel caught the eye of Community Policing's tech supervisor, a burly middle-aged man of unfailing good cheer and deadpan wisecracking abilities by the name of Paul Gaffney. He raised his eyebrows, miming a la-di-dah gesture that made Rachel smile before she hastily schooled her features.

She listened to the pleasant timbre of the prime minister's voice as he offered assurances to Khattak.

'I want you to know how grateful we are for the work you've done,' he was saying. 'The portfolio we landed you with is a minefield. You haven't had the kind of ministerial support you're entitled to for being bold enough to take it on. As of now, that will change. You will still report to the minister of justice, but we will be amending the legislation that governs CPS's mandate to make it simpler and clearer. We don't want a repeat of what happened in Algonquin. I've also told the minister that you're to have a direct line to me in case of any obstruction.' He flashed his charming smile at Rachel. 'Should Esa be out of commission for any reason, it's been made clear to the minister that you are to have unfettered access.'

Rachel expressed her thanks. In the politest politician-speak possible, the prime minister was letting her know that he thought the inquiry into their work had been a fiasco. What was the point of bringing on someone like Khattak only to constrain him at every turn?

She breathed a sigh of contentment. Rachel's personal philosophy was liberal in every sense. The prime minister didn't need to charm her – he already had her vote. She listened as Khattak thanked him in his deep, attractive voice. He was dressed in black tie, his dark hair smoothed back across his head. He looked more like a television star than a policeman.

'It was kind of you to invite our team to dinner.'

The dinner was being held in honor of a delegation from South Asia, so Rachel suspected Khattak's presence served the government's interests, as much as anything else.

The prime minister hailed RCMP Superintendent Martine Killiam across the room. She didn't smile, offering a quick nod of acknowledgment. When her gaze landed on Rachel, one corner of her mouth quirked up. Martine Killiam kept her eye on promising women in law enforcement: Rachel was on her radar. Not quite sure what to do, Rachel sketched a non-military salute that brought the prime minister's attention back to her.

'I see you know Superintendent Killiam,' he said.

Rachel cleared her throat. Any mention of the murder at Algonquin Park would cast a dark cloud over a festive occasion, so her reply was cautious.

'A little.'

'She speaks very highly of you. And she's not the only one.'

The prime minister raised a hand, inviting a latecomer to join their conference.

Rachel recognized him at once. It was Nathan Clare as she'd never seen him, formally dressed in evening wear, a serious look in his eyes.

The prime minister turned a rueful glance on Khattak.

'Politicians always have ulterior motives. Our government owes Nathan a debt – one he's come to collect. I thought I'd make it official, so this time there's no confusion with regard to your involvement.'

Rachel's sense of awkwardness fell away; she observed the prime minister with interest.

'A case?'

And then she looked at Nathan in alarm. He was Khattak's closest friend, a public figure very much in demand, but her attachment to him was personal.

He didn't look at her, his attention focused on Khattak.

'You have to help me, Esa. Something's happened to Audrey.'

2

Ottawa, Canada

THEY MOVED THEIR DISCUSSION TO the Café France, a quiet bistro overlooking the canal. The three of them were seated in armchairs clustered around a wooden table, a hastily conjured pot of coffee placed at Nathan's elbow. Nate had pressed Rachel's hand, but otherwise ignored her.

She took out her notebook and began to make notes as she listened to the two men talk. Nate's pleasant face was tight with strain; one hand worked to loosen the bow tie from his neck. He threw it down on the table, and for a moment Rachel's thoughts were of her own preoccupations.

Nate had never seen her dressed in evening wear. She didn't kid herself that she was a heart-stopping beauty, but even her younger brother Zachary had taken a look at her trying on her dress and whistled his appreciation. She hadn't expected to see Nate tonight, but she thought he might have noticed the difference in her appearance.

She swallowed her disappointment. It was only right he was thinking of his sister.

'You've been away,' Khattak said. 'Searching for Audrey?'

'I should have shut down that NGO months ago,' Nate said. 'Part of this is Ruksh's fault.'

Rukhshanda Khattak was Esa's sister. Their younger sisters were as close as Nate and Esa were.

Khattak didn't react. The panic beneath Nate's accusation was palpable.

'Start at the beginning. What can you tell us about Audrey's disappearance?'

'You've been away,' Nate said impatiently. 'Audrey got herself involved in the government's push to bring refugees from Syria to Canada. She wanted Woman to Woman to play a leading role in resettlement work. She went to Greece last December, to facilitate the intake process. There was a lot of pressure to meet the government's end-of-year deadline.'

'I remember. Why are you so sure she's missing?'

'Let me tell it, then you'll know,' Nate snapped.

Rachel poured him a cup of coffee and passed it across the table. He took a sip.

'Her e-mails and phone calls stopped. Lesvos was her last known location. No one has seen her or talked to her. No one knows where she is.'

Khattak asked a blunt question. 'How does this fit with Community Policing's mandate?'

Nate swore out loud. 'You can't possibly be thinking of your jurisdiction, this is *Audrey* we're talking about.'

'Nate.' Esa laid a hand over Nathan's. 'There's more to this, isn't there? That's all I'm trying to get at. There's a reason you have the prime minister's backing.'

The same thought had occurred to Rachel. Their handsome young prime minister had his own reasons for asking them to the dinner.

Nate took a shallow breath. 'Two people were found dead at Woman to Woman headquarters on the island of Lesvos. One was a French Interpol agent. The other was a young man from Syria whose case Audrey was supervising. Their bodies were discovered the same day she went missing. The Greek police believe there's a connection.'

Rachel looked up from scribbling in her notebook. 'So

Audrey's implicated. They think she's responsible.'

Nate's hands clenched around his coffee mug. He spoke to Khattak. 'You and I know that's not possible. She's been taken. And I don't know what to do.'

Rachel swallowed. There were tears in Nate's hazel eyes, and fine lines etched on either side of his mouth. He was drawing dire conclusions based on minimal evidence.

She knew this moment, this feeling – her brother Zachary had been missing for seven years. His absence had hollowed out her life, an agonizing period of dislocation between the stages of missing and returned.

She was overcome by a powerful surge of emotion. She wished she were alone with Nate. She wanted to show him she understood, in a way that Khattak couldn't.

Instead, she cleared her throat and said with forced cheer, 'It's important not to give up hope.' She meant to infuse him with her strength of belief, but he turned on her at once.

'Is it? This isn't like Zachary going missing on the streets of Toronto by choice. This is Audrey in a camp on the islands, or dead somewhere in Izmir, or God forbid, taken hostage at the Syrian border. There's no reason for your optimism.'

'Nate, stop.'

Khattak cut across this catechism. Rachel swallowed back her hurt. Nate's attack wasn't personal. He was thinking of his sister, just as she'd spent years thinking first and foremost of Zach. She focused her attention on her notebook, letting Khattak take Nate through his story.

Audrey had visited the island of Lesvos in her capacity as chief operating officer of an NGO called Woman to Woman, funded by the Clare Foundation. The NGO had been operating on Lesvos for a year, staffed by a young Canadian named Shukri Danner, herself a former refugee.

Audrey's visit was meant to assist in speeding up the intake process, identifying refugees with documentation from the United Nations High Commission for Refugees. Syrian refugees fleeing their country's civil war could be fast-tracked for resettlement in Canada, if they met certain criteria. Audrey had met with UNHCR representatives, with dozens of local volunteers, and with hundreds of refugees, not all of them Syrian. She'd spent time assessing Woman to Woman's needs; she had also evaluated Shukri Danner's effectiveness in her role as lead agent on the ground.

She'd been in Greece since December, and though she'd called and written her brother regularly, often about some aspect of the NGO's work, she hadn't returned to Canada in the months before her disappearance. Nor had Nate found the time to visit Greece. His last contact with Audrey had been two weeks ago.

'You spoke to Shukri yourself?' Khattak asked.

'To Shukri, to volunteers she passed me on to, to anyone I could get hold of by phone. No one will admit to knowing anything.'

'Was Shukri at headquarters when the bodies were found?'

Nate gave a bitter laugh. 'Do you know what headquarters consists of? It's a white tent with these plastic windows that ridiculously resemble the ones at our house. There's a logo, there's communication equipment, there's a few cots and desks, and a few boxes of paperwork that have nearly been shredded by rain. No, Shukri wasn't there. She was in Mytilene, the capital.'

'Do you know why?'

Nate's expression became sullen. 'She wouldn't tell me.'

Small wonder, Rachel thought – if he'd spoken to Shukri Danner with the same combination of misplaced anger and blame he was using on Rachel, Shukri would have been reluctant to tell him anything. Though Nate had helped with their cases in the past, he wasn't a trained investigator. She wasn't sure he could recognize when a suspect was lying, or how to break through layers of defensiveness or fear.

She could see why the prime minister had given them carte

blanche. She was thinking of Shukri as a suspect, and that was the least of their troubles.

If a prominent Canadian's sister had disappeared while working to facilitate resettlement, it would bring the entire Syrian refugee program under scrutiny. There were persistent voices in Canada who'd decried the government's campaign promises from the outset. The prime minister had been accused of rushing the resettlement through without sufficient vetting of prospective refugees. This was the kind of ammunition needed to pressure a shutdown of the program.

The whole thing made Rachel's head ache. She had to remind herself that it was a Syrian who had been found dead, not Audrey Clare. It was a lesson in perspective, but she was a seasoned enough officer to comprehend the optics.

If the program went without a hitch and refugees were resettled in Canada without incident, it would shower the prime minister with glory. But if problems cropped up – a breach of national security, an unexpected drain on resources, the inability of newcomers to find suitable employment – the ensuing outcry could bring the government down.

The prime minister had staked a great deal on Canada's global reputation.

And on Canadian values, Rachel reminded herself. They had started all this with assistance to the Vietnamese in another era.

The response to the government's Syria initiative had been overwhelmingly positive. Ordinary Canadians had lined up to organize private sponsorships of refugees, angry at the government for not doing enough to alleviate the refugee crisis.

It had come to a head with the shattering image of a dead child on a Turkish beach. Aylan Kurdi had drowned attempting to cross the Mediterranean with his family. When news that the Kurdis had applied for refugee status in Canada and been refused became public, it resulted in a national outpouring of support for the resettlement of refugees in Canada.

The voices in opposition had been silenced for a time, but their private outrage at the influx of refugees hadn't dimmed. Wherever possible, they used the term 'migrant' instead of 'refugee.' And whenever an opening provided itself, they raised the specter of terrorists slipping through the net to wreak havoc on Canadian soil.

Khattak's sharp question cut into Rachel's reflections.

'Where is Shukri now?'

'She's been detained by Interpol in Greece.'

Khattak's eyebrows went up. 'She's alone?'

'Not quite. I found a local lawyer and interpreter to represent her.' That sounded more like the Nate she knew.

'We'll fly over at once, now that we've been asked to speak to Interpol. And we'll get Gaffney and Byrne to do some digging here.'

Nate's gaze had drifted to the glow of lights above the canal. Now it returned to Khattak.

'I'm just wondering –'

'What?'

It seemed to Rachel that Nate was consciously turning away from her. He hunched up his shoulders, shifting his long limbs in his armchair. 'Before you take that step, there may be something worth pursuing in Toronto.'

'Tell me.'

The warmth in Khattak's voice would encourage the most reluctant witness to come clean, Rachel thought. Nate was his dearest friend – there was no reason for him not to speak.

'Audrey wrote me about this boy from Syria, the one who was killed,' Nate said.

'I thought a man was found dead at Woman to Woman.'

'He's young so it's hard to say. It's sometimes difficult for refugees to collect the necessary documents. Audrey thought of him as a boy. She was hoping to establish he had family in Canada, otherwise his chances of getting through were slim.'

24

'Were they difficult to find?' Rachel asked, wanting Nate to involve her. He directed his answer at Khattak.

'That's just it. When I tracked the family down, they denied knowing the boy.'

'Couldn't that be true?'

There was a faint aura of tension in the café – Rachel knew it was due to how Nate was interacting with her. He was uncomfortable, even a little angry, as if he didn't want her there; maybe he'd speak more freely if she left.

She contemplated getting up and offering him some privacy. But there was a dogged persistence about Rachel: she'd worked hard at her relationship with Nate. She wasn't going to abandon it at the first hurdle. She cared about Audrey and she had expertise to offer, both as a police officer and as a sister who knew what it meant to search for a loved one.

Khattak intervened. 'I'll need to see your correspondence with Audrey. And I'll need you to take me through everything you remember from her phone calls.' He addressed Rachel. 'Could you make the arrangements for our travel to Lesvos?'

Nate scowled at Esa. 'You're not going to interview the family?'

'I know it's not easy, but try to look at it clearly. We'll follow every lead, but we need to prioritize the prime minister's request. We should speak to the Greek police and to Interpol as soon as possible. We'll also need to interview Shukri Danner.'

Nate straightened up in his chair. 'I'll give you everything I have. And I'll make arrangements for you, you don't need to trouble Rachel.'

Startled, Khattak answered, 'I'll need Rachel's help.'

Nate flicked a shamefaced glance at Rachel. 'There's someone else on Lesvos who'll be able to help you.' He pushed his coffee cup away. 'I sent Sehr to Mytilene to find Shukri a lawyer, she'll meet you when you get there.'

Khattak should have been glad, Rachel thought. Sehr Ghilzai was a friend of his, and she was Woman to Woman's legal counsel. She'd cut through any red tape they might face, sort the jurisdictional issues. But a faint reserve settled in Khattak's eyes.

'You sent Sehr to the islands?'

'She speaks Arabic, Esa. She's indispensable to our work.'

Was he wondering if Nate was trying his hand at matchmaking? Nate's explanation was reasonable, and Rachel, for one, would be glad of Sehr's help. She was smart and insightful without being intrusive. She was also in love with Khattak.

'That's great.' Rachel hurried past Khattak's reluctance. 'Why was an Interpol agent found with a kid from Syria? Do you know how they were killed?'

Nate stumbled over the answer.

'Audrey took a firearm to the islands, I bought it for her protection. Both the Interpol agent and the boy were shot with Audrey's gun.'

3

Ottawa, Canada

ESA WALKED ALONG THE CANAL, Rachel and Nate at his side. They approached the Chateau Laurier, where Nate was staying. He and Rachel were booked in more humble accommodations, but given his friend's state of worry and preoccupation, he thought it best to walk with him to the Chateau. He was glad Nate was flying back to Toronto in the morning; he'd appeared at the state dinner as a courtesy to the prime minister, but his thoughts were frantic with worry for his sister, just as Esa's were preoccupied by Ruksh. Esa's sister was a doctor, specializing in infectious diseases. He couldn't see how she would be involved in Audrey's disappearance.

'What did you mean about Ruksh? Why do you say she's to blame?' A late night in spring meant the city was still cool, though the trees that lined the canal had begun to bud, their shapely limbs stretching to the stars. He had turned up the collar of his coat, and was careful to accommodate his pace to Rachel's less practical footwear. He didn't know why Nate was trying to distance himself from Rachel, but he would find out when they were alone. Their lives were getting tangled up in ways that weren't confined to the fact that they worked together. Esa supposed it was inevitable. He'd long since concluded that his relationship with Rachel was unlike any other in his life.

Nate shrugged his shoulders inside his cashmere topcoat. 'I'm sorry, that was a stupid thing to say.'

'But?'

Nate shrugged again. He kicked at a stone in his path, watching it sail into a gutter.

'She's the one who got Audrey worked up about the war. She talked about the refugee crisis until it was the only thing on Audrey's mind. You didn't know this?'

Esa shook his head. He and Ruksh hadn't spoken since before he'd left on his trip to Iran. He'd called her several times; she'd refused to answer. But he *had* seen the effect his sister's engagement with the refugee crisis had on their mother: Angeza Khattak was a member of a private sponsorship group; she dedicated a great deal of her time to working with the family her group had sponsored.

A bitter note in his voice, Nate added, 'Audrey was the one who visited the camps, while Ruksh hasn't left Toronto.'

Esa didn't point out that his mother had strenuously discouraged Ruksh from volunteering. She didn't often impose her will on her children; that she'd been successful in this case surprised him. He knew Ruksh likely held him responsible for their mother's position, but in this instance he was blameless.

'They'll have been in touch. I'll talk to Ruksh and find out.'

Nate grimaced. 'You should have Rachel talk to her. She's more likely to get through.'

'Why? Won't Ruksh talk to you, either?'

A fleeting grin crossed Nate's face. 'She sees us as one and the same: overbearing older brothers.'

Esa smiled too. 'We've had to be. They were a pair of nitwits in their teens.' There was an undercurrent of laughter in his voice.

He caught Rachel's sideways glance. She looked a little wistful, but the moment she caught his eyes on her, she smoothed out her expression. Rachel had never had anyone to watch out for her, but she hated the thought of his feeling sorry for her, something he'd learned the first time they'd met.

'She *would* talk to you,' he said to Rachel. 'She owes you her life, after all.'

His sister had a knack for making him lose his temper, no matter how he tried to keep his cool. If he did, it would shut down any discussion in a heartbeat. And it had occurred to Esa that despite Nate's worry, it was possible Audrey had disappeared for reasons of her own.

Like Ruksh, she was inquisitive, independent and stubbornly insistent on doing things her own way. Suppose the Interpol agent had raised questions about the boy who'd fled Syria as a refugee. If Audrey had formed an attachment to him, she might have been looking for answers. Or she might have found the bodies in the tent, and fled for her own safety.

There were a limited number of explanations for her disappearance, and though she wouldn't deliberately cause Nathan to worry over her, it might not have occurred to Audrey that Nate would assume the worst. Nate was ten years older than Audrey; he'd taken care of her since their parents had died in an accident abroad. Nate and Audrey were much closer than Esa and Ruksh were, but there had been times when Audrey had chafed at her brother's close supervision, particularly as their professional lives were entangled. Woman to Woman was run by Audrey, but it was funded by Nate. It was possible Audrey had wanted to resolve the situation on Lesvos on her own. It was what Ruksh would have done.

But would Audrey have left Shukri Danner to the mercies of a foreign authority? He didn't think so. If she had, her reasons must have been compelling.

'I don't think your sister likes me much, sir,' Rachel ventured.

'Audrey did.'

It was the first thing Nate had said to her that contained his usual warmth. Rachel didn't demur. Nor did she point out that he'd spoken in the past tense.

'Well, in that case, I'll do my best to talk to Ruksh.'

The lobby was filled with guests who'd returned from Rideau Hall. A bouquet of exotic perfumes filled the space, echoed by the fragrance of dahlias. The chandeliers and wall sconces were lit; they cast a throbbing light over deep-cushioned velvet chairs.

The concierge hurried to supply Nate's room key, a simper on his face. His eyes widened as he caught sight of Khattak in evening dress; Esa offered a non-committal smile. The concierge leaned over to Nate, adopting a confidential tone.

'Miss Stoicheva won't be joining you tonight?'

Nate's hand froze in the act of reaching for his key. 'What? No.' His face stiff, he didn't look at Esa. But he cast a swift glance over his shoulder. For a moment something had broken through his consuming fear for Audrey. If he'd rekindled his affair with Laine, he didn't want Rachel to know. He wouldn't want *Esa* to know. Nate was a terrible liar, so Esa didn't afford Nate the opportunity to lie. Audrey's safety was paramount. He asked a different question.

'How did Audrey get a gun into Greece?'

4

Toronto, Canada

PAUL GAFFNEY SAUNTERED OVER TO Rachel's desk. He'd been seconded to Community Policing from the RCMP's cybersecurity division. The work he did at CPS was less challenging than his portfolio with the RCMP, but two successive cardiac arrests had ensured he didn't mind the change of pace. He was nearing sixty-five, but he was far too valuable for anyone to suggest his retirement. The secondary posting to CPS was the RCMP's version of compromise.

Gaffney had been verging on obesity before his hospitalization. A new diet and a healthier attitude toward exercise had seen him shed the excess weight. Rachel had begged him to join her on the ice for a game of scrimmage, but he'd taken up snowshoeing instead. He'd told her it was safer on his knees, and he had a cottage in Huntsville at the gateway to Algonquin. Now his sharp blue eyes twinkled down at her as he hefted himself onto her desk.

'It's good to have you back, Gaff.'

'Wasn't expecting a parliamentary welcome, was I?'

Gaffney wore the uniform he wanted to wear, in his case a pair of slacks and a decidedly ugly Christmas sweater, topped by a navy blue Maple Leafs ball cap that Rachel thoroughly approved of.

'Not so bad for a man in your line of work. Rideau Hall and a lovely lady on your arm.'

31

'I'll have you know that lady was my wife.'

Rachel grinned. She knew Gaffney's diminutive wife, Meera, quite well. They'd kept each other company in the cardiac unit during Gaffney's operation. She was every bit as bossy as Gaff was laid-back and slapdash. Meera had convinced her conservative Indian parents to allow her to marry Gaffney when she was only nineteen. He freely admitted to anyone who would listen that Meera was his whole life.

'Do you want to take a look?' Gaffney dropped a pile of stapled-together papers on her desk. Rachel moved her cup of coffee to make sure it didn't spill on the printouts.

Nate had given them unfettered access to his e-mail account. Khattak had asked Gaff to separate out the e-mails that dealt with three subjects: Audrey's discussions with Shukri Danner, any reference to the young man from Syria or any allusion to the Interpol agent from France.

Nate had supplied them with the relevant names: the boy was Sami al-Nuri, the woman Aude Bertin. The rest of Nate's correspondence with Audrey needed to be read in chronological order, dating from her departure to Lesvos. The search had taken Gaff less than five minutes. Now, while Rachel sorted through his findings, he'd trace the origin of each of Audrey's e-mails.

Khattak wasn't in, he was driving down after his meeting at the prime minister's, so Rachel settled in for a long read, munching the chocolate-dip donut she'd collected on her way to work, while Gaffney tut-tutted her breakfast choices. Rachel ignored him: there was nothing worse than a reformed junk food addict.

She felt a little guilty about reading Nate's private e-mails, but as she made her first scan through the printed material, she saw that though the Clare siblings had written each other most days, their e-mails were short and to the point, primarily occupied with the business of their NGO. At his most affectionate, Nate called his sister 'sprite,' and Rachel now remembered that the first time she'd met Audrey Clare in a bar as the prelude to an uncomfortable scene between Khattak and his friends, Khattak had called Audrey by the same nickname.

She was a little startled to discover that most of the e-mails were about money. When Audrey had first arrived on Chios, she'd taken stock of the efficacy of Woman to Woman's work, and promptly decided they were short of everything: staff, supplies, interpreters, and the basics for making it through the winter. She'd sent an itemized list of her requirements to the NGO's accountant, and copied Nate on the e-mail. He'd signed off on the request the same day, transferring additional funds into the NGO's account.

Rachel read the list closely. It included winterized tents and camping equipment; generators; portable printers, copiers, and fax machines; a surprisingly large order of flashlights and batteries; blankets; winter clothes and shoes; a sundry list of office supplies; and a catalog of pharmaceutical drugs. There was also a request for two hundred mobile phones, with the pay-as-you-go cards to supply them.

Rachel pondered this. She knew the NGO had minimal staff on the islands, too few to make use of Audrey's inventory. A follow-up e-mail confirmed her hunch. The supplies were given to refugees. As the new year came and went, Nate continued to accept requests for additional stores. His casualness made Rachel wonder at the extent of the Clares' wealth. Over the course of a few months, he'd authorized spending to the tune of three hundred thousand dollars. That kind of money led to complications.

Sure enough, Rachel came across a tense exchange between the siblings in February. Audrey had asked Nate to approve a single large expenditure, the cost of a forty-thousand-dollar motorboat. Nate had responded that such a purchase could not be attributed to the NGO's work, or registered as a legitimate expense. Rachel read through the transcript, highlighting certain passages.

From: AudreyClare@womantowoman.com
To: NathanClare@nathanclare.com
Date: Saturday, February 12, 2016 at 9:12 am
Subject: Island cruise

Hey big brother, I'm still waiting on approval for the speedboat requisition. I don't have the money, and I don't want to divert the funds we spend on intake. Please approve by tonight.

From: NathanClare@nathanclare.com
To: AudreyClare@womantowoman.com
Date: Saturday, February 12, 2016 at 9:15 am
Subject: Re: Island cruise

Why do you need it, sprite?

From: AudreyClare@womantowoman.com
To: NathanClare@nathanclare.com
Date: Saturday, February 12, 2016 at 9:20 am
Subject: Re: Island cruise

I've told you. I need to get around the islands. What is the issue? So we'll do a little creative accounting. What does that matter when lives are at stake?

From: NathanClare@nathanclare.com
To: AudreyClare@womantowoman.com
Date: Saturday, February 12, 2016 at 9:22 am
Subject: Re: Island cruise

That's precisely what I'm worried about. There are smugglers out there on those waters. I don't want you intercepting them, or doing the work of the Coast Guard. I know you. You'll use the boat to pull people out of the water. That's not what you're there to do.

From: AudreyClare@womantowoman.com
To: NathanClare@nathanclare.com
Date: Saturday, February 12, 2016 at 9:30 am
Subject: Re: Island cruise

Nate, I'm 30 years old, I'm not a child. You have no idea what I'm down here to do. I need the boat. Having my own boat increases my independence and my safety. You've never been miserly before. If you won't release the money, I'll take it out of my trust fund.

From: NathanClare@nathanclare.com
To: AudreyClare@womantowoman.com
Date: Saturday, February 12, 2016 at 9:33 am
Subject: Re: Island cruise

You know me better than that, so I won't take offense. You need my permission to access money from your trust fund – I'm sorry but I'm not giving it. You're all I have left in this world, I won't let you risk your life. You don't deny my suspicions: you do intend to go out there like the Coast Guard. You should be pushing cases for the people who've made the crossing.

From: AudreyClare@womantowoman.com
To: NathanClare@nathanclare.com
Date: Saturday, February 12, 2016 at 9:41 am
Subject: Re: Island cruise

I hate when you get like this. Ruksh and I both do. How long do you and Esa think you can keep sheltering us from the world? You have no idea what I've seen. I need the boat to help Sami, I promise that's all I'm doing. His situation is desperate. You wouldn't understand because you didn't come, you didn't want to leave Rachel. Don't think you can guilt me by making me think you're alone. I need the money, you have to let me have it. Otherwise, I'll ask Ruksh.

From: NathanClare@nathanclare.com
To: AudreyClare@womantowoman.com
Date: Saturday, February 12, 2016 at 9:42 am
Subject: Re: Island cruise

Ruksh won't have it to give you. I'm sorry, but my answer is final. I
don't want you out on the water. You need to be at headquarters,
supervising Shukri. Have you resolved your issues with her? Tell me
about Sami; I'll do what I can to help.

From: AudreyClare@womantowoman.com
To: NathanClare@nathanclare.com
Date: Saturday, February 12, 2016 at 10:01 am
Subject: Re: Island cruise

Forget it. I'll figure out another way. I'll talk to you later.

Rachel found it all very interesting, not least the mention of her
name. It sounded as if the Clare siblings had talked about her, and
though the thought made her squirm, she couldn't deny a twinge
of pleasure. Nate hadn't responded to his sister's provocation,
but she wondered if her name would crop up again. She admired
Nate for having the openness to share these e-mails, knowing
Rachel would read them.

She swallowed the last bite of her donut, her sense of
contentment dimming. Perhaps he'd felt able to do so because
he hadn't mentioned her at all. She knew it was selfish to think
of these things, when Nate was worried about Audrey. She hadn't
forgotten her search for Zach, but Zach lived with her now,
their relationship improving by the day. There was no point
in revisiting the agony of that bleak period before she'd been
recruited to work with Khattak.

Rachel grinned to herself. She hadn't made the best first
impression, but one of the nice things about Khattak was that he

seldom lost his temper; when he did, he inclined more to quiet displeasure. Her childhood had been defined by her father's anger. Khattak's manner was different: thoughtful, courteous, slow-burning. She'd never heard him raise his voice.

She brought her attention back to the e-mails. That couldn't have been the first mention of the boy Sami, could it? The way Audrey referred to him made it clear he'd been the subject of previous discussions.

His situation is desperate.

Of course it was. The situation of anyone who risked crossing the sea in a raft was desperate. But how did Sami stand out from the thousands of refugees who struggled to get to the islands, in hopes of reaching the European continent? There had to be something more to it, something linked to Sami's death.

She didn't dismiss the possibility of Audrey's guilt – she knew Khattak wouldn't want her to. Their different perspectives on a case were the key to their partnership's success.

She set aside the e-mail in question for further discussion with Nate. She went through and read the rest of his correspondence with single-minded focus. There were no earlier or later mentions of Sami, though Nate persisted in asking questions that Audrey chose to ignore. She didn't raise the issue of the boat again, but ten days later there was another query from Nate.

From: NathanClare@nathanclare.com
To: AudreyClare@womantowoman.com
Date: Thursday, February 22, 2016 at 4:16 pm
Subject: Bank withdrawal

Have you been getting some rest? It's been a few days, and your phone goes straight to voicemail. I received a notice from your bank. You've withdrawn $3000 from your personal account. Why?

I hope to God you haven't done something crazy and found yourself
a second-hand boat. I'd give you the money for something top of the
line if I thought you'd do anything so foolish. Please reassure me. Is
Sami OK? You still haven't told me.

There was no corresponding reply from Audrey. Her next few
e-mails resumed her updates on the progress of her work. No
reference was made to other refugees or to Aude Bertin.

Rachel made a note to ask about Nate's banking arrangements.
Why, for example, had he received notification about Audrey's
bank withdrawal? It suggested there was a more controlling side
of Nate she hadn't been exposed to. She didn't like the thought
of it, because it struck too close to home. Audrey was right. She
was perfectly capable of making her own decisions, including
decisions on how to spend her money.

Rachel scribbled on her note pad again. It was worth exploring
whether Audrey received a salary for her work at the NGO, and
how much that salary was. If she didn't, Nate likely held the
purse strings to Audrey's trust fund, and possibly to the bulk
of the Clare wealth. She wondered how such wealth had been
acquired – through his own fame as a writer, or through their
parents' estate? How much wealth were they talking about, when
it wasn't the cost of the boat Nate had balked at, but the uses his
sister might have put it to?

Rachel's resources were adequate for her needs. She wasn't
struggling, but neither was she anything close to well-off. And
now she was supporting Zachary as well, until he made some
headway as an artist.

She felt a secret kinship to Nathan Clare: even if Zach failed
at his chosen profession, she would never kick him out. She
suspected that if Nate was the source of Audrey's financial
independence, he felt the same way about his sister.

He hadn't batted an eyelid at the increasing demands for funds
related to Audrey's pet project. Though the money was being

used for a worthwhile cause, and was doubtlessly tax deductible, not everyone would have agreed to these expenses.

So she'd have to ask questions, nosy, intrusive questions, but she'd better run them by Khattak first, in case he knew the answers. She didn't much like the idea of Nate being involved in this mess – her line of questioning would make him feel like a suspect.

She sighed to herself, drawing Gaffney's attention from his work. He had his feet propped up on his desk, his keyboard in his lap, and he was scrolling through a long line of numbers that made no sense to Rachel.

'What's the matter? Man trouble?'

Rachel narrowed her eyes at him in warning.

'Why do men think that if a woman's a little preoccupied, it's always about a man? I could be thinking of a woman or I could be thinking like a police officer, which is how I spend most of my time.'

Gaffney's blue eyes sparkled with humor. 'I've read the e-mails, remember? I know about you and Nathan Clare.'

'There is no me and Nathan Clare.'

'That's what you think.' Gaff tapped his keyboard. 'What makes you think I gave you *all* the e-mails?'

Rachel paused. Then she realized she was being teased. She'd fallen for it.

Her face flushed bright red.

'You wouldn't be a very good detective if you didn't.'

'I'm not a detective,' he assured her. 'I'm the guy who knows everyone's secrets, remember? The tech guy.'

'Hardly,' Rachel scoffed. 'The tech guy is that guy in the Geek Squad who helps recover your hard drive. You're this under-the-radar genius the RCMP loans out.'

'Exactly.' Gaff tapped his keyboard again. This time the gesture contained a wealth of meaning. 'I didn't just look at the e-mails our friend Mr Clare volunteered. He seems to think that if you delete your e-mails, they vanish from the internet for good. He gave his account a pretty thorough cleaning before he granted us access. Or at least, he tried to.'

Rachel pushed back her chair. She walked over to Gaffney's desk.

'You're saying he deleted e-mails to Audrey? E-mails related to our case?'

Gaffney rubbed his hand over his chin. 'I don't know if they're related to the case, but yes, he deleted a fair bit of his correspondence, most of it to do with financials, some of it to do with you.'

'With me?' Rachel was stalling for time.

'Do you want to take a look at it?'

'Don't we need a warrant? Seems a bit tricky if we're going beyond the parameters of consent.'

Part of her leapt at the opportunity to read Nate's private thoughts. That part she squelched, disgusted with herself. The other part knew that if Nate had deleted some of his e-mails to Audrey, that was relevant to their case.

It made her a little frightened for him. He was hiding something. It might have to do with the gun.

Or it might cast a suspicious light on Audrey's involvement in the deaths of Sami and Agent Bertin.

She was about to cross a line.

'Yes,' Gaff said. 'We'd need a warrant or consent. That's why I didn't hand them over. This chat we're having is off the record. So. Do you want to know about your boyfriend?'

Rachel shot him an exasperated look. 'No, I don't, Gaff. I want to know about the gun.'

Gaff stretched his hands behind his head, balancing his keyboard on his lap. 'There's some administrative correspondence with the Greek authorities about firearm permits. Do you want to see that?'

Rachel thought about this. Her first boss had had no problem with cutting corners or coloring outside the lines; as a result, his unit had acquired a reputation for corruption. Some of the mud had stuck to Rachel; it had taken time to wash off. She knew Gaff would show her the e-mails without mentioning it to anyone else, but she took a certain pride in her own integrity.

'Just collect the e-mails in a folder: all correspondence between Nate and Audrey since December. We'll get consent.' She bit her lip, seeing the pitfalls ahead. 'Or we'll get a warrant.'

5

Ottawa, Canada

ESA'S MEETING AT THE PRIME minister's office ended up taking place with a senior advisor who clearly had better things to do. A dynamic young Quebecois who introduced himself as Jean Cordeau and responded to Khattak with an air of inattention, he paged through several folders on a delicate desk as he spoke. He ushered Khattak to a seat, finally allowing his eyes to come to rest on Khattak's face. Khattak waited to speak until Cordeau passed him the folder in his hands.

'Is this everything I need?'

'Everything: names, dates, contact information for all relevant authorities. I'm sure I don't need to impress upon you the need for discretion in this matter. There are *so* many potential pitfalls, I'm not sure we shouldn't leave the matter alone.'

'I doubt that would be possible, M Cordeau. Better to face Interpol on their ground than ours, if discretion is our priority.' He glanced at the light breaking over the Ottawa River through the windows behind the golden desk. The desk was so delicately sculpted, so graceful in its lines, he catalogued it as an antique. He wondered who'd chosen it. 'And of course, there's the question of Audrey Clare. Even if Interpol wasn't involved, Nathan Clare would raise the issue of his sister's disappearance.'

'Of course.' Cordeau took a sharp breath. 'Which is why the prime minister has extended himself.' He gestured at the folder. 'It's all there. The PM said to make it very clear that you aren't on your own in this. Should Interpol cut up rough, there *will* be contact at the highest levels.'

Khattak tried to set the other man at ease with his assurances. Cordeau looked down at Khattak with a frown. 'My father was a police officer,' he said. 'In the Sûreté. I know these investigations tend to be unpredictable – a double homicide, good God. I don't think the prime minister understands what he's setting loose.'

Khattak had the sense that Cordeau was sizing him up, and wasn't entirely pleased by the conclusion he'd reached. 'You've made quite a name for yourself, Inspector.' Cordeau flicked a hand at the stately stretch of parliament buildings that blocked the view of the river. 'The way you handled Mr Manning at the Drayton inquiry.' He gave Khattak a sudden, shrewd look. 'You don't brush anything under the rug, do you?'

Esa rose to his feet. 'I didn't think the prime minister would want me to.'

Cordeau shrugged, a blithe, dismissive gesture. 'That's how you look at things in law enforcement – this is politics, Inspector.'

He was beginning to sound as if he regretted handing over the folder that contained Khattak's authorization. Khattak moved it to one side.

Cordeau was hailed by someone at the door. He raised a hand in welcome.

'Madame Ambassador, come in, he's all yours.' He gave Khattak an envious glance. 'I was just leaving.'

But he wasn't quite finished. To Khattak, he said, 'I won't pretend I'm glad you're looking into this. Everything about our Syria policy has been political; its ramifications are political as well. It was never about that little boy who washed up dead in Turkey.'

Khattak flinched at this unnecessary candour. Cordeau closed the door behind him.

'Always the drama queen, that one.' The new arrival shared Khattak's disapproval. Canada's ambassador to Lebanon,

Camille Mansur, was a dashing woman in her sixties, dressed in a navy blue skirt suit, her Avon blouse pinned at the throat with a fine-spun filigree brooch. She advanced on Esa with a smile of welcome, kissing him on both cheeks.

He held her by the elbows, smiling down at her. 'Madame Ambassador. It's been too long.'

'Don't you dare call me anything but Camille. Shame on you, you devil. You haven't been to visit us in ages. Michel misses you.'

Khattak held out a chair for her. She sank into it in a single fluid movement, not troubling to look at its placement. Her natural elegance reflected the mannerisms of a dying generation, the foreign-born sons and daughters of diplomats who were equally at ease among the elite of Canadian society as they were in their families' olive groves.

Camille came from a well-respected Lebanese family that had settled in Canada four generations ago without losing touch with their Lebanese Christian heritage. Camille had trained in the diplomatic corps to arrive at her present posting. Khattak couldn't think of a better choice for Canada's ambassador to Lebanon: she spoke five languages fluently, having studied at the Sorbonne and the Kennedy School of Government; she had come home to Canada declaring her fatigue with the French and Americans alike.

'The one too self-important, the other far too earnest. I'll leave you to sort out which is which, darling,' she often said. In anyone else, such a comment would have ruffled diplomatic feathers, but Camille was a grande dame of the old school. Her wit was received in the spirit intended, and with the desire to curry her influence.

She laughed a great deal at everyone, yet always in a spirit of kindness.

'*Habibi.*' Her voice had dropped into a lower, more roguish register from a diet of cigarettes and cognac. 'Tell me everything.'

Khattak smiled again and she fluttered a hand at her heart.

'Spare me such debonair glances, *mon cher,* and tell me why you travel to Greece.'

She was as wily and well informed as ever.

'It's rather for you to tell me, I think. This wasn't an accidental meeting, I take it?'

She patted his arm with a comfortable familiarity. He curled his fingers around her little claw.

'The young one asked me to step in, given my work in Lebanon.' Her shrug was classically French, an elegant displacement of her shoulders. 'I could hardly refuse, could I? His father asked me to keep an eye on him.'

The current prime minister's father had been a former beau of Camille's, a lion of the old guard. Canadian politics had never seen such a personality. Khattak doubted they would again.

She leaned forward, patting his knee. The nearly transparent skin at her neck tightened, throwing the tendons into high relief. In the jewel-like glow of sunlight through the windows, the ambassador looked her age.

'I wouldn't have refused in any case, you are without a doubt my favorite policeman. So what is it you need to know?'

'Anything you can tell me. You know Nathan and Audrey Clare, of course. Do you have any idea what Audrey was doing on the islands that would see her linked with these deaths?'

'I knew Aude Bertin, as well. She was the most tenacious Frenchwoman one was likely to meet. She had a way of collecting names. And quite a long list of favours.'

In addition to her accomplishments, Camille had a memory like a strongbox: nothing ever escaped from it.

'Are you suggesting an impropriety? Was Aude Bertin corrupt in some way, is that what you mean when you mention favours?'

'*Au contraire.* She was, in fact, the most incorruptible person I've ever met. She used her contacts to one end, and that was her work as a police agent. She bullied no one except those who deserved to be bullied – her mission was to represent the weak.'

If Aude considered you to be in the business of exploitation, then look out! Once she caught the scent – *quelle tigresse*. She never let anything go. Her connection to the boy, I cannot say, but she was involved in tracking the progress of refugees to France. Perhaps that was the link.' She hesitated, miming a familiar gesture with her fingers. 'A cigarette, *habibi*?'

Khattak feigned a note of severity. 'In a parliamentary office, madame? I think not. And besides, think of your health.'

'I assure you I am not going anywhere. The Syrian people need me back in Lebanon as soon as it can be arranged. I have promised them I will live forever, so I must. I'm home for a few days at the temptation of seeing my grandchildren. So many sticky fingers, but how they adore *Grand-mère*, and the pretty things I bring them.'

Khattak smiled, as he was meant to. A moment's thought made him ask, 'Why was Agent Bertin tracking refugees to France?'

Again, the ambassador shrugged. 'She was French, after all. France was her bailiwick, as you would say. But you know about that dreadful Jungle, Esa, yes? I think Aude viewed it as reprehensible. It was a dead end. No one moved on from Calais, she didn't want others to risk their lives on a futile journey to the north. They are cruel there, *n'est-ce pas*? They don't want outsiders in their country – they barely tolerate the native-born.'

The ambassador had seen a great deal in her time: the civil war in Lebanon, the Israeli strike on the south, the destruction of Beirut, the attack at the UN base in Qana, the devastating collapse of first Iraq then Syria – and the present refugee crisis, unparalleled in her lifetime, though Lebanon knew more than its share about hosting a refugee population. The Calais Jungle in northern France was one of the flashpoints of the crisis. It served as a point of departure for the UK via the port of Calais, through the Eurotunnel, or through the dangerous practice of stowing away on transport headed to the UK.

Though the camp at Calais had been in existence in some form since the 1990s, the Syrian refugee crisis had swollen the numbers of those who transited through the camp. Not all who ended up in the 'Jungle' were refugees fleeing war and persecution. Some had fled dire economic circumstances in pursuit of a more hopeful future, either for themselves or for the families they'd left behind. Both groups were referred to as 'migrants' by the European press, a shift away from the possibility of legitimate need.

Khattak privately believed both groups represented different kinds of necessity, just as he knew that the Convention on Refugees defined refugees stringently for well-considered reasons. The sixtieth anniversary of the treaty couldn't have fallen at a darker moment: an unprecedented 62.5 million people around the globe had been displaced from their homes, 21.3 million of whom qualified as refugees.

So if Camille Mansur found the Calais Jungle problematic, he trusted her judgment. But he asked himself what Agent Bertin's perspective had been, and whether any of this touched on Audrey Clare's disappearance.

He was trying to think within the analytical framework of a police officer because if he made it personal, he wouldn't be able to focus. Audrey was as much a sister to him as Ruksh or Misbah.

'This young man who was found dead alongside Agent Bertin.' He checked the name in the folder Cordeau had given him. 'There's very little information about him. Is it possible Sami al-Nuri was trying to get to France?'

Camille took the folder from him. Khattak didn't protest. Whatever the prime minister had told Esa, he would have confided more openly in Camille. The ambassador to Lebanon had worked night and day to fast-track refugees to Canada. She had very little patience for bureaucracy. If something didn't make sense to Camille, she cut through it like deadwood. That included personnel. She was more popular with the new people she'd brought on board than with staff who'd become entrenched in their way of doing things. She'd hired new blood who knew how to streamline the process in time to meet the deadline.

She leafed through the folder and closed it.

'I don't recognize this young man's name. Or his application.'

'Is it likely you would remember him?' Thousands of applications for asylum would have crossed Camille's desk.

'Probably not. But no one wants to end up in France. Austria, Germany, Scandinavia, the UK – these are the destinations of choice. They have a kinder refugee policy, and better institutional support. Not to mention the more pressing concerns facing France.'

Khattak didn't pursue this. He knew well enough what she meant, but the rise of the far right in Europe was irrelevant to his investigation. He would visit Michel and Camille soon – they were old and dear friends of his parents – and when he did, he would unburden himself. There was so much he wanted to share – things he hadn't talked about since the death of his father, things he couldn't say to his mother for fear of causing her pain. His relationship with Camille was a close one. Though she teased him no end, she treated him like a son.

'So where would you suggest I begin? Nathan did mention this young man might have a Toronto connection.'

Camille's exquisitely made-up face looked sorrowful for a moment. 'He seems more like a boy than a man, but how quickly these boys have had to grow up. A third of their lives have been war.' She twisted the heavy gold rings on her fingers. 'This Sami was a boy, no different than Aylan Kurdi, but because of his age, he would be among those least likely to be granted asylum. Families with children, yes. Women on their own, of course. A boy on the verge of manhood fleeing Syria – a boy like you were at one time...' Here she smiled a nostalgic smile at Esa. 'Why, he's the most dangerous creature in the world. There *is* no refuge for these boys.' Now she spoke briskly, raising her chin. 'But if he was going to meet his death on an unforgiving shore, this is *not* how I would expect it to happen.'

A glimmer of sympathy in Khattak's eyes indicated how well he understood her.

'You must speak to the director at Sanctuary Syria. Sanctuary helps process these cases. If there was a family connection in Toronto, the case will have crossed their desk.'

Khattak knew the organization. His mother had worked with Sanctuary to sponsor a family from Damascus. The ambassador gave him further details, which he noted in his phone.

'A warning, if you'll hear it. Whatever you're going to do, do it quickly. It would be better for you to knock on Interpol's door, before they knock on ours. And little Miss Audrey – you must find her before she gets herself into any further trouble.'

He didn't dare tell her that this wasn't one of Audrey's or Ruksh's adolescent pranks. Audrey hadn't gotten herself into trouble – trouble had come for her.

'I promise I will, Madame.'

He placed a hand beneath her elbow to help her rise to her feet, inhaling the delicate scent of her French perfume. She was as divinely feminine as he remembered from boyhood, when he'd been hopeful of her notice. She had always had a sweet for him in an expensively gloved hand; she had also taught him to widen his appreciation of his heritage. Camille had taken his cultural education in hand, improving on a foundation laid by Esa's father.

She offered him a mischievous rendering of a *qasida* of the Syrian poet Nizar Qabbani, as he escorted her to the elevator.

'As long as you love me, my green-eyed boy, God is in the sky.'
He took her hand and kissed it. '*Chère* Camille, always.'

6

Toronto, Canada

SANCTUARY SYRIA WAS LOCATED ON the fourth floor of an office building in the downtown core not far from the CBC News building. Each corner of the intersection was accented with a mid-rise glass-fronted office building; there was no view of the harbor.

The staff was arranged around clusters of desks in an open-concept space, where it was clear that the bulk of the funds allocated by the government had been used to further the non-profit's work, and not on public perceptions of their enterprise.

The office staff was an interesting mix. The handful of full-time senior staff was joined by a group of students and retirees who could be called on to work consistent daytime hours.

The staff reflected the city's ethnic diversity – Rachel could hear a smattering of languages. The volunteers were of different backgrounds, working toward a common purpose, facilitating the resettlement of Syrian refugees in various parts of Canada.

Rachel took in the scene with a glance. There was an atmosphere of cheerful cooperation in the office, a buzz of excitement and purpose that made the co-workers seem more like a family. Even the senior staff, who were boxed in by veritable mountains of paper, seemed relaxed and approachable as they chatted with two college-age designers working on a visual presentation. Everyone greeted Rachel as she was ushered through the small reception area to the executive director's office where Khattak was waiting. He got to his feet, as he always did, to pull out Rachel's chair. She thanked him with a quick smile, searching his face for signs of strain. He'd known Audrey Clare all her life; it would be natural for him to be worried. If he was, he didn't show it, and she thought something about his meeting in Ottawa must have improved his spirits, which surprised her. Nearly all their work had political implications, and their last few cases had been trickier than most. Rachel would have guessed that an investigation touching on refugee policy would be exceedingly sensitive, but Khattak couldn't have seemed more confident and relaxed – almost light-hearted.

Rachel couldn't help herself; she wondered if a woman was behind his sudden contentment. His sharp, green eyes probed her face; she realized she'd let the silence drag on too long, he'd be wondering at her preoccupation.

The organization's executive director stepped into her office to greet them, and Rachel was glad of the reprieve. If she worked up her courage later, she might venture to tease Khattak about his love life.

'Welcome. I'm Linh Pham. I'm sorry Suha can't be here, as well. We're co-chairs of Sanctuary at present as we're in the middle of reassigning staff.'

Linh Pham was perhaps five feet tall, with a small, neat build and an inquisitive face, marked by a pair of dimples. Though there was an ageless quality to her skin, Rachel knew she was forty-five. She had been evacuated to Canada with her family during the Vietnamese boat crisis of the 1970s.

A former child refugee, Pham now ran the most effective resettlement program in the country. Rachel wasn't familiar with the name Suha, though to be fair, she'd just been notified by Khattak to meet him at the agency. The information Gaffney had pulled for her hadn't included a full list of staff.

She settled into her seat to let Khattak work his magic. Her

51

boss was exceptionally attractive; people paid scant attention to Rachel when he was conducting an interview.

'Thank you for seeing us on such short notice, Ms Pham. I hope that as the executive director of this organization, you'll be able to help us.'

'Please call me Linh.' She transferred her gaze to Rachel, who was dressed in a pressed green suit, her hair disciplined into a ponytail, her eyebrows newly groomed. She seemed to like what she saw because her dimples deepened as she smiled.

'You said on the phone you were curious about a case Sanctuary may have worked on. Suha Obeidi is our case coordinator – if this young man is a reunion case, Suha would definitely know.'

Rachel looked over at the companionable cluster of desks. If one of the staff in the outer room was Suha, Linh would have called her over.

'A reunion case?' Khattak's pleasant voice deepened. 'I'm not familiar with the term.'

'I'm sorry, it's an in-house term we use to refer to refugees who are sponsored by family in Canada.'

That tied in perfectly to their inquiry. Linh Pham seemed to know it.

'Do you have a photograph to show me?' she asked.

Khattak removed it from the folder, but before handing it to Linh, he offered a warning.

'This is in strictest confidence. The young man's name is Sami al-Nuri. This is a photograph of his body; you might find it a little unsettling.'

Linh accepted that without comment. She took her time examining the photograph, and when she returned it to Khattak, there was a hint of perception in her face.

'You know him,' Khattak said. He edged forward in his seat. Linh opened a drawer of her desk and fished out a small, white card from its interior. This she passed to Khattak. Rachel pressed closer to him to read it: it was the contact information for Suha Obeidi.

'I recognize the face, I don't recognize the name. I'm not sure what name his case would have been processed under.'

She entered the name into her computer, frowning at the results.

'No, we don't have a record of Sami. If he does have a relative in Canada, it won't be under that name. Do you have any other information you can share with me? Something that would help me track him down?'

Rachel's thoughts leapt to Nate's e-mails. Sami al-Nuri had been mentioned only once in the e-mails Nate had shared. But what if Audrey had used a different family name in the e-mails Nate had deleted? She needed a moment with Khattak to discuss this. And to ask about consent.

He missed her signal, focused on Linh's response.

'But you *do* recognize the face.'

Linh ran a finger over the photograph. 'He may have been part of a reunion case, but I can't say why I think so. I'm just as likely to be wrong.' She considered her screen. 'I wouldn't know how to search, and I'm sorry, thousands of profiles cross my desk. You'd do much better to speak to Suha.'

Rachel glanced back at the group of volunteers. 'But she's not here today, is that right? Is she out sick, do you know?'

The other woman pressed her lips together. Rachel had the feeling she was treading on difficult ground.

'She asked for some personal time. She's worked all hours in the past few months, so of course she deserved a little time off.'

Rachel studied her brightly. That didn't sound like the phrasing of someone who considered herself a co-chair, or an equal partner in an enterprise. It sounded very much like a boss speaking of an employee. Though Khattak didn't throw his weight around in their particular arrangement, he'd picked up on it, too.

'Ms Obeidi reported to you? Her work hours weren't

discretionary, then.' He smiled his devastating smile. It had no effect on Linh, whose eyes had become opaque. Rachel guessed she was arranging her answer in her mind, deciding how much to tell them.

'We've had some bumps along the way. No one would deny this is life-changing work, rewarding in its own right. But there have been some staffing and oversight issues.' Her tone became dry. 'You may have read about it in the papers.'

A light came on in Rachel's head. *Sanctuary Syria, of course.*

The organization had come in for some unfavorable press early on. The problems had arisen because board members of the organization had interfered with day-to-day operations, hindering Linh's independence and efficiency as director. Later, several of the board members had resigned.

Sanctuary Syria had set out to do its work in the tradition of Operation Lifeline, the 1970s campaign on behalf of the Vietnamese. Linh Pham's professional life had been dedicated to supporting and enhancing Canadian refugee policy – the organisation couldn't have asked for a better candidate to coordinate Canada's response to the Syrian crisis. Once new board members had been elected, she'd been left to do her work in peace.

Rachel wondered how Suha Obeidi might fit within this picture. If she was a co-chair, how did the organization's reporting structure work? Khattak was right to ask.

'Originally, we were co-chairs. But when the new broom came in to sweep out the old, it was decided the organization should have a single administrative head, and I was chosen for the post. To her credit, Suha doesn't get hung up on these issues. She's entirely focused on the work.' She nodded at the card she'd given Khattak. 'You can reach her on her cell phone. She should be able to tell you what you want to know. And if you leave me your contact information, if I come across anything related to your inquiry, I'll give you a call.'

'Thank you.' Khattak passed her his card. She read it and looked at him quickly.

'Your name seems familiar. You're not related to –'

'Angeza Khattak? She's my mother. You handled a private sponsorship for her group last year.'

But Linh Pham was shaking her head. 'I was going to say Ruksh Khattak, but yes, of course I remember your mother.'

'Ruksh?' Khattak's voice acquired an edge. 'She's my sister. Was she here? She wasn't involved in my mother's sponsorship efforts, as far as I know.'

Linh slipped Khattak's card into a drawer. 'She consults with us, on occasion.'

'In what capacity?' Rachel asked.

She questioned why a specialist in epidemiology would be needed at Sanctuary Syria. Perhaps because refugees were required to have clear medical results before they could enter Canada, unless they were given dispensation by the government.

Linh was swift to enlighten them. 'She was recommended as a consultant by Audrey Clare. I don't know if you know the name, but Audrey runs an NGO called Woman to Woman. They're one of our funding partners. When we were struggling to meet the prime minister's resettlement deadline, Woman to Woman was invaluable in helping us fast-track cases.'

She clapped her hands together in sudden recognition. 'The photograph. I know where I've seen that young man before. I've seen his picture in a case file referred to us by Audrey.'

Rachel tried to prevent her excitement from showing. They now had a solid link. She glanced over at Khattak.

'And Ruksh?' he asked again, distracted. 'What role does my sister play?'

Linh's calm expression broadened into a smile. 'The Khattaks are quite a family. Your mother is responsible for growing our list of private sponsors. And your sister runs a clinic on the weekends for our new arrivals. She's formed a network of volunteers –

doctors, dentists, much-needed specialists like OB-GYNS, and psychologists –'

'Psychologists?' Rachel broke in.

'We've resettled Syrians from nearly every part of the country. Aleppo, Daraa, Ghouta – the things they've seen or experienced... how can I describe them? They're war-traumatized. And war isn't the only trauma they've had to face on their journey.'

Khattak's hands unclenched from the arms of his chair, a small gesture Rachel noticed. The relationship between Khattak and his sister had not warmed up over time. He'd been so preoccupied by the mention of Ruksh that he'd passed no comment on a subject that would normally engage his interest. And, from what she knew of him, his sympathy.

'I'm surprised you didn't know that, Inspector. Ruksh has been an inspiration.'

Rachel tried to make light of it.

'I live with my brother and I never know what he's up to.' She tried out a grin, noting the tension in Khattak's face. 'At least your sister is a credit to you. I'm not as confident of Zach.'

In fact, the reverse was true. Ruksh had caused Khattak an insupportable amount of distress over the past year, whereas Rachel had never been happier than to have her brother at home again. Of course, she wouldn't say that to Khattak. She was trying to lift his spirits.

'I've been out of the country recently,' Khattak answered. 'How long has Ruksh been working with you?'

Linh Pham paused to consider. 'Not that long. She first came to see us when we began operations, but in the middle she had her exams and couldn't devote her time. For the past three months, she's been operating the clinic on Fridays and Saturdays.'

Rachel had a pretty good idea of what might have distracted Khattak's sister – it wasn't her exams. Ruksh had been inextricably involved in a case Rachel and Esa had worked the past winter. Some would even say implicated.

It was strange Khattak hadn't known about his sister's work. If Ruksh wasn't speaking to him, his mother or his sister Misbah surely would have raised the subject, if only to grant him peace of mind.

Rachel tried to redirect the conversation. Linh Pham had given them two excellent leads. Anything else was a bonus, though she could appreciate that Khattak would need to talk to Ruksh about whether Audrey had mentioned Sami or Agent Bertin. An unpalatable thought struck her.

There was bound to have been copious contact between Ruksh and Audrey Clare – via phone or e-mail or text. It wouldn't be enough to ask Ruksh to tell them what she knew; they'd have to see the correspondence for themselves. And if Rachel's past encounters with Khattak's intractable sister were anything to go by, Ruksh wouldn't be inclined to help, even if they were able to convince her of their need.

Her mind boggled at the thought of Khattak having to subpoena documents from his own sister. But he'd been through worse; perhaps this wouldn't even register.

She stole a glance at his sensitive face. He'd crossed one long leg over the other and was looking down at the hands he'd folded over his knee. His thick, dark lashes fanned his cheek. She couldn't read his expression, but the faint wrinkling of his forehead told her he'd thought of something she'd missed.

He thanked Linh Pham for her time. When he and Rachel were at the door, he turned back and asked the question he'd seemed to be weighing.

'Do you have the address of the clinic, by any chance?'

Linh Pham showed her surprise, her dimples disappearing as she compressed her lips.

'Inspector, the clinic's open now. I'm sure you'll find Ruksh there.' There was a pitying note in her voice. 'I believe it's the address of your father's former practice.'

There was silence in the car as they left the lakeshore to drive toward the city's more affluent neighborhoods. They weren't heading back to their offices, but Rachel wasn't about to ask Khattak any questions. He would tell her what he wanted her to do when he was ready.

She slipped a hand into her handbag and closed her fingers around a packet of Sesame Snaps. She debated with herself for a moment. The interior of Khattak's car was spotless; Sesame Snaps were sticky and known to crumble. With a reluctant sigh, she dropped them back in her purse.

She caught the quirk of Khattak's smile from the corner of her eyes.

'Go ahead, Rachel. We'll break for lunch soon, but there's no need for you to suffer. You don't do your best work on an empty stomach.'

It was Rachel's turn to grin, a sense of relief behind it. This was an overture she was happy to take up. She made a show of opening the packet.

'You just don't remember,' she said mournfully. 'Breakfast, lunch, three meals a day. You're a bit of a tyrant, if you don't mind me saying so, sir.'

'It seems more like six meals with you, Rachel.'

The teasing note was back in his voice so Rachel offered him a Snap.

'You must be kidding.' His black-gloved hands were on the steering wheel. 'If I didn't respect your basic human rights, I wouldn't be letting you eat in my car.'

'Noted.' Rachel made quick work of her snack. She found a tissue in her purse to wipe her hands on. 'I'm still a bit sticky, sir.'

'Then don't touch anything.'

At the bantering note in his voice, Rachel felt utterly happy. This was what she loved about her work. She had a partner who didn't take his moods out on her.

The car made steady progress along Avenue Road. They

turned off and passed the campus of Upper Canada College, where Khattak had gone to school. Its gently groomed four-square lawns lay under a mantle of snow, as perfectly edged as a postcard. The reddish brick of its Georgian façade had received a similar dusting; the graceful hands of the clock were etched in black against the snow.

'Spring,' Rachel said. 'I think the good Lord mislaid his magic wand.'

'It will come, Rachel. This is the mildest weather we've seen for some time. And I didn't know your deity was a sorcerer.'

'Hey, whatever works.' Rachel judged the time was right to question Khattak. 'So we're heading up to your father's practice? We're *not* paying a call on Suha Obeidi?'

Khattak turned down another street toward a small complex at the end of a road lined with maples. A bit of green, Rachel observed. Tiny shoots coming to life, taking their chances that winter had ended. The parking lot in front of the complex was half full, three young men loitering outside its doors, one smoking a cigarette.

On one end of the complex was a pharmacy, on the other a women's spa and a small eatery called the Istanbul Café. Sandwiched between these was an upscale bakery and a bookshop with a whimsical display.

The largest section of the complex was in the center, its rounded entrance constructed of thick, bluish-green glass. There was no sign above the façade, but a makeshift banner bore the logo *W2W Clinic*. It was printed in a green that matched the glass.

Khattak pulled up in the parking lot of the complex. He studied the banner before he answered Rachel's question.

'I know I said that you should interview Ruksh, but given what we've just learned, I think it's best if I talk to her. Perhaps in this environment she won't be quite as obstructive. You could order us some lunch. And set up that meeting with Suha Obeidi.'

They turned to face each other in the car. At the close proximity,

Rachel was struck by Khattak's unequivocal attraction. But unlike most women, she wasn't itching to get closer by penetrating his reserve on matters related to his family. He'd been open about the troubles he'd had with Ruksh, a close regard she cherished. So much so that she sometimes asked his advice about Zach. But she didn't know exactly where the line was.

Carefully, she said, 'You don't want me as backup?'

She was thinking of the disaster at Algonquin. She looked him straight in the eye.

The way he looked at her in return made her blush. Khattak had the uncanny ability to read her thoughts; she didn't want him to at this moment.

With just as much care, he answered, 'If you don't mind, Rachel, I'd like to do this alone.'

There was a hint of vulnerability to the curve of his mouth; Rachel gave in at once. To break the solemnity of the mood, she rubbed her sticky hands together and pulled on her toque.

She opened the car door and tossed over her shoulder, 'You trust me to order your food?'

Khattak's answer was stunningly sweet.

'I'd trust you with anything, Rachel. You know I already have.'

7

Toronto, Canada

ESA WALKED THROUGH THE GLASS doors with a strong sense of nostalgia. His mother owned the building, but she had closed his father's practice after his father had died. Esa hadn't crossed its threshold in years. He saw from a framed register on the wall that the building had been leased to several new practitioners, none of whom were connected with his father's old practice. At the bottom, the words 'Woman to Woman Walk-in Clinic' had been added to the register in white letters.

The reception area was spacious. Leather button-down couches had been added to the waiting area, and across a gleaming quartz floor, several curly-headed boys were absorbed in a game of building blocks in the children's play area.

Khattak took in the changes: expensive but characterless prints on the wall, a raised glass countertop that gave the receptionist privacy. An artfully arranged coffee table hosted a selection of miniature pastries – it struck a homespun note in contrast to the quartz and white glass.

One of the boys darted from the play area to help himself to a pastry. He wiped his hands on a napkin before returning to play. He flashed Esa a naughty smile as he picked up a colorful block. Esa returned the smile with one of his own.

The office manager was a comfortable woman with a welcoming manner and a pair of lively blue eyes. She might have been in her sixties but her silky-smooth, rose-pink complexion made it impossible to tell. She spoke with a mild Scottish brogue that softly rolled her Rs.

'And who might you be, my handsome stranger? Not a regular patient, I wouldn't forget a face like yours, though come to think of it...' She frowned as if she were trying to place him.

Khattak produced his ID. 'I'm not a patient. I'm here to see Ruksh Khattak.'

The receptionist clicked her tongue, her eyes refusing to stray from his face. 'That would be *Doctor* Khattak, you mean. Do you have an appointment?'

Khattak leaned his elbows on the glass counter. He placed his ID on her desk. She immediately lowered her voice.

'Police? And you're here, why? Is it about *them*?' She tipped her head at the group of boys who were building a structure with their blocks. A frosty note tinged her voice. 'They're good boys, they're no trouble. Neither are the parents. I'll not have anyone say otherwise.'

Khattak took an immediate liking to her. Her streak of protectiveness would benefit the newcomers. So many doors had closed on them. In his father's clinic, one had opened.

'My name is Esa Khattak. I'd like to see my sister, if she's not busy with a patient.'

The woman sat back in surprise. This time she clicked her tongue at herself.

'You're alike as two peas in a pod, I don't know why I didn't see it. Though I must say neither one of you resembles the little one.'

'Do you mean Misbah? Is she here, too?'

The receptionist introduced herself as Holliday Baines. 'A ridiculous name, I know, the good Lord bless my parents, but they always said that having me in their lives – I was a late arrival, you know – was something akin to a miracle, and so why shouldn't they celebrate it like a holiday... though Heaven knows a late baby is no picnic, but there you are, and here I am.' She paused before launching herself into an answer to his question.

'Missy's in here all the time, babysitting, cleaning up, talking to the mothers; she's very good with the mothers, especially the ones who don't speak English.' She broke off this flow to glance at Khattak's ID. 'My dear Inspector Khattak, here I am rattling on when you've come to see the doctor. I'll ring her to let her know you're here. She's catching up on her paperwork.'

She returned his ID and Khattak thanked her. 'That won't be necessary, I'll surprise her.'

'Then I'll just bring you both some tea, shall I? It's right through there.'

Khattak gave her one of his slow, warm smiles. 'Thank you, I know the way.'

Her ringing 'gracious me' caused the boys to look up from their game.

Esa watched Ruksh from the doorway of their father's office, the knot of pain in his throat making it hard for him to speak. Ruksh was seated at their father's old desk, adding patients to the clinic's database. She was wearing her lab coat over a blue dress, her hair loose and her face bare of makeup.

She hadn't changed anything in the single office their mother had left untenanted, except for adding a vase of blue dahlias and bringing in a chair. Their father's leather chair had been pushed to one corner; it waited there, expectant.

Esa blinked the moisture from his eyes. He wished he'd known the office had been reopened. He wished he'd had a chance to come here again and sit quietly among his father's things before the office reacquired its air of purpose. There was a carom board in the corner; he'd spent many an afternoon playing the game with his father. The shelves were full of medical books, a crystal sculpture of a pair of devoted swans, his father's medical degrees framed on the wall, and below these accomplishments, Esa's.

On one corner of the desk, in the same spot they had sat for years, a collection of letters was drawn up in a bundle: blue and red aerograms bound with a ribbon. It was a set of old correspondence between Esa's father and his grandfather. As a boy, Esa had wanted to know what the letters contained: his father's mood was always brighter after receiving a letter from Peshawar. But his father had held them close.

He'd smiled at Esa and said, 'This is between a father and his son. One day they'll pass to you, but not now.'

After his father's death, Esa's mother had asked if he wanted to read the letters. He'd asked that they be left where they were until the day he was ready.

Seven years had passed, yet Esa wasn't ready.

Memories crowded his mind – he didn't want anything to change them.

Many times, his mother had urged him to read the letters, just as she urged him to remarry and to start a family of his own.

'You should have children, these letters will be their legacy.'

Esa didn't contradict his mother, no matter his own thoughts. He'd learned his code of behavior from the father he'd idolized as a child. He treated his mother the way she had always been treated: with great respect and love. They were partners in their grief; she had lost her husband, he had lost his wife. But beyond thought of her own desolation, she'd devoted herself to helping her son overcome his burden of grief.

It was Ruksh who defied her at every turn, Ruksh who caused her worry.

But if Ruksh was running a clinic at their father's office, his mother must have been consulted. She'd be relieved that Ruksh had seemed to find a purpose. It would take Ruksh out of her bitterness, or so Esa now hoped.

He cleared his throat. Ruksh looked up, a lock of dark hair falling against her throat.

He waited for her response. She was surprised, he could see, but not immediately hostile. Her pale green eyes narrowed, a look he was familiar with, as so many of his sister's expressions chanced to mirror his own.

She watched him for a moment and then she sighed, waving her hand at the empty chair. When she offered him her *salaam,* Esa scooped her up from her chair and hugged her.

'I've missed you, Ruksh.'

She hugged him back for the briefest instant. 'Yes, well. This isn't the family visit on *Survivor.*' She smiled her sharp-edged smile. 'I wasn't exiled to a desert island.'

Esa held on to her. She hadn't spoken to him in months. He hadn't seen her or heard her voice or received so much as a text. If she was thawing, he wasn't letting go. He'd been without the friendship of his closest friend for two years – he wouldn't relinquish his sister.

'You exiled *me,*' he pointed out. 'Something I didn't want.' Holliday Baines knocked at the door, bearing a tea tray. Esa took it from her with thanks.

She winked at Esa as she closed the door.

'I should be courteous, I suppose.' Ruksh passed Esa a mug of tea. 'What brings you to Dad's office? Did Mum tell you I was here?'

Esa sipped his tea. Ruksh set hers on the desk, blanking out the screen behind her.

'Ami didn't tell me,' Esa answered, using his name for their mother. 'I learned of the clinic from Linh Pham. She suggested you might be able to help me. But I would have come to see you in any case.'

'Why?'

Ruksh leaned back in her chair, fingering a locket at her neck. It was an oval-shaped locket set with small diamonds that Esa had given her as a graduation gift. His mouth quirked up at the corner: if Ruksh was still wearing it, things between them weren't as bad as he'd feared.

'What kind of a question is that? You're my sister, why else?'

Ruksh was shaking her head; the warmth she'd shown him had cooled.

'That means it's about a case.' She swiveled her chair, turning her back to him. 'I think you know I prefer not to be involved in your cases.'

'Ruksh,' he said gently. 'Don't you know Audrey is missing?'

Ruksh swung back to face him. 'What are you talking about? Audrey is fine. She's on Lesvos, there's no need for you or Nate to be so intrusive. So she doesn't call him for a day.'

'It's been two weeks, Ruksh. The circumstances of her disappearance are troubling.'

He looked at Ruksh with the assessing eye of a police officer. 'Are you saying you didn't know this?'

Ruksh gripped the arms of her chair. Her delicate features hardened, a familiar dislike in her eyes. 'You haven't seen me in months, and the first thing you do is accuse me of lying?'

'I'm simply asking you a question.'

'None of your questions are simple. Don't think I've forgotten. The last time you entangled yourself in my life, it ended in disaster.'

'Not for you.'

Esa couldn't stop himself from saying this. Ruksh knew exactly how to hurt him; he didn't see how she'd earned his restraint.

'What does that mean?' she demanded.

He didn't back down. 'Your life was saved, Rachel's was at risk. In fact, Rachel was at risk from the moment she met you. In the months you've spent blaming me, tell me you've thought of that. Tell me you've considered what *I* faced. I killed a man for you. I've never killed before, I never want to do it again. And what about the rest, Ruksh? The Drayton inquiry, the press. I was suspended, demoted, not knowing if I had a job –'

Ruksh leapt to her feet, jostling her cup of tea. 'That job is all you care about – I'm just another obstacle in your way.'

She cast around the office for something to vent her anger

on. Her gaze fell on the letters. Esa quickly whisked them out of reach. She snatched a photograph instead, and smashed it down on the desk. It was their father's favorite photograph, the one he'd kept beside him in a painted Kashmiri frame, a photograph of his children holding on to each other and laughing.

Ruksh looked at the shattered frame in horror. She cleared out the glass with care, raising her eyes to her brother, something forlorn in her look.

'Esa –'

'How could you do that, Ruksh?' The pain in his voice brought her to her senses.

'I'm sorry,' she said. 'I never meant to –'

'You do a lot of things you don't mean to.'

She sat down again, a feverish flush on her cheeks. She avoided looking at him, until he said, 'It's not me you haven't made peace with. You haven't come to terms with yourself.'

He weighed the letters in his hand. 'Is that why you started the clinic? You'd done something terrible, so you wanted to make amends?'

Ruksh's face went white. Esa had never spoken to her like this; she'd been protected from the consequences of her actions. This calling to account was long delayed.

'You accuse me of acting as a police officer, instead of as your brother. This time, I'm afraid it's true. I can't let you obstruct my investigation – it would jeopardize Audrey's safety. The fact that you'd do so just to prove something to me – I expect better from you, Ruksh.'

Ruksh swallowed. She didn't answer. He took that as permission to proceed, outlining the facts of Audrey's disappearance.

'Did you know she was carrying a gun?'

'No.' Her reply was stunned. 'Audrey never mentioned it.'

'But you were in frequent correspondence, which is what I would expect. When was the last time you heard from her?'

Ruksh straightened her shoulders. She had gathered her

composure, and he knew that she would overcompensate, to seem as reasonable as possible.

'She sent me an e-mail two weeks ago. I assumed there were communication issues. We didn't talk much by phone, but we e-mailed each other often.'

'What were the e-mails about?'

'They were follow-ups. She was checking on the status of arrivals – cases she'd supervised from the islands.'

'"Arrivals" meaning refugees from Syria?'

'Yes. She wanted to make sure new arrivals were seen by a doctor. Some of these children haven't had medical or dental care in years.'

She was hoping to soften him by expressing her compassion. He had no intention of making it so easy. He pressed ahead.

'Did she mention any of the applicants by name? Did she ask for your help with a boy named Sami al-Nuri?'

Ruksh looked relieved. Because she'd found something she could help him with? Or because these weren't the questions she'd expected him to ask?

'I think I remember that name – but from some time ago; several months ago, it would have been. She might have asked me to find out about his family here, whether they were willing to sponsor him, I think it was something like that.'

A consistent line of inquiry from Audrey, the one he would follow up next.

'Did you do as she asked?'

Ruksh frowned, a delicate pleating of the skin between a pair of eyebrows shaped like wings. 'I didn't. She wrote me again, almost at once, to tell me to leave it alone. She didn't explain why, and I never thought to ask.'

'What about the name Aude Bertin? Does that mean anything to you?'

'No,' Ruksh said in a whisper. 'Audrey didn't say she was in trouble. The one thing she talked about that she seemed to find upsetting –' A trace of uneasiness entered her voice.

'Go on.'

Ruksh took an audible breath. 'She was worried about money. She spent it like water, but she said it was never enough. And she said that Nate had put his foot down – he refused to release more funds. She sounded a little desperate so I sent her a bit of my own money –'

Esa cut her off. 'Did she say why she needed the money?' He suspected she would confirm what Rachel had already told him. Audrey Clare had needed a boat.

Ruksh had forgotten her tea, her gaze dwelling on the shattered Kashmiri frame.

'The money was for plane tickets.'

Her answer was unexpected. 'For herself?'

'I can't say. And not because I'm trying to obstruct you – Audrey didn't tell me.' What was left of her poise deserted her. 'You don't believe she's guilty of these murders, do you? You know Audrey's not capable of that.'

Esa didn't answer. He made her no assurances, because he had none.

'At the moment, I'm concerned she's missing. I'd rather it was because she's chosen to disappear than because she's come to some harm.'

'Do you think that's p-possible?'

She said the last word with the hint of a stutter, a nervous habit that resurfaced now and again. He didn't reassure her. She had told him she didn't want to be misled, so he'd take her at her word. He was treating her like an adult. He hoped it would make a difference.

'It's possible, though it's not the only scenario. You'll need to show me your e-mails. There are things you might have forgotten.'

He got to his feet, expecting her to comply.

For a moment, Ruksh looked torn. Then common sense overruled her desire to prove herself above her brother's influence.

As he'd said, he wasn't acting as her brother. He was speaking as a police officer.

'I'll do anything I can to help, but you must know my e-mails are private. There's no reason for you to read them.'

'Then they'll be subpoenaed. I'll have them by the end of the day. And Ruksh – if you try to delete them, I'll consider that obstruction. And we'll retrieve them regardless.'

She put a hand on his arm, entreating him, shocked at the side of himself he was showing her. 'Esa, it's not that. I don't want *you* to read them. Could Rachel look at them instead?'

It was Esa's turn to hesitate. There might come a moment when he'd have no choice but to read her e-mails for himself – yet he hadn't intended to cause irreparable damage to his relationship with his sister. He gave her a quick nod, though he clarified, 'For now.'

'Thank you.' She wrote down the information he'd need to access her e-mails and placed it in the pocket of his jacket.

Silence fell between them. Esa's gaze moved beyond Ruksh to the shattered frame on the desk. 'You'll get that fixed, I trust.'

Ruksh shook her head helplessly. 'I'm sorry. I don't know what made me do it. I just – haven't been myself.'

At last, Esa relented. He gathered his sister close. 'The past can't hold you back forever. You're worth so much more than that. Especially to me.'

Tears formed in Ruksh's eyes. She hugged Esa back, clinging to him like a child. 'How do I stop blaming you? Or myself, for that matter?'

Esa tugged at a lock of her hair. 'If that's a serious question, I have a couple of suggestions.'

Ruksh reached for a tissue and blew her nose. 'It is.'

'Keep doing what you're doing. The more you think of the needs of others, the more you'll be able to recalibrate the way you look at things. As for blaming me...' He gave a rueful shake of his head.

'Try reading the press coverage of what happened in Algonquin. And maybe find out what I was doing in Iran. If that doesn't bring you out of this, I can't say I know what will.'

He kissed the top of Ruksh's head. Then he took the letters and left.

8

Toronto, Canada

RACHEL HAD ORDERED A HEARTY lunch of Adana kebabs with all the trimmings. The lamb was served on a round of bread topped with tomatoes, sweet peppers, and onions. A meek bowl of salad and a cup of soup were poised beside this culinary splendor.

Khattak hung up his coat and sat down. Fascinated by the flavoring of her carrot-ginger soup, Rachel's sympathy was minimal.

'So? Was it World War Three? Or has the enemy decided to surrender?'

Khattak grinned. He couldn't help himself. Rachel had a way of deflating the most serious subjects that no one he worked with could equal.

He took a bite of his food.

The café was new. It hadn't been around in his father's day. It was on the fashionable side, with its exposed brick walls and rustic chalkboards – he wouldn't have identified anything about the Istanbul Café as Turkish, except for the line of copper *cezves* perched upon a sill. The little engraved pots with their long brass handles were used for making Turkish coffee, and a delicious earth-baked aroma wafted through the café.

'I wouldn't say surrender. A truce would be more accurate.' He held up the piece of paper Ruksh had given him. 'Ruksh has given us access to her e-mails, but she's asked that you read them and report to me.'

Rachel's soupspoon splashed into her bowl. He could tell she had plenty to say, though she had learned that sometimes discretion *was* the better part of valor. It didn't stop her from trying to comfort him.

'I know how it is with younger siblings, sir. They run you down every chance they get, but that doesn't mean they don't need you.'

Which was her way of saying she fully expected to find Ruksh railing against his tyranny in her e-mails. He sighed. As he cleared his plate, he brought Rachel up to speed on everything he'd learned.

He could tell from the way she tilted her head that she was picking up the scent.

'So we have two things, sir. The money – was it for a boat? That would be good to know. And this family connection that can't be traced. Audrey personally brought his case to the attention of Sanctuary Syria. Why this one? Why a boy who ended up shot by Audrey's gun?'

Rachel swirled her spoon in the bowl, letting the soup grow cold. 'Sir –' She shot him a diffident glance. 'We need to talk about Nate. This is all a bit messy, isn't it? He's your friend, Audrey's your friend, your sister's involved...'

'I won't let that sway my judgment in the slightest, Rachel.' The warmth in his voice cooled.

'You know that that's not what I meant – actually, what I'm suggesting is quite a bit worse than you fuzzing the lines.' She paused, choosing her words.

Khattak's smile was wry. 'Naturally.'

Rachel plunged ahead.

'Did you know Nate deleted quite a bit of his correspondence with Audrey? Gaff recovered a cache of e-mails.'

'Did you read them?' Khattak's tone was sharp.

'I thought I'd better check with you first. Something isn't adding up. Why would Nate hamstring us? Is he hiding something?'

Rachel dropped her voice. 'And then, what if there's something in the deleted e-mails that's, well, incriminating. What if Audrey's not missing? What if she's fled the scene of a crime?' Now she gestured with her hands, building to a conclusion. 'The only way to know that is by reading the e-mails Nate deleted, so that raises consent issues, and ultimately, sir, we're talking about subpoenaing the private e-mails of your oldest friend. The two of you have been on rocky ground before. I'm not sure how to proceed.'

The waiter came to remove their plates and Khattak asked for coffee. It gave him a second to think. He wasn't happy with himself for doing it, but his first instinct was to deflect the question.

'What about you, Rachel? I know you and Nate have grown close. Working this case could upset that. Do you want me to ask Declan to step in?'

Declan was the youngest member of their team. He was also the most eager to impress Khattak with his initiative. Rachel treated Declan much the same way she treated Zach: like an overgrown kid brother. But she was conscious of his shadow, Esa knew. The dynamics at CPS had changed with Declan's and Gaffney's renewed responsibilities. It was no longer Esa and Rachel on one side, with everyone else ranged against them. There was more openness, more collegiality, and less of a feeling of being battened down. Esa wanted that for Rachel. His battles shouldn't be hers.

Rachel cleared her throat, a film of sweat glistening on her upper lip. 'That won't be necessary, sir. Nate and I are just friends.' She turned the words back on him. 'I think I can weather the storm better than you can.'

Khattak thanked the waiter for his strong, dark coffee. He didn't try to sweeten it as Rachel had done, almost choking at its potency.

'We shouldn't assume things,' he said. 'Nate may have withheld those e-mails quite innocently, if he thought they were unrelated to our case. All we have to do is ask him.'

He didn't believe his own words. The mention of Laine Stoicheva at the Chateau Laurier had come as a shock to Esa. He'd read a certain sensitivity in Nate's face – the way he'd interacted with Rachel, his discomfort at getting caught – Nate was hiding something. Khattak hoped it concerned Laine, and not Audrey's disappearance.

Rachel was right. He and Nate were overdue for a chat.

'Did you get hold of Suha Obeidi?'

She nodded. She finished the piece of baklava served alongside their coffee, not at all embarrassed that her fingers were sticky again.

'She's at Eglinton West, maybe twenty minutes away. She said to come any time.'

Khattak checked his phone. It had buzzed with a message from Nate. Their travel arrangements had been made. Their flight to Greece was first thing in the morning.

He frowned. That didn't leave him much time to track down the family Nate had spoken of or to speak to Suha Obeidi. Or to sort through the e-mails, though he supposed he and Rachel could make their way through most of them on the plane. And he still had to let his mother know he'd be out of the country again.

He sent back a brief message.

Need to speak with you about your e-mails before we leave. Send me the information for the Syrian family you met with. I'll drop by Winterglass tonight.

Nate texted back, *OK*. A second later, he texted again. *Don't bring Rachel.*

Esa slipped his phone back in his pocket, his caution reawakened. What wasn't Nate telling him?

He advised Rachel of their travel arrangements. Like him, she would have expected a day or two more in Toronto to follow up leads from the e-mails and to interview the Syrian family who claimed not to know the boy named Sami al-Nuri.

'Should I call them, sir? Set up a time to see them?'

'I don't think so, Rachel. If they lied to Nate about knowing the boy, it may be better to give no warning.'

Suha Obeidi lived in an apartment block on a small street close to the intersection of Yonge and Eglinton. The thoroughfare was lined with boutiques and restaurants, the corners anchored by a busy subway station and a shopping complex. A bookstore and theater ate up the rest of the block.

Khattak found paid parking on Lillian Street. Rachel noticed the name with a pang. It was her mother's name. She hadn't seen or heard from her mother since she and Esa had returned from Iran.

Suha Obeidi buzzed them into her apartment, where she lived alone.

A dynamic woman in her thirties, she wore jeans and a blouse with a bow at the neck, and a head scarf that matched the tight blouse. Her skin was milk-toned, her eyes as dark as Rachel's. She didn't seem surprised to see them; she didn't seem worried either, her attention preoccupied with finding them somewhere to sit. There were stacks of folders on the sofas, chairs, and tables. Each was stamped with Sanctuary Syria's logo and a file number.

Her apartment was otherwise rather bare, as if she'd just moved in. There were no knickknacks or family photographs, just a book with a bookmark jammed halfway through it. Rachel glanced at its cover: it was called *The Calligrapher's Secret*, and it featured an image of Islamic architecture.

Looking around the small apartment, Rachel guessed Suha did most of her work on the plain wood dining table, where more of the folders were stacked.

It was an open-concept space and Rachel could see through to the kitchen, as well as to the small bedroom. It was as neat as the rest of the apartment, with a night table, a lamp, and a twin bed, the décor strictly neutral, and to Rachel's critical eye, even a little bland.

Suha cleared a couch with some haste and invited them to sit, asking them to call her by her name.

'Linh said you wanted to speak with me. She said you're trying to track down a case.'

She spoke with a Niagara-region accent. Rachel was familiar with it because her hockey team included a couple of worthy stalwarts who drove in for their games from west of the Welland Canal. Perhaps Suha had moved to Toronto from Grimsby or Lincoln, or some other small town farther west.

Khattak gave Suha the photograph with the same warning about its graphic nature that he'd given Linh. She looked at it without flinching, though not without dismay. Her expression of concern made her seem more approachable.

'Do you know who he is? Linh Pham didn't know his name. Or at least she didn't recognize the name we gave her.'

Suha tilted her head at Khattak. 'What name was that, Inspector?'

'What name do you know him by?'

She dropped the photograph onto a stack of folders. 'I haven't said I recognize him.'

Her reply was surprising. They had counted on Linh Pham's certainty that Suha would be able to help them.

'But you do, don't you?'

Her mouth twisted. She was an attractive woman; the worry that had crept into her eyes was at odds with her offhand elegance.

'Linh must have told you I would. I'm not surprised. As case coordinator, I've had each one of Sanctuary's cases cross my desk at some point.'

She hugged her arms to her torso, warding off a chill that only she felt.

Khattak asked a different question.

'How long have you been with Sanctuary Syria, Ms Obeidi?'

He didn't take up her offer to call her by her first name. Nor had he offered her a conventional *salaam*.

She didn't seem to expect one, which meant she didn't recognize Khattak's name, nuances Rachel had come to understand through her training at Community Policing. Khattak was a Muslim of South Asian background. Suha clearly wasn't, though Rachel couldn't hazard a guess as to her ethnicity.

'Is that relevant to your inquiry about this boy?' She avoided looking at the photograph again.

Rachel followed Khattak's lead. 'We'd be grateful if you'd just answer our questions, Ms Obeidi. We're investigating a murder, time is of the essence.'

Restlessly, Suha Obeidi rose from the couch, tugging at the sleeves of her fitted cherry blouse. It outlined her figure with some clarity.

Rachel wondered at the contrast to the woman's hijab, but otherwise passed no judgment.

'I see.' Suha paced in front of the living room windows. 'I've been with Sanctuary since its founding; I've worked for the organization in several different capacities. Case management coordinator is a kind of catch-all because I've had to try my hand at a lot of different things.'

Khattak gave a non-committal murmur. Rachel wondered if this had anything to do with the staff reorganization Linh Pham had mentioned.

'I was brought in to grow our sponsor base. Community engagement, additional partners, that kind of thing. But we've always been a little understaffed, and when our volunteers returned to school in the fall, we were under a great deal of pressure.'

'I feel like I've seen you before,' Rachel said, studying the other woman's face.

Suha took that in her stride. 'You may have done. Sanctuary gets a lot of media requests, and for a time, I handled media liaison as well.' A self-mocking note entered her voice. 'Case management, partnership development, communications, social media, hiring volunteers – I've done *all* those things at one time or another. I think that's why they gave me the title of co-chair. They know I can step into any of those roles.'

She wasn't boasting, simply running down the facts. And her onerous responsibilities might have been the reason she had asked for a little time off.

Rachel wondered what she was doing with this backlog of files if she needed a break.

'Are you a lawyer? Are you responsible for fast-tracking these cases?' Rachel glanced around the small apartment. 'I'm wondering why these files aren't at your offices.'

The question didn't faze the other woman. Which meant that in this respect at least, she wasn't holding back.

'I'm a paralegal, not a lawyer, and these aren't active cases. These files represent refugees who've been in Canada for some time. I'm trying to build a database of those who might be willing to volunteer to help more recent arrivals – acting as translators, and so on. Helping to lessen the fear and anxiety a little.'

A reasonable explanation that provoked a question from Khattak. 'I've heard that after they've been resettled, refugees from Syria don't necessarily wish to congregate. They haven't established their own communities.'

Suha raised her well-defined eyebrows. 'That may be true of some of our arrivals, particularly the reunion cases. We've tried to settle them in neighborhoods with mosques and halal grocers, places where community has already been established – and not just Syrian communities, mind you, but other Muslim communities. They haven't been keen to mingle.'

She raised her hands and let them fall. 'It's a mistake, I think, to make assumptions about what would benefit refugees immediately upon arrival. They may be traumatized, they may be frightened. They certainly don't want to relive their most recent experiences. Mixing with other refugees reminds them of the horrors they've left behind, things they're trying to shut from their minds.'

'I don't think that's the only reason.'

Suha paused in front of the window, her troubled gaze fixed on Khattak. 'You seem to be acquainted with the subject.'

'I've met a resettled family through a private sponsorship group. To put it bluntly, it seemed to be an issue of trust.'

Suha nodded. 'I suppose that could be true. Syrians have fled from different parts of their country, they don't necessarily know what others were fleeing or what role they may have played in the civil war: soldier, civilian, Assad supporter, revolutionary. Or someone who wanted to keep out of it, and was praying for the carnage to end.'

Bashar al-Assad was a name as familiar to Rachel as it would have been to anyone who'd watched the news the past five years. He was Syria's ruler, and she used that word advisedly. Syria wasn't a democracy. A single family had ruled the country for nearly fifty years. Bashar al-Assad's father had been a dictator. The son was immeasurably worse.

'An Assad supporter wouldn't qualify for asylum in Canada, surely?'

Suha's response was dry and a little bleak. 'Barrel bombs don't take names. The damage they do is indiscriminate.' She turned to Khattak. 'But that's not what you were getting at, is it? Or maybe it is, a little. You think that even over here, far removed from the war, Syrians might have reason to distrust each other.'

Khattak watched her closely. 'Do they?'

'That hasn't been my experience.' She made a helpless gesture. 'It's more that they want to leave it all behind. They don't want the stigma of being known as refugees. They've made a choice, they've risked everything for that choice. They want to be known as Canadians. They want to *become* Canadian.'

Khattak rose to his feet. From his glance at her, Rachel saw he wanted her to stay put. He moved closer to Suha. He'd picked up the photograph and now he handed it to her again.

'*Do* you know this boy? His name was Sami al-Nuri.'

Again, the lift of her eyebrows indicated her surprise.

Without looking at the photograph, she said, 'I'm very sorry that he's come to this end, and sorrier than I can say that he's the subject of your investigation. I processed his case myself.'

'Processed?' Khattak's voice sharpened. 'He'd been granted refuge in Canada? A single young man on his own?'

Suha looked confused for a moment. 'I'm sorry, that was a clumsy choice of words. I meant I opened a file on him – he hadn't gotten very far through the system, I believe. And you're right. He was alone, he wasn't going to be approved. But I did it as a special favor to a member of one of our partners. A group called Woman to Woman. They have a long-established record as a sponsorship agreement holder. This isn't the first time we've partnered with them. Sadly, I doubt it will be the last.'

Suha threw open the window to let in the fresh April breeze. The plangent noise of traffic floated up from the street.

'Did you speak to Audrey Clare? Was she the one who asked you to process Sami al-Nuri's case?'

Suha nodded. 'She called from Lesvos sometime in late February. She said the matter was urgent, a case of life and death.' The corners of her mouth drew down. 'Isn't that the way of things? Every one of our cases is a question of life and death. That's what Sanctuary deals in.'

This was an overstatement in Rachel's view. Canada wasn't a destination of choice for *all* of Syria's refugees. Most had sought asylum in Germany, given Chancellor Merkel's promise of government assistance. Rachel remembered the magazine cover that had cast Angela Merkel as Mother Teresa, a saintly figure wearing a blue-and-white wimple. Refugees called her

Mama Merkel, mother of the Syrian nation.

'Did she say why?'

'Not in any great detail. I had the impression she was reluctant to do so on the phone. But my general impression was that this particular young man was a target. He was known to Assad's forces and they wanted him dead.'

This struck Rachel as peculiar. 'But he was out of Syria.'

Suha grimaced. 'So are a lot of others.'

'Then weren't you concerned that Sami wasn't properly vetted?'

'That never crossed my mind.' She studied Sami's photograph. 'I know Audrey quite well. If she vouched for someone, if she *worried* for someone, I had no reason to doubt her.'

Fair point, Rachel thought. She waited to see what Khattak would make of this.

'I understand the young man might have had family in Toronto. Do you have the file with you here? Or anything else that might help us?'

Just as he hadn't mentioned it to Linh Pham, he didn't tell Suha that Audrey was missing. It was vital they keep that information from as many people as possible. But Suha proved to have an intuitive grasp of the facts.

'Audrey would in fact be the best person to speak with you about this case.'

'We'll be speaking with her soon. But we do need to see his family here.'

Suha brushed past him to search out a file on the dining table. She sorted through several before finding the one she wanted. She gave it to Khattak, who flipped it open to find a picture of the same young man, his eyes bright and searching in the photograph, his face otherwise somber. He was wearing a thin black sweater and blue jeans, the same outfit he'd been killed in. Khattak scanned the file, waiting for Suha's answer.

'I kept the file here because I was trying to schedule an interview with his contacts.'

'You haven't been to see them?'

Suha shook her head. 'I've tried several times. They keep canceling the appointment. I actually brought the file home so I could call to reschedule.'

Khattak was paging through the file she'd given him, oblivious to the worry on her face. He paused at a handwritten page signed with a familiar flourish. It was Audrey's signature.

'What does this list of numbers mean?' He'd taken a good look at the files. Each had a six-digit number attached, prefixed by the letter G. The numbers on the handwritten list followed a different protocol. 'Are these Sanctuary cases?'

Their heads bent together over the list.

Rachel watched their inadvertent closeness with a sensation that bewildered her. She'd had these feelings before – during their investigation into Christopher Drayton's murder, and more recently when she'd joined Khattak in Iran. Was she jealous? Of anyone who encroached upon Khattak's attention? Or was she jealous of any woman she suspected him of being attracted to, no matter how scant the evidence?

She felt dismayed at the thought. She needed to sort herself out before her confusion cast a pall over their partnership. He didn't seem to suffer from similar reservations, quick to encourage her with Nate.

Suha ran her finger down the page in the folder, her sleeve brushing Khattak's arm.

For a hijab-wearing woman, she wasn't preoccupied with maintaining her distance, Rachel thought sourly.

'No, you're right,' Suha said. 'That's not our numbering system.' She tapped one of the stacks. 'You see the "G" designation?'

Khattak nodded.

'Once a case goes to the central processing office in Winnipeg, it gets a case number. G-246891, for example. Then it takes a few months to get to a visa office – though with current delays, that processing time is closer to a year. The numbers you're seeing on this list – they're a different tracking system. They must be numbers Woman to Woman assigns internally. I'm not sure how their system works, or what their numbers mean.'

The numbers were written in numerical order, but with gaps between them.

215   216   220   227   235   248   (601)

The number 601 was circled. Khattak looked up. Easy enough to check with Nate. And with Shukri Danner once they reached the island.

'What number was Sami al-Nuri assigned? I don't see it here.' Suha took the file from him.

'There's no G-number here. That means you *didn't* file this application.'

'I've told you – it would be futile to do so on its face. But if we were able to turn the application into a reunion case, it would have been a different story. That's why reaching the family was so important.'

Khattak closed the file. He nodded at Rachel to indicate they were done.

'We'll contact the family ourselves. I'd appreciate if you would hold off on reaching out to them, until you hear from me.'

A wry twist to her lips, Suha braced her hands on the dining table. 'I have plenty to keep me occupied. As long as you let me know what happens.'

But Rachel knew they wouldn't be handing back Sami's file.

9

Mississauga, Canada

THEY WAITED IN THE CAR for an hour before knocking on the door of the Fakhri family's home, at the address gleaned from the file. In the car, Esa told Rachel a little about his relationship with Audrey, how he'd viewed her as a third sister, who was just as likely to get into trouble as Ruksh, and even more likely to beg to be bailed out of it without facing the consequences.

'She had a crush on you once,' Rachel reminded him.

He smiled. That had been so long ago now: he was proud of how Ruksh and Audrey had turned out, proud of the contribution each was making in her own way. The thought of Audrey in danger – lost, frightened, threatened somehow – was an urgent knot of worry that he could only resolve by seeking answers.

He waited for the Fakhris' car to pull into the driveway of the drab two-story town house in a busy part of Mississauga. It hadn't taken them long to get to the west end; he'd driven with more speed than care, certain that the Fakhri family was an integral part of the puzzle.

There wasn't much information in the file. Declan had unearthed a few more details: the Fakhri family had been in the country for just over a year. They had landed status, the official term for which was 'permanent residents.' They hadn't yet met the residency requirement for full citizenship. Since they'd landed in Canada, they hadn't traveled. Khattak had asked Declan to check if the family had visited Greece. They hadn't even crossed the US border.

The Fakhris were not well-off. The father worked at a local grocer's, the mother stayed home with a small child. Further details were not available.

Ahmed Fakhri was carrying groceries in his arms. Esa and Rachel caught up with him on his doorstep. Esa introduced them, holding up his police ID, and, after a moment's consideration, offering a quiet *salaam*.

He noted Fakhri's reaction with a swift pang of conscience. The other man wasn't well. He was gaunt, his frame delicate; the bags in his arms seemed to bear their weight down on his wrists. He had a pronounced cough, and though he was young, his face was haggard and his hair was sparse and gray. Esa's *salaam* did nothing to reassure him.

He swallowed twice before he unlocked his front door, calling out to his wife in Arabic. There were footsteps, a child's cry, the sound of someone fleeing up the stairs.

Fakhri dropped the grocery bags on a small plastic table in the kitchen. He ushered them into a cramped room where a toddler was playing with a toy inside a playpen. Everything inside the apartment was tidy. A few children's books were piled in a box in one corner next to the playpen. There was a television and a single couch. And in an opposite corner on a narrow baker's rack, a collection of ornaments and photographs.

Fakhri gestured for them to take the couch. He remained standing in front of the playpen, his body blocking their view of the child, a curly-headed girl who called for her father's attention.

Esa shifted his position so that Rachel was closer to the rack. He remained on his feet, his eyes on Fakhri. The man hadn't spoken except to call to his wife. There was no mistaking the fear in his eyes; underlying it was another emotion Esa couldn't decipher.

In slow and careful English, Esa explained why they'd come. He opened the folder to show the man the photograph, but Fakhri held up his hands to ward off Esa's approach.

'No, no. I don't want it.'

His hands gripped the playpen's rail. His skin had turned a ghastly color, his legs were visibly trembling. Before Esa could react, the man fell down with a thump. The little girl began to cry. The man didn't speak, making gasping movements with his mouth.

Rachel called up the stairs to the woman who'd fled. As Khattak helped the man to the couch, Rachel fetched him a glass of water. Khattak held it as the man drank. His hands were trembling too much for him to take hold of it.

The child's wails increased. Rachel strode over to collect her from the playpen, raising her high in her arms. She found a tissue in her pocket and wiped the child's wet face, cooing at her without missing a beat.

The woman – Fakhri's wife? – came flying down the stairs, her pale face outraged.

'Don't you touch my child!' Then she saw her husband, trying to speak but unable to.

Esa could see the struggle in her face. The child had quieted down, taking a liking to Rachel. Her curly head was tucked into Rachel's neck. At a nod from Esa, Rachel disappeared into the kitchen.

The woman rounded on Khattak.

'Get away from him. I'll call the police.' She snatched the glass from his hand.

Khattak gave her a little room, holding up his hands in a placatory gesture, easing away from the couch. He let her speak to her husband. She gave Fakhri the glass. Her voice as she comforted him was gentle, a stark contrast to the way she had snapped at Esa, the endearments she used in Arabic expressed with exquisite tenderness. Khattak studied her. From the photograph he'd seen of the family, she was a hijab-wearing woman, but as she crouched before her husband her head was bare, her hair tumbling over her sweater. They were young, the woman in her mid-twenties, the man no more than thirty.

Khattak waited until the atmosphere had calmed before he asked if they wanted a doctor. He held up his police ID and called Rachel back, introducing her as his partner.

The sight of his ID stopped the woman from saying whatever she'd meant to say next. As threatened as she felt, she wouldn't call the police. Curiously, neither Ahmed Fakhri nor his wife asked to take the child. Fakhri watched the child tucked up in Rachel's arms, his body freely sweating. His wife clung to his hand with a grip that looked as if it might snap his delicate bones. Neither said a word.

There was a chair at the back of the room; Esa hooked it closer with his arm. He sat down facing the Fakhris. He'd called Rachel back in because he didn't want anything about his presence to frighten Fakhri's wife. Rachel indulged the child with nonsense-speak that had no effect on the couple – they didn't relax, they didn't look away from his face.

He began again, this time addressing himself to Fakhri's wife. 'We haven't come here to harm you. You haven't done anything wrong, you aren't being arrested. We're simply wondering about this young man who was seeking to come to Canada.'

He showed them the photograph from the file. 'His name was Sami al-Nuri. Was he a relative of yours?'

The woman exchanged a quick glance with her husband. He raised a hand to speak, she captured it in her own to stop him. She turned to Khattak with a glare.

'You may talk to me. I'm his wife, Dania.'

She straightened her back, caught Khattak's eyes on her hair, and tilted her head. She wasn't embarrassed to be without her head scarf; her glance at him was scornful.

Khattak repeated his introductions and described the reason

for their visit. Like her husband, she didn't look at the photograph. Her answer was clearly evasive.

'We don't know him.'

Khattak's reply was mild. 'He listed you as possible sponsors on his request for asylum in Canada.'

Dania Fakhri tensed. 'I've said we don't know him. I don't know why he said we would be his sponsors.' Her English was fluent, unbroken, very faintly accented.

Stymied by this, he asked, 'Where in Syria are you from?'

The child in Rachel's arms had discovered her mother's presence and let out a shout, demanding to be transferred. Still, neither parent asked for the child. Rachel set her down in her playpen, wiggling a toy and making animal noises. Distracted, the little girl settled in to play.

Khattak kept his attention on Dania Fakhri's face.

Her lips were so dry she had trouble forming words. But when Rachel set down the child, the tension in her body eased. She shifted her posture to shield her husband from his gaze. Something about his presence was terrifying to Ahmed Fakhri, yet he could see Dania's natural instinct was defiance.

'It doesn't matter where we're from. We don't know this boy.'

Khattak persisted. Sooner or later, they would have to tell him something.

'I understand your husband was a teacher. What subject did he teach?'

A painful wheeze issued from Fakhri's lips. Dania Fakhri flicked a glance at Rachel, playing with her child. She asked her husband to take the child upstairs.

His hands were trembling so much that Khattak asked Rachel to help him. He didn't want the child to be hurt as a result of Fakhri's obvious distress. It would also give Rachel an excuse to take a look around.

When they were alone, Dania Fakhri turned on him.

'We don't have to tell you,' she flared. 'We don't have to tell you anything.'

'But that sounds like you have something to hide,' Khattak said reasonably. 'When all we want to know is who this boy is to you – can you confirm his name is Sami al-Nuri?'

Dania Fakhri paused for a heartbeat before she gave him a quick, jerky nod. She had made up her mind to something, fighting back her fear.

'My husband taught geography. Maybe this boy was my husband's student and used his name.'

'Was?'

Did Dania Fakhri know the boy was dead?

Now Dania looked frightened. 'Yes. In Douma, near Damascus,' she supplied, and something about the nervous way she offered additional, unsolicited information, as if to stave off anything else he might ask for, made Khattak experience a sense of distaste and a sharp dissatisfaction with himself.

The feeling deepened when Dania Fakhri's demeanor changed. Her tone became appeasing. She held his gaze with her own, softening her manner.

'My husband isn't involved in politics. I hope you will believe me.' She left her mouth parted after she spoke the words.

Khattak looked away.

'Mrs Fakhri,' he said. 'Something has happened to this boy. That's why we're asking about him. That's all we want – a little information.'

He'd said the wrong thing. She flushed deeply. Her hand went up to her hair, miming a habit she must have had of tucking it away in the presence of a man who was not her relative.

'What's happened to him?' she asked. 'This boy you speak of – Sami al-Nuri – he's dead?' He couldn't quantify her expression: were her dark eyes anxious or wretched with pain? 'And you know this – you know this for certain?'

She came closer, placed a pleading, promising hand on his

arm, a gesture he knew was unthinkable for her. He didn't touch her. He took a step back, releasing himself, raising his voice so Rachel could hear.

'Yes,' he said. 'Sami al-Nuri is dead. He was killed on the island of Lesvos. Did you know he was on the island? Did he contact you to ask for your help?'

She took the photograph from his hand.

There was something subtle and immutable in her face. That stark communication of fear was gone, to be replaced by what? Agony?

Or a sense of reprieve?

She met his eyes and spoke with the ring of truth. 'This boy, he didn't contact us. He wasn't our family, I don't know why he used our name. He looks so young, I'm sorry he's dead.'

'So there's nothing you can tell me, nothing you know about Lesvos.'

'We didn't come through Lesvos.' She said the words with a strange emphasis. He wondered if it was pride.

'What was your route, if not through the Greek islands?'

'We flew from Lebanon. We applied from a camp in Lebanon.'

It had the air of recital to it.

'Did you leave family behind in Syria?'

She looked at him as if she couldn't believe he'd asked her such a question. In her blazing defiance, she was beautiful.

She picked up the card he'd given her husband and crumpled it with contempt. 'We came with nothing but ourselves. We left the whole world behind.'

There was nothing to be gained by pressing her. She brushed past him to the stairs, meeting her husband as he came down. They spoke to each other in Arabic, then Dania Fakhri ran up the stairs to see to her child.

Rachel joined Esa at the door. Fakhri followed them outside. When Rachel had gone ahead, Fakhri tugged at Khattak's arm, bringing him to a standstill. Khattak apologized for bothering his family. Fakhri was oblivious to these courtesies. He leaned in closer to Khattak and whispered, 'Is it that you want money? I can get you money, if you give me another day.'

Esa was overcome by remorse. How could he have let Fakhri arrive at such a conclusion?

He offered a gentle, conciliatory phrase in Arabic, one of a handful he knew, trying to find a way to connect. The words offered little comfort, so Khattak tried another tack. 'You're in no danger from us. We're police officers; we're here to protect you, Mr Fakhri.'

The man shook his head. Something Esa had said had driven the hope from his eyes.

'I can't pay for protection, I don't have any money. My wife, my child, they need it. I can give you something else – something that you want.'

A sob in his voice, he offered, 'I can give you names. I can give you all of their names.'

Rachel could see how angry Khattak was from the pulse that beat at his temple. His hands were clenched on the steering wheel. He didn't swear, he didn't say anything, he wasn't angry at Ahmed Fakhri, or what he'd failed to tell them. He was furious with himself.

Not knowing what to ask, she said, 'Sir?'

'Community Policing,' he said, in as bitter a tone as she'd heard from him. 'I couldn't have been more callous if I tried. We should have gotten background. We have no idea what this family has been through. We made this man think we were no different than the men who work for Assad. He was terrorized. *I'm* the one who terrorized him. And his wife.' Now he did curse at himself. 'God knows what she must have thought, what she's already been through.' He glanced over at Rachel. 'I wish you hadn't left the room.'

Before she could respond, he went on, 'Dania thought it was

deliberate. They're terrified of something. They tried to buy my silence.' He hit the wheel with one hand. 'They think that's how things are done. In Syria, the Mukhabarat act as the people's enemy. They have more to fear from the security services than they do from violence or crime. Fakhri tried to buy me off with money he doesn't have. He must have spent it on bribes to get himself this far. And his wife...'

He dropped the subject, suddenly aware of what he was confiding. Rachel picked up on it at once. 'His wife, sir?'

He met her gaze briefly. 'I've no doubt she thinks the police in this country are no different than the ones she left behind.'

Out of respect for Dania's dignity, he chose not to elaborate. Rachel understood without the need for words.

10

Mytilene, Lesvos

ALI TRIED TO TAKE PART *in the conversation in the bar. The volunteers had come to relax before going out to meet the boats; he saw several familiar faces – Freja, Hans, and Peter Conroy, who was stationed on Chios. They worked for different organizations, trying to help out with the skills at their disposal. Peter had come from Australia. His NGO was low on resources, so he doubled as Audrey's assistant. When Shukri and Audrey were on Lesvos, Peter took over operations on Chios. He was friendly and well-meaning, though he became markedly unpleasant after he'd had a few drinks.*

Octavio was the owner of the bar. He didn't mind if Ali didn't drink, as long as he didn't bring Aya into the bar. Aya was asleep, so Ali had come down to see if there was news of Israa.

He was trying not to think of his siblings. He had four older brothers and a sister. He hadn't seen any of them in years. He would see them in the Akhirah now; they would never meet in Syria again. He couldn't lose Israa, too. She was his love, his life – her absence was his tragedy, an accounting on a scale of losses in a system that knew no measurement.

He was like Qabbani's willow tree, always dying while standing.

Two members of the Italian Coast Guard joined him at his table. Commander Illario Benemerito and Vincenzo Sancilio were serious about their work – they volunteered off-duty in Greece. Benemerito was gathering information on refugee flows to help with the Coast Guard's work, though the Aegean was beyond his jurisdiction. The Italians were looking for solutions: their patrols on the Mediterranean had made them well acquainted with the horrors of the crossing.

Benemerito had taken Ali under his wing. If there was news of Israa, he would be the first to tell him. He never parted from Ali without giving him a meal or pressing money into his hands. Ali tried to refuse, but the price of dignity was too high. He needed money, he needed the help of others. One day, he'd show others the same benevolence.

'I'm sorry about Sami.' Benemerito patted his shoulder. 'That's why you look so sad. Two of your friends are gone. It could be it's time to move on.'

'The borders are closed. Even if I could get through, how could I leave Israa?'

The Italians exchanged a glance. Last week, six hundred people had drowned on the crossing from Libya to Italy. Ali's belief that Israa had survived flew in the face of these realities: he couldn't give it up, no matter how they tried to persuade him.

'You have to think of Aya.'

Ali couldn't muster the energy to argue with the commander, so he offered, 'Don't worry. I've been writing letters to God.'

They didn't recognize Qabbani's poem. He tried again. 'He only responds to letters of love, I know He'll find her again.'

Eleni Latsoudi entered the bar, her grave eyes searching for him. She'd just come in from the sea. When he got up to meet her, hopeful of news, Benemerito murmured, 'When will he learn? The dead are the lucky ones.'

11

Scarborough, Canada

Esa's conversation with Nate took place on the terrace at the back of the house on the Bluffs. The weather had turned fine and Esa, after excusing himself to pray, had returned to his comfortable lounger to look out at the waves whispering under the crescent of the moon, the night sky spangled with currents of swirling stars. Leaves rustled on the wind, the first scent of spring edging the purity of the air.

Nate was on edge, his hand clutched around a balloon-shaped glass, its contents lending a smoky flavor to the night.

'I'm coming with you,' Nate warned him. His half-packed suitcase was sitting on a chair. When Esa had arrived at the house, he'd been flinging personal items into it with scant regard for what he actually needed. Esa had asked him to take a break, and now, at Nate's words, he didn't demur. There would be things Nate could do on the Greek islands that would be useful to their investigation, people he could approach without offering the specter of authority, a lesson Esa had learned from his interview with Ahmed Fakhri.

But before they got to that place, there were several questions he needed to ask Nate – clarity he needed in his own mind, a certain frank communication that had always been possible in the days before Laine Stoicheva had come between them. His former partner still cast a shadow between them, a shadow Esa hoped to banish.

He began with what seemed to him to be simpler things. He

asked Nate about his deleted e-mails. As he'd guessed, Nate was surprised to hear them mentioned.

'Did your tech expert say I'd deleted them recently?'

'Didn't you?'

Nate looked a bit sheepish. He hitched a shoulder at Esa in a shrug, a familiar gesture that was easy for Esa to interpret, given the history of their friendship. Nate's motives had been personal; he hadn't been double-dealing.

'So?' Esa studied his friend keenly. 'What's been on your mind, other than Audrey's lack of communication? What else *could* be on your mind?' He tried to imagine himself in a similar scenario: understanding was swift. 'This was about Rachel? You thought the e-mails would reflect badly on you?'

Nate kept his gaze fixed on the ragged shoreline of the Bluffs. The waves left it whole, then erased it in spiraling loops, the Bluffs that rose from the shore, a series of sharp, white cliffs.

'Nate?' Esa prodded. 'If you want me to find Audrey, you'll have to tell me everything.'

'Yes, all right.'

The two men were childhood friends. They had seen the best and worst of each other, the bond between them deeper for it.

'I'm not proud of myself,' Nate began.

'You never are.' There were a handful of people Esa felt comfortable enough to tease. Nate was the first outside family. Rachel had become another.

'Esa, listen. You're going to be angry. And of course, you'd be perfectly within your rights.'

Esa could guess where this was heading. He picked up his glass, and muttered his doubts into it. 'I'm far from perfect at anything. Who knows that better than you?'

When Nate didn't take that as an invitation to come clean, Esa brought matters to a head.

'I haven't read the e-mails you deleted, Nate, I wouldn't without your permission. But I realized at once in Ottawa – you've seen

Laine, haven't you? You've slept with her. That's why you're concerned about your e-mails.' There was a break in his voice he couldn't control. 'I don't want you to do something stupid, but as far as it concerns me, I don't care.'

'Dammit, Esa. Is there anything I can tell you, you don't already know?'

'I *am* a detective, Nate. The concierge at the Chateau wasn't what I'd call discreet.'

'No.' Nate's response was sheepish. 'I didn't mean for it to happen. When you were in Iran, I thought I could help by reaching out to Laine. Stupidly, I thought I was immune – she's different now, not that I'd try to convince you of that...'

Esa shrugged. 'You don't have to. She helped me over that business in Algonquin, but frankly, I don't care what her motives are. I *do* care about Rachel.'

'Rachel?'

'She's the reason you deleted those e-mails, isn't she? Unless there's some other reason?'

'None whatsoever. I wish I'd known you'd take it this well, I would have told you as soon as you returned.'

'Tell me now.'

'It's nothing. It happened once. It was the thought of Rachel knowing that made me feel a bit shabby.'

'Rachel is the last person to pass judgment.'

Nate glanced over at him with a sudden frown. 'Of course, you know her better than I do. You've grown very close.'

Esa shook his head at Nate. 'Don't make me your excuse, I'm not in your way. I'm only making it clear to you that I need to read Audrey's e-mails.'

Nate didn't take this in. He looked up at the clouds assembling over their heads, the familiar rolling darkness that collected over the Bluffs, blanking out the white light of the stars.

'Yes, fine. Read anything you want. Read it all, there's nothing there.'

Esa got to the point of his visit. 'There were a lot of e-mails about financials.'

'You mean the boat? Surely you think it's reasonable that I refused her the boat.'

'I do.' He said this with the certainty of a man with two younger sisters, neither of whom he wanted out on the Aegean attempting the work of the Coast Guard. 'But I wasn't thinking of the boat. Woman to Woman burned through several hundred thousand dollars in the past four months. Do you know where that money went?'

'Every cent of it. We didn't burn it, Esa. It went to relief and resettlement work.'

He looked shamefaced as he said this and Esa grinned. Nate hated being praised. He would do anything to avoid congratulations.

'And plane tickets?' he asked, recalling something Rachel had told him.

'Plane tickets?' Nate looked at him. 'To come home, you mean. I booked Audrey an open ticket so she could come home when she was ready.'

'What about that withdrawal from her personal account? And why are you notified when Audrey spends money from that account?'

'Why do you move into the Forest Hill house whenever your mother is away?'

Their eyes met in acknowledgment of their brotherly guilt. They were prone to overstep their bounds; Ruksh and Audrey frequently fought their interference. In Nate's case, the intrusiveness was understandable – he'd become Audrey's guardian when their parents were killed. Esa preferred not to examine his own protectiveness too closely.

'So you've been monitoring her bank account,' he said. 'What else? Credit cards?'

'And a satellite phone.' Nate anticipated his next question. 'The last time she called me was two weeks ago. Since then, the

99

phone's been out of service. No one picked up at first. Now the phone is dead.'

Khattak took the number down. He would get Gaffney working on phone records, and assign Declan to sort out Audrey's financials.

'You think she bought a boat?'

'I do.'

'What do you think she did with it?'

Nate's sigh was deep and worried. 'I'd like to think she used it to help this boy in some way. Perhaps he had family on the Turkish coast that she wanted to bring across. Knowing Audrey, she wouldn't stop there. What if she was doing her own patrols?' He swallowed. 'What if her boat capsized at sea, and she drowned like so many others?'

Esa was following his own line of thought. He used it to distract Nate from his fear.

'I can think of a reason why someone would kill a French Interpol agent. Agent Bertin may have been asked to stem the tide of refugees en route to Calais – she would have been a threat to smugglers. But what I can't fathom is why someone would shoot the boy. What threat could *he* have posed? And why were they shot with Audrey's gun?'

'I shouldn't have given it to her,' Nate said with great bitterness.

'How did you get it?'

'Legal means. I applied for a license for Audrey, I had her take the test. I picked the gun myself, to clear international customs.'

'There was no forensic report in the file I received,' Esa mused. 'How did the Greek police connect the gun to Audrey?'

They made their way back into the house. Little arrows of lightning had begun to pierce through the clouds. The rain would be on them soon.

'Another stupid decision. I had the gun engraved with Audrey's name.'

Esa bit back the words that rose to his tongue. Nate blamed

himself as it was. He didn't need to tell him he should have consulted Esa.

'There is one other thing, Nate.'

Nate stopped to look at his friend. His face was tired, his gold hair uncombed, his shirt and slacks were rumpled.

'You reviewed Audrey's requests for money – you flagged the money for the boat. Did anything else strike you? Any smaller, regular transactions?'

Nate frowned, trying to remember. 'There was payroll – I was a bit embarrassed at how little we spent on payroll, but Audrey wanted the bulk of the funds to be spent on the people she'd gone there to assist, not on administration. Most of our staff are volunteers. We pay expenses, but we don't pay salaries.'

'So on the islands you'd have how many salaried staff members?'

'Only one, I think. Shukri. Audrey didn't take money from the foundation. We have offices on two islands: Lesvos and Chios. Audrey split her time between them, but I don't know if she had some particular reason for being on Lesvos that day.'

'Maybe something took her there,' Esa said. 'Something that involved Interpol and this boy that nobody knows.'

Nate walked him to the door. 'You don't think Audrey is involved, do you? You must know there's a reasonable explanation for her disappearance.'

'She didn't kill an Interpol agent, I know that. But she's involved in this somehow – we'll figure it out, Nate.' He gripped his friend's shoulder. 'Try and get some rest before the flight.'

He was almost at his car when he looked up at the house again. The outdoor lights were on, illuminating the circle of the driveway. Nate stood on the porch, his eyes reflecting a curious amber light.

An unaccustomed impulse flickered through Esa's mind. He hadn't been entirely honest with Nate. Nate caught his mood at once.

'What is it?'

'It's really done this time, isn't it. You and Laine.'

Nate came down the steps, his face oddly anxious under the outdoor lights. Rain was falling in a drizzle, glazing the stones on the driveway. Diamond drops studded Esa's hair.

'There's something wrong with Laine, something different about her. I have to admit I'm worried, I wish I could say otherwise.'

Esa had noticed it too, though he didn't view it as his business. And he wondered if this was ground they were going to tread again, when they both had more pressing concerns.

'What?' Nate looked worried, this time on Esa's account.

'You care what Rachel thinks of you, you've taken an interest in her.' He held up a hand before Nate could deny it. 'It's none of my business, I know. But I know Rachel better than you do, and I can tell you she hasn't had it easy.'

'I know about Zach, I've met him.'

Esa shook his head. 'It's not just Zach, so you need to be careful.' He unlocked his car, searching for a way to say what he meant, thinking of both his friends. He decided to be frank even if it caused Nate some injury.

'Don't hurt her,' he said. 'The things you break aren't easily repaired.'

Toronto, Canada

Khattak let himself into his mother's house. He knew she would rouse herself in the middle of the night if it meant she could see him before he left for Greece.

The lights in the entrance hall were on; he heard the quiet clink of china from the living room, accompanied by feminine laughter. His mother was entertaining. He must have been so preoccupied with making arrangements that he missed the car on the street.

When he'd placed his keys on a table in the hall and entered the room, his mother's face brightened with joy. He walked over and embraced her, kissing the soft skin of her cheek. He greeted her guest, a dynamic woman his mother's age, by the name of Emily Banks. A retired defense attorney, she was married to Justice Kelly Morgan, a luminary of the court. Khattak had never appeared in her courtroom without wishing he'd been better prepared. Kelly Morgan and Emily Banks were known for hosting salons where the glitterati of the legal world gathered to gossip and to drink unfathomably expensive champagne. His mother had met Emily at one of these salons, invited by mutual friends. Emily and Judge Morgan were two members of her group.

When Khattak had met Emily before, he'd found the encounter as challenging as when he'd crossed swords with Judge Morgan. She was a well-dressed, elegant woman with an imperious manner of speaking that made him feel like a boy. He smiled inwardly when he realized he was gripping his mother's hand. He kissed it lightly and settled her in her seat.

The preliminary courtesies concluded, he explained he'd be leaving for Greece, but wasn't expecting to be away long.

Angeza Khattak passed him a cup of tea and placed a bowl of *savaiyaan* at his elbow. This was a dish of vermicelli noodles cooked in milk and saturated with sugar. It was Khattak's favorite dessert: he associated it with his mother's love, and with his father's joyful return to their home in the wake of Friday prayers.

His mother was wearing a Kashmiri shawl over traditional clothing. Embroidered with soft pink paisleys, it made her look young and fresh. She was telling Emily that Esa had been summoned by the prime minister, and as always in his mother's hands, his accomplishments were embellished in the telling. Emily inquired about his trip with a skeptical lift to her brow.

'Are you conducting the prime minister's business or your own? Or are you looking for another family for your mother to sponsor? Come to think of it, Inspector, why aren't you a member of our group? Or of any other private group?'

He finished his dessert before answering, taking a moment to consider. Emily was too sharp to be given a hint of what he was about. He couldn't lay the blame on Nate, and he couldn't mention Audrey's disappearance.

He settled for the briefest explanation by calling it a routine inquiry, and focused on the second part of her question. 'My line of work is quite sensitive. It's possible that because I'm a police officer, my involvement in a sponsorship group would raise a conflict of interest. But if you don't mind, I'd like to ask you some questions about the process.'

He'd realized that Emily might be able to shed some light on the Fakhris' refusal to speak.

'I know you sponsored a family as part of a private group. Is there a difference between a private application and one with a family sponsor?'

Emily Banks set her teal and gold cup in its saucer with a clink. Esa's father had purchased the Elizabethan Lucerne tea set on the occasion of Esa's birth. His mother used it whenever he came to see her.

'You've really kept yourself aloof, haven't you?'

This was too much for his mother to bear. 'Emily, please. I rely on Esa completely. He's too modest to tell you the details.'

Embarrassed, Esa brushed aside this praise. He'd given his mother the funds to support the sponsorship at the level she wished, but it was an action he preferred not to advertise.

He waited for Emily to continue. A little surprised, she did.

'Yes, there's a difference. A private effort can be difficult. You raise the funds and you volunteer your time. There are also other issues – interfering in the lives of strangers isn't easy. Family cases, on the other hand, are fast-tracked because sponsors are invested in the outcome. There's less pressure on the government, so the sponsorship process is streamlined.'

A distinct advantage, then, to the boy who'd hoped to come to Canada. An advantage the Fakhris had refused him. If there *was* no family connection, it made sense. There was also the possibility that the responsibilities Emily was describing – emotional and financial – were too onerous for the Fakhris to handle. Denying the connection might have been their only way out. He couldn't shake his impression that Dania Fakhri had lied.

'Do private sponsors take on individual applicants?'

Emily Banks looked doubtful. 'Girls, maybe. Otherwise, I wouldn't think so. Our group, for example, sponsored a family whose circumstances were extreme.'

'In what way?'

Emily waved a hand. 'Their medical needs. The children still need counseling. They were traumatized by the crossing. Their father suffered an injury – a peculiar one for a lifeboat passenger.'

Esa frowned. 'A near-drowning? Not so peculiar, surely?'

'His injury resembled strangulation. When we asked him to explain, he claimed he hadn't been attacked.'

Esa noticed his mother's concern. He decided not to share his theory: it was possible the man's boat had capsized. His children might have panicked in the water, clawing at their father's throat. He may have wanted to protect his children from the knowledge that they were the ones who had harmed him.

'He didn't tell you anything else?'

Emily's reply was dry. 'A Syrian man is not about to discuss his personal issues with a group of unknown women.'

Esa glanced at his mother. 'I thought there was a man in your group. Someone who runs your errands.'

Emily laughed at this, a satirical sound of amusement. 'He's really no help at all, you know how reclusive he is.'

Surprised, Khattak said, 'I do? How?'

Emily's sharp glance quizzed him. 'I thought Nathan Clare was your friend.'

105

When Emily had gone, Khattak took a seat at the breakfast bar while his mother fussed about the kitchen. His eye fell on the portrait of his wife, a photograph he'd never felt he could ask his mother to remove. He swallowed a familiar knot of pain.

'What can I make you to eat?'

'Nothing, Ami. I had dinner with Nate.'

'He came to see me while you were in Iran.'

'Did you ask him to join your group?' He found it strange that Nate hadn't mentioned it.

'He insisted when I told him about it. He thinks he's been given too much, so he wants to help.'

'He personally funds Woman to Woman.'

His mother smiled at him. 'That's not enough for Nathan. You know how he is, Esa.' She waited before she added, 'I'm glad to have him back.'

Esa gave her hand a squeeze. 'I am, too.'

He'd missed his friend. Nate may have kept his counsel because he feared Esa's censure. Perhaps he thought Esa would suspect him of trying to ingratiate himself. But the truth was simpler and worthier of Nate. His bond with Esa's mother had deepened with his own parents' deaths. The consideration he showed her was a mark of his friendship with Esa, but also of his sense of loss.

Esa felt a quick stab of fear. If he didn't find Audrey, Nate would lose everyone he loved.

His mother sensed his concern.

'What is it, Esa?' She sounded afraid. 'Is something wrong with Nate?'

He denied it at once. He wouldn't add to her worries by making her share in his fear.

12

RACHEL WAS FINDING IT HARD to believe where she was ending up. A few weeks ago, she'd been in Iran. Now she'd just landed in Athens, where meetings with the local police had been arranged.

The bodies of Aude Bertin and Sami al-Nuri had been moved to a morgue in the city. After she'd had a shower and a change of clothes, a member of the Greek police force was to take her to the morgue, while Khattak handled an Interpol interview with the discretion he was known for.

She wasn't quite sure what Nate would be up to, but she didn't mind the division of labor. She knew what to do at a morgue. She wasn't quite sure how to handle cross-jurisdictional issues, and her blunt style of engagement might not go over well with their Greek counterparts.

She stretched out her shoulders in the comfortable expanse of the limo Nate had hired. He wasn't ostentatious with his wealth, but he did take certain things for granted. The Eleftherios Venizelos airport had been crowded: it was Greece's largest and busiest airport, a regional hub that served as the base for Aegean Airlines. Rachel had expected to compete for one of the dozens of yellow taxis that circled the airport in a loop. Instead, Nate had hired a private driver in a very expensive car, who was depositing them at their hotel.

She could smell the sea in the air as they passed the broken arches of a set of oak-gold ruins, and shifted in her seat to see if she could catch a view of the Parthenon at the peak of a stone-studded hill. Across from her, Khattak's eyes were closed. Rachel assumed he'd been to Greece before, and wasn't quite as awestruck as she was by the wide boulevards, the vast roar of traffic, or the commingled sight of cypresses and olive groves.

She looked up to find Nate watching her. There was worry and fear in his face – the emotions she would expect from a man whose sister was missing in deeply disturbing circumstances. She wanted to offer reassurance, but didn't think he'd welcome it, not after the way he'd rebuked her in Ottawa. He hadn't spoken to her on the private flight he'd chartered, but then he hadn't spoken to Khattak either.

For an hour or two on the plane, Khattak had read through Nate's recovered e-mails, while passing on to her the task of combing through Ruksh's and Audrey's correspondence.

She'd fallen asleep quickly; she'd get back to the task after her meeting at the morgue.

'Will you be waiting for us in the hotel lobby?'

Nate shook his head, his pale gold hair falling into his eyes. He spoke quietly so as not to wake Khattak.

'I'm meeting Sehr. The four of us can have dinner at the hotel. By then we should be able to come to some conclusions.'

Rachel hoped that would be the case. But what she understood from Khattak was that Interpol was pressing them for answers, rather than the reverse.

The pathologist at the morgue was a friendly man who was six inches shorter than Rachel, and where Rachel was strong and well muscled, the excess weight on his body was distributed so that he gave an impression of compactness. His English was fluent, his accent deep and melodic. Keeping up a steady flow of conversation, he told Rachel as many facts about Canada as he could pull from his memory.

Rachel's smile was warm and genuine. She knew it was Dr

AUSMA ZEHANAT KHAN

Giannopoulos's way of making her feel welcome. He was now quoting facts about Chris Chelios to her, miming the motion of a hockey stick. Nothing was guaranteed to get past Rachel's defenses faster.

'You come from the place of ice hockey, yes?'

Rachel happily agreed. If nations could be distilled to their essence, and Canada's was hockey, what would Greece's be? Olive groves? The Acropolis? Or the foundations of democracy?

Dr Giannopoulos explained that the city morgue was actually a hospital mortuary attached to a pathology lab. He led the way through the cool, dim halls to a bank of refrigerated cabinets in a spacious, well-organized room adjacent to a smaller viewing chamber for relatives, police, and others, usually medical trainees.

He pulled a clipboard down from the wall and read through his written conclusions. Then he pulled Sami al-Nuri's body from its cold chamber. Together, they viewed his face in silence.

It was the boy from the photograph provided by Sanctuary Syria. The fragile bones of his face and his fine, slender jaw suggested he hadn't grown into manhood; his neck and shoulders hadn't yet acquired adult musculature. His hair was curly and thick, his face white and without distinction, as was common to many of the bodies Rachel had seen: the experience of life erased by the moment of death.

Dr Giannopoulos gave her an anxious look. 'Are you certain you want to see the rest?'

Confused, Rachel said, 'The gunshot wound, you mean? I do need to.'

He shook his head. 'There's a lot more to this poor boy than his cause of death.'

He pulled back the sheet that covered Sami's body with a prayerful murmur. Instantly, Rachel knew why.

The boy's body was scarred and bruised, marked and discolored from his sternum to his toes. Puckered round scars that peppered his torso looked like cigarette burns. There were jagged slashes through his flesh, wounds that hadn't been stitched... they looked more like they'd been cauterized. Some of the flesh looked sick, as if it had begun decaying long before his death. There were other signs Rachel recognized: broken bones that had never had the chance to knit or be repaired.

And the boy's testicles were missing.

She choked back the sob that rose in her throat, casting the good doctor a horrified glance. He was still praying to himself.

'Nearly all his major bones were broken,' he told her, pointing to bruising on the thighs. He twitched up the sheet, his hand above the gunshot wound. Feeling sick at the wholesale torture inflicted on the boy, Rachel forced herself to focus on the wound at the heart.

'Shot at close range?'

Sounding sad, he answered, 'Very close. Not more than two feet. You see the precision of the shooter's aim.'

Rachel accepted this. 'Is there anything else I should know? Anything that's medically relevant?'

Dr Giannopoulos shook his head. 'A single shot. It would have killed him instantly.'

He showed her Aude Bertin's body in the next cabinet, and here Rachel was able to tell a little more from the body. She'd been an older woman, her light brown hair cropped short, her eyebrows and fingernails groomed, the slight groove of a scar denting her upper lip. Her face was frozen not in an expression of fear or surprise, but rather in defiance. Her wound was similar to the boy's, precise and small, directly above the heart.

'We have the bullets,' Dr Giannopoulos told her.

Rachel nodded. 'Can you tell me this? I didn't see the bodies before they were removed. Could you tell whether the boy or the woman was shot first?'

Dr Giannopoulos nodded. 'The woman, I think, though that is not an official conclusion.'

'What makes you think so?'

He turned over Aude Bertin's left arm. There was distinct bruising along the forearm and shoulder.

'Her body was found to the right of the boy's, so close together they were nearly inseparable. But hers a little in front.'

Rachel studied the bruising for herself. She could see the distinct grip of a thumb just below the left shoulder, and at the wrist, a tight band of red that was now discolored.

'I see,' she said. 'You think she tried to protect him, shield his body somehow.'

'And then she was pulled aside and shot before the boy was. Bang bang. Two shots. No other bullets at the scene.'

It was possible, Rachel thought. If the boy had been shot first, Aude Bertin would have had the chance to reach for her gun. She'd been armed, her gun found with her body.

'What else can you tell me, Dr Giannopoulos? Was anything taken from the agent's body? Were there any other injuries, any question of drug use?'

She'd been thinking about the detailed list of pharmaceuticals on Woman to Woman's requisition list.

The little doctor shrugged. 'This will take me a while, Miss Getty. And I cannot keep both the bodies. The French government has asked for their agent's body to be released. They want a separate report compiled by their own examiners. This poor lady is about to board a flight.'

It felt terribly intrusive to do so, but in light of this information, Rachel thought she should snap a few pictures to review. She didn't expect that Khattak would be sending her to France.

Dr Giannopoulos was reluctant to allow this. Rachel talked him round with a promise of discretion.

When she was finished, he shooed her out of the room, back to his private office.

'I can only tell you about the body. Your other questions, you must speak to the police. They will tell you about the scene.'

'You would have photographed the scene,' Rachel said hopefully. The doctor shook his head.

'I am for the body,' he told her again. 'The police captain will tell you the rest.'

'Who's in charge of the local investigation? Lesvos police or Athens?'

Dr Giannopoulos arched his heavy eyebrows, giving his face a look of comical consternation. 'No, no,' he said. 'This investigation has been taken over by the International Police Cooperation Division. Because of you, I think.' He made a shoving motion with his hands. 'This will not be easy. Not for our Captain Nicolaides.'

'Why is that?'

'The Interpols,' he said. 'They are calling the shots.'

Rachel took a break in her hotel room. She didn't want to eat, sickened by her discoveries. She drank a bottle of water as she waited for Nate and Khattak to return. They were staying at the ruinously overpriced King George Hotel. Rachel pinched herself just to make sure it was real.

Her room was so luxurious and so richly appointed that she was afraid to place her suitcase on the bed. The windows were open and a glorious April breeze carried the scent of the Aegean into her room, along with the evocative perfume of blossoms Rachel couldn't identify. They were thick and curling, their petals feathery as they drifted over her balcony.

She settled herself in a plush white armchair, her laptop open on her knees, her eyes taking in deep gold curtains brushing daffodil walls. In the other room, the bathroom was paneled in original Greek marble; she'd promised herself a soak in the tub at the end of the night.

She couldn't have imagined such luxury; she'd only seen it on reality television. She hadn't envied it or felt its absence. And she wasn't sure she felt comfortable with it, especially in light of what she'd just seen – and knowing they were headed to the camps. The contrast was too cruel, the luxury unmerited and wasteful.

She wrote up her conversation with Dr Giannopoulos for Khattak to review, trying not to betray her sense of horror, and then, sipping at her water, she read over the bulk of Audrey's correspondence with Ruksh, making additional notes.

A vein of affectionate humor ran through the e-mails as the two women discussed the challenge of keeping up with each other across time zones, or pondered the kind of clothes Audrey should have packed for Greece.

As Ruksh had told Esa, much of the e-mail simply contained Audrey's follow-up questions about the well-being of the families who had arrived in Canada. Ruksh would respond with a brief account of their health and a diagnosis of the obstacles before them. Rachel found herself warming to Audrey and Ruksh in a way she hadn't before: despite their teasing and their occasional self-absorption, both women were concerned about the welfare of new arrivals. Both took an interest in the needs of individual cases. And both made suggestions on how resettlement could be humanized. Ruksh wrote of not making the sponsorships seem like charity, though Woman to Woman held all sponsorship funds in trust. Occasionally the friends disagreed, but one or the other would eventually be convinced of her friend's point of view.

Finally Rachel found the reference to Sami al-Nuri she was searching for. It was more detailed than Ruksh had suggested to Khattak, though to be fair, it had been sent in December. Rachel read it several times, then she sat back in her chair to do a little thinking about the warning Audrey had sent Ruksh.

Dania is his sister. She's the only one who can help him, the only one who knows how valuable he is. He trusts her. Please tell her Sami has run out of time. Tell her he's waiting for help. Tell her she has to convince her husband. There is no other way.

So why had Dania denied knowing Sami? How could she have been unaffected by news of her brother's death? Khattak had guessed she might be lying, but hadn't been able to determine her motive for doing so.

Rachel looked for a reference to plane tickets. There were frequent discussions of how Woman to Woman could best direct its funds, but no specific mention of Audrey needing tickets. Nate had told Khattak that he'd booked Audrey an open ticket back in December. So why had Audrey told Ruksh she needed money for travel? Where had she been planning to go? Home to Toronto? Or somewhere that wasn't on their radar yet?

While searching for the exact reference, Rachel came across the reason Ruksh had asked Khattak not to read her e-mails. At the end of January, Ruksh had written Audrey an e-mail that shed some light on her personal feelings about her brother's involvement in her life. It was strongly worded and harsh with pain – reading it brought a lump to Rachel's throat. But Ruksh's message also stirred in her a sense of anger at how unfair Ruksh was to Khattak, how she saw only her own interests. Rachel was most struck by the e-mail's conclusion. It was so wounding, she knew she'd do her utmost to keep Khattak from seeing it.

What am I supposed to do about Esa? He wants absolution, he calls and writes to the point I can't stand it. I don't need his shabby excuses. He works against my happiness every chance he gets. Do you know why I'm not there with you? He convinced Ami I'd get into trouble – she begged me not to go. She cried her heart out. There's no room in my heart to forgive him. After what happened with Hassan? I wish Esa was dead.

Audrey's response was brutal. Rachel liked her all the better for it. It was the kind of thing she'd have written herself.

Shut up, Ruksh. You didn't care about Hassan, you do love Esa. Don't ever let me hear you say something that outrageous again.

Rachel closed her laptop and set it aside. She rubbed the cool neck of her water bottle against her overheated skin. She'd never told Khattak much about her parents, and she knew he also preferred to keep his affairs to himself. But he *had* told her about Ruksh, and he spoke of his sister with a mixture of respect and indulgence. He loved both his sisters deeply. He'd told her he cherished his family more closely in the aftermath of his wife's death. She could picture how much his sister's words would hurt him. She knew something about that kind of pain. Rachel's mother had once told her she would have suffered less if Rachel had disappeared instead of Zachary.

Rachel cursed in the quiet of her hotel room. 'Stupid bloody fool. She doesn't know her brother at all. He *could* be killed in the line of duty, then she'd have that on her conscience.'

She muttered a few other choice phrases. With a sigh, she opened her laptop again and began to make notes. She typed up each reference to Sami al-Nuri, noting the dates Audrey had raised queries, putting down words to see if they formed a pattern. In one of the last e-mails sent before her disappearance, Audrey discussed funds for a boat – except the reference wasn't explicit.

You know that big purchase I hoped for? Nate turned me down. But I met a guy who says he can help me out, I won't have to break the bank. I think this is going to work. Pray for me, Ruksh, because I've been taking on a lot… maybe too much. But you know me – always tilting at windmills. Let's hope I don't get blown away. And keep your eye on Nate, in case I'm not around. Make sure he doesn't blow this thing with Rachel. Love you, be good, and for God's sake, patch up this stupid thing with Esa. To you, your Overlord, to me, my Bumbling Lamb.

The e-mail ended with a string of tiny hearts.

Rachel found herself smiling at her screen, when she should have been focusing on the apparent reference to the boat. She stored her discovery away for a later moment when she could examine it, and made a note of her questions: Who was the man who'd helped Audrey out? And why had she suggested she might be difficult to reach? More importantly, what had she taken on that might have turned out to overwhelm her?

One good thing had come of Rachel's invasion of Ruksh's privacy: they now had a reason to believe Audrey had vanished for her own reasons. Which meant there was a good chance she would reappear in due course.

A tap on her door distracted her from her thoughts.

'Rachel? Are you ready?'

It was Khattak. She wasn't certain what time it was. Dusk, from a glance out her window. He had promised to collect her on his way to dinner.

She scrambled off the chair, searching for her shoes.

'Be right there, sir.'

A quick thrust of a comb through her hair, the exchange of one jacket for another, a little bit of powder on her face, and she was ready.

She didn't want to alarm Nate with her concern for Audrey, but her priority was to make certain Khattak didn't read his sister's e-mails for himself.

13

Athens, Greece

SEHR GHILZAI HAD JUST RETURNED from the prosecutor's office in Athens, where she'd had a frustrating discussion with the prosecutor affiliated with the International Police Cooperation Division. The circumstances of Audrey's disappearance had been referred to Yannis Andreadis; it was in his hands to determine if a warrant should be issued for Audrey Clare's arrest.

Well-built and bluntly handsome, he'd hit on Sehr within minutes of their meeting. She'd been relieved to see that her IPCD liaison, a much older gentleman by the name of Philip Nicolaides, had shut down the prosecutor's attempts to make her feel uncomfortable. Even as soberly dressed as she'd been, Sehr hadn't been able to make Andreadis treat her like a colleague.

After a few minutes of listening to Andreadis, Philip Nicolaides barked something at the other man in Greek, then turned to Sehr with an expression of smooth and deliberate politeness.

'What are you wishing Mr Andreadis to tell you?'

Sehr was grateful for his help. Since arriving on Lesvos two weeks ago, she'd worked her way through an unfamiliar chain of command to try and determine whose jurisdiction governed the double murder at the camp. The Interpol agent who'd flown in to investigate had refused to meet with her. Nate had called her and told her not to press because the prime minister had asked Esa to act as the government's representative. Fair enough. She still needed to know the legal ramifications for Audrey personally, and for Woman to Woman.

The Greek authorities might shut them down. It had been difficult to get a permit to set up shop; the extension she had filed for was tied up in red tape.

'Is there a search on for Audrey Clare? Does Mr Andreadis have any leads?'

Not a body, she prayed. *Don't let them have found a body.*

What she needed to know was if the prosecutor had issued the warrant or not; asking about it might precipitate it, if he'd decided on another course. There was no way she could sweet-talk her way to an answer under Nicolaides's eye, and no way she wanted to, regardless.

She could tell from the smirk on Andreadis's face and the calculation in his near-black eyes that he was expecting a return of service for service. She was used to solving her own problems, but in a foreign jurisdiction without language skills, she was out of her depth. She admitted she was grateful for Nicolaides's presence. There was a long exchange in Greek before Nicolaides turned back to her.

'They are searching. They will continue to search.' He relented a little at her obvious anxiety. 'Audrey Clare is a person of interest at this point. We would like to know about the gun. We have her declaration at customs.'

Sehr wanted to see that declaration. She wanted to confirm for herself the caliber of the weapon used on Aude Bertin and Sami al-Nuri. She knew Andreadis had the gun in his possession – she'd just thought of a way to flatter him.

'The Interpol agent was much too high-handed.' She'd gleaned this from gossip flying around Lesvos. 'You had every right to secure the crime scene and the weapon. I'm glad that you received the customs declaration so quickly. It must have helped confirm you were right to reserve jurisdiction in this case.' She allowed her lips to curve in a smile. 'Without the gun,

Interpol will have to work harder at cooperation.'

'Yes,' Andreadis said at once. 'They think they can throw their weight around, they don't know what the situation is on the islands. They haven't been to Lesvos once in the past year.' He gave a fastidious shudder. 'The noise, the traffic, the garbage these *metanastes* leave behind.' He used the Greek word for migrant. 'The camps are an abomination.'

Sehr made a non-committal sound that could have passed for agreement. Responding to it, Andreadis snatched a form off his desk, brandishing the customs declaration in her face. Taking it as an invitation, Sehr reached for the form and skimmed it. Her heart dropped at the familiar sight of Audrey's well-formed handwriting. Audrey had declared the gun, a Browning Buck Mark Camper, a weapon often recommended to women.

Nicolaides stepped in again. 'It's the same gun. The prosecutor's office has registered it as evidence. Perhaps it was stolen from Miss Clare. Violence isn't unknown in the camps.'

Andreadis dropped his mantle of cooperation, suspicious of Sehr now. He held his palm open for the form; she passed it back. She ventured another question. 'How many bullets were fired from the gun?'

Andreadis scowled at the form. She could see the question had taken him by surprise.

'Two bullets, as you already know,' he said with fine disdain. 'The cylinder holds five rounds.'

Nicolaides wanted to see the form for himself. He snapped his fingers and at once, Andreadis handed over the paper. He smoothed his hand over his vibrant head of hair, watching Sehr as he did so.

At Philip Nicolaides's shoulder, Sehr read the form again, collecting as much detail as she could. Whatever he'd gleaned from the customs declaration, Nicolaides was not inclined to be forthcoming. With a distant politeness that reminded Sehr of

Esa, he made her a formal bow and escorted her out of the office to the car park.

'We have your contact details,' he told her. 'I will call if there is anything to tell you.'

Sehr chose her words carefully. 'Please understand, Captain Nicolaides. I represent Miss Clare's interests. I'm acting as her legal representative.'

The watchful look in his eyes told her he knew as much.

She tried a more personal touch. 'Audrey is also my friend. I'm worried about her safety.'

Captain Nicolaides's stern expression didn't ease. 'I checked the date of your arrival in Athens. You landed after the bodies on Lesvos were found, otherwise this would have been a different discussion.'

He opened the door of her cab. When she'd buckled her seatbelt, he leaned into the window and said, 'Attorney or friend, whichever you are, I am sorry for you, Miss Ghilzai.'

Sehr wasn't staying at the same hotel as the others. She refused to let Nate pay her way; she'd found an affordable boutique hotel outside of the city center. A brief stop to shower and change for dinner, a hasty cab ride, and she was just in time to meet Nate at the rooftop restaurant of the King George Hotel.

The terrace was a beautiful space. Their table was in a corner against a snow-white balustrade, a spot where the evening view of the Acropolis was spectacular. Lit from below on a rocky promontory, the Parthenon showed up as a series of amber columns under an incandescent sky. In Athens, the blues were deep purples, the sunset a ravishing pink.

The table was laid with white linen and silver candelabra. At its center was a vase of chrysanthemums the color of pale yellow corn silk. Their heavy heads curved down as if they carried the weight of nostalgia.

Nate came forward to embrace her, and Rachel as well, to

Sehr's surprise. At the last moment, she let her gaze linger on Esa's face. She hadn't seen him in the weeks since his return from Iran, and though the distance between them pained her, she had learned to accept it.

She thought of a word in a language they shared – *judai*.

It described the loneliness of separation.

They were always apart.

Not that Esa was suffering. He looked lighter in spirit than she'd seen him in some time, despite the circumstances of their meeting. His dark hair was brushed to one side, his green eyes calm and watchful. He was wearing an evening suit and looked so handsome that she bit the inside of her cheek. She let him take her hand and pull out her chair, thankful she was seated beside him and not across the table. She couldn't bear those watchful eyes on her face, dissecting emotions she was careful to hold in check.

Wine was served at the table, yet it failed to lend a festive air to the occasion or to Nathan Clare's spirits. He must have been worried, probably far more worried than he was showing, and if Esa was more hopeful and more deliberate in his discussion of Audrey's disappearance, she knew it was for Nathan's sake.

She could hear Esa's voice in her ear – he was too close for her to feel at ease. He didn't shift his chair, his arm occasionally brushing hers, and Sehr's hand trembled on her crystal glass.

She looked up to find Rachel watching her, compassion in her bold, dark eyes.

Did Rachel know?

Or was it the compassion of a woman who knew herself secure in Esa Khattak's affections? Plates were brought to the table as others were cleared away, with Sehr scarcely conscious of what she'd ordered or tasted. Rachel moved them from subject to subject, and Sehr admired the way she assembled the facts into a cogent narrative.

Rachel glanced at Esa once as she talked about Ruksh, hurrying over the words. Ruksh must still be a sore subject, though Sehr wouldn't know. Esa didn't speak about family to her; after Samina's death, she hadn't been invited to his home again.

She missed those days. She mourned the fact she could never get them back.

Esa listened to Rachel with penetrating attention, asking questions at the right moments. Finally, it was time for Sehr to speak, and she posed a question to Nate.

'Did you know Audrey's gun was loaded when it was found, except for the rounds that were fired? Was she in the habit of carrying a loaded gun?'

Nate's eyebrows shot up. He was dressed as he always was, his clothes subtly expensive, but he was looking a little worn around the edges as though he hadn't slept in days, his jaw slightly rough, his eyes deep-set and shadowed behind his glasses. Sehr wished there was a way to comfort him.

'What's wrong with that?' Sehr accepted the faint hostility in his voice; she wasn't bringing him news he wanted to hear. She was pointing out the case the Greek authorities were building against Audrey. 'I'm the one who bought Audrey the gun.'

'Was she experienced at handling a gun? It was found with the safety off.'

'Why wouldn't it be?' Nate demanded. 'If someone had just fired two shots?'

'Nate.' Esa's voice was warm at Sehr's side. 'It takes time to gather that information. Sehr is doing what you asked her to do – she's looking into what the Greek police have on Audrey.' He touched Sehr's wrist lightly. 'Do they have the gun in their possession?'

Sehr tried not to tense her hand. Half turning her head toward him, she said, 'Yes. But they wouldn't let me have it tested.'

'Did you ask them if you could?' Nate's voice was tense. He'd finished two glasses of earthy red wine, and recklessly poured a third. Rachel raised her hand to stop him, then evidently thought better of it.

Sehr arched her eyebrows at him, her tone cooler than it would have been if she hadn't had such a trying day – a trying two weeks of being obfuscated, with the growing suspicion that much of it had to do with the fact that she was a woman.

And knowing that Esa and Rachel would come, and worrying over that as well.

'I've asked. They only allowed me to see the customs form because the IPCD is involved.' She hesitated. 'If the IPCD is running things, that means matters are serious.'

Speaking like the prosecutor she'd been, she asked her companions to bring her up to speed on what they'd uncovered so far. When they were finished, she summarized the facts.

'Audrey wanted to expedite the case of a young man with family in Canada. They deny knowing him – we should determine why. Since the Fakhris refused to help her, perhaps Audrey was trying to figure out another way to ensure Sami's resettlement. The money she withdrew from her bank account may have been intended for Sami.'

Rachel nodded. 'It's possible.'

'To me, it seems likely that Sami is at the center of this case. Agent Bertin was caught up collaterally, or she knew something about Sami, such as who was responsible for his torture. From Rachel's interview with the coroner, it sounds as though Agent Bertin was trying to shield Sami from his killer. That could mean he was valuable to Interpol.'

Rachel looked at her with new respect. 'Not your first double homicide, then.'

'No.' Sehr had fiercely enjoyed her work as a prosecutor; she had dedicated her life to it. She missed the collegiality, the sense of purpose it had given her. Her life had a different purpose now, but her striving had been to one end.

She'd lost her job in an effort to help Esa, a decision she'd made for herself. She didn't blame him, because given the same situation, she knew she'd do it again.

Nate's unsteady voice cut into Sehr's thoughts.

'And Audrey?' he asked. 'What do you think's happened to Audrey?'

Sehr considered Audrey's withdrawal of funds, her calculated silence. 'I think Audrey's disappearance is something she orchestrated herself.'

She said it with conviction. She knew how to influence others to her point of view; it was the foundational skill of a prosecutor.

Briskly, she went on, 'You need to hire a local brief. An experienced criminal defense attorney, preferably a Greek. When Audrey turns up, she's going to have to account for why she fled the scene, at the very least.'

Her words galvanized Nate into action. He excused himself to attend to her suggestions; a moment later, Rachel excused herself, too. Sehr wondered if it was so she could keep an eye on Nate, or because she thought Esa would value some time alone with Sehr.

Sehr gathered up her handbag, thinking of the next day's work.

'Wait,' Esa said. 'We should talk.'

They moved away from the table, walking along a terrace drenched in flowered sweetness. It was a night without a moon, the sky a polished sapphire, the tangled glitter of the waves unbearably romantic. She was conscious of Esa's presence at her side, conscious of a thrum of excitement.

She wanted him to speak of what lay undeclared, this tentative trust they were building. He would have asked her to stay for this reason. She looked up at him, unaware of the glow in her eyes. When he'd needed her to, she'd thought of Samina, or of Ruksh. Now she thought of herself.

Tell me, Esa, please. Please, just say the words.

She was so engrossed in these thoughts that she didn't take in his reproach.

'You need to go easier on Nate. He deserves a little compassion.'

Her hands clenched on the balustrade. She bit back the words on

124

her tongue to stop herself from recounting every minute of the past two weeks. He'd been dining with the prime minister, while she'd been at work in the camps.

'That's what you wanted to speak to me about – how I handled Nate?'

'What else? I want you to be careful in the future.'

'What else?' Her throat tightened, the words like straw. Realization flooded his face. It tightened his expressive mouth, the mouth she longed to feel pressed against her own. It was a beautiful, vanquishing mouth, but Esa had never kissed her.

He took note of their surroundings: the candlelit terrace, the blazing light of the stars, the scent of bougainvillea, his hand next to hers on the rail, his shoulder brushing the dark sleeve of her dress.

He took a breath – was he steeling himself to face her?

'I don't want to hurt you, Sehr, but haven't we had this out? It's not going to work between us, that's not how I feel about you.' He gave her a moment to absorb this. 'I'm sorry, I wish it were different.'

Sehr didn't believe him. The past was more tangled than Esa would concede.

'No, you don't. You value your solitude too much. You *know* what this is… what it could be. I never took you for a coward.'

His face grew dark, his courtliness erased.

'How does not loving you make me a coward?'

She let the pain of that sink in, felt the tears start in her eyes, falling back on the bitter comforts of poetry – *to move the seas from their customary places, to make the Shah of Persia one of her admirers* – to once have power over Esa. She dismissed the thought as unworthy; she viewed love as an accession, not a tyranny.

She didn't intend to visit past humiliations – she needed Esa to face the truth.

'You won't *let* yourself feel anything, because it's easier to live in the past. You won't let yourself move forward. But I loved Samina too, I miss her as much as you do –'

He cut her off in a voice harsh with pain.

'Don't *ever* compare your loss to mine. Don't ever speak about my wife. I'm done with this, Sehr. I don't want to see you again.'

She made a strange little sound of protest. 'Esa, I'm not –'

He turned away. 'Just go, Sehr. Don't make me say something that we'll both regret.'

When she'd gone, Esa stood at the railing, alone with a grief that seemed to expand the longer he thought of Sehr. He'd never spoken to a woman like that, raising his voice, striking where he knew it would hurt. It was worse that he'd done it to Sehr. His friend, Samina's friend. She might encompass the things he wanted, but Sehr was not for him.

He'd let it get to this point. He should have seen the signs, should have known that Sehr was misreading him. They'd worked together in the past, he knew their paths would cross again, it was inevitable – he'd tried to bring things between them back to a normal footing, tried to relax his guard.

She'd seemed to view him as just another friend, treating him much the same as Nate.

Now it was clear her feelings hadn't changed.

His shoulders slumped. He looked up at the great jewels of the stars without taking in their beauty. He didn't want Sehr in Athens, entangling herself in his work.

Then why when he'd made her cry had it felt like a fist through his heart?

14

ALI HUNKERED DOWN TO WAIT. *The ferry from Athens followed a steady course to the port. He wasn't surprised he couldn't see passengers on deck. The rain was cold and persistent, the kind of rain that drilled through your clothes to make its way into your bones. But even the rain in April was better than the winter just past. He shivered inside the jacket Audrey had bought him in Izmir. A windbreaker, she'd called it, turning up the collar of the one she'd bought herself in yellow. His was black and it was versatile, good for the rain or for sleeping on when circumstances called for him to improvise. Audrey had bought him a heavy winter jacket too, thick and fur-lined, indescribably warm, with gloves, a hat, and a scarf. He'd given the extras away; he couldn't pass by children who'd dug into ditches for warmth, their bodies like bundles of bones. Ali's father had said of the war, 'What is the difference between my son and someone else's? A child who is not my son is like my son.'*

The gloves, the scarf, the hat – the children had taken them without speaking, too frightened to show him gratitude. He didn't need it. He didn't need anything from kids who'd risked a journey like his.

The Afghan boy at Moria looked like he was used to being beaten, flinching from every touch, every unexpected sound. The camp manager held up a clipboard; the boy expected a whip. Ali read it in the boy's face, he knew that cowed look: the world was cruel, softness came at a cost. The boy's legs were covered in sores, his teeth had gaps and his gums looked diseased. Ali had given him his gloves. A week later, a newcomer had beaten the boy for the gloves.

Though it twisted Ali's heart, there were things he couldn't give up. If the Afghan boy couldn't hold on to what was his, Ali couldn't help him – he couldn't afford to part with anything else. He needed his jacket and his shoes. He had to be ready to leave the instant he heard about Audrey – night, day, it didn't matter. He had to stay dry and alert, ready to leap into danger.

He chewed his lower lip. Nothing could be more dangerous than what he'd already faced.

The escape, the overland crossing, the checkpoints, the sea in the dinghy where no one stayed afloat. The first safe sunrise in years.

The rain had found its way into his collar; its chill reminded him of the sea, of the boat he'd taken, of the foghorn and the blinding lights in the night, of the bodies reaching shore, some dead, some alive, someone pulling him to shore. After that, he'd gone to the beach to help. He'd become someone who handed others to safety.

Children who cried; the ones who would never cry again.

Ali didn't cry, because tears didn't serve as a release – they were a punishment that stung his sores. The sea was still a nightmare in his mind; he wouldn't add to the sum of his injuries. He wanted to be like the others, and the others tried not to cry. The Hellenic Rescue Team volunteers, the Christian peacemakers, the pretty Danish girls with long blond hair.

They scooped the children up and dried them off. They wrote down names and dates of arrival, wrapping the children in blankets that reflected the moonlight off the waves. They were cheerful and full of encouragement.

They weren't like him. They hadn't seen what Ali had seen.

They hadn't done what Ali had done.

He'd heard the horror stories about the crossing but he'd told himself the others were describing the passage from Libya. The *journey across the Aegean was short – he could see Lesvos from the Turkish coast. He'd spent the last of their funds arranging passage for his group: Aya, Israa, Sami, and himself, the four limbs of a body, each essential to survival.*

The call from the smugglers had come early in the morning on a night when the wind was high and a bleak rain pelted their faces. He'd refused to go, insisting on a safer crossing because he had to think of the girls. The smugglers hadn't cared. They told him if he stayed behind, he wouldn't get another chance – they'd keep his money and leave him stranded in Izmir.

He'd talked it over with Sami, but the calls had come one after the other, pushing, pushing, persisting. Finally, Israa had kissed his cheek and said, 'Our dreams are beginning to fade. I want to reach the other side.'

On the sea, the night had choked his hopes. Four boats had launched at once, the smugglers hustling them along. He'd been given a quick lesson in operating the engine; Sami had been handed a flashlight.

'Wait until you're nearly there,' the smuggler said. 'Don't waste the battery on the torch.'

They'd shrugged into their life jackets, ill-fitting and damp with cold. The smugglers began to load them into the boats, a scene of noise and confusion. Once Sami was on the raft, Ali passed Aya into his arms. Israa's turn was next, but suddenly he couldn't find her. She'd been at his side a moment ago. He craned his neck, searching the crowd of passengers struggling to find a seat. He began to shout Israa's name. Sami climbed down from the raft.

'No!' Ali shouted. 'Don't leave Aya!'

He called for Israa until a smuggler shoved him in the back. His head was wrenched sideways. The smuggler pointed to a boat up the beach. 'She's there.'

He caught a glimpse of a white scarf, though he couldn't see Israa's face. She was climbing into the boat; she didn't hear him over the wind.

He yanked the smuggler's hand. 'We're together. Get her back here.' Israa's boat was pushed out onto the waves, overcrowded with bodies.

The smuggler shrugged. 'Go, don't go, your choice.'

Aya called for him, crying.

'We're going to the same place?' He insisted the smuggler tell him.

The smuggler pointed out into the darkness. 'You all go to Lesvos.'

He couldn't see the outline of the island; the rain was falling in sheets. His life vest was already soaked. 'Push us off,' he said. 'We need to catch the other boat.'

He hurled himself into the raft, pushing past others to get to his seat. The engine sputtered before it caught, rain lashing the sides. He looked at Sami with dread in his eyes. He'd never steered a boat, and here in the dark with the rain and the rising waves – there were thirty or forty people in the boat. Their lives were in his hands.

'I can't see,' he called to Sami. 'Get closer, shine the flashlight.'

Sami and Aya pressed through the crush of bodies, the raft pitching with each step. An older woman took Aya onto her lap. Sami held up the flashlight. When he flicked it, nothing happened. He switched it on and off. The batteries were dead.

The smugglers had tricked them. The engine was weak, the light didn't work, the boat was too heavy – the waves were crashing the boat. Some passengers were prepared. They'd brought plastic cups to bail with.

He looked at Aya's terrified face and thought about turning back.

But Israa was out there on the waves. She needed him now more than ever.

He counted the bodies in the boat. He counted his own and decided. There was no going back from this point. It was only four miles across.

'*Does someone have a cell phone?*' he shouted.

Hands in the boat went up.

The phones cast a limited light on the waves. He saw the shadows of the other boats, carving a path for him to follow. He turned the boat too fast; the passengers cried out. He didn't dare cut his speed in case the engine refused to catch.

He didn't know how the next hour passed. His arms and back ached with effort, his eyes straining against the darkness. Cell phones were swept away with their belongings, the waves black, the boat half submerged, the passengers shivering, their lips blue with cold.

Lightning forked through the clouds, a silver slash against the night. Aya screamed, but Ali held on to the rudder, willing the engine to last. On the Mediterranean, pirates stripped the engines from the boats, leaving passengers to die at sea. He prayed that wouldn't happen here.

He thought of the risks he'd taken: no one chose the water unless the place they'd left behind was too perilous for them to remain. Sami's stories of Aleppo were the most harrowing Ali had heard. Apart from his own hands' work.

A huge wave caught the raft. They were flung into the dark. He kicked to the surface, coughing water, his life vest hanging from its straps. Sami had Aya in one arm; he was kicking his legs furiously, but he wasn't making headway. Ali swam back, calling to the other men. It was impossible to flip the boat, but together he and Sami dragged children to the raft.

The life vest felt like it was choking him, but it was suicide to take it off. He wasn't a strong swimmer. Some of the passengers were drowning, succumbing to the drag of the waves. He clutched Aya and Sami to the raft. Thunderclouds rumbled overhead, an ecstatic color like the sea.

The waves were pulling him down; he couldn't stay afloat.

His frantic thoughts were for Israa. Please, God, Israa had made it. *His cold hands slipped from the raft, thunder crashing in his ears.*

Sami held on to Aya. He heard her high-pitched scream.

He was drifting down, no matter how hard he kicked his legs, his limbs heavy and weighted, so cold and thick he couldn't move.

A ghostly white light appeared; he tried to blink it away.

Israa needed him – and Sami…

A fair-haired figure reached for him, coaxing him to the light.

'I've got you,' she said, 'I've got you.'

He fought the desire to give in, but in the end the angel took him.

He was dragged onto a boat, his life vest stripped from his body. When the dark mist cleared from his eyes, he saw Sami and Aya on deck.

He hadn't been dreaming of an angel.

He'd just met Eleni Latsoudi.

What an agonizing time it was taking the cars to disembark. Passengers followed the cars in little clumps. He was looking for a reed-thin black woman who wore a canary yellow scarf. The scarf meant he would spot her against the backdrop of the antiseptic dawn.

He reached for the apple in his pocket, forgetting he'd eaten it hours ago when he'd first begun his vigil.

A scuffing of feet on the path below alerted him to action.

Aya had come to find him, guessing he'd be at his favorite perch, looking over the water. She'd brought him a little Styrofoam cup, but because the climb up to his perch was a rough one, she'd spilled half the contents on the way. It didn't matter. Even half was good on a morning like this, the rain like a chilly warning, flattening the stench of the camp. He might have caught the scent of olive trees on the breeze, or he might have been remembering his home.

He sipped at the hot chocolate, a subversive effort of the Danish girls, who insisted on providing rations beyond the limits of their NGO.

'Did she come?'

He smiled at Aya. She was doing her best to pick up English, practicing every chance she got. She wasn't shivering, because he'd given her his winter jacket, the one Audrey called a parka. It was so big on Aya that she wore it like a dress, her hands stuffed deep into its pockets.

He was cold, but Aya was warm, and that was what mattered. He'd kept one of his promises to Israa.

'I don't know yet.' He let the hot chocolate slide down his throat. When it was finished, he picked Aya up and hoisted her onto his lap.

'Look for the yellow scarf.'

They watched the passengers come and go – tourists from the region, a handful of police, the agent in a special uniform with the crest of a globe on her shoulders. The globe was held in the grip of a pair of olive branches; Ali snorted to himself.

There was no such thing as an olive branch. There was only a ruined orchard.

'There!'

Aya's finger shot out from her pocket to point. She was thrilled to be of help, pounding his leg with her fist.

'Careful,' he warned. 'That hurts a little.'

'Oh, sorry, sorry.' She smoothed a hand over the sore spot.

Ali picked her up and settled her on her feet. 'You're right,' he said. 'That's Shukri. Let's find out what she's learned.'

Aya danced from one foot to the other. Her shoes were a size too big, in danger of slipping from her ankles.

'You think she knows about Audrey?' Her eyes went round and wide. She fluttered her long, thick eyelashes, an imitation of her sister.

Ali felt a quick stab of pain. With her curly hair and long-lashed eyes, Aya was the image of Israa. She would grow up to be as beautiful, one day. And that day would come, God willing.

'Yeah,' he said, helping Aya navigate the hill. 'I think she knows. She must know. But even if she doesn't, I'm going to make her help us.'

He frowned. Two passengers from the boat had caught up to Shukri, a tall woman and her companion, a dark-haired man with a face that reminded him of the Afghan boys on the hill.

The woman was holding on to Shukri Danner's arm. The man was blocking her path.

She'd been about to hail a taxi; now she turned back to the newcomers, making for a building near the dock.

They weren't wearing the Interpol insignia.

Who were the strangers then?

15

Mytilene, Lesvos

'ASSALAM-U-ALAIKUM, SISTER.'

Khattak's greeting did nothing to set Shukri Danner at ease, Rachel noted. She had a beautiful round face, her skin so smooth it appeared seamless. It was her expressive black eyes that gave away her sense of discomfort at being asked to speak to them about Audrey's work.

Shukri was tall like Rachel, though her proportions were more fragile. She wore a white headband beneath a flowing yellow head scarf that draped the top half of her body. Her small brown hands darted in and out of this covering with quick, sparrow-like gestures.

'I need to get back to headquarters,' she advised.

'We just have a few questions. Once we're done here, we'll take you there ourselves.'

They'd found a small café near the beach and were warming themselves up with strong Greek coffee and pastries. The ambiance made it seem less like an interview and more like a meeting of friends. As Khattak continued to speak in low, soothing sentences, Shukri began to relax. She drank her coffee, giving them her full attention.

As they'd expected, she was horrified by the murders and worried about the implications for Woman to Woman's work.

'There is a lot to do here,' she told them. 'There's never a shortage of need.'

She spoke with an accent that lightened the emphasis on vowels, drawling them out so they were soft and almost tangible. Her voice was so delicately pretty, it could have soothed a child to sleep. Rachel had gathered some preliminary information about Shukri. She was a Somali-Canadian married to a man of German background. In addition to her native language, she spoke English, French, and Arabic, and was an invaluable asset to Audrey's NGO.

When asked to describe her role, she told them it was a little bit of everything. Providing translation services to help refugees at the intake point fill out paperwork and acquire accreditation, tracking down and reuniting families that had been separated at border crossings and checkpoints – or, more unforgivingly, on the Aegean Sea. Requisitioning supplies, maintaining inventory, helping out in the volunteer kitchens, offering rudimentary first aid.

Her primary responsibility had been to select cases that were suitable for fast-tracking to Canada, but as she spoke, it became clear that despite her commitment to her work, she was wearied by the changing demands of bureaucracy – internally within W2W, and, in a broader sense, with the Canadian government.

'People are angry,' she said in her fine, soft voice. 'They want families *now*, they want to answer the need, they've raised the funds and they don't understand what could be taking us so long. It isn't us,' she explained with a sigh. 'We do what we can. I wear so many hats, I sometimes forget I have a head.'

Khattak laughed at this, and at the warm and pleasant sound, a smile escaped Shukri, slowing her harried recital.

'Yes, I'm funny, that's what the children on the island tell me. Miss Shukri, you are funny, you always make us laugh.' She sighed. 'I wish I could keep them laughing, because I have some idea of what they've seen. They've suffered, Inspector Khattak. I've run out of languages in which to tell you how.'

Gently, Khattak brought her around to the subject of Audrey Clare, and the rumored disagreement between them. Shukri folded her hands over her breast. Her prayerful posture made her look like a golden Madonna. She didn't seem like a woman with anything to hide, an assessment supported by the frank disclosure that followed.

'I wouldn't just say we disagreed, my dear Inspector. We were fighting – actually fighting. She's a foolish, headstrong girl. It wasn't easy to keep her in check.'

'In check how?' Rachel asked, wondering at this unexpected description. The Audrey she had met on several occasions was a bright and lovely young woman, self-confident and poised, and, by all accounts, successful at her work.

Shukri tapped the table with her palms, exasperation plain on her face.

'She was meant to come to Lesvos and assist us. To coordinate efforts between the two islands where we have set up offices: Lesvos and Chios. She was supposed to take over management of the budget, but she spent so much money. So many supplies. Where did they all go? I began to notice discrepancies.'

'With the medical supplies?' Rachel asked. Her first thought had been of prescription drugs, an easy thing to traffic to raise additional funds.

'No,' Shukri said, surprised. 'The medical supplies are kept under lock and key – I hold the key. I'm careful about inventory because the authorities do spot checks. Your paperwork has to be in order, everything has to add up.'

'Where were the discrepancies, then?'

'Life jackets, office supplies. What a girl she is for using up our office supplies. Our printers running until the generator blew out. I don't know how many boxes she filled with what she was printing, and when I asked her, what is this, where is it going, she didn't have anything to say. And what she did say I didn't believe.'

Rachel edged forward in her seat, the pastries on her plate forgotten. 'What *did* she say, Ms Danner?'

'She said it was shadow paperwork for the Greek immigration authorities.'

'Shadow paperwork?' Khattak frowned. 'I'm not familiar with the term.'

'No one is, Inspector. Audrey said the Greek government wanted copies of every application we filed for asylum in Canada – additional registration paperwork.' She shook her head doubtfully. 'Even if that were true, it wouldn't have added up to material that needed to be stored. And it's a violation of an applicant's privacy. Refugees get registered in Greece so they can move on. They don't need to make their case with the authorities of two separate countries.'

'How big were these boxes?' Rachel was thoroughly intrigued.

'Not that big. The size of shoeboxes, I suppose, perhaps a little wider. But there were so many of them, twenty, maybe twenty-five in all.'

Khattak rose to his feet. 'We'd like you to show us these boxes. And if you could point out anything else that you may have found odd, that would be helpful.'

Shukri rose as well, adjusting the flowing yellow scarf with a practiced flick of her hand. Rachel noticed a colorful hairpin near her ear: a clump of white-and-yellow daisies.

'I wish I could, Inspector. Those boxes are no longer on Lesvos. Audrey moved them from the island two weeks ago. The day before she disappeared, in fact.'

Khattak paused to look at her. 'They're at your offices on Chios, then?'

Shukri folded the remaining pastries into a napkin. She tucked them into her capacious yellow handbag. 'Waste not, want not,' she said with a smile. 'No, not on Chios either. I don't know where she took them – perhaps, as she said, to Athens. That girl is never in one place for long.'

'She was back and forth from Athens, you mean?' Rachel said. Shukri looked from Rachel's face to Khattak's. 'You really don't know very much about what she was doing here. I thought you'd come to ask me where Audrey has gone.'

Khattak tensed. 'You don't think she was taken?'

Shukri shook her head with emphasis. 'The arguments we had were not about me taking Audrey in hand, though perhaps this is what you were led to believe. I was trying to rein in Audrey's tendency to distraction. And more importantly, to extravagance.'

Rachel was flummoxed by this. It didn't sound as though they were talking about the same person. To be sure, she pulled up a photograph of Audrey on her phone and held it up to Shukri Danner. 'This is Audrey Clare. Is this the woman you mean?'

Shukri's beautiful, round eyes widened. 'Yes, of course. I *know* Audrey, I've known her for many years. She hired me personally as W2W's refugee resettlement coordinator.'

Then why had Audrey lost faith in Shukri's efforts on Lesvos and Chios? What had prompted her to send her complaints to Nate via e-mail?

'You said you were worried by Audrey's extravagance. How was Audrey spending the NGO's money?'

Shukri led them to the door, her yellow head bobbing. 'She was supposed to oversee our efforts to fast-track cases. But truthfully, she'd been taking holidays, booking plane tickets with the funds set aside for refugees.'

An odd note in his voice, Khattak asked, 'Was she going anywhere in particular?'

'Everywhere,' Shukri said firmly. 'France, Austria, Germany, Holland. And back and forth to Turkey nearly every week, as if we didn't need her help here on Lesvos.' She made her hand into a fist. 'We need volunteers, we need paid staff so badly. The major relief organizations – they're hardly present on Lesvos. Everything you'll see at camp is managed by volunteers.' She paused, taking in the island's green hills. 'And of course, by the great kindness of the Greek people. The islanders have shown a compassion beyond anything we expected.'

Though Rachel wanted to know more about the crisis, she directed Shukri back to the subject of Audrey.

'Do you have any idea why she went so often to Turkey? Was that where she purchased supplies?'

'I think it was more than that, because she had those two children in tow.' She paused for a moment. 'They might even be here now; they haven't been processed yet, at least not through Woman to Woman.'

'Two children,' Rachel said in a neutral tone of voice. Sami al-Nuri may have been the first. Who was the other?

'Yes. I guess that's something else Audrey didn't tell her brother. There was a boy with her – a young man, I suppose. And a very pretty little girl. To see a child in these conditions – cold, hungry, frightened – to see any of them suffer what they've experienced, and what they don't yet know is coming – it breaks your heart, Sergeant Getty. It breaks your heart every damn day. So if I don't seem too worried about a woman who couldn't commit to the work she came here to do, that's the reason why.'

She wasn't callous or indifferent, Rachel thought. She was overwhelmed. And when they reached the gates of Kara Tepe, Rachel understood why.

Kara Tepe, Lesvos

They'd been described as hordes, as swarms, as a flood, as an invasion, as groups of gangs, as 'rapefugees,' with the British press leading the charge. These debates framed refugees as migrants: in England they called for gunships to be used to intercept the boats at sea. For the Calais Jungle in France, the prescription was sending in dogs.

It was the flipside to the mainstream Canadian coverage of the same issues, though perhaps this was because the crisis was so far from Canada's shores. Canada was upholding its Refugee Convention obligations, and the angry counterpoint to this proud internationalism was a murmuring many Canadians had rejected.

It could change, Rachel knew. It *would* change if refugees were accused of serious crimes. The voices of the extremist right would emerge. Part of Rachel's work at Community Policing was to keep track of the impact of hate groups on minority communities. She wasn't oblivious to what had transpired in the country in the past decade. She'd seen the effect of creeping anti-Muslim hate on her partner; she knew it affected his work. Elements of that sentiment had bled into the parliamentary inquiry, and into Khattak's suspension from Community Policing. She was on the watch for it now, in a way she hadn't been before she'd started to care so deeply for Khattak, making his burdens hers.

The little taxi driven by a friendly local resident named Dmitri pulled up at the gates of the camp. Her first look at Kara Tepe gave Rachel reason to reconsider the framing of these issues. She was brought face to face with the urgent realities of the crisis.

Two things struck her at once: the muddy ground beneath her feet and the securitized aspect of the shelter. The Kara Tepe camp was designed to host a thousand refugees transiting through, in hopes of resettlement in another country. The camp resembled a miniature town, with shelter tents laid out like houses on a street grid, and designated waiting areas for those who needed their paperwork processed. But the entry point for those hoping to enter was presaged by a concrete border that ran below a barbed-wire fence.

A drizzle of misery coated the camp: people stood in long lines where makeshift cardboard signs designated a long list of country names. Whether these were processing directions or someone's humorous attempt to point the way home, Rachel couldn't tell. She had expected the camp to be a hub for Syrians fleeing their country's civil war. But the list was more expansive than that: Iraq, Iran, Lebanon, Libya, Afghanistan, Pakistan, Sudan, Yemen, Somalia, and Eritrea were all represented on the signs.

Rachel began to question her knowledge of current affairs.

It wasn't just young, single men who formed the queues. There were mothers and fathers, grandparents, cousins – dozens and dozens of children.

Their credentials passed inspection, and as they left the checkpoint behind, the sprawling nature of Kara Tepe became apparent to them both. Khattak was as silent as Rachel, watching families gathered around bonfires contained by sleek black oil drums, and children darting out to play from the haphazard shelter of their tents.

The UNHCR had organized a few neat rows of their sturdiest, most spacious white tents. Beyond these, scattered across a horizon of dirt-brown, shrub-studded hills, were thinner, colorful tents pitched upon patches of land. A handful of NGOs had attempted to impose order upon the confusion: there were tents for food and clothing, tents that dispensed tea, tents for medical evaluations and paperwork.

The cement wall that supported the official complex was covered in graffiti and slogans. Children had painted hopeful pictures of sunshine over gardens of bright purple flowers, others had written slogans: *No Borders, No Walls. Freedom of Movement.* Those who were too tired to wait in queues, holding children or a fragile bundle of possessions in their arms, had slumped down against the barrier, exhausted by the journey they'd taken to arrive here.

Volunteers moved around the camp, most with purposeful expressions or cheerful smiles of welcome. A few looked frazzled as they were asked for help with translation; Rachel could see translation was one of the greatest needs of the camp.

She found the sights and sounds overwhelming. Laundry hanging from the stunted branches of trees, families huddled together in the cold, children inadequately dressed for the weather. A startlingly pretty child crossed in front of her path, beaming a smile at Rachel. She was wearing a heavy black coat that was too big for her – she might have been seven or eight years old, petite for her age but with a bold personality behind her mischievous eyes. She cupped her hands together to form a heart above her own. Rachel smiled back at her and waved.

Shukri showed them the tent that formed Woman to Woman's base of operations. It was cordoned off by official police tape, though the seal at the entrance was broken.

Khattak looked around the camp, searching for something he didn't find. 'Where did Audrey sleep? Where are her personal possessions?'

Shukri nodded at the tent. 'Everything is there. Audrey stayed on Lesvos, I was over at Chios. We haven't been allowed back in, so Audrey's things should still be there.'

'You haven't been allowed in on whose authority?'

A woman came out of the tent. She was dressed in a blue jacket with the Interpol insignia: a globe held by a pair of branches, not dissimilar to the United Nations logo, if one discounted the sword thrust down behind the globe.

'*My* authority,' she said. 'Come in, I was told to expect you.'

'The scene's been cleared?' Khattak asked.

'Yes. The technicians have been and gone.' She pointed a dismissive finger at Shukri in her pretty yellow head scarf. 'You can come back when we're done.'

To Khattak she said, 'Follow me.'

Rachel entered last, a shivery sensation causing her to glance over her shoulder.

The child in the black parka was watching her, her large dark eyes unblinking.

16

THE INTERPOL AGENT WAS A French national of the same rank as Khattak in her nation's police force. She had the whipcord energy of a greyhound, and a narrow-eyed, edgy approach to international cooperation. Her name was Amélie Roux, and because she treated him so brusquely, he took his time looking over the tent, ignoring her bristling impatience. He wanted to set the tone for the interview, to settle the ground at once.

The tent was partitioned into two sections: a front area for intake work, consisting of two tables and a handful of chairs, and a back end with several cots and additional blankets spread over another plastic chair and the ground. Audrey's suitcase was missing, as were her laptop and any personal effects, though he spied a familiar pair of sunglasses on a pillow on the cot. At the very back, a locked cabinet displayed a selection of first-aid supplies: bandages, tubes of antiseptic ointments, an assortment of over-the-counter medication. Khattak frowned at this. Did the meager contents of this cabinet match the inventory Shukri had described? He didn't think so, though he didn't say as much.

Officially, he'd been sent to cooperate. Unofficially, he would not support either the Greek authorities or the French in an assumption of Audrey's guilt. When he'd satisfied himself that he hadn't missed anything, he offered Roux a plastic chair, helping Rachel to another before he took one himself.

He didn't break the silence. Though he and Rachel hadn't been shown photographs of the scene, he could tell from discoloration of the plastic tarp what the position of the bodies had been. He made a mental map in his mind, trying to reconstruct the scene from the few facts in his possession. He waited until Inspecteur Roux had lit her cigarette, then he said, 'I'm very sorry about your colleague, Agent Bertin. Please accept our condolences.'

Inspecteur Roux held her cigarette away from her mouth, between the tip of her thumb and forefinger. It wasn't a studied gesture or an elegant one; Khattak guessed it was second nature to the woman he'd already pegged as an adversary.

She blew smoke through teeth that were stained with nicotine. 'Tell me about Audrey Clare,' she said.

'What can you tell us about your investigation so far? When exactly was Audrey taken?'

'Taken?'

He'd used the word deliberately to sound her out.

'What makes you think she was taken?' Roux held up her hand, counting off on her fingers. 'She was the last person seen in the tent. Two people were killed here – she was in contact with both. They were killed with her gun, and the next thing you know, our Canadian friend disappears from the scene. So I ask you again, police officer to police officer. What makes you think she was taken?'

Rachel made an awkward sound of interruption. 'I suppose my first response would be this. Two gunshots would resound through this camp – the way everything's packed together so tightly, the sheer number of people. If Audrey Clare had shot two people in this tent, wouldn't someone have seen her flee the scene?'

Roux stared at Khattak. 'You let your subordinate speak for you?' Khattak stifled a grin. He could almost see Rachel's raised hackles. 'Sergeant Getty is my partner. And I think she's asked you some excellent questions. I can rephrase them, if you like, but it will come to the same thing in the end.'

He caught Rachel's startled expression from the corner of his eye. She hadn't expected him to take this tack: direct and confrontational. And if Rachel thought he was being discourteous, he probably should recalibrate. He was still on edge from his disastrous conversation with Sehr – with the helpless sense of not knowing how to regroup.

The crushing reality of the refugee crisis should have wiped his personal affairs from his mind; he was disturbed it hadn't.

Amélie Roux rested her palms on her knees, her cigarette precariously held. The cool insouciance of her pose reminded him of Marlene Dietrich. He could see she didn't give a damn what they were doing here; she certainly didn't intend to share her findings.

'Where are you from, Inspector?'

'Canada.'

She dismissed this by flicking the ash off the tip of her cigarette. 'You look like those boys on Afghan Hill.'

Khattak made no reply. She must have seen his distaste, because she let the subject drop. If it had been a genuine inquiry into his background, he would have given her a forthright answer. It wasn't, and they both knew it.

She took a deep drag of her cigarette, stubbed it out, and now she leaned forward so that her face was close to Rachel's.

'The gunshots were heard just after midnight. It was dark, no one saw Audrey Clare leave the scene. No one saw anyone, for that matter, so that in itself is not exculpatory.'

'What about those streetlights at the perimeter? They look like they light up the camp fairly well.' Rachel had noticed them on the ride in.

'Not this far up the road. It's nearly pitch-black at night here. These tents don't have an independent electricity source, people muddle through as best as they can.'

Rachel pointed to the generator at the back of the tent. 'This one does.'

'So the light goes inside, eh? Not outside.'

Khattak could see this was plausible. And it was a little more cooperation than he'd expected. He decided to be more forthcoming.

'The Canadian prime minister enjoys a close relationship with your president. It's in the interests of both our countries to resolve these murders quickly. I'm happy to tell you what we've learned on our end, just as I want to assure you of the personal interest the prime minister has taken in the welfare of Audrey Clare.' He tried a smile – its only effect was a narrowing of Roux's eyes.

But she must have seen the wisdom of his remarks, because she offered more.

'We are not at this point treating Mademoiselle Clare as a suspect. We have issued a Blue Notice.'

'What's that?' Rachel asked. 'An arrest warrant?'

Almost pityingly, Inspecteur Roux said, 'You think we are some kind of international spy force – James Bond with French accents, *n'est-ce pas*? It is not so. We are mainly bureaucrats, technocrats. We do not have supranational powers, we do not make arrests. A Blue Notice is the equivalent of looking for someone who can help with an investigation. You call this a person of interest, I think. I watch American television programs. I like them, in fact.' A hint of humor transformed her attitude. 'I am sorry, Sergeant, to disappoint you.' She mimed a shoot-'em-up action with her hands. 'We are liaison officers coordinating officers in different jurisdictions. We also serve as a clearing house, do you follow?'

Rachel nodded, interested in this explanation.

Khattak saw an opening. 'Am I correct in thinking that homicide doesn't fall under Interpol's mandate?'

'You, at least, are well informed. Yes, Inspector, you are correct.' She didn't elaborate.

'Then your presence on the island…?'

Amélie Roux glanced around the tent, her gaze lingering on the stained plastic tarp.

'Aude Bertin was a friend. I recruited her, I trained her – I want to know how it came to this. Who did this to her? Her death may be inconvenient to my government, but it is a tragedy to me. Your condolences, I appreciate them, but they are not enough.'

Khattak felt ashamed. How quickly he had judged her and how sensitive he'd become. He resolved to do better at once.

'I understand better than you may realize. Audrey Clare is a friend. I know she couldn't have done this, just as I know that if she fled, it was to protect herself. If Agent Bertin and Sami al-Nuri were killed at Woman to Woman headquarters, to me it's very likely that Audrey is in danger. That's why we're trying to establish this connection between Audrey and your friend. Why was Agent Bertin on Lesvos? What was Interpol's reason for sending her?'

He thought of the likeliest possibilities: drug trafficking, piracy, organized crime. But there were other possibilities, including genocide, terrorism, or war crimes. It was possible that any of these things connected the boy, Sami al-Nuri, to the others.

What had brought these three people together at the camp on Lesvos?

'Come.' Inspecteur Roux got to her feet. She led them out of the tent to a smaller tent behind it, this one with an armed Greek police officer at the door. 'Let me show you something.'

The police officer stood aside. The interior of the tent was just a collection of seemingly random materials stacked on a plastic table, each in a labeled plastic bag with a sign-off sheet attached. An expensive black suitcase was open under the table, its contents half displayed: a woman's clothing and her personal toiletries – simple, sensible items.

'She didn't take it with her, but two things are missing: her laptop and her phone.'

'That's not all,' Khattak said. He told her about the missing boxes, and about Audrey's expenditure of funds. Roux already knew. She handed him a plastic bag that contained a clipboard.

'It's been printed.'

'What is it?' Rachel asked.

'I pieced together her itinerary – everywhere Audrey Clare traveled since she arrived on the island. Look at this.'

Khattak followed her pointing finger. Apart from a list of travel dates to European cities, Roux had flagged three bus tickets to a place called Hatay. It was a trip she'd taken four days before she'd disappeared.

'Hatay?' The name was unknown to him. Rachel didn't know it either. Khattak remembered that Shukri had mentioned the Netherlands.

'Is it in Holland?' he asked her. 'She took the bus from Germany, perhaps?'

But he could tell from Inspecteur Roux's posture, the intensity in her narrow face, that Hatay was the key to Audrey's disappearance.

'No, *cher Inspecteur,* Hatay isn't in Holland. It's a city in Turkey, close to the Syrian border. What's more one of us will have to go there. I'd rather it was you.'

Then she picked up another file on the table. She placed it before them with a warning: its contents were confidential.

When they read the file, they knew why.

By the time they'd finished going over the elements of the case, Roux's manner had transformed. She took Khattak by the elbow.

'Inspector Khattak, I am sorry, eh? What I said about the Afghan boys. You didn't like it, I think, this comparison. I apologize, it was discourteous.'

Khattak's expression warmed. 'Not at all. In fact, we likely do share a wider heritage.'

He sketched a movement in the air. 'Do you remember the

imaginary line the British drew to delimit their sphere of influence – the Durand Line?'

Inspecteur Roux nodded.

Khattak smiled. 'Sometimes it's hard to know on which side of it you belong.'

17

RACHEL'S LONG WALK FROM KARA Tepe to Moria had left her alarmed and disheartened. She'd intercepted any number of volunteers, but no one had answers to her questions. Though Audrey had made an impression on everyone she'd met, the urgencies of camp life, and the sheer volume of people transiting through, meant that very few volunteers could recall their encounters with any precision. She kept at it, trying to orient herself, trying to understand what had motivated Audrey – what she'd thought she could accomplish at either camp.

The more she witnessed of camp life for herself, the harder she found it to accept the good cheer of the volunteers, or Moria's system of management, tumultuous yet evidently functional. She'd followed the signs up Afghan Hill, where she'd been surrounded by a circle of children, boys and girls alike, pestering her with questions before their parents had caused them to scatter and leave her alone.

She'd learned that Syrian refugees were processed separately at Kara Tepe because the war in their country had given them priority: at Kara Tepe, well-established crisis organizations played an important role. Refugees were registered at a steady, streamlined pace and referred to numbered tents or offered medical care by Médecins Sans Frontières or Medicins du Monde. Most moved on quickly to the ferry at Mytilene's port.

But the camp at Moria had been a prison before taking on

its new incarnation as a hub for refugees. The need was so great that this modest attempt at bureaucracy was overwhelmed. The facilities were inadequate, far outmatched by need. Whether this was deliberate or whether it was a symptom of a crisis that knew no comparison in terms of scale, Rachel wasn't well informed enough to know. She could question why the UNHCR had erected so few shelters when there were thousands of people in need. It was possible, she supposed, that there was a concerted effort by the authorities not to make Greece more welcoming as a destination.

And she wondered what lies the people who'd undertaken the perils of the journey had been told – what refuge or earthly paradise they'd been promised.

People were mainly encamped in the muddy rows of the olive groves, where campfires soldered the darkness in bursts of hot orange light. The olive trees were sparse, the grove stripped for firewood; when there was nothing else to burn, plastic was fed to the fire, creating an acrid haze above the camp. She found herself coughing and wondered at the respiratory effects. Because shelter was so limited, people slept outside huddled around the fires.

Worse than all of this was the fact that no adequate arrangements had been made for human waste. A strong stench permeated one section of the camp where outhouses and portables had descended into disaster. There was no question of dignity or privacy; it had become a matter of survival and anything extraneous to that thought had been discarded.

The children played like children: teenage boys engaged in a game of volleyball, a pair of little girls shared a coloring book under a bank of barbed wire. Rachel eavesdropped on a volunteer who was speaking to a translator she'd dragged over to the girls. With them was an older man in scarcely adequate clothing, without shoes. He'd taken the turban from his head and wrapped it over his hands to warm them.

The volunteer explained something to the translator, who

tried to convince the man of the sense of the volunteer's earnest words. She was wearing a jacket with a patch on one shoulder: the Danish flag. Though she looked young, she spoke with an air of experience.

'Don't leave your daughters alone,' she warned. 'There are too many strangers, people you don't know. Anything could happen.'

The translator offered a few blunt phrases to the man.

When he stared at the young woman with his empty, exhausted eyes, she insisted, 'You must protect them. You must not let a stranger approach your daughters.'

His look of surprise was such that Rachel wondered if he had fled a place where, despite its dangers, the thought of a close community causing harm to its own was unthinkable. Or whether he was a man to whom life had offered no opportunities for education or for coming to terms with the cruelties of the world.

The volunteer broke it down into two simple words.

'Bad men.' She said it again. 'Bad men.'

She pointed around the camp. Then she bent down and hugged the girls, much to their surprise. They giggled at the embrace.

'Keep them close.'

Finally, the man understood. He sank down beside his daughters on the muddy ground, staring into the distance at something the others couldn't see.

To the translator, the Danish volunteer said, 'It's not getting better here, is it?'

The translator – Rachel didn't recognize the language he'd spoken, but she thought the man was an American either of Arab background or Iranian. He nodded.

'Believe me, Freja. I've tried to warn them. I heard there was an incident in Kara Tepe.'

The volunteer named Freja sighed. 'There are so many people here, it's hard to keep track of who's coming or going. There have been thefts, and occasionally fights have broken out, but this is new.'

'Why? What happened?'

'Someone grabbed a girl, she fought back pretty hard. She couldn't say who it was, but she scratched him up pretty bad.'

They told each other to keep a weather eye out.

None of it surprised Rachel. Stealing from those with nothing to steal. Harm done to those who were desperate. Refugee status wasn't a badge of sainthood any more than it was a choice. She couldn't discount that crime and predation were possible in the camp. She viewed the world through the lens of a police officer, the lens of someone who'd imagined terrible outcomes for her brother. She expected cruelty from the world, she'd known her share of it, though she'd done her best to move past it. She expunged her father's violence from her mind: it had made her who she was. She was lucky it hadn't *un*made her.

As she watched the girls playing in the mud, her despair was overcome by self-contempt. Each person in this camp could likely tell her a story more painful than her own.

Children under barbed wire, an image that would never leave her now.

She asked herself what else she didn't know as she left the camp for the beach, the scene of other disasters. The temperature had dropped and the water was cold, the pristine shoreline marred by detritus on the beach: black flotation devices resembling rubber tires, stacks of orange life jackets, the occasional dinghy that would never float again, odd bits of clothing, mismatched shoes, a single sock.

She had left the stench of Moria behind, breathing in great, gasping gulps, trying to focus on Audrey, when suffering was all around her.

She wondered how Khattak felt – could his composure rise to this occasion? He'd said nothing as they crossed the gate, nothing outside the parameters of the case, until he'd spoken to Roux about the Afghan boys.

She'd tried to decipher his emotion and failed. Whether he felt anger, regret, bitterness, he was often a mystery to her. But he couldn't be indifferent to what they'd witnessed. He'd left her at the hill to put his language skills to use. Boys had urged him to join in their game. She'd seen another side to Khattak, laughing and affectionate with children who were thrilled to find someone who spoke their tongue – someone who looked like them, as Amélie Roux had observed. They'd teased him mercilessly, delighted to be teased in return.

'Walk around,' he'd said to Rachel. 'Get a feel for what we're dealing with here.'

Doubtfully, she'd warned him, 'They might become too much for you to handle.'

He'd waved her off with a grin, teasing her as well. 'They're not as fearsome as you think. I'm certain I can manage.'

Maybe Khattak's life wasn't as sheltered as hers; maybe he'd been to places like Moria before. Kicking aside a life vest with her toe, Rachel asked herself if there *were* other places like this. She needed to educate herself. Until she did, she wouldn't be able to figure out the motive behind the murders, or to puzzle through the role Audrey might have played. There had to be someone on Lesvos who could tell her why Audrey had risked a trip to the Turkey-Syria border, and why she had taken two children to such a dangerous crossing.

She was also thinking of the missing boxes. What was in them? Who had taken them? Sehr had made it clear that the local police were choosing not to be helpful. Rachel wondered if she should try speaking to them as a colleague.

'The boats come here at night.' The voice spoke to her from nearby. Rachel looked over her shoulder. A boy and a young girl were picking their way along the shore. She recognized the girl. She'd been watching Rachel at the Woman to Woman tent.

The girl had bright brown eyes, wide and long-lashed, and thick curly hair shaped into a mop. Her face and clothes were clean but her hands were dirty, her fingernails torn. She saw

Rachel looking at them and shoved them behind her back.

'Who are you?' Rachel asked the boy.

'Let's play a game,' he said. She tried to pin down his age. He could be anywhere from sixteen to twenty, she thought. He was slim and wiry, with a clever, suspicious face. The little girl looked hungry. Rachel offered her an apple. She took it with a bright, beaming thanks.

'What kind of game?' she asked.

'You tell me your name, I'll tell you mine.'

'Easy enough. I'm Sergeant Rachel Getty.'

'Sergeant? You're police?'

'I am.'

He looked at her plain blue windbreaker. 'Not Greek,' he said. 'Not Interpol. American?'

'No, I'm from Canada.'

A light went on in his eyes. 'Then you came because of Audrey.' The little girl clutched his hand; he gave her a reassuring smile. He whispered to her in an undertone: something he'd said made the girl jump up and down.

Rachel spoke to him sharply. 'I'd like to know who you are.'

'That's fair,' he said, still watching her. 'My name is Ali Maydani.'

They walked along the shoreline, the boy speaking to Rachel of his journey, the little girl playing a game of hop, skip, and catch up. Rachel noticed the way Ali kept his eye on the girl, even when his attention was focused on Rachel.

'Is it slowing down?' She meant the arrival of refugees on the island.

He nodded. 'You wouldn't think it's only four miles across to Lesvos's northern shore. There's a moment when you're out on the raft on the open sea, and you feel like you've fallen off the edge of the world. You can't turn back, and you don't know what's ahead.'

Rachel knew he wasn't talking about geography.

'You risked it anyway. With your little sister in tow.'

The boy spoke English well, the little girl not as well, though she seemed to understand their conversation. She was so endearingly good-natured that Rachel wanted to hug her. She wondered if these were late-developing maternal instincts, then asked herself how she could think that with all she'd been to Zachary. All she'd had to be.

'Aya isn't my sister,' Ali said. 'She's my friend's sister.'

'And your parents?' Rachel asked. 'Her parents?'

'Gone,' he said, without elaboration. 'They won't be coming.'

He asked her why she'd come to Lesvos, so Rachel told him the truth. Nothing she said seemed to surprise him. She had the feeling he'd known who she was, and that he'd expected her to come. When he told her he'd been on Lesvos since January, she guessed he'd found her for a reason.

'You've been here a long time. Why haven't you transited through?' Ali planted his feet. He faced Rachel squarely, studying her open face – making calculations, she thought, as he pulled a photograph from his pocket.

'I'm waiting for Israa,' he said. 'She's Aya's sister and my friend.' Rachel looked down at the photograph. If Aya was pretty, the older sister could have given Helen of Troy a run for her money. The wide, clear eyes, the stunning symmetry of her bone structure, the rich, dark curls that framed her face. It was a face that was older than her years, the expression anxious, her hand raised as if to stop the photographer from capturing her image. She was a girl in motion, sixteen or seventeen years old.

'Friend?' she asked Ali, a humorous emphasis on the word.

Ali flushed, his fingers curled around the edge of the photo.

'I was going to marry her,' he said with all the stout conviction of first love. He met her eyes with such grown-up clarity that Rachel adjusted her perceptions. 'She's missing. We fled Damascus together. When the smugglers took us to the boats, we were separated. I've been looking for her ever since.'

He took a deep breath, his words forced into a sharp, hard point. 'Audrey Clare said she would help me find her.'

He turned the photograph over and pressed it into Rachel's hand. It was covered in a jumble of figures that resolved themselves into names.

Rachel looked up with a frown. 'What is this?' she asked the boy, alarmed by his sudden pallor.

'This is everyone Audrey asked about Israa before she disappeared.'

18

Douma, Syria

THE SEA WAS THE ENEMY *he'd thought about, the enemy he'd prepared himself to face, the enemy he'd convinced Israa was one they could overcome, fighting its remorselessness together. She hadn't wanted to make the crossing; she'd said they should stay in Izmir, find work, find others who might bring word of her parents and brothers. Someone would know if they were trapped in Douma, or if they'd managed to escape.*

Israa returned home to search for her parents. While the jets had flown past, she'd rushed from street to street, calling out their names. She'd searched hospitals, clinics, bomb shelters. She'd chased after ambulances, crying for her little brothers.

Sometimes the drivers answered her questions; other times, their sirens brought the echo of a storm in their wake – the double-tap carried out by helicopters and fighter jets: the first strike against the people, the second against the paramedics who raced to the people's rescue.

'Go back, go back,' they shouted. Israa could only obey.

She was his next-door neighbor. He'd been in love with her since they were children. They had played together without disrupting the strict conventions of their culture, their mothers keeping an eye on them, the children of the two families so closely intertwined that Ali and Israa's love affair had passed beneath their mothers' notice.

Or so Ali had assumed. One morning he'd heard his mother decide his future across a cup of coffee. She promised there would be an engagement as soon as Ali enrolled in college. She told Israa's mother not to worry, Ali was too deeply in love to look at another girl, even if he left for Damascus. If he tried, she'd straighten him out.

So plans had been made, comfortably and without fuss, neither he nor Israa consulted. Later that night, he'd told Israa the news – the two of them had giggled at their mothers' presumption. At the end of the conversation, they'd smiled into each other's eyes, knowing they'd make the promise good.

All this before the siege of Ghouta.

Before Ali had gone to study in Damascus, his family falling afoul of the regime. His father dead of 'respiratory failure,' his oldest brothers conscripted into the army, the younger ones disappeared for joining in the protests. When they came for Ali, they forced him out of school, recruiting him to the kind of work he couldn't wipe from his mind, in an effort to demonstrate his loyalty, and to keep them from Israa's door.

The destruction of Douma escalated. Finally, the morning came. Ali's uncle decided he had to get them out. He paid for transport to the border: Ali and the others had been allowed to transit through, but his uncle was detained, accused of being a spy. Ali had friends on the other side to receive him, friends who knew the importance of getting him out. They paid bribes to the guards to look the other way, but something about his uncle had flagged the guards' attention.

Ali's parting from his uncle was bitter, no words of consolation spoken, his tears a counterpoint to Israa's despairing cries. He'd held her close and urged her to silence. She was wearing a niqab, her beautiful face hidden; he didn't want to give the guards an excuse to demand a strip search. He'd seen perversity he couldn't imagine on the long journey north. It had taught him to weigh the costs of each action he undertook.

He yanked on Aya's and Israa's hands and left his uncle with the guards. In the camp on the other side, they found a moment of respite, pretending to be siblings. They'd made friends their own age, and heard all kinds of promises about a golden life in Europe: a life free of war, a life without Syria.

The pain of it struck him in new and vulnerable places. He was leaving his history behind. The city of jasmine, the country that desolated childhood. In Turkey, everything was different: a mixture of fear, loneliness, desperation, hunger, ridicule, and cruelty; exploitation leavened by occasional kindness.

People were no longer seeing the boy Ali, in love with the girl, Israa. They saw a young man on the prowl, a predator who might strike, who needed to be contained. Kindness had become happenstance, too illusory to be prized. Except for the friends who had promised him safety. But they had promised it only to Ali, and not to the people he loved.

He wouldn't give his newfound friends what they'd come for unless they made arrangements for the others. While they took their time deciding, he was running out of options. To get the others registered, he'd have to risk the crossing. He'd pay the smugglers to take them to Mytilene, where they'd catch the ferry to Athens. Once he had papers for the others, the friends who'd met him at the border would return. They'd get him across to the continent, in exchange for what he'd promised them. Nothing could go wrong. He'd told himself this every step of the journey: nothing could go wrong.

They'd been stopped at a dozen checkpoints between Douma and the border. His uncle paid the bribes, while the girls huddled together, muffled to the eyes. A few times the car had been searched. A few times, Ali had been abused. A few times, the money had been enough to wave them on.

Then they were through and Ali's uncle was on the other side of the barrier, in the hands of Assad's men.

He knew the fate that awaited his uncle; its imprint had scoured his mind.

And implicated his body.

19

Mytilene, Lesvos

ESA AND RACHEL FOUND A table in the bar of the Sirena Hotel, where they'd asked Ali Maydani to join them. He'd left Aya in Shukri Danner's care, promising to return within the hour. The hotel was really a guesthouse, and its bar was pleasant and homey, the tables a warm, polished wood. There was no overemphasis on the Greek identity, no plastic flags in shot glasses, no framed photographs of Mykonos or Santorini. The proprietor had an air of benevolent goodwill, dispensing drinks behind the bar, including a bitter beverage known as raki, while his wife bustled comfortably between the tables, her face and figure soft and round. The apron she wore around her waist was patterned with a floral border; Khattak guessed that the lovely, feminine touches in the bar were due to her artistic eye. Pots of violets adorned the wooden tables.

They were using the hotel's Wi-Fi to touch base with Sehr and Nate, both tasks Khattak had passed on to Rachel to give himself distance from the others. Rachel had introduced him to Ali; Khattak had felt an instant sense of connection to the boy. The depth of experience in the boy's eyes, the sensitive cast to his mouth, made Khattak realize he was more fragile than the image he tried to project. He felt protective toward the boy, though he warned himself against it. He went through the list of names Ali had given them, making his own notes.

The bar served plain, hearty food, the flavors wholesome and savory. He didn't think Rachel had eaten so many olives in one sitting before; the bread and goat cheese that rounded off their appetizers were just as flavorful. There were small seeds in the bread that gave it an enticing, earthy scent.

However hungry Rachel may have been, the boy was ten times hungrier. He was a charming, good-looking boy with a pleasant manner, but the waitress treated him with marked contempt, saving her smiles for Khattak, who was too preoccupied to notice. Disgruntled, she set down their main courses and flounced off.

Minutes later a loud and hearty group of men tumbled into the bar, bringing with them an atmosphere of friendly chaos. They chaffed each other in different languages; Khattak's ear picked out Greek, Italian, German, and bits and pieces of the lingua franca – English – through which they all communicated.

Seeing Rachel at their table, the only guest in the bar who was a woman, the group of men stopped and took notice. A raffishly attractive man with speaking dark eyes doffed his hat and gave Rachel a smile of welcome. He and one of his friends wore navy jackets with the insignia *Guardia Costiera* on the breast. Members of the Italian Coast Guard. The older man's jacket had a thick orange stripe on each shoulder, the same color as the jacket's hood, and a single star on the inner lapel. A commander or captain, Esa surmised, watching Rachel offer a smile of her own.

The men proceeded to a table close by, calling out greetings to the proprietor. Having struck out with Khattak, the waitress proceeded to try her sulky charm upon the men. In no time, she and a German medic named Hans had established a familiar rapport.

The men at the table noticed Ali and waved. He waved back, his face a little anxious. He called out something in Italian but the man who was a member of the Coast Guard shook his head, his easy smile dimming into sadness.

Ali pointed to a name on the list. Illario Benemerito.

'That's him. He's a commander with the Italian Coast Guard.'

Khattak nodded. 'We'll speak to him before he goes. Who else?'

'Eleni Latsoudi will be here soon. She took me across to Turkey a couple of times before the HRT made her stop.'

Rachel had used the intervening time to read up on her laptop. She leaned over her plate of eggplant moussaka to brief Khattak.

'The Hellenic Rescue Team, sir. They've done phenomenal work during the crisis, stepping up when no one else would. I don't mean the Coast Guard of the nations who are chiefly involved – Greece and Turkey. I mean the European continent. The places where walls went up.'

'You call it a crisis?' Ali turned his dark eyes on Rachel, his mild warmth erased.

Khattak guessed where this was going. 'Sergeant Getty doesn't mean anything by it, Ali. Where we're from, this is how the conflict has been framed: the civil war in Syria is responsible for the refugee crisis. It's accurate as far as it goes, which is not far enough, I know.'

The boy put his long head in his hands, his fingers buried in the curls. 'I find it hard to think of myself as the victim of a crisis. I feel like a person – do you think the war erased that?'

Khattak looked at the boy with great compassion. These were thoughts he hadn't wanted to own to; this wasn't the first time he'd had them. The question of *ummah* was always with him; it was a question of community, of rootedness in a common history, and the sharing of a present moment of crisis and decline. It was why he'd chosen to go to Iran, why he followed the news in the time he had free from his work. It was instinctive to him as a man of his faith to be deeply concerned about the *ummah*. He thought of the cruelty that characterized the abuse of dissidents in Iran. He knew the situation in Syria was worse on a scale that defied imagination – of a nature to wring tears from a statue of the Madonna.

Assad was engaged in the wholesale slaughter of his people. Set aside for the moment the destruction of Syria's cities: their colleges, hospitals, and schools, their mosques and ancient souks. Even if that wasn't totted up in a column of unthinkable loss, there was the question of Syria's people. Syria had been a nation of twenty-two million. Fully half that population was displaced: seven million internally, while five million had fled Assad's incalculable violence. The abject misery of Syria's prison system needed to be weighed on a separate scale of horrors.

He'd known this, he'd followed the escalation of the war closely, he'd supported his mother's efforts with the family she sponsored, but for all that, he'd kept the distance and silence of a member of Canadian law enforcement. He was beginning to feel the strain of this compartmentalization, of not acting where he felt action was called for as he'd done as a student, when he'd imagined a different future for himself.

In the past, he'd shared his inner turmoil with Samina or his father. Often, he'd visited the mosque to find the devotional warmth of community, speaking to the imam when his heart was burdened most.

Now the touchstones of his life were gone, he was working his way back to the friendship he'd shared with Nate, and as much as he admired and respected Rachel, he didn't believe she could understand. She couldn't understand what it felt like to be in his skin, to be proud of who he was while despairing that perhaps there was no longer anything to be proud of – anything to claim except this sense of oppression.

Looking at Ali's young face and imagining the desperation of his journey, Khattak experienced a familiar weight of shame at daring to think these thoughts. Here was this boy who hadn't begun to speak of his losses, and he could set that aside to think of a girl he loved, a girl he feared for with all his heart.

Where was she? What had happened to the girl named Israa, the beautiful girl in the photograph?

Police officers with their government's backing were searching for Audrey Clare, dispatched by the fame and resources of her brother. Ali was searching for a girl among thousands of refugees, a girl without money or family, a girl whose dismal fate Esa envisioned as only a police officer could: she had drowned at sea, she had fallen into prostitution in Izmir, she'd been snatched back across the border, or she'd disappeared in the hands of smugglers.

One life was sought with crushing urgency; the other had vanished unremarked.

These were scales Esa had been weighing all his life, an actuary of the dead and disposable. The boy would trade his life for Israa's. But Esa could search only for Audrey.

Perhaps reading something in his face, Rachel palmed the list for herself. 'The Hellenic Rescue Team took you on board? Why?'

'To take me back to Turkey. I've done the crossing a dozen times searching for Israa. I only found the smugglers who brought me across once.'

Rachel raised her eyebrows at Khattak, who caught her meaning. 'Movement into Europe is strictly controlled. Why would anyone agree to take you across and bring you back? How could you circumvent the authorities on either side?'

Ali made a familiar gesture with his hand, rubbing his thumb against his fingers.

'Money?' Khattak asked. 'You bribed the volunteers?'

'We paid bribes on the Turkish side. On the Greek side, I had papers. The rest – the people who helped me – it was because of Audrey. They were helping *her*. She told them she needed a translator, she said what we were doing was important.' He glanced around, sounding surprised at his own words. 'I don't know why, but sometimes people are kind. Sometimes, they look the other way. And I think – I think Audrey is important, yes?' He looked directly at Esa, and for a moment Esa caught a glimpse of something troubling in the boy's eyes.

A somber note in his voice, he answered, 'Yes, Audrey is important.' Rachel directed Ali back to his reason for risking the crossing.

'You say you met the men who smuggled you across. What did they tell you about Israa?'

His voice broke over the words. 'They told me she drowned the night we crossed.'

Rachel reached a hand across the table, patting Ali on the arm. She hated having to ask the boy something so callous, but they wouldn't get anywhere if she didn't focus. 'I know it's a hard thing to face, but how do you know Israa didn't?'

'I've checked with all the volunteer organizations.' Ali nodded at the other table. 'I've spoken to the Coast Guard – Commander Benemerito has become a friend. Between Eleni and Illario, I've had a lot of help, until they were told not to help me. I've checked the shoreline on both sides. Those who drown wash up on the beaches. Israa isn't among the dead.'

Rachel wished she could believe the answer was as simple as that. Some of those fleeing Syria drowned without ever turning up. Ali couldn't cover each place of landing or visit each morgue. Her trek between Moria and Kara Tepe had given her some sense of the scope of the problem. Ali didn't have access, he didn't have resources. If the Coast Guard and the HRT had shut him down, he didn't have transportation.

An answer streaked through her mind.

'When was the last time you made the trip across?'

Ali named a date in early March. 'They need each available spot on their boats. They can't afford to keep helping me, because others need their help more.'

Two days after that date, Audrey had written to Nate asking for money for a boat.

Rachel studied Ali's determined face. He wasn't going to give up. She knew exactly what that felt like. She also knew emotional stress could precipitate a crisis. What she didn't know was if Ali had broken under the strain, and done something he couldn't confess.

'Did Audrey Clare buy a boat so she could take you across?'

Ali looked a little uncomfortable. 'How did you know?'

'How many times?'

'Every day. Every day she was on the island. Sometimes she went by herself if there was no one who could watch over Aya.'

'And Hatay?' she persisted. 'Did Audrey take you and Aya to Hatay?'

Ali shook his head. He pushed his plate away, moistening his lips. Rachel could see he was lying. She left it aside for now.

'When was the last time she took you across on the boat?'

Ali named the date.

Khattak and Rachel exchanged a glance. It was a few days before Audrey's disappearance. They needed to pin the boy down.

'Did you hear the gunshots?'

Again, he shook his head. 'I was on Chios that day. I came back to find out she was gone.'

'What were you doing on Chios?'

'Checking the beaches.'

Though he spoke the lie with assurance, Rachel caught the telltale glance away.

'I'll go, if you don't mind. I want to talk to Illario.'

He moved off to the other table. Rachel observed the line of his back, nervous and tight with tension.

'He knows more than he's telling us. We need to talk to him again.' She pointed to the list. 'What about these names, sir? Do we send them to Nate or what?'

Khattak scanned the list. 'Yes. Send the list of everyone who's off-island to Nate. I want you to talk to Benemerito – I have a feeling you might make some progress.' He talked over Rachel's mild protest. 'I'll tackle Eleni Latsoudi. Then we should check out Audrey's office on Chios.'

Rachel wanted to say something more about Ali, something

about the pressures that were driving him. But if she did, she might have to explain a little more about herself, about the long, dark years without Zachary. She evaded Khattak's questioning glance. Sometimes she had the feeling he knew her a little too well.

20

'TALK,' ELENI LATSOUDI SAID. 'OR the water will break your heart.' She had a home on the island and she'd invited Khattak to join her for coffee on the patio that overlooked an olive grove above the sea. The hills were a luxuriant green, slashed with purple shadows. A night breeze had sprung up, swaying the trees. The brush of the leaves against a thin shell of moon painted a picture of heartbreak: life jackets lay under that moon.

'So many,' she mused. 'So many risked their lives to come.'

The coffee was bittersweet on Khattak's tongue, rough with a bit of drag that kept him wide awake, his senses alert against the wind, heavy with the scent of flowers. Eleni Latsoudi was a graceful woman his own age, with a beautiful fall of blond hair and eyes as dark as the coffee. She was dressed in her work clothes: a waterproof red jacket and pants, over which she wore a neon safety vest. Her yellow helmet with its flashlight rested on a small stone table nearby. When she got a call from the Greek Coast Guard, she'd have to be on the water in less than twenty minutes.

She was a seasoned paramedic who was responsible for training the Hellenic Rescue Team's influx of volunteers. A call had gone out after the chaos of the crossings in 2015: the HRT's contribution was vital. He could see from Eleni Latsoudi's calm description of her work that she was the right person for the job. The Aegean at night was dark and unforgiving – it was easy to

170

panic at the sight of an overturned boat. The small teams that went out together required coordination and discipline to meet the challenge at sea. In addition to search-and-rescue skills, Eleni had incorporated counseling into the training of her volunteers.

They saw too much heartache on the sea – when bodies washed up on the shore, especially those of children, her young volunteers couldn't cope.

This was what she'd meant when she'd encouraged him to speak: *Talk or the water will break your heart.*

'When was the last time you saw Audrey? What did she want to talk to you about?'

Eleni turned to face him, the breeze lifting a skein of gold hair across her cheek. 'She came out scouting with us when we let her, which truthfully wasn't that often. We need every available spot on our boats in case the scouting run turns into a rescue. Once or twice we let her accompany us because she wanted to chronicle the course of the crossing as part of her NGO's work. She wanted to make sure Woman to Woman had the right response tools. A few times, I took her across to Turkey when I went to meet with my Turkish counterparts – we need to stay up to date about rescue efforts on both sides. Once, when I couldn't take her, she took the ferry to Izmir in the morning and returned to Lesvos on the last boat across.'

'Was she with Ali Maydani?'

'Not to my knowledge. She used a strange phrase. She said she was going to beard the lion in his den.'

'Do you know whom she meant?'

'I don't. But a shipment came over for Woman to Woman on the ferry, a package fairly large in size. Two days after she received it, Audrey made that trip to Izmir. I liked her,' Eleni added, speaking in the past tense. 'Every child, every person on this island mattered to Audrey Clare – islanders and refugees alike. She could sympathize with those who felt the island was overburdened, as much as she could with those who were struggling to reach our shores. Tensions have risen in Greece – we don't have the resources to support a refugee population in such numbers, and the European Union is refusing to do its share.'

She smiled a beautiful, full-lipped smile at Esa. 'The poorest country taking on the ones who are outcast. Is that how you say it, outcast?'

Esa nodded. Something about this woman, with her grave dark eyes and unflustered spirit, eased the despair that had engulfed him since he'd arrived on the island.

'People fill in the gaps, I find.' She smiled that intimate smile again. 'When governments won't act, people open up their hearts and find a way. There's a wonderful baker on the island of Kos, perhaps you've heard of him. Every morning he drives around in his little van to hand out food to those who've made the journey. So many times I've seen young and old alike, refugees who come here with nothing except their hopes, kiss him on his cheeks, as if the bread is a benediction. His name is Dionysus. We keep in him in our prayers.'

Khattak noticed the tiny gold cross at her neck. 'He'll be in mine now, as well.'

He was trying to think of Audrey, but in his mind's eye he kept seeing the curly-headed little girl who'd clung to Ali's hands, her face full of distrust as he'd passed her off to Shukri Danner. He thought if he witnessed this baker handing out bread to children in the cold, he would have kissed him, too.

Eleni touched his hand. As Amélie Roux had done, she asked him about his resemblance to the boys on Afghan Hill.

'Is it my imagination?' she asked. Briefly, he explained the connection. The boys he'd met on Afghan Hill were Pashtuns or Pathans, as was Esa himself. Pashtun tribal links extended across the Afghanistan/Pakistan border; physical similarities that suggested this heritage could sometimes be discerned.

'Ah.' She took a sip of her coffee. 'Then you are experiencing this search for your friend in a more personal way – I can see it in your eyes, Esa.' She used his name with a warm-hearted familiarity.

'Perhaps.'

If he started to speak of these things, he didn't know where it would end. His thoughts moved to Sehr's accusations. If he didn't want her – and he didn't – why had her words struck so deeply? He had a quickened moment of insight into his reticence with Eleni: it was Sehr who would understand, Sehr whose warmth he sought.

Eleni's phone rang. She spoke into it urgently, assuming a brisk competence. She stood up, fastening her helmet in a practiced move.

'I don't know if I can help you more than that. I do know the package that came for Audrey is still at her office on Chios. A friend called and asked me if I wanted to take custody of it. I head out there tomorrow if you need a ride.'

Esa thanked her, emotion deepening his voice. He didn't examine it. He knew it wasn't about Eleni, despite his admiration of her work. It was about the swirling blue waters beneath them, and what Eleni was setting out to find.

They parted ways at the gate to the road, Eleni lingering for a moment.

'Talk,' she said again. 'Don't let Lesvos break your heart.'

21

Eftalou Beach
Lesvos, Greece

THE BREEZE THAT BLEW OVER the island carried the scent of almond blossom. The island's trees were heavy with birds whose cries were like an exultation. Spring was coming to Lesvos much earlier than it was to Toronto; it draped the island in a dreamy warmth accented by grape-colored clouds. Rachel was in her element discussing sports with two well-built members of the Coast Guard. Though hockey was her holy grail, she was conversant in soccer, or football as the Italians called it, and the subject took up most of the walk to the northern beach. She'd asked them to spare a little time; Commander Illario Benemerito had invited her to accompany them. If they were taking a break from their work, she decided she might as well enjoy the fresh air.

She marked off a familiar set of questions: How well had they known Audrey? Could they pinpoint the last time they'd seen her on the island? Did they know if she'd had any success with her inquiries about a missing girl?

Though Benemerito offered his condolences on Audrey's disappearance, he didn't have much to tell her. Vincenzo Sancilio was a cadet who was learning the ropes of his profession; he'd seen Audrey with his commander, but hadn't spoken to her. Together, the two men were voluble, joking with each other despite the difference in rank, though it was Vincenzo who came in for the bulk of the off-color teasing. He wasn't at ease in Rachel's presence: when she offered an opinion on anything from the weather to Barcelona's famous football club, he directed his response to Illario instead, his English not quite as fluent. She wouldn't have called his demeanor deceptive, but something more uneasy.

Benemerito, on the other hand, was forthright and respectful, though a warm glint in his eyes let Rachel know he had noticed her as a woman and approved. He offered a strong hand to assist her on the rockier parts of the descent, keeping her hand in his a second longer than necessary.

At five foot nine and with the build of an athlete, Rachel wasn't used to chivalrous treatment. Trying not to smile, she found she was enjoying it. This must be what Khattak felt like all the time, basking in admiration – though she had to admit, she couldn't really accuse Khattak of basking. His poker face was quite good.

She gave herself a mental pat on the back. If she was comparing her conquests to Khattak's, she was heading up to the big leagues.

She'd thought Illario meant to show her the leisure craft he'd used to come across. He and Vincenzo had a few days' leave; they were on the island to offer their assistance at the camps. Rachel admitted she hadn't expected members of the Italian Coast Guard to be so moved.

When she said as much to Illario, he shrugged off her praise. 'When you've seen what we've seen, when you've rescued people stranded at sea, it leaves its mark on you. The volunteers here, the Greek people –' He made an expansive gesture with his hand. 'They're the heroes of this crisis. We do a little here and there, but they're the backbone of the effort to save lives. You might be able to do a little yourself,' he added with a smile. Rachel noticed a gold tooth – the gleam from one of Illario's incisors gave him the air of a pirate.

She demurred, a little embarrassed. 'I'm a member of Canadian law enforcement.'

'I'm a commander of the Guardia Costiera,' he said easily.

'That doesn't stop me. Don't you want to know what we're doing on this beach?'

Rachel looked around. This wasn't the same beach she'd explored before. Illario and Vincenzo had brought her some distance in the dark, the moon sunk low over the curl of the waves. The wind whipped up along the water. Rachel shivered a little inside her jacket. Unselfconsciously, Illario placed an arm around her shoulders, offering the warmth of his body. Rachel hesitated briefly before accepting.

She was alone on the beach with two men who were strangers, but she wasn't afraid. One, she had her gun strapped in the holster at her waist. Two, she had expert qualifications when it came to self-defense. Three, she was an excellent judge of character. Illario's warm and casual manner posed no threat to her. He was a man used to taking care of others.

'I thought we were out for a stroll.'

Vincenzo took out his flashlight. He swept it over the water in wide, concentric loops.

'Do you think we're here to waste our time?' he said rudely. 'We come here to wait for the boats. We don't only think of ourselves.'

Now Rachel noticed that both men had zipped up their jackets, and were wearing waterproof boots. A flashlight flickered from farther down the beach where a team of volunteers worked, members of a Christian mission. Each white vest was marked with a bright green cross. They were pulling a cart over the stony beach, but stopped a few yards away and began to unload blankets. A few members of the group played their flashlights over the blankets' reflective surface, creating a glare that could be seen from a distance.

His arm still around her shoulders, Illario marched Rachel toward the group.

'Come on,' he said. 'They'll need our help. They're mostly girls – they're not strong enough to pull the boats in.'

He pulled her into a circle of volunteers and released his hold, observing a professional decorum. Greetings were exchanged, with brief introductions, and soon their little group was assembled at the edge of the water, facing out over the waves. Rachel made inquiries about Audrey, and though some of the volunteers knew her, none could offer any knowledge of Audrey's private activities beyond experiences they'd shared as volunteers.

Rachel tugged Illario aside. 'Why did you take her across? Audrey was making regular trips to Turkey. She wouldn't have been traveling through Italian waters.'

'No,' he agreed. He pulled out a pair of binoculars, scanning the silent waves. 'She was educating herself about the refugee journey. She learned the routes over the Aegean, but she also wanted to know what was happening on the Italian side. Most of the migrants we rescue have fled from Libya across the Mediterranean; they're mainly young black men: Ethiopians, Sudanese, Somalis, Gambians. Their experience at the hands of smugglers is the worst of any group that's passing through. There's a strong element of racism to all this.'

'Migrants?' Rachel noted the deliberate word choice.

He lowered his binoculars for a moment. 'Yes, some are refugees – particularly those fleeing Eritrea. But many are economic migrants who wouldn't qualify as Convention refugees.' He shrugged his broad shoulders. 'The poverty and corruption they are fleeing is no less a danger to their survival, in my opinion; I'm not trying to be political.' He spared Rachel a smile. 'It's just important to be accurate, so we neither understate nor overstate the magnitude of the crisis.'

Rachel remembered the conditions at Moria. 'I don't think anyone is in danger of overstating things.'

Vincenzo broke into their conversation.

'You haven't seen the Italian ports. They're sweeping through our cities, sleeping in our parks, chasing the tourists away.

Families can't go out in safety anymore. Wherever *they* go, they leave their garbage behind.'

Illario rebuked him. 'No one asked for your opinion.'

Vincenzo scowled. 'Free country,' he muttered.

Illario turned back to Rachel. 'It is true that this year more refugees are reaching Italy than Greece.'

There was a heavy sterling cross at his neck that he raised and kissed. 'When you've pulled as many people from the water as we have, you're in a constant battle with death. I can't say we're winning it.'

This time when he raised his binoculars, he let out a shout. He extended his arm out to the sea, pointing. 'There! Vincenzo, move!'

He passed his binoculars to a volunteer, striding out into the water, Vincenzo at his side, the water sloshing up against their boots.

At first, Rachel couldn't see the boat. It was half-submerged and darker than the water. The first sign she had that the boat was headed to shore was the sight of orange life jackets dipping against the waves. However the dinghy was powered, it wasn't moving forward now, just buffeted by the waves. Vincenzo and Illario lost their footing a few times before they regained their feet. Vincenzo swam out ahead to meet the boat.

In the glare of the volunteers' flashlights, Rachel had her first look at a boat arriving from Turkey. It was a small rubber craft designed for twenty people, but double that number were crammed aboard, sitting on each other's laps, children packed into the middle, silent and numb with cold. A few of the older boys who could swim were clinging to the sides of the boat, treading water to prevent the boat from sinking under the weight of such a load. Families were squeezed together – the elderly, the middle-aged, the young – small children and babies gripped in their mothers' arms.

The faces of the travelers were white in the glare of the lights, filled with dread and panic. Illario reached the boat. His strong arms began to pull it in, Vincenzo swimming around to push the dinghy from the back.

Farther up the beach where the land met the road, Rachel heard the honking of horns. Two or three white vans were driving down the road close to the edge of the beach. One of the volunteers had gotten a fire going on the beach, the smoke rising to meet the waves.

It was a scene of chaos and noise, and Rachel couldn't stand by and watch. She ran into the water, her steps slowing as they met the drag of the waves. She took the opposite side of the dinghy, using her upper-body strength to help Illario pull it in. The young men who'd been treading water did the rest. How they found the strength, Rachel didn't know. Even this limited attempt was wearing at her muscles. At the rear of the dinghy, Vincenzo shoved the boat ashore. The minute it was out of the water, its occupants began to clamber out.

They were met by volunteers with blankets and urged toward the fire. Some did as they were told, others looked blankly back at the dinghy, searching the faces of those who hadn't stirred. A young woman whose lips were blue unclutched her freezing hands from the baby in her lap. The man beside her – a husband, a brother? – reached down and passed the baby to Rachel. She unzipped her jacket and pressed the child to her chest, struggling back to the shore. The baby's skin was cold, its eyes closed. She passed it to a volunteer, and stumbled back to the boat to help the mother.

So the next half hour passed – hands meeting hands, life jackets being unzipped and abandoned on the rocks, paramedics attempting a makeshift triage. A hastily contrived stretcher was brought from one of the vans to assist an elderly woman whose long black *abaya* was soaked. A little boy translated anxiously for his silent, stoic parents.

The last of the men treading water next to the boat now

staggered ashore and fell to his knees, kissing the rocky ground. He raised one finger high above his head, his body racked with sobs. He was praying, Rachel saw.

Others were crying as well – the absence of a reply to names that were called out, fathers diving back into the boat to search for children they couldn't find. When Rachel spun around next, the woman who'd passed Rachel her child was sitting alone near the fire, her face empty as she stared into the flames. The baby was beside her on the ground, its small body covered with a blanket. The paramedics had moved on to those who were still alive.

Rachel caught a glimpse of Illario crouched down next to two little boys who appeared to be alone. He stood and craned his neck, playing his flashlight over the crowd. He was making a count of how many had arrived on this particular boat.

Rachel was wet and cold, but she couldn't have faced herself if she didn't pass off her coat to the little boys who were shivering together by themselves. She draped the coat around their shoulders and zipped it up over their bodies.

'Here,' she called to a volunteer. 'Help them. They need to get dry right away.'

She was surprised when Vincenzo shouldered her aside and scooped them into his arms.

'I'll take them,' he said. He lumbered up the beach to the waiting vans. Rachel lost track of him as another arrival tugged her hand.

The night seemed endless. The rescuers as much as the new arrivals were cold, tired, and hungry – helping, processing, calming, and reassuring. Finally the beach was empty. The living had been driven up the road to the camp; the dead would have to wait for the van's return.

Exhausted, they huddled beside the fire, listening to twin sounds: the waves slapping the shore, and the paltry spitting of the fire. Rachel had never felt so wretched, or so grateful to have a man's shoulder at her side. This had been one night out of her life.

What of those who made the crossing? What of the longer journey they'd risked in the name of sanctuary?

Her lips and her fingertips were numb. She wanted to cry but didn't. How could she? She was remembering that Audrey Clare had been on this island for months, seeking to make things better. Trying to improve conditions. Trying to make sure her NGO could do its part to meet the overwhelming need.

She said as much to Illario, who nodded, telling her stories of how deeply Audrey had been engaged, of the survivors she'd interviewed, of the police officers, Coast Guard, asylum lawyers, and officials she'd spoken with in order to create a comprehensive picture of the crisis.

'She came to Italy several times in the beginning. After that I didn't see her. I heard she'd joined up with the Hellenic Rescue Team.' He smiled down at Rachel, whom he'd sheltered inside the warmth of his jacket, his shoulder strong and steady against hers. 'By the way, you can't give everything you own away. The NGOs have supplies, especially for the kids. I go up there to check on them regularly. Members of the Guardia Costiera are always sending things across with me. You have to stay well, Rachel, so you can help others.'

Beginning to warm up again, Rachel saw the wisdom of this, though she couldn't square it with her conscience. It was one thing to read about a crisis whose scale you couldn't fathom; it was another to take a child from its mother and find it dead on a pile of life jackets.

'I don't know how you do this,' she said. She was looking at the wet pile of life vests, a spark of recollection striking. She puzzled it through. When refugees landed on the shores of Lesvos, they left what they no longer needed behind. They expected their next step to be the chance to catch the ferry from the Mytilene port to Athens – a well-equipped and safe means of transportation. So then why –?

'Illario, what do the islanders do with these life jackets? Do they have any further use?'

She remembered now that volunteers had used discarded life jackets to make art: on a hill on Lesvos was a giant rendering of a peace sign formed by the orange vests.

Illario wasn't listening. He'd let go of Rachel and now had his binoculars raised to his eyes again.

'Come on,' he said to the group. 'I see another boat.'

22

Aegean Sea crossing
Lesvos to Chios

'COME ON, AYA.'

Ali lifted her onto the boat. Audrey had purchased it from a fisherman who'd done the deal in cash. Ali was always finding problems with the boat, not least the fact that Audrey no longer piloted it.

She'd steered it with the competence born of a lifetime's experience, her gun stowed in the hold in case they ran into trouble on their way to Izmir. They'd discovered things in Izmir, bad things done to innocent people, refugees burned like matchsticks on first use.

He wouldn't accept that as his fate. He was going to fight for Israa, the way he knew Audrey would fight.

Aya was with him, because Shukri claimed to be too busy to keep her eye on her. After what had happened with Audrey, he couldn't risk leaving Aya on her own. She was all that was left to him now, the only thing in his life not stained like the blood of a poem. He wondered if Nizar Qabbani had envisioned this future for Syria when he'd written, 'O my sad homeland, how in a moment you changed me.'

He shook off the thought. It was daylight and they were safe. He'd be able to steer them to Chios. He was following the detective who'd tousled his hair with a smile that reached his eyes, and a look of pain about his mouth that said he understood him.

The man's name was Esa.

It was a Muslim name, an Arab name, a name to live up to, the way Ali had tried to live up to the example set by his brothers. They'd disappeared inside Sednaya, where he prayed they had met their fate at once. These were terrible prayers to make – the only ones he could summon from the knowledge of what he'd fled. He loved his brothers like pieces of his heart; he prayed for their release from the evil of the torturers, the kind of evil that lurked in hell, banished for eternity, except that the torturers, like Assad himself, still reveled in their earthly pleasures. On the day that Aleppo was pounded into submission, the nightclubs in Damascus were packed.

The material journey was a brief one. In the eternal life of the Akhirah, his brothers would reunite at the foot of the Prophet's throne, and Esa, the son of Maryam, would call them home as companions.

He was following a less saintly Esa to Chios. If this one proved reliable, he would tell him what he knew about Audrey's journey to Hatay, and her subsequent visit to Holland. He would also confess about Audrey and the van.

23

Souda refugee camp, Chios

THE SOUDA CAMP ON CHIOS occupied the rough trough of the moat of a ruined castle, close to the central plaza of the main town, Chios, locally known as Chora. The castle was a heritage site that had housed previous generations of refugees. Recent arrivals were confined to its outskirts, a camp designed for a thousand people overflowing with thousands more; the attendant health and sanitation problems had become unmanageable.

A row of UNHCR shelters ran along the trough, service tents on the opposite side. Electricity was minimal, most of the tents were unheated; men and women often had to share makeshift public showers and toilets. The first thing Esa noticed as he looked down the length of the trough was a concrete barrier painted over with slogans that read like cries of despair: no borders, no borders, no borders, the prayer of the stateless.

The Greek islands were bearing the brunt of the crossing: some sixty thousand people were trapped, with no assistance from the European Union to boost the islanders' best efforts. An appalling lack of asylum services coupled with a refusal to assist in relocation had resulted in growing tension between the local population and the refugees who were detained there. The pace of asylum proceedings was too slow to accommodate the flow of arrivals from Turkey.

A generation was losing its childhood: six thousand children were trapped on Chios without access to education or adequate health care. All around the camp were groups of people, young and old, with no occupation, no chance of earning a livelihood, unable to return, unable to move on. The camps were not a permanent solution, yet no other solution had been proffered. They were so far below humanitarian standards, the camp on Chios the most crowded on the islands, yet the demands to improve could scarcely be met by Greece, one of the EU's poorest members.

No wonder tensions were rising. Despite the best efforts of those who understood the extent of the humanitarian crisis, the current situation was unsustainable. Islanders had been pushed to the limit of their goodwill and resources; refugees were facing mental and physical health crises from enforced isolation.

Khattak could read the danger signs from a distance. A group of Greek men were gathered around a fish restaurant's patio, smoking, talking, and studying the refugees encamped in a nearby lot with expressions of judgment.

Khattak had hired a taxi to take him to Souda, parting from Eleni Latsoudi with thanks. She'd gone on to meet with her volunteers, he was making for the Woman to Woman service tent at Souda.

The tent was occupied by an Australian exchange student named Peter Conroy, who offered Khattak a hearty handshake and a seat on a plastic chair. The tent was open to the alley that ran between the service tents and the UNHCR pre-fab shelters. People passed in front of it in groups; Khattak's conversation with Conroy was frequently interrupted by people asking Conroy for his help with myriad problems.

Despite the urgency of his search for Audrey, Khattak let the interruptions flow. Now that he was here, it was better to see for himself the nature of W2W operations. Peter Conroy handed out maps, he occasionally translated English terms into Arabic, he pointed applicants in various directions, and with cheerful warmth, he offered children sweets from a stack he kept on his desk, which was no more than a plastic table with two sets of plastic drawers. He had a habit of leaning back in his chair, catching himself just before the chair up-ended. Khattak suspected that a good deal of the time, Peter Conroy was bored.

'Woman to Woman doesn't usually recruit male volunteers,' he said. 'It's a little at odds with their mandate.'

Peter Conroy smiled a broad, gummy smile. 'Oh, I don't work for Audrey Clare. I'm actually here with an Australian NGO, but they're overstaffed at the moment and Shukri asked me if I'd keep an eye on things. Just the basics, mind you. I don't know a heck of a lot about operations.'

Khattak looked around the service tent, searching for signs of the package Eleni had mentioned. There was a pile of boxes at the back, half-hidden by a large canvas roll.

'How long have you been filling in?'

'Since last December, I would say.'

Khattak asked how well Conroy had known Audrey and when he'd last seen her, but he learned nothing new or of value. Apart from Shukri Danner, everyone either he or Rachel had spoken to about Audrey had the greatest admiration for her work. Conroy knew none of the details of Audrey's travel, though he confirmed that several of the names on Ali's list were known to him, friends to the islanders – people who regularly assisted with intake work, despite the fact that it fell outside their purview.

'We all have to be a little improvisational here, you know? There's a different need at every hour of every day. If we could just get more translators – I honestly think we need them more than medics, though OB-GYNs and dentists are really in demand. Most of these kids haven't had dental care in years.' He let his chair tip forward, speaking with the great earnestness of the young. 'I mean, this is a tragedy compounded by fresh tragedies every day. And people get so upset, I don't get it.'

'The islanders, you mean?'

Conroy took a moment to answer this. 'To be fair, there's no way as many refugees would have transited through as they have *without* the assistance of the islanders. For the most part, the people here have been incredible. But every other day or so, I get wind of a new complaint. Like, why is this five-year-old kid getting dental treatment when no one cares about me?'

Khattak had heard similar sentiments in Canada, particularly through social media, when Canadian dentists had offered free dental care to new arrivals. One of his friends had taken the challenge head on by inviting anyone in need of treatment to make an appointment at her office.

It came back to a hierarchy of need, and a balance of competing interests.

He didn't believe it was a case of people not wanting to help, or of not having empathy for what refugees were enduring. The marginalized existed among every group of people. If their voices cried out in need, he couldn't blame them, and he didn't. He tried to understand, he tried to extend solidarity where it was needed, regardless of personal affiliation.

He thought of the graffiti on the concrete wall: *no borders.*

There were no boundaries to human need; there should be none to his compassion. This was how his faith governed him, and he thought perhaps his despair could be eased by turning back to prayer – he'd heard there were mosques on the islands, but he didn't know if they were in operation. Or if they were, how wise it would be for him to join the congregants, in light of present tensions.

He could see the Greek people couldn't solve the crisis on their own. They needed and deserved help. More than that, they deserved gratitude from an often irresolute world, unwilling to contend with what Assad had done in his deadly desire for power. The question remained: What other losses would Assad inflict?

The ripple effects of the war in Syria had spiraled out.

But here to this island? To the death of an Interpol agent who'd kept company with a refugee; to the kidnapping of a foreign citizen?

Had Audrey been kidnapped? Or was she following a trail of her own?

'Did Audrey receive a package a few weeks ago? Something on the bulky side? Perhaps she stowed it behind that canvas. I'm also looking for a group of boxes – maybe the size of shoeboxes – at least twenty of those. Would Audrey have stored them here?'

Good-natured and obliging, Conroy got up to look. Khattak joined him. He wanted to see what else was behind the canvas.

Conroy kept up a pleasant stream of conversation as they searched the pile together. 'Apart from Audrey's team, I haven't seen that many Canadians.'

'What about Australians? You mentioned an NGO.' Khattak picked up a box that was larger than the others. It was empty. He set it aside.

'Yeah, Australians are really feeling it. The boats where the kids wash up dead? It's like decent people won't have it, do you know?'

The blithe assurance behind this remark made Khattak suspicious. Peter Conroy had come a long way to volunteer with an NGO with limited resources. Supposedly this left him free to help out at Woman to Woman, but he could have made himself useful to anyone on the island. Why, then, had he brought himself specifically to Audrey's attention? And what had made Audrey believe that Conroy could be trusted with her NGO's work? What had made them compatible?

'If you wanted to help, you didn't need to come halfway around the world,' he said.

'How'd you mean?' Conroy sounded aggrieved. 'You've had a look at this place. You can see what the need is like.'

'Surely, Australia has a crisis of its own?'

Conroy's blank look confirmed Khattak's suspicions. For someone who'd traveled to Greece with a volunteer's zeal, Conroy seemed oblivious to problems at home.

Khattak tested his theory. 'There's Nauru,' he said. 'And Manus Island.'

Conroy began to shift things around the tent, searching for

Audrey's package. If he was invested in the refugee crisis, he'd be aware of Khattak's meaning. His sudden, frantic search could mean he was giving himself time to come up with an explanation.

Nauru and Manus were two islands in the Pacific where asylum seekers were detained at the Australian government's insistence. None had been settled in Australia. The offshore processing policy meant that asylum seekers innocent of any crime faced mandatory detention in warehouse facilities on the islands.

But in the past year, explosive leaks from within Nauru had revealed that assaults and self-harm were prevalent at the detention center, with more than fifty percent of the assaults against children. An opposition movement had risen up against the so-called Pacific Solution. Khattak wondered why Conroy hadn't joined it.

When Conroy straightened up from his search, his face was deeply flushed. His tone defensive, he said, 'If Australia is guilty of mistreating refugees, we're not the only ones.'

It was a deflection. It didn't explain Conroy's decision to travel to Greece. His trip and his room and board would be costly, spending resources that could be better used to enhance the efforts of established organizations. Or the effort back home.

'I'm not sure what you mean,' Khattak said. He was pushing Conroy, but if there was something Conroy was hiding, he needed to uncover it now.

Conroy's eyes narrowed against the glare of the sun.

'Canada, mate. Don't you detain refugees in jail along with convicted criminals? Doesn't sound much better than Nauru.'

Khattak didn't deny it. A lack of legal status in Canada meant that refugees could be subject to detention for status offenses indefinitely. There had been hunger strikes by detainees, and protests by NGOs who championed humanitarian solutions. Thanks to their efforts, the criminalization of refugees was under renewed scrutiny, though the needle had hardly moved.

So Conroy *was* aware of both countries' refugee policies; something for him to consider.

A little nervously, Conroy moved away. He shuffled around the boxes until he uncovered a bulky yellow envelope. 'I think this is what you're looking for.' His tone made it clear he was anxious for Khattak to leave. Khattak studied the package.

Audrey Clare's name was scrawled on the outside. It was addressed in care of Woman to Woman, and extra postage had been paid for personal delivery.

Khattak took the package and opened it, mystified as two orange life jackets with the Yamaha logo fell into his hands. As so often happened when he and Rachel were working a case and their discoveries synchronized, Rachel chose that moment to call him.

He went to stand outside the tent for better reception on his cell phone.

She sounded tired and frazzled, as if she hadn't slept. She was on her way to Chios. She'd hitched a ride with Commander Benemerito, and she hurried over preliminaries.

'Remember those inventory lists Gaffney got us from Audrey and Nate's e-mails?'

'Yes, why?'

'I've been on the beach twice in the last twenty-four hours, but I didn't take it in right away.'

'Take what in, Rachel?' he asked patiently, waving at a little girl who darted down the alley. He was looking over the trough to the castle, and thinking how precariously placed the camp was – vulnerable to torrential rain or to an attack from higher ground. But what made him think of an attack? The Greek men at the restaurant with their closed, suspicious faces? Surely their grievances were minor and would not amount to harm. He made a note to check in at the UNHCR office to get a better sense of relations between islanders and refugees.

He could also ask Eleni Latsoudi for her opinion. Perhaps she could meet them for dinner. Though, based on the exhaustion in Rachel's voice, he wasn't sure Rachel would last that long. He'd booked accommodation on Chios, in case their inquiries delayed their return to Lesvos.

'Are you listening to me, sir?'

He admitted his attention had strayed and asked her to repeat her conclusions.

'There are life jackets all over the beach. Ali told me there's a peace memorial made from these jackets up on a hill on Lesvos. The site is called "The Dump."'

Khattak frowned at the jacket in his hands. It was new, the tags still attached, and it looked capable of surviving the sinking of the *Titanic*.

'That package that came from Audrey contained two Yamaha jackets.'

'Yes!' Rachel sounded triumphant. 'That's exactly it. I was asking myself why Audrey had invested money in life vests for refugees. She was already on the island, Woman to Woman was working from the island.'

'Go on.' Minute by minute, it was becoming clearer to Khattak. But he preferred to hear how Rachel had arrived at her conclusions.

'Refugees dump their vests when they get here. They don't intend to stay on the islands. In fact, the only person I've heard of who made the reverse crossing to Turkey is Ali. Most people take the ferry to Athens and move on. So why was Audrey ordering life vests on Lesvos?'

Khattak looked at the jacket in his hand and offered a suggestion. 'She wanted to test one for herself before it was put into use? Or she was smuggling people across on her boat, as Nate thought – she needed supplies for them.'

'Why order them from abroad then? Why not get them in Turkey like everyone else, especially when she'd made so many trips to Izmir in recent weeks?'

Khattak tested the strength of the life vest's buckles with his hand. 'Those are good questions, Rachel. I'm afraid I don't know the answers.'

'That's because the answers aren't on Chios. I hope you're ready for another trip, sir. I think we need to be on the other side of this journey. But mostly I think you need to get Ali to tell you what it is that he knows.'

When he'd made arrangements to meet Rachel at a restaurant, Peter Conroy came out of the service tent to join him, conveying an eagerness to be of assistance that was at odds with their earlier discussion. Khattak weighed it, but it was too soon to draw definitive conclusions. Being questioned by the police disturbed the innocent and guilty alike, albeit for different reasons. Conroy gave him a small piece of paper: the receipt for a storage facility, charged to Audrey's credit card. But the facility wasn't in Greece, as Khattak would have expected. It was in a town called Delft. And if Khattak's memory was correct, Delft was not a town in England, Germany, or France, lining up with Audrey's plane ticket purchases – it was a city in the Netherlands.

The boxes Shukri had described weren't in Athens, to his knowledge, and they weren't at W2W headquarters either on Lesvos or Chios. Was it possible that Audrey had shipped the boxes to Delft? Could she have stored them at the facility mentioned on the receipt?

He thought about the e-mail correspondence between Audrey and his sister, and between Audrey and Nate. He needed to give Gaffney a call to find out what he'd learned about where her e-mails had been sent from.

Conroy helpfully urged him to turn the receipt over. A name was printed on the back. Perhaps the printing was Audrey's, Khattak couldn't tell.

CIJA.

He had no idea what it meant.

24

RACHEL WASN'T ALL THAT HUNGRY after her choppy ride to Chios with Illario. She'd warmed to him during the short boat ride, enjoying his humor, enjoying the fact that he had any humor at all, given the things he saw every day: the condition of the living nearly as wretched as that of those drowned at sea, their names and histories lost.

It was getting to her, this place. She felt bad about it but she longed to be off-island, and back with Nate and Sehr, picking up the friendship they'd established when Khattak had been in Iran. Vincenzo, Illario's subordinate, hadn't warmed up to Rachel at all; the more comfortably she chatted with Illario, the stormier the glances he cast in her direction. She suspected him of having a crush on his commander.

They left her at the pier and went on to the camp, making the most of their few days' leave. Rachel hadn't asked but she guessed that Illario made a point of checking the number of survivors that made it across to the islands in the northern chain each day. She wondered if he was comparing those numbers to the crossings to Italy.

Rubbing her tired eyes, she let Khattak order a late lunch for them. She described her efforts during the night, and he listened to her with his familiar combination of close attention and warmth, interpreting her emotions from her terse recital of the facts.

'I never meant for you to become so personally involved, Rachel.' Before she could flare up, he added, 'Though I wouldn't have expected anything else from you.'

They talked about the life jackets and agreed that their next step would have to involve tracing Audrey's steps in Turkey. The restaurant didn't have wireless access or they could have checked for messages from Gaffney – they were waiting on his summary of locations, so they'd have a better understanding of what Audrey had been chasing.

During the course of the night's work, she and Khattak had lost track of Ali Maydani, who, for all they knew, had the answers. Their food came and they helped themselves to brined fish whose quotient of salt was an acquired taste. When they finished, they were served the ubiquitous Greek coffee. Khattak told her about Conroy and showed her the receipt.

'The boxes are there, I think,' Rachel said. 'Unless the Greeks aren't cooperating.' She grinned at Khattak. 'I know you had a rocky beginning, but maybe Inspecteur Roux would be willing to be more candid with you. She's ahead of us in terms of putting pressure on the Greeks.'

Rachel and Khattak both knew that despite the prime minister's endorsement, the Greek authorities had primary jurisdiction. She thought of another idea.

'Sehr didn't seem to have much luck with the IPCD. Maybe you should give it a shot.'

Khattak considered this in silence. Finally, he said, 'I don't want to infringe on relationships Sehr has established. She might think I'm questioning her competence.'

Rachel shook her head, her ponytail bouncing. 'Why would she, sir? We all want the same thing – a quick resolution to this, and answers about where Audrey may be, if she's still alive.'

Her words caught the attention of a group of men on the patio – most in their twenties, wearing ball caps. They were dressed in black, their T-shirts imprinted with a logo that contained a cubic emblem within a pair of laurels. The backs of their T-shirts were printed in Greek.

'Sir.' She lowered her voice. 'Is that something we should be worried about? That emblem looks like a swastika.'

Khattak had his back to the men. Rachel didn't think it was a good idea for him to turn around. These men wouldn't take Khattak for an Italian or Greek. She reached across the table and grasped his hand.

'I'm tired, love,' she said, adopting an affectionate tone. 'Should we head back to our hotel?' Under her breath, she muttered, 'The Athena looks pretty good. That's where you booked us in, right?'

Khattak picked up on her cue at once. He ran a caressing hand along Rachel's arm, a gesture that caused her to gulp her coffee, scalding the back of her throat. He summoned the waiter and paid the bill, escorting Rachel out from the far side of the patio. They walked hand in hand, Rachel conscious of a strange new tension.

'You don't think we should head to Lesvos to look for Ali?'

They walked to the Athena, a guesthouse ten minutes down the road, built like a miniature castle with two arched windows at the summit of a flight of stone stairs. A Greek flag flew beside a medallion of the goddess Athena.

'No point in delaying, sir. Let's see what Gaff has sent us, then let's get across to Turkey on the first boat. We could fly but I think we should follow Audrey's exact route.'

They were far enough from the restaurant that Rachel could raise the issue of the men in black. 'They're watching the camp,' she said. 'They're watching you. Any idea who they are?'

Khattak looked back. The group of men had been joined by several others. One was looking straight at him, his strong face set with enmity. He'd brought a black staff with him and laid it on the ground, its red flag tightly furled.

'I haven't seen them before. When I arrived at Souda there was a different group of men sitting there, older and more vocal. They were watching the camp as well.'

'Maybe we should talk to the police.'

'It might be enough to warn the proprietor of the Athena. I'm sure they don't want trouble around here.'

Once inside the hotel, Rachel freed her hand from Khattak's. He'd been holding on to it as an afterthought; she could see that he was preoccupied. The proprietor, a man named Nikos Papadakis, wasn't forthcoming about the police, but he gave them advice about ferry crossings. They had missed the afternoon ferry; the next one wasn't until the morning.

They checked into the hotel for the night but stayed together in the lobby.

Khattak had received the message from Gaffney. He forwarded it to Rachel so they could make comparisons. Nate had also sent him an e-mail containing scans of Audrey's credit card purchases from the time she'd left for Greece. Together, these comprised at least four months of records. Rachel borrowed a pencil from the front desk and began to chart a course that followed the location tags attached to Audrey's e-mails.

When she'd finished cross-referencing e-mails and credit card purchases, there were two separate trips that she'd tracked.

The first was a trip Audrey had made by boat from Mytilene, Lesvos, to Izmir, Turkey. She'd stayed in Izmir for several days before catching a flight to Paris. From Paris, she'd taken a trip to Brussels, and from Brussels she'd flown back to Izmir, then crossed back to Mytilene.

That had been in January. In between, Audrey had sent numerous e-mails from the Greek islands, and just as many from Izmir. A week before her disappearance, she'd taken the second of two complicated trips: Mytilene to Izmir, where she'd purchased bus tickets to Hatay. She'd stayed in Hatay for a day before returning to Lesvos. Then she'd flown to the Austrian-German border, where she'd taken a series of train trips that had seen her end up in Delft. For the two days she was in the Delft area, there were no transactions recorded on her credit card and no e-mails from her account. She'd flown back to Greece; a day later she'd sent an e-mail to Nate from Lesvos. There was no record of her journey from Mytilene to Izmir; Rachel suspected she'd used her private boat for that trip.

Audrey had purchased three bus tickets for Hatay – who had she taken with her? Ali and the little girl? Why would Audrey have taken two refugees who'd fled Syria back to the Syrian border? Were these roundabout trips attempts to find Israa?

One thing was clear. Only after the trip to Hatay had Audrey rented a storage unit in Delft. The boxes that were missing from Woman to Woman's offices on Lesvos were likely stored in Delft. Rachel believed whatever was in those boxes had something to do with Audrey's trip to Hatay. One week after her return to Lesvos, she'd disappeared, and Aude Bertin and Sami al-Nuri had been found shot with Audrey's gun.

Had something in Hatay precipitated this outcome?

She studied the receipt Khattak had passed her.

CIJA.

What did it mean? A Google search brought up the Center for Israel and Jewish Affairs, and the Center for Investigative Journalism in the Americas. Could Audrey have been trying to break a story on the refugee crisis?

There were other acronyms Rachel needed to check as well. She bookmarked the page and looked over at Khattak.

'Hatay, sir. I don't get it. What's there? It's not near the coast, it's near the Syrian border. Why on earth would Audrey have risked a trip to the border? Especially if she was traveling with Syrian refugees?'

He shook his head. Neither of them knew enough about the refugee crisis, or what Audrey had been doing with her time. Khattak was sorting through information on his laptop and now he angled the screen in her direction.

He'd done a search on Hatay, trying to find a link to the refugee crisis. There were dozens of refugee camps in Turkey; one of them was a heavily guarded camp close to the Syrian border called Camp Apaydin. Reading about it had confirmed something to Khattak – the muscles in his face were taut.

'Sir,' she said. 'What's special about Apaydin?'

'It's guarded by Turkish patrols.'

Rachel was confused. She was having a hard time following the politics involved.

'Is the Turkish government trying to prevent people from moving on?'

'It's trying to protect the inhabitants of this camp from other refugees. And from questions from the outside world.'

Rachel's eyebrows shot up. 'Why? Who's being held at that camp?'

Khattak's tone was thoughtful. 'It's a camp for Syrian defectors. Defectors from Assad's forces, the Syrian Army.'

25

ESA WASN'T ASLEEP. THE FERRY to Cesme was so early in the morning that he hadn't been able to snatch more than a few hours' rest. The sky was still black, the stars erased by the glare of streetlamps on the harbor. He'd woken early out of habit to pray, then he'd searched for background information on Camp Apaydin. He judged it was time for a call to Ambassador Mansur, who might have information on the camp. She was due an update on his investigation anyway.

She would ask him whether Audrey was safe, a question he couldn't answer.

The thought he didn't allow himself to examine was that Audrey could be dead, her body irrecoverable. Nate had sent him an e-mail, advising that he'd hired a team of private investigators to continue the search on the islands. He had another team working in Izmir.

He updated Nate on his findings. As an afterthought, he sent a politely worded e-mail to Sehr. He didn't know if she was still in Athens or if she'd returned to Lesvos. He couldn't guess where Nate would find her skills most useful. Perhaps Rachel was right and he should have used his influence with the police in Athens. He shouldn't be tiptoeing around Sehr. But she was pushing past his boundaries when he viewed her only as a friend.

Samina's friend.

Wasn't that the issue?

Sehr was attractive, accomplished, yet he denied her ability to compel anything deeper from him: affection, desire... love. He'd told her it wasn't possible.

She'd asked this of him too soon; he blamed her for pushing past his grief. She'd come to the hospital to visit him, but Esa had refused to see her. She'd waited outside his room, passing messages to him through his mother. Later, when he'd recovered, she'd gone with him to the cemetery, a visit he paid each Friday.

He'd taken selfish consolation from the fact that while he was in Iran, Samina had had Sehr to keep her company. She'd been going to visit Samina long before he'd been discharged, the injuries he'd sustained nearly healed. Samina was her oldest friend. A sister, she'd said at the ceremony, after the funeral Khattak had missed. He'd been in surgery. Samina's parents had refused to delay; he couldn't bring himself to ask them to wait. He accepted the expedience of the funeral, it was merciful; more than that, he wouldn't have taken any step that caused his in-laws further pain.

Sehr had spoken of these things at the grave. She'd spoken of their long friendship, she'd told him things Samina had said, confidences shared between friends, things he hadn't known that had lightened his spirit, easing his grief with love.

When he'd wanted to mourn in peace, she'd respected his wishes and left him at the grave.

A few months later, when his father died, Sehr had come again, this time to aid his mother. She assisted in carrying out the customs that followed upon a funeral, bringing food, company... solace. She'd spoken with his family long into the night.

At the forty-day mourning ceremony, he felt Sehr's eyes on him, felt the gentle caress of her glance, and with sudden clarity, he'd known. He'd understood that she loved him: his suffering and loss were personal to her – she ached for him and longed to console him.

He viewed it as a betrayal.

201

Of his trust in her, of the way Samina had loved her.

He said as much at the cemetery on the anniversary of Samina's death. They hadn't come to the grave together as they'd done in the past. He'd stopped seeing her, his rage and grief bound up in a festering knot.

He assumed she'd come not for Samina's sake, but his.

She'd listened to his bitter evisceration of her motives, drawing her scarf over her hair. The gesture was frozen in his mind: her delicate hands pulling up her scarf, staring down at Samina's headstone, her lashes dark on her cheeks.

To this day, the sight of a woman drawing up her scarf caused him acute distress.

When his torrent of rage had expunged itself, he'd felt the knot in his chest dissolve. He'd wanted to say these things for so long. He wanted her to accept the crushing weight of blame so he'd cease to blame himself.

Sehr had reached for his hand. Numbly, he let her take it. She wasn't wearing gloves; her thin, strong fingers were cold.

'The accident wasn't your fault. But it wasn't my fault, either. From God we come, to God we return. Doesn't that help you at all?'

'Don't pretend,' he said, with the last vestiges of a desire to hurt. 'I know why you've come.'

He caught the shimmer of tears on her lashes. It didn't check his anger. He cast her hand away.

Sehr pressed her palms to her eyes. 'So what's my crime, Esa? What are you punishing me for?'

'Do you need me to say it? Are you really so lacking in shame?'

'I didn't realize loving you was something to be ashamed of.'

After that, he didn't see her at the cemetery. But when he came on Fridays, there were flowers at Samina's grave. They lasted a day or two, then a new arrangement would be laid.

Sehr was still coming. She was just avoiding him, the way he avoided her at his parents' house. A casual word in his mother's ear resulted in a plea that he treat Sehr with kindness, with something approaching the gratitude she deserved.

'I'm trying to be kind,' he said.

There he'd left it, until matters had come to a head.

Doubting whether he should, he passed the information on to Sehr: the details of the storage unit in Delft, and the word written on the back of the receipt. *CIJA*. Or was it Cija, a person's name? A Greek name? If so, *who* was Cija?

The smell of smoke reached his nostrils, accompanied by a noise that sounded like a log being split. The windows of his room led to a tiny balcony, and through these the smoke drifted up in a curl of black cloud. There was a sudden silence, like a breath being sucked in. The exhale came like a hammer blow: a full-throated, heavy chant, shouts of alarm and cries of fear, the unmistakable crackle of fire. The smell of burning plastic singed the air. Something was thrown down hard into the ground. Khattak raced to his window to see.

It was Souda. Souda was on fire, its entrance ringed by two dozen men in black, wearing the same insignia as the men in the restaurant. They'd struck their red flag, and on its banner was a Greek meander, a design with a clear resemblance to a swastika.

Khattak threw on his clothes. He pounded down the stairs to Rachel's room at ground level. Papadakis met him in the lobby.

'Call the police,' Khattak shouted, hammering on Rachel's door. She appeared fully dressed, her gun holstered, her bright, brown eyes alert, responding to Khattak's alarm.

Papadakis didn't move to the phone.

'What are you waiting for?'

He shook his head. 'They won't come. These men are connected to police.'

'Call them,' Khattak demanded. 'I'll speak to them.'

The call was put through as Rachel scouted the street.

'They have torches, sir,' she called. 'They're not armed.'

Khattak spoke curtly into the phone, relaying who he was and what he was witnessing. He promised a call to his country's prime minister was next.

'Let's go, sir.'

He told Papadakis to bar the front entrance, following Rachel up the road to the camp. They heard the wail of a siren in the distance.

If not police, at least the fire brigade was on its way. But they were too late, whoever they were. The tents were burning, families were scrambling to find safe exit from the trench. Hundreds of people had fled to the perimeter, blocked by men who formed a human chain.

If the chain wasn't broken, the camp's inhabitants would burn. From the corner of his eye, Khattak caught sight of Peter Conroy, shepherding families through the trench. He was joined by a dozen volunteers, each working to clear the tents.

He could see the fire truck hurtling down the road, but there was still no sign of the police. Like Rachel, he had his gun, and after motioning to her to take shelter behind a concrete block, he fired over the rise.

The gunshot so close at hand startled the men who formed the chain. The attackers wheeled, threatening Khattak with their fists. Rachel stepped out into the street, her gun poised and sighted. Abruptly, the men fell back.

'The police are on their way,' Khattak warned.

Conroy caught sight of him and shouted at the men in Greek. They moved against the barricade; Khattak raised his arm to fire again.

A second siren joined the first – this time it was the police. Khattak murmured a prayer of thanks. The men began to disperse as a whooshing sound came from the hill. Khattak looked up at the ruins. A handful of men were stationed on the hill, hurling stones down at the camp's panicked residents. A man lay bleeding from his head.

Khattak made for the hill. Conroy followed his movements, calling up the hill.

'*Astynomia!*' he shouted, cupping his hands around his mouth. '*Astynomia, astynomia!*'

A man flung a block at Conroy, who ducked in time. The men on the hill vanished into the darkness, their chants echoing behind them.

They'd left one of their flags behind in the pandemonium created by ambulances, fire trucks, and the police car that had finally appeared on the scene.

The Greek police officer who took his time disembarking approached Khattak with his handcuffs in his hand. Conroy clambered over the barricade to meet him, speaking at a furious pace, gesturing at Khattak. The police officer spit at his feet, but he put the handcuffs away. He signaled to the fire crew to proceed.

For the next hour, Souda burned. Refugees huddled in clusters along the edges of the camp, bewildered that the world had more cruelty to offer. The sight of children lost and scared, their faces grimy with smoke, was captured on camera by a furious volunteer who looked little older than the children, but who had the tenacity of a bulldog.

'I'm sorry, I'm sorry,' she kept saying as she snapped her photographs. 'It's to make them see.' She was talking to herself; the children didn't understand. Firefighters barked at her to get out of the way, and she clambered up the hill for a better view.

Khattak called a warning after her. 'There are others up there, be careful.'

'Just let them try anything,' she shouted back.

Khattak, Rachel, and Conroy gave what assistance they could. At the end of the night, when the clamor had died down, Papadakis showed up at the entrance to the trench. He took a look at the children who hadn't found anywhere to rest. He offered beds to women and children, taking down names on a pad.

When the police officer tried to interfere, Papadakis waved him off. 'Give them our rooms too,' Khattak said. 'We're heading out. We'll be there in a minute to get our things.'

Rachel picked up the abandoned flag and held it up. 'What in the holy héll was that, sir? A sea of fucking *swastikas*?'

Catching herself, Rachel apologized for her language. She wasn't just upset. He could see that she was shocked.

'What were they chanting?' he asked Conroy. 'Who were they?' Conroy brushed back his hair, leaving a black mark on his forehead.

'That was Golden Dawn, the local neo-Nazi variant. They were chanting something along the lines of "People! Army! Nationalism!" There's been a lot of unrest in Greece because of the economic situation. The flow of refugees onto the islands has exacerbated tensions, but I didn't know they were so close to boiling over.'

The coordination and volunteer effort went on around them as they followed Conroy to the W2W service tent on the far side of the alley. Most of the refugees' tents had burned to the ground, the scant possessions within destroyed, the smoke hanging low and heavy over their heads, leaving traces of grit on their faces, acrid and painful to the throat.

On the service side, the tents had escaped damage – a matter more of luck than anything else. Had the sirens not sounded, the whole camp would have been destroyed.

Khattak came to a halt in front of the Woman to Woman tent.

It was the only tent on the service side to lie in ruins. He'd told Conroy he'd return to the tent in the morning to collect Audrey's package.

But everything in the tent had burned; Khattak couldn't find any sign of the jackets among the wreckage. Either they had burned, which he thought unlikely given the flame-retardant material used on life vests – or someone had stolen the package from the tent.

Someone had taken advantage of the destruction of Souda, someone close at hand, who'd been monitoring his activities.

He looked over at the Australian volunteer, a single question on his mind.

Was that someone Peter Conroy?

26

Port of Chios

THEY MET NATE AT THE ferry. He was arriving on Chios just as they were leaving, the silver-gray of the sky overshadowed by livid clouds.

'I hope this means no crossings today,' Rachel said. 'The waves will overturn any dinghies that set out.'

She studied Nate's face for some sign of his mood. His private investigators hadn't turned up anything new. He'd sent them into Moria, Kara Tepe, and Souda, where they'd frightened the camps' inhabitants, who were so often at the mercy of the authorities that they'd closed their ranks in silence. Nor were the islanders much help – some had their own reasons for refusing to cooperate. Rachel guessed that those reasons were tied to the Golden Dawn raid.

She knew Nate was casting about for a lead, for anything that could make him feel like he was doing something useful. Khattak tried to reassure him. Nate had brought word of Sehr's discussions with the Greek police. They hadn't issued an arrest warrant, though Sehr believed it was coming. They needed to push ahead; they needed answers before the Greek police decided what those answers were.

What had Audrey meant when she'd said she was going to 'beard the lion in his den'? Who *was* the lion? All they knew was that Audrey had gone to Izmir for this purpose. They'd have to find out why. They were hoping Amélie Roux would help them. She was meeting them on the ferry. She'd agreed to come along, but Rachel wondered if her reason for doing so was to keep abreast of their discoveries. She might not trust them to share information that implicated Audrey. Funny, given that she wasn't all that forthcoming herself. But fair enough. Cooperation on both ends would need to be earned. She could only hope that Audrey didn't pay the price of their discretion.

She didn't say this to Nate, who took her by the arm and led her away from the ramp. Cars were being loaded; the process would take some time.

'Go ahead,' she said to Khattak. 'I'll catch up.'

Rachel looked up into Nate's worn face and felt a familiar stab of compassion. She was attracted to Nate in a way she couldn't explain. A frank examination of her feelings told her it wouldn't end well. The minute she'd stepped out of place, Nate had spurned her closeness.

Nate thrust a hand through his hair, a nervous habit Rachel recognized.

'Look, I get it,' she said. 'Audrey is your sister and you have the right to call the shots. I was talking like a cop before, not being a friend the way you've been to me.'

Nate dropped his hand. He stared at Rachel searchingly. 'Don't say that, Rachel, it makes me feel terrible. What I said to you was uncalled-for. You faced something much worse, yet you didn't fall apart. That should be a lesson to me.'

Rachel's reply was quiet. 'There's no right way to handle this.' They looked at each other without speaking, though it was obvious there was more to be said. Nate locked their fingers together. 'I don't know how you kept the faith. When I think of you looking for Zach on your own I'm ashamed of how I behaved.'

He tugged her closer. Rachel let him, her stern lecture to herself swept aside by Nate's desire to be forgiven – more than that, by his ability to empathize with the suffering she'd never described, the time she thought of as the lost years.

'You don't need to apologize. Believe me, I understand.'

She remembered how she'd turned on Khattak when they'd met, how insubordinate she'd been, which Khattak had taken in his stride. He'd handled her rudeness with such careful consideration – he'd learned about Zachary, something she hadn't known then.

Nate released her hands, slipping his own around her waist. Rachel froze in the circle of his arms. He was crossing that line – that careful dance between them where they could fall back upon friendship as an excuse.

He was taking a risk. Rachel didn't know if she was ready.

What if he was turning to her because he felt abandoned without Audrey? What if this had nothing to do with her? She didn't belong in Nate's world. She couldn't picture herself in his life. But that didn't necessarily mean she wanted to push him away.

'Nate, are you sure –'

'Rachel.' His gold eyes gleamed. 'I wish you'd stay with me. Let Esa handle Izmir, I could use your help. You're a lot less clumsy than I am when it comes to asking questions.'

So it *was* about Audrey – and how could she blame him, even if she'd hoped for something else? She sighed to herself, chancing a glance at Khattak. He was leaning against the rail, deep in conversation with Roux, whose change in manner suggested that she was succumbing to Khattak's pervasive charm. Why was everything so easy for him? A little angry at the contrast, Rachel freed herself from Nate's arms. She promised him she'd be back before he had a chance to miss her. She didn't ask herself whether he *would* miss her, doubtful of her own attraction. When she'd told her father that there was a man in her life, her mother had said, 'Rachel has to take what she can get.' The words had burrowed inside her, wounding places she couldn't protect.

Nate needed to focus his efforts, and she was about to tell him how. 'We're going on to Hatay from Izmir. We need to know why Audrey went there. If it's dangerous, I need to be there to help.' She filled him in on Camp Apaydin. 'I don't think the people you've hired are going to have much luck at Souda. The people in the camp won't know your investigators or have any reason to trust them. You, on the other hand, are less threatening.' She signaled to Khattak that she was about to board. He waved back, unconcerned. 'If you have a photograph of you and Audrey together, that's what I would show around. Find a translator to help you.'

Nate accepted this, just as he accepted her withdrawal. Rachel wished he wouldn't. She wished he would demand something or tell her where she stood, though she was no less impaired when it came to expressing herself. She turned the conversation back to Audrey.

'I don't mean to scare you, but you need to ask your people to check on last night's raid. See if they can find out more about who organized the attack. Usually, there's a ringleader. And he might not have been kindly disposed to Audrey or her work.'

Nate recoiled from her words, though he didn't quarrel with her conclusions. He reached for her hand again, eager to make up for his behavior.

'Thank you, Rachel,' he said. 'For telling me the truth when you know I don't want to hear it.'

He turned up her palm and kissed it, an inherently romantic gesture. Rachel was too bemused by his tenderness to panic, or to fully accept it.

'Don't give up on me, Rachel. Don't let this come between us. I wanted to show you – I *want* to show you… well, I think you know what I want.'

He tilted up her chin and kissed her mouth.

Rachel was still for a moment. Then, eagerly, she kissed him back. His technique was impressive. She tried to match it from her scant experience.

Raising his head, Nate said, 'What about Esa? Is there something I shouldn't get in the middle of?' His tone was a little embarrassed. 'We've been down that road before.'

'Esa?' she echoed in a daze, the name completely unfamiliar.

Nate smiled, his gold eyes crinkling at the corners. 'Good,' he said. 'Good. That's just what I was hoping.'

Rachel's eyes widened. She'd never heard a man express himself in quite that way before. Nate's warm smile was self-deprecating and sweet, but his use of the word *hope*... she felt a tremulous flutter of happiness. No one had ever hoped for anything from her.

'You spend so much time with Esa,' he said thoughtfully. He was studying Esa's body language, his earnest conversation with Roux.

Rachel suppressed a smile. 'That's why I'm immune.'

When he kissed her again, he muttered his fears against her lips. 'This trip away won't change that?'

Rachel surprised herself by laughing out loud. 'Just how irresistible do you find my boss?'

He laughed too, and suddenly everything between them was easy. He saw Rachel off to the ferry with a wave, a relaxed set to his shoulders that told her more than she'd hoped to learn.

Now all she had to do was try not to ruin something good.

27

THE FERRY CROSSING WAS SO choppy that a sickly green color invaded Rachel's skin. When Khattak expressed his concern, Amélie Roux suggested Rachel take up a spot where she couldn't see the motion of the water. Rachel hastily agreed, so Khattak turned back to Roux. They were retracing Audrey's steps as best as they could with the limited information at hand. Her activities in Turkey puzzled them: they raised questions that required immediate answers. How did Audrey's activities connect her to Sami al-Nuri? And what was it about her trips to Izmir that might have placed her in danger? Retracing her steps, talking to the people she'd spoken to, might provide those answers. It might also give them more background on Sami.

Esa put a question to Roux. 'What else can you tell me about Audrey's activities?' They had progressed to first names. Esa found much to admire in Amélie's assessment of their operations. She'd kept an eye on their work, and her insights were invaluable.

She was serious about her work, committed to bringing Aude Bertin's killer to justice. To further her cooperation, he told her about the life vests he'd found at Souda, and she offered a theory of her own.

'This is about organized crime. I think this impressionable young woman thought she could push back against forces more powerful than she realized. Perhaps because that's how things work in Canada. And in France, as well.'

'You're saying it's different in Turkey?'

From Roux's face, he could see he'd missed the significance of what she'd just told him. He was following a tangent, but it was one he thought was necessary.

They were facing the Turkish coast, its craggy outline looming up against waves crested with white tufts of foam. Esa couldn't see any sign of the smugglers' activities or of boats that had recently been launched. Some distance away, one of the Hellenic Rescue Team's boats was in the water. A blond-haired woman on the deck was scouting the waves, radioing news of conditions on the water to volunteers on the islands. He wondered if the woman was Eleni Latsoudi. She was too far away to tell.

Rain began to fall, thick fat droplets spattering the deck, until the horizon disappeared in an iridescent silver streak. He and Amélie retreated to the lounge, where Rachel was huddled at a table, shivering as she sipped her watery tea. She'd bought a coat for herself on the island, but it wasn't as warm as the one she'd brought from Canada.

He understood the impulse that had driven her to give hers away. It was the same impulse he was fighting: the desire to return to Moria and put his language skills to use. The needs of the Afghan children on the hill, contrasted with the prospects for their future, was something he couldn't erase with a donation. He felt the stirring of an old calling, the sense there was more he could do – *must* do. He would ask for another meeting with the prime minister. But even that wouldn't subdue the anguish of his thoughts.

Amélie Roux brought coffee in Styrofoam cups. They rejoined Rachel, whose pallor was beginning to fade.

'Turkey is the most beautiful country I've visited. Its history is fascinating. Izmir – Smyrna – is famous for its association with Alexander the Great.' Amélie returned to the question Khattak had asked. 'But look at the neighbors, my friend. A dangerous neighborhood, as the Americans would say.'

Khattak was familiar with this characterization, though it wasn't one he used. But if Amélie was speaking of the border, he could hardly disagree.

'You were speaking of organized crime,' he reminded her, trying to determine what he'd missed.

'Already well established in Turkey. The refugee crisis has opened up new opportunities for profiteers.'

'What kind of profiteers?' Rachel raised her head from her cup. Amélie leaned forward confidentially. At the table behind her, Khattak caught sight of the same group of men who'd assembled in the café on Lesvos. A mix of Germans, Danes, Italians, and Greeks, joined by Peter Conroy. Despite the rain and the chilly ambience, their conversation was lively. They were headed to Izmir for a break from their work, dressed in civilian clothes.

'Smuggling refugees across from the Anatolian coast to the islands of Greece has been profitable for organized crime. Someone gets the boats together, someone delivers them to the beaches, someone collects refugees from Izmir and drives them to the coast. Someone organizes the routes and keeps an eye on the weather. Well...' She shrugged. 'I can't say that the smugglers are concerned about a safe passage; their job is to collect money – as much money as they can. That's why they overcrowd the boats. The point is, all of this is a very big operation, a well-*coordinated* operation. Somebody is running it, someone's making money.'

Rachel played devil's advocate. 'At least someone's getting refugees across. They're not having to do it themselves, and after all, don't the people who want to cross have the option of remaining in Turkey?'

She wasn't expecting Amélie's fierce response. 'That's no more of an option than the Calais Jungle. There are no jobs for such a huge influx of people. Those who exploit them can take their pick, paying one-half, one-third of normal wages, sometimes not paying at all. It's a machinery that thrives on desperation.'

Khattak didn't know what Amélie Roux had seen, but he disagreed with some of her conclusions. 'Do you think Greece should be expected to cope with the crisis on its own?'

Amélie crumpled up her cup and tossed it into a bin. 'Absolutely not. How could they?'

'It's no easier on Turkey. Turkey hosts nearly three million refugees. It doesn't have resources to sustain them.'

Amélie bristled at this. 'That's an easy way out, Esa. Turkey has responsibilities under the Convention.'

'So does France,' he rejoined.

'Turkey is a near neighbor. More importantly, the people of Turkey and Syria have more in common.'

'I don't disagree. What I'm saying is that a disproportionate burden has fallen on Turkey.' Khattak kept his voice low, conscious that the men at the next table had fallen silent to listen. 'And let's not forget, the European Union has just paid Turkey billions to shut down the flow into Europe. That's led to people taking increasingly desperate chances on the sea.'

Amélie pulled out a cigarette and lighter. She kept her eyes on Khattak's face as she lit her cigarette and inhaled.

'Your eyes,' she said to him. 'They tell me a lot more than this very polite way you have of speaking. You hate this, I think. You hate everything about this.' She took another draw of her cigarette, then said, 'Yes, I agree. The record of France as a member of the European Union is terrible. It's a dreadful thing that's been happening with Le Pen and her neo-Nazi following. The force she represents is continuing to gain strength. Another Bataclan or Nice, who knows where we'll end up?'

She was referring to the terror attacks that had devastated France. 'This cycle we are in is ugly – the French do not want

Muslims. They don't want Arabs, they don't care whether they are born in France or not. The same thing applies in Turkey. Refugees will go to their graves in these camps. The Turkish template, the Jordanian one at Zaatari – these are not solutions. Calais is even worse.' She turned her head so the smoke would blow away from her companions. 'These words... refugees, migrants... maybe they have some legal effect, they don't mean anything to me. They didn't mean anything to Aude. She thought of people as having rights, no matter who they were, and now she's dead.'

Khattak was sorry he'd pushed her so hard. The shine of tears was in her eyes. Respectfully, he looked away, giving her a moment to gather her composure.

'There's plenty of blame to go around,' he said. 'Enough for France... Canada... Turkey. It takes our attention away from the man responsible for this.'

'The lion in his den?' Rachel asked, a little pale herself.

'Assad,' Khattak supplied. 'Though I suspect debate on that subject would be just as heated.'

Amélie crushed out her cigarette. She took an envelope from inside her jacket pocket and placed it on the table. Rachel opened the envelope and slid its contents onto the table between them. Three pairs of eyes studied the photograph of Sami al-Nuri.

Every inch of his torso was mutilated.

'Assad will be at The Hague soon enough. There's too much evidence to come to any other conclusion. If you think of Sami al-Nuri as an emblem of Assad's Syria, his broken body is all the proof we need.'

Someone dragged a chair over to their table and sat down next to Rachel.

It was Ali Maydani: he was on his own, Aya nowhere to be seen. His curls were standing on end, as if he'd brushed them with some force.

'Am I allowed to speak? I know my country better than you

do. Better than Interpol, better than whatever it is *you* represent, Inspector.'

Khattak heard Rachel gasp. A fury as stark as the endless war was bottled up inside the boy.

He placed a hand on Ali's shoulder. 'You're right, of course, forgive me. I didn't mean to hurt you.'

He noticed that Commander Benemerito at the neighboring table had risen from his seat, a frown of concern on his face. He gestured to reassure the other man. Benemerito nodded.

'It's nothing new,' Ali said. 'You all do it. The UN, the volunteers, the border agents, people on the news. You make choices that affect us, you decide what our lives will be, you decide what we should *think* about those choices. All you see is a problem.' His voice became rough. 'Even you, Inspector Khattak. You said we're a burden to Turkey. We're a burden to the islands, to every country we've fled to. We're a burden within our own borders because we continue to exist.'

His eyes caught sight of the photograph on the table.

'Oh God,' he said. 'Oh God, oh God. Is that Sami? Is *that* what he wouldn't tell me?' He buried his face in his arms.

Khattak's instincts took over. He didn't say anything, just rubbed the boy's back with his hand, trying to give him comfort. It was clear now that Ali's connection hadn't been only to Audrey. He knew Sami al-Nuri, and judging from his grief, knew him well. He signaled Rachel to bring something for Ali to eat.

Benemerito was on his feet, undecided.

Amélie came to the rescue. She tucked the photograph away, lighting a cigarette she passed to the boy. 'Here,' she said. 'You need this.'

He didn't raise his head until he'd exhausted his tears. Then he looked up, half-defiant, half-ashamed, rubbing at his face with his sleeve. Khattak handed him a napkin.

Ali took the cigarette and smoked it, his face closed, his eyes shifting from theirs.

No one spoke until Rachel brought a cup of tea, accompanied by a roll stuffed with lamb. Ali finished his cigarette. He bolted down the roll.

The ferry was winding down its speed; at the Turkish coast Khattak's phone gained service. It rang loudly in the silence. He frowned as he saw Sehr's number. He shut off his phone to give Ali his full attention, blaming himself for his carelessness.

How stingingly accurate the boy's denunciation was.

He'd said as much to himself many times while watching news of the Middle East or other parts of the world. What he saw on his screen invoked a familiar refrain: *Iraq without Iraqis, Afghanistan without Afghans, Palestine without Palestinians, and now Syria without Syrians.*

Commander Benemerito joined them at their table, bearing a second tray of coffees.

He glanced gravely at Khattak and Roux. 'We don't discuss politics in public, it's painful to our Syrian friends. I'm sure you can understand why.' He didn't wait for an answer, though Khattak took his mild reproach to heart. 'You want to come with me?' Benemerito asked Ali. 'I can drive you into Izmir to take a look around.'

Vincenzo had risen to his feet, murmuring something in Peter Conroy's ear. Khattak began to appreciate how close the volunteers were. They worked together, they took time off in each other's company. What he didn't understand was the scowl on Vincenzo's face.

'No,' Ali said at last. 'I'm all right, Commander. It's okay. I want to talk to the police.' He couldn't muster a smile. 'Don't worry about me, thank you.'

Benemerito nodded his acceptance. 'Fine. If you have any trouble with your papers, let me know.'

He left them to themselves. Khattak attempted a more thorough apology for his words. Ali listened to him, but he didn't say anything at the end, and Khattak knew better than to insist on absolution. His comfort was irrelevant. He wanted Ali to know his thoughts to the extent it would offer the boy any solace from his pain.

Rachel gave them a reprieve by asking about Audrey's package. 'How do the life jackets fit into all of this?'

The ferry's engines powered down as it began its docking procedures. Passengers began to empty out of the lounge, preparing to disembark. Khattak's eyes followed Conroy and Vincenzo as they left the lounge, Benemerito behind them.

'It's part of the operation I was telling you about – it has to do with organized crime.'

'They've jacked up prices for life jackets?' Rachel guessed. 'There must be a black market, given the need is so dire. I bet it's hard for supply to catch up with demand.' She said this carefully, keeping her eyes on Ali to see if she was giving offense.

Ali's eyes were still red, but his breathing had evened out. He looked from Rachel to Amélie Roux. 'What's this?' he asked. 'What are you talking about?'

'Audrey Clare,' Khattak explained. 'She ordered Yamaha life jackets. I thought they were for you and Aya for the crossing.' He kept his eyes on Ali's. 'I also thought it was possible that you and Audrey were bringing others across from Turkey.'

Roux interrupted before Ali could answer. 'The smugglers have locked down the beaches. They would sink any boat that cut into their profit.'

Khattak was watching the boy. 'You know something,' he said. 'Please tell us. The longer Audrey is missing, the less likely it is we'll find her.'

The color drained from Ali's face. He gasped out Israa's name.

Esa was aghast. Twice in ten minutes, his thoughtlessness had injured the boy.

Israa had slipped his mind. What he'd said applied equally to Israa, and Israa had been missing longer than Audrey Clare.

The boy's heart was in his eyes. It was clear that Esa's assessment carried weight. And he'd just heard Esa confirm his deepest fears. Israa wouldn't be found; Israa was lost forever. A fresh set of tears rolled down his cheeks, this time in total silence.

'I thought this was about the life vests. I didn't know what it would cost me.'

28

Izmir, Turkey

'HOW DO WE KNOW WHAT we're looking for?' Rachel asked Khattak. He nodded at Ali, but he was also looking at something on his phone.

He showed it to Rachel. It was the list he'd made of places where Audrey had used her credit card; they fell within a discrete circle.

They reached Izmir without incident, renting a car in Cesme, and now Rachel had the opportunity to see what Roux had meant. The city was overdeveloped with ranks of repetitive apartment blocks, but what Rachel couldn't take her eyes from was the boulevard that swept the curve of Izmir Bay. It was lined with palm trees whose blade-like leaves slashed the mirage of the sea. She hadn't been expecting palm trees.

It was an exciting, vibrant city, the coastline gorgeously sectioned into parks and colorful marinas. It bustled with all the business of a port – container ships, cargo holds, cruisers sailing into the harbor. The clouds had passed and the air had become mild and balmy, little plumes of mist stroking feathery green palms. Rachel felt a thrill of discovery: she hadn't expected to end up in Turkey as an outcome of Community Policing. In the course of a single year, her life had turned inside out.

Some of her euphoria left her as Ali directed them to his point of arrival. A helicopter swung low and Ali looked up. 'If this was Syria, it would be dropping cluster bombs.'

He was from a place where children heard planes and thought of bombs.

They passed a circular park reached by two thoroughfares, the Gazi Boulevard and the Fezvi Pasha. They found parking in the Basmane neighborhood, popular with Kurds and Syrians. Ali led them along an alley between shop fronts, two-story buildings whose upper floors were residential, in contrast to the activity on the street. The alleyway was formed of paving stones. Single cement blocks mounted up to each shop. Patches of green turf on the blocks lent a dash of color to the street.

Internet cafés were a common sight. Shop windows carried notices in multiple languages: Turkish, English, and Arabic were prevalent. Chalkboard signs were set up on the street, offering money-changing services. There was a raft of plastic chairs on little patios for those seeking the refreshment of Turkish coffee or the apple tea served to tourists.

Rachel noticed the life jackets. Along the crowded pavement, bundles of jackets were wrapped in plastic. As they moved up the street and crossed the thoroughfare, fancier stores featured mannequins dressed in men's suits on one side, and in life jackets on the other.

'It's deserted here,' Ali said. 'After the deal to seal the border, it no longer makes sense for people to come. Before, you could hardly walk down this street – people were sleeping in the alleys, in the parks, waiting for smugglers to call them to the boats. There was so much life packed in here.' A smile drifted across his lips. 'We made so many friends.' He told the story of his little group, and how they'd agreed to make the crossing. He'd admitted his friendship with Sami: they'd met in Basmane, and the four of them had grown close.

Ali's head was turning from side to side. He was staring down each blind alley, craning his neck to peer into shops. Then Rachel noticed something else. Wherever there was a signpost or a free spot on a wall or shop window, a flyer with a photograph on it was posted. It was a picture of the girl Israa, and underneath it the words 'HAVE YOU SEEN HER?' were printed in three languages above a phone number. A substantial reward was offered for information.

Rachel frowned at it. 'Sir.' She drew Khattak's attention to the flyer. 'That number.'

Khattak recognized it at once. 'Audrey's satellite phone.'

They stopped to look at the boy.

'Yes,' he said. 'She helped me. She was serious about the search for Israa.'

'Did you get any calls on that phone?'

Ali jammed his hands into the pockets of his jeans. 'They were all dead ends, people wanting money. Sometimes families showed up with girls who looked like Israa. I couldn't blame them. When you make this journey, you're pushed into doing things you never imagined were possible.'

He didn't make eye contact, scanning the nearby park. He wasn't wasting a moment in his search. As Khattak and Roux peeled away to speak to store owners who might have interacted with Audrey, Rachel kept her attention on the boy.

'You're saying it was busier than this when you first arrived in Turkey?' To Rachel, the streets seemed crowded.

A few young men were sitting with their backpacks leaning against the wall. Ali pointed to them. 'The undesirables. As single travelers, we can't get anywhere. I have an Afghan friend in Moria who made it to Sweden before he was refused.'

'How do you stay in touch?' Rachel asked.

Ali held up his cell phone. 'Everyone uses WhatsApp to stay on top of the routes. But a lot of rumors get spread. One of the worst was that a Swedish ship was coming to collect us. We learned it was a lie at the coast.' His eyes met Rachel's. 'You meet good people during the journey, but you also see the worst.'

He explained how refugees found their way to the coast. If they came by bus, they were met by smugglers who pressed them into making an immediate decision about crossing to Greece. The smugglers provided boats and some basic guidance on steering. They insisted the journey was safe, even if they didn't issue life vests.

'They have it worse on the North African side. If you make it to the boat, the smugglers take you out on the open sea, and leave you there to die. One of the men I met said the captain of the boat kicked his son into the sea. He was picked up by the Coast Guard and sent back to Libya, where he tried another route. Usually, by that point they've taken all your money. They feed off your desperation.'

Rachel thought this over. 'What happens when you get to somewhere like Basmane?'

'You make contact with the smugglers. First you go to the money-changers, then you go to an insurance office where you deposit your payment in cash. At night, you head to a park for further instructions from the smugglers. Everyone is waiting for a call. With any luck, your handler is a Syrian trying to save up funds to get his own family across.'

Rachel could picture the type. Enterprising young hustlers who moved the machinery along, the last ones to leave because it was more important to move their families to safety.

She remembered Dania and Ahmed Fakhri, and their claim to have flown from Lebanon. But what if they'd lied and come through Turkey? Had Sami stayed behind in order to ensure their safe passage? Had he tried to desert his bosses and ended up dead? She asked Ali if he'd heard of the Fakhris. He stumbled over a young man in his path. There was a rapid exchange in Arabic, which ended with Ali's apology. It was followed by the same question. Ali held up a flyer and asked the young man if he knew where Israa had gone.

His shoulders sagging, he turned back to Rachel. 'It's beginning to seem hopeless. This deal with Turkey – if it's finalized, no one else gets through. I don't know if I should bring Aya back to

Izmir to try and find some work. But who could I leave her with? What kind of future would we have?' He crumpled the flyer in his hand. 'Or maybe we should move on and pray that Israa finds us.'

Rachel didn't know how to advise him. As a police officer, she believed the law should be obeyed. No one country could resettle refugees. By that standard, even Canada's contribution was minimal. There had to be a better solution than choosing between someone like Ali with Aya in his care, or someone like the youth they'd left in the alley. She remembered Suha Obeidi, the paralegal at Sanctuary Syria. Suha had said Sami al-Nuri stood little chance of being accepted on his merits; he needed a family connection that the Fakhris had refused to establish.

Despite leads from Canada, Turkey, and Greece, Rachel was no closer to untangling the truth.

'Where's Aya?' she asked suddenly, following the progress of a little girl across the alley. She had dark hair and eyes that stood out in contrast to her magenta sweater. She was clutching colored pencils in one hand and packs of tissues in the other, a fanny-pack around her tiny waist. Her sunny smile and confident manner stood her in good stead. Strangers were willing to indulge her in the sale of her various goods.

Her throat constricting in pain, Rachel gave the girl a twenty-euro note for a pack of tissues, refusing to take her change. The little girl danced away. She called to her father, who was watching for her at a stoplight. He led her into a park surrounded by tall, dark trees.

Rachel felt a surge of embarrassment when Ali looked at her.

'I told you,' he said. 'There are good people, too.'

She made a dismissive gesture. She'd tried to salve her conscience by giving the little girl money, but she would have felt worse not doing it. 'I needed tissues. It wasn't charity, if that's what you're thinking.'

'I was thinking you are kind to have noticed her. Kind like

226

Miss Audrey to be helping me look for Israa.'

'Do you think we'll find Audrey and Israa together?' If the boy knew something, his answer to this question would tell her what it was.

'No.' He shook his head, causing his curls to bounce. 'They're not together.'

Before she could ask him how he knew this, Khattak and Roux rejoined them. Khattak was holding a life vest he'd just purchased.

'We bearded the lion in his den,' he told Rachel. He explained he'd bought the vest from one of the Turkish vendors. Ali nodded as if he knew what Khattak meant.

'The life jackets weren't for me and Aya. Audrey *wasn't* taking people across, she didn't want to get her NGO kicked out of Greece. It's just that I told her what was happening at sea. The day I crossed, for example.'

Rachel noted Khattak's grim expression. She studied the logo on the life vest. The logo was misspelled, and suddenly she knew.

'The life jackets are fakes.'

Now, at last, Amélie Roux ventured to offer information. The little she told them made it clear that in fact, she knew a good deal more. 'The factories are run by organized crime. They make money by selling knock-offs stuffed with foam. The vests are hydrophilic. They become a weight around the neck. They can cause serious injuries – not just drowning injuries, but also strangulation.'

Khattak's head came up. '*A peculiar injury to occur in a lifeboat,*' he said with strange emphasis. He recounted what he'd learned in Toronto from Emily Banks.

'What are you saying?' The horror of it was too vast for Rachel to grasp. She tested the life vest in her hands. 'They *deliberately* sell jackets that cause refugees to drown?'

'Real vests cost upward of a hundred and fifty euros. The knock-offs are as little as ten. People buy them for the illusion of safety – at least they'll have something, they think.'

'My God.' A chill ran down Rachel's spine. 'You knew this?' she asked Ali.

He shrugged it off like it was nothing. 'We crossed with vests like these. Our boat sank, we nearly drowned. If Eleni hadn't found us, I wouldn't be here now.'

He looked at their shocked faces and tried a smile.

'By far,' he said, 'that wasn't the worst part of our journey.'

He took them to Sinbad restaurant; it was popular with refugees because the food was tasty and not too expensive.

'This neighborhood is amazing,' he told them. 'Kurds, Turks, Syrians. So many language barriers, yet here we all are. Many of these people have become my friends. They've done good things – they've helped us when they're struggling themselves. As a refugee, you learn how people hate, but also about how they love. This neighborhood reminds me of before.'

Rachel was starving so she let Khattak ask the questions.

'Of your life in Damascus, you mean.'

Ali nodded, swallowing a bite of his kebab. 'The most beautiful place on earth. I miss everything about it. The way it smells, the way it looks when the sun sets. The jasmine trees in our courtyards. The closeness of the old city walls.'

'I'm so sorry,' Khattak said.

Ali shrugged. 'How we thought we could take on a regime that began by murdering the schoolchildren of Daraa – we were crazy to think there was hope. Look what's happened to us now.' He snapped his fingers. 'I never thought a Syrian could kill another Syrian, but that's a mistake we all made.'

The revolution had begun in the city of Daraa, near the Jordanian border. Schoolboys had painted slogans against the regime – the children were arrested and tortured. When Daraa's tight-knit community had demanded the boys' release, the governorate had shunned them. Protests had broken out in

Daraa, then across the country. As one young activist had said, 'Daraa lit the spark. The children's courage was contagious.'

Rachel ignored her meal, reflecting on Ali's story – the Syrian border wasn't out of reach, but the Syrian catastrophe seemed a world away. On this boisterous street, Turkish pop music blasted through the alleys, with families strolling through the parks, under the leafy cover of the palms. If she didn't have so much to think about, she would have found it fascinating. The call to prayer sounded all at once, the music fading away.

Khattak looked over at Ali. 'Shall we go to the local mosque?' They excused themselves, Khattak with his hand on the boy's shoulder, the gesture of an older brother. Amélie Roux watched them go.

She turned to Rachel with a speculative look. 'A handsome devil, that one.'

Rachel forbore to answer, focusing on her food.

Inspecteur Roux prodded her again. 'So you two – is that something?'

Rachel swallowed hard. 'I have a boyfriend,' she said weakly. She was thinking of Nate. Nate had kissed her, but he wasn't her boyfriend – a word she wasn't sure was grown-up enough to use. She felt that same little flutter of happiness as she contemplated whether that would change. *When, not whether,* a small voice insisted. She told herself to have a little faith.

Roux shrugged. 'A lot of temptation to resist.'

Rachel changed the subject. 'What did Inspector Khattak mean? When he said you bearded the lion in his den?'

Roux swept a hand in the direction of the shops. 'We learned something from our tour of Basmane. Your friend Audrey visited nearly every store and sidewalk operator selling life jackets. She tracked down the main purveyor plagiarizing the Yamaha logo.'

'So the life jackets on Woman to Woman's inventory…'

'Were ordered for the purpose of comparison. She had to make her case. She told the Coast Guard, who'd had similar suspicions.

The Coast Guard confirmed the bodies in the water were wearing counterfeit jackets; they notified the Turkish police.' Sounding impressed, she continued, 'Eventually, because of the police operation, two of the factories were shut down.' She grimaced. 'It turned out the children of refugees were being employed to make the fakes.'

She rubbed the back of her neck, signaling the waiter she wanted another coffee.

'I shouldn't say "employed,"' Roux went on. 'In fact, these children were indentured. The police put an end to that.'

Rachel listened to this recital with growing suspicion. This was more than Khattak and Roux could have learned in their interviews with shop owners. It sounded like the kind of background available to an Interpol agent.

'You already knew this.' She gestured at the busy restaurant and the streets beyond. 'So why didn't you just tell us on the ferry? Or on Lesvos? You could have saved us a lot of time.'

Unperturbed by Rachel's accusations, Roux leaned forward in her seat. 'I wanted to see where your leads would take you. You might have found something I missed. After all, it was your partner who discovered the life vests at Souda.'

Rachel didn't buy the explanation. Either Roux didn't trust them, or this was Interpol's version of a power play. Interpol was in charge – Roux's job was to make sure it stayed that way.

Assessing Roux's expression, she asked, 'What else do you know about the factories? What exactly was Audrey's role in uncovering this operation?' Her tone left no doubt that she knew Roux was holding back.

The sharp edge of Roux's smile acknowledged Rachel's suspicion. 'You think your friend did all this on her own, putting herself at risk?'

'I *know* she put herself at risk.'

'So did my agent, Aude Bertin. Your friend was clever enough to contact us, so Aude was sent to investigate.'

Rachel considered this explanation. It didn't take her long to find the gaps in it. Horns sounded from the street beyond the little park, but she kept her attention on Roux.

'You sent an Interpol agent to do the job of the Turkish police? I don't think so, Inspecteur Roux.'

The other woman's face closed up. Beneath the slash of emphatic black brows, her shrewd eyes studied Rachel. Rachel was being weighed. But whether as an adversary or a confidante, she couldn't tell.

'Audrey's tip-off was enough to lead us to something bigger. It's not just the factories, there's the whole operation, how it's all connected – the smugglers, the Syrians who slip into their nets. She was tenacious, your friend. She wanted answers to dangerous questions.'

Rachel nodded to herself. Quietly, she said, 'She would have been a thorn in the smugglers' side. Doesn't that suggest to you Audrey was taken? And she hasn't run away.'

'Perhaps.' Roux lit a cigarette as she waited for her coffee. 'There are other reasons she may have been taken. She comes from a wealthy family, her brother is well known.'

'To you?' Rachel's voice sharpened.

Roux smiled a smile she didn't find in the least encouraging.

'Yes. He bought his sister a gun, after all. Why did he think she would need it? What was he expecting, I wonder?'

Rachel's poker face was no good. She knew it telegraphed her fear. She took a moment to collect herself, to stop a defense of Nate from tripping off her tongue.

'You've just mentioned kidnappers,' she pointed out. She looked around the bustling square – ordinary families doing ordinary things, the absence of police. 'This doesn't seem like a place where someone could be kidnapped.'

Roux leaned over the table, blowing smoke in Rachel's face. 'I wasn't thinking of Izmir. Audrey took a trip to the border with her Syrian friends in tow. The border areas are not as controlled as one might think. If Audrey went there, she was at risk.'

'Why would she take that risk?'

'Think it through for yourself, Rachel.' The older policewoman spoke kindly, as if she regarded Rachel as a protégée. But Rachel couldn't think of an answer.

'Do you think it's tied to these trips she took to Europe?'

Roux nodded, stubbing out her cigarette in her saucer. 'The question you should be asking is this: What was Audrey looking for at the border?'

Rachel picked up on this thread. 'We haven't explained Sami al-Nuri. Surely he's the missing link.'

Roux shrugged. She gazed in the direction of the mosque, impatient for Khattak's return.

Rachel studied her air of distraction; she was beginning to suspect it was an act. Roux wasn't interested in Khattak. She was interested in what he might know, or what else he might uncover. Her eyes flicked back to Rachel with an undercurrent of warning. Rachel's mouth went dry.

Roux knew more than she was telling them.

Or she wasn't what she seemed.

29

THE URGE TO TELL ESA the truth was pressing against Ali's thoughts. Esa was a man of faith; he'd shepherded Ali to the mosque, finding them a place on the prayer rugs without seeming to feel out of place. The Çorakkapi mosque was lovely and elegant in the manner of Turkish mosques, but on a quieter scale, with a miniature five-domed façade and a simple, emerald green carpet. The mosque had opened its doors to refugees. Ali's little company had slept in its courtyard for weeks.

After he made his supplication, Esa turned to Ali. 'I prayed for Israa and for you all.'

He wasn't looking for thanks. He was reminding Ali he wasn't alone, that the ummah hadn't abandoned the Syrian nation.

Ali had done the same, praying for the ummah in Iraq, in Palestine, in Burma and South Sudan – wherever he knew there was suffering. Once he'd come to know the boys at Moria, he prayed for the people of Afghanistan. Nor was his compassion restricted to those who shared his beliefs. Syria was a multi-ethnic, multi-faith society; an Armenian family had been his family's closest neighbors. The bombs had fallen on them both.

Whether you were against Assad or against the jihadis who'd usurped the revolution, one way or another, you ended up on a list.

He thought maybe he could trust Esa, because Esa hadn't asked him to explain his affiliations, or to account for the war. He treated Ali as a friend, not as a boy boxed in by his past, defined by a history in which he'd had no part.

He was ready to talk to Esa. Especially when Esa added, 'I also prayed for Audrey. Did you know I've known her all her life?'

Esa hadn't said this to win his confidence. It was something he wanted to share in case it helped Ali to know. Ali wanted to trust him, but the last time he'd been in this mosque, it was Sami who'd been at his side. Sami had warned him they couldn't trust anyone – the imam, the smugglers, the Turkish guards, the Syrians at the checkpoints. The one person Sami had trusted was him. They were bound together now by a bond that couldn't be severed.

Sami wasn't from Damascus. He'd been sent to Damascus by Military Intelligence in Aleppo. He didn't explain his situation further. His description of his work served as explanation enough.

Sami had nightmares, calling out the names of his friends. His small, close group had lived together in Aleppo. He was a paramedic with the Aleppo Civil Defense. For two years, he'd lived at a factory in disuse, a station protected by a wall. The station was at risk of mortar fire, exposed to frequent bombardment. Sami's group had survived the season of massacres, to find it followed by another.

Their truck was riddled with bullet holes, the windshield splintered like a web. Any day it would give, but otherwise the truck was sturdy enough to cope with the massive craters on the road. Sami had been to more impact sites than he could count. His work had centered on search and rescue. When the bombing of Aleppo was reinforced by Russian jets, the group's priorities had changed. The Civil Defense was the only active group to rescue survivors from the blast zone. Sami's team had learned to be wary of the double-tap: the site bombed again after rescuers arrived. They'd lost two team members before they'd adapted. From the sound of aircraft they'd learned to identify, they could forecast the scale of the attack.

Barrel bombs were taking out the city's apartment blocks. The station had been hit by mortar shells, but it had been spared the thousand-pound bombs packed with shrapnel. When the collapse of their station house had come, the team had been out on a rescue. Sami's home had fallen behind regime lines – they couldn't take shelter there. His brother Shahoud had suggested they establish their new base inside an abandoned school. More experienced in the war's barbarities, Sami had warned against it. 'Schools are a target. They've almost gotten them all.'

No functioning hospitals were left; even the underground clinic had been shredded. The most dangerous job in Aleppo was working as a doctor or nurse.

The sky had fallen in Aleppo. No corner of the city was spared. There was nothing Sami hadn't seen over the course of the war: barrel bombs, clusters, Scud missiles, mortar fire, snipers, chemical weapons. From one day to the next, a house on a well-known route would disappear. And now that their station house was gone, they'd have to begin again.

They were committed to the people of Aleppo.

Just as well that they were.

Nobody else was coming.

It had taken Sami time to gain the strength to risk the journey to the border. Ali didn't know the details of Sami's experience – Sami refused to describe it, so Ali left it alone. He knew East Aleppo had been starved out by the siege. Sami had admitted as much. When Israa had cradled Sami's head in her lap, he'd let slip, 'I've been dreaming in fruit.' Another time, doubled over with stomach cramps, he'd said, 'Hunger is the real assassin.'

He hadn't told them the worst until Ali had confided his horrors. When they took Sami to see the ruins of Israa's house, Sami didn't react.

'It's just like this in Aleppo. Every block, every house. There are no more roads left to walk on. When you come back from digging out the wounded, there's no water to wash off the blood.'

Ali didn't ask who Sami had fought with or where his loyalties lay. Since he was a member of the Civil Defense, they couldn't be with Assad. As for the rest, the rebels who held the east, the increasing fundamentalism that characterized the different groups who were the backbone of the rebellion, it had been enough for Sami to say, 'Nothing's worse than the black flag of ISIS. We saved Aleppo from that.'

But what was left of Aleppo? When he posed the question to his friend, Sami's response was hopeful, underscored by his courage.

'As long as we resist, they can't say they've beaten us down.' He smiled at Ali. 'Even if Aleppo is gone, they can't defeat Saladin.'

But Saladin couldn't save them now. His legacy was shrouded by phosphorus gas.

Sami refused to concede. 'It matters that you survived. You owe it to us to resist.'

Ali shook his head. 'I'm guilty of things that will send me to the fire.'

'We've already been through the fire.'

He wanted to be consoled. He wanted absolution from Sami, so he said, 'There's nothing worse than what I've done.'

'You think so?' Sami lit a cigarette. He passed another to Ali. 'You know my brother was with me in the Civil Defense?'

Ali hadn't wanted to ask about Shahoud. 'Is he with the Mukhabarat?' Sami squeezed his eyes shut. 'After we trained in Turkey, men signed up to volunteer – men like me, tailors, mechanics, schoolteachers like my brother. He had a fiancée on the regime side, did I tell you?'

Sami hadn't talked about his brother at all; it was one of those lines Ali knew better than to cross.

'We divided the team into shifts. I was on the night shift.' Sami mimed putting on eyeglasses. 'Shahoud had bad eyesight, he thought he'd see better in daylight. The next strike, they dropped two bombs. Shahoud went out after the first hit. The damage was *so massive, they called for another team. When we got there, you should have seen it. The bomb had peeled the city block like an egg. You could see inside the shell, bodies everywhere, a mountain of rubble – we were searching through the thickest fog. So many people called for help, each member of our teams was active. Their faces were caked with dust, some of them were bleeding. They went to the site too soon, they were lucky they missed the second strike.'*

Ali shook his head. No one in Aleppo was lucky.

Sami dug out a staircase. He found a girl whose throat was sliced by shrapnel; she was holding her sister's hand. The rest of her sister's body was scattered under the stairs. He used the flashlight on his helmet for visibility. The staircase was in danger of collapse; someone was calling from below. He attempted a vertical rescue. It was like an excavation, digging through blocks of concrete, trying to avoid the twisted steel.

After the strikes' pulverizing roar, quiet engulfed the street. It was a kind of death, this absence of the people of Aleppo. So eerily quiet, it reminded Sami of that Friday, the first time in thirteen hundred years that the call to prayer hadn't sounded.

The war had swallowed the Adhaan, divesting the city of its essence, the moment of Aleppo's death. Unless that moment had come later, with the building's final collapse.

They'd worked with too much urgency and not enough skill. By the time they reached the bottom, no one was calling out. The dust was so thick, he felt like he was swallowing metal. He'd never forget the taste, razor-edged and cruel. They found the body at the bottom; its legs were severed by the blast. Sami checked to see if the boy was still alive... his blood was the one bit of color able to penetrate the dust.

Ali didn't want to hear the rest.

Sami's recital was remorseless.

'I turned him and found his glasses. It was my brother, Shahoud.'

Behind them, Israa was crying, deep, convulsive sobs, Aya cradled in her arms.

Sami stubbed out his cigarette. 'There are worse sins than the ones you've claimed for yourself.'

Ali tried to embrace him. He knew Sami didn't like to be touched, but in that moment, he'd forgotten. His body stiff, Sami moved away.

'There's nothing left of my life in Aleppo. There's nothing left of Aleppo. Well...' A ghostly smile creased his mouth. 'There was one thing I wanted to keep. Intelligence sent it to Damascus.'

'What was it?' Ali couldn't disguise the anguish in his voice.

Sami flicked his cigarette away. 'It was my brother's white helmet.'

30

Calais, France

THE CALAIS JUNGLE WAS EVERY bit as oppressive as Sehr had expected it to be. In some ways she was reminded of Moria. From the neat white containers at the heart of the concrete grid, a forest of tents spiraled out, and farther out from the center there were mounds of garbage and abandoned plastic sheeting. The makeup of the camp's inhabitants was more diverse than on the islands, but here the hopelessness had set in more deeply. There was little sign that the camp's inhabitants had anywhere to go beyond the northern perimeter. Purportedly, there were mosques and shops available to the camp's residents, though not all those who ended up in Calais were Muslims. There were also distribution centers, but not nearly enough to meet the need.

Every road at Calais was blocked – there was no work to be had and no hope of a permanent address. No chance of crossing the Channel, and nothing but risk involved in trying to stow away on the vehicles crossing into England.

She'd scheduled a meeting with Matthieu Arnaud, the French government's liaison with the camp. He treated her to a breakdown of numbers and ongoing problems. He did his best to be fair, passing no judgment on those who sought the camp's protection, or on those who were clamoring for the Calais Jungle to be destroyed.

He couldn't have been more than twenty-five, and had

a censorious cast to his face that wasn't reflected in his straightforward speech.

Sehr asked about Audrey's visit to the camp earlier in the month, and the young man began to rummage through quantities of paper on his desk, searching for the agenda where he kept his appointments. When Sehr asked if his calendar was backed up on his phone, he gave a weary shrug. 'My phone is stolen once a month like clockwork, so it's best I rely on my notes.'

His office had a view of the English Channel. He glanced out the window at the peaceful expanse of waves and the miles of untouched beachfront.

'We built this camp for fifteen hundred people – it's acquired a life of its own. We've had to work to contain the sprawl. We've had fires; we had to raze the southern part of the camp at the insistence of a certain segment of the population, and now there are tensions around the northern zone – what can I tell you, mademoiselle? We are heading to a point of conflict. These migrants cross agricultural lands, they fight with each other, there is a lot of violence spiraling out from the inside, and our trade unions and truck drivers have had enough. If migrants want to go to the UK, *bien,* the British government should build the camp on their side of the Channel, instead of telling us *we* aren't doing enough. These are their words, not mine, but to be frank with you, the Calais Jungle is a nightmare.'

Sehr's family was from Afghanistan. Her parents had come to Canada as refugees fleeing the Soviet invasion. In a soft voice, she said, 'If only they could have stayed in their own lands.'

There was no judgment behind the words. Arnaud flashed a sharp glance at her, his hands stilling in their work, but as he saw her expression, he took her words at face value.

'Yes,' he agreed. 'If only. There's a balance to be struck, but it seems to me it's struck on the backs of those who have very little say in what's decided.' He paused for a moment in thought, then concluded with, 'They are at the mercy of too many forces, with very few choices available. The making and unmaking of all of this – that is beyond my purview.'

Yet he had a role to play, Sehr thought. A critical role, perhaps. His hands settled on his agenda. He snatched it up and paged to the week in question.

'I'm sorry,' he said to Sehr. 'I should remember your friend, but the number of people who pass through this camp tests my personal recall.'

He read quickly for a moment, half-whispering to himself.

Sehr waited, her hands clasped in her lap.

'She made an appointment to speak with me about the Jungle, though she never called it by that name.' He gave Sehr a sudden smile. 'I remember her now. She was very pretty, very charming, very much in command of her facts. She knew a lot about the camp before she arrived. And she came at a tumultuous time – two weeks after we closed the eviction zone. She was concerned that we had done that.'

'Why? My understanding is that the French government bussed out the inhabitants of the eviction zone to other parts of France. The barrier to the highway, that's relatively new, isn't it?'

He nodded. 'To prevent stowaways from creating problems for our drivers, we cut off their access to the road.' He sighed deeply. 'Your friend wanted to look at our records. How many people in, how many people out at any given time.' He paused. 'She was interested in children, but we don't keep records like that. It's impossible – a lot of people are dodging the authorities, they don't want to be pinned to a place.'

Sehr thought of things her parents had confided about their journey to Canada, their long delay in north-west Pakistan.

'It's more than that, wouldn't you say? Many of them come from places where the authorities are corrupt or dangerous. They may not know whom to trust.'

Arnaud agreed. 'Yes, we can't discount that. The point is I

couldn't give Mademoiselle Clare the figures she was looking for – our response in France has been reactive, improvisational. The main concern has been "How do we get these people out?" A lot of the population has been transient, evading registration, so our estimates are just that.'

Sehr wondered how Audrey had received this news. She thought she could guess what Audrey had been chasing. 'Did she say why she was focused on children?'

'There have been many unaccompanied children who've made the trek.'

Sehr puzzled this through, staring out at the waters of the Channel. From here, the camp looked like a colorful assortment of blocks, flung carelessly over a patch of land. She could accept that unaccompanied children ended up in countries that neighbored Syria – Lebanon, Turkey, or Jordan. But it seemed unlikely that they made it as far as France. When she asked this question point-blank, Arnaud tugged at his tie.

'We do the best we can. Our welcome center is overwhelmed.'

'Was she looking for anyone in particular? A girl named Israa, by any chance?'

His tone was one of genuine surprise. 'She didn't mention anyone by name. She wanted an overview of operations. She was trying to build a picture in her mind of what happens at each stop along the route.'

But a picture of what, precisely? Sehr wished she had answers. 'Is there anything else you can tell me, Monsieur Arnaud?'

'There is one thing. When Mademoiselle Clare came, she seemed to know the roadblocks refugees encounter. She knew keeping the camp intact has been a major point of contention between France and our neighbor across the Channel. The pressure to close Calais comes from the English as much as it does from locals. When Mademoiselle Clare expressed interest in the children in the eviction zone, I told her the best thing she could do was take her concerns to the British.'

Sehr frowned. She was getting close to it now – she could almost put her finger on it.

'The British insisted we wait to close the zone until they relocated the children with their relatives in the UK.'

'And did you?'

Frustrated, Arnaud flipped his agenda shut. 'We had no say over the eviction, it was in the hands of the police.'

Sehr stood up and collected her briefcase. 'So what happened to the children in question?'

Arnaud passed over a business card to Sehr. It was the address of a mission in Brussels, but contact details were scant. Inwardly, she sighed. She needed to book a flight. As she made her calculations about her itinerary, she realized Arnaud had yet to answer.

When she looked at him, she saw that he was sweating.

'Monsieur Arnaud? What happened to these children you say were never counted?'

His answer sent a frisson of fear down her spine.

'I'm afraid I don't know.'

In the taxi that took her to the ferry, Sehr tried Esa's number again. He didn't answer her call, she tried a third time. When it went to voicemail, she sat back in her seat to consider her options. Should she set up a meeting at the mission, or should she report back to Nate? If she did go on to Brussels, was there anything the others had discovered that would tell her what questions to ask?

She decided to call Rachel. She tried not to think about that painful altercation in Athens. The things Esa had said... the harsh way he'd spoken to her... why would she put herself in a place where he could treat her like that again? Her heart beating faster, she realized she was angry. After all this time, she was angry: weary of being a supplicant, weary of having given herself where there was no appreciation of her gifts, of the risks she continued to take for a man who could shut her out of his life as easily as he shut off his phone.

By the time Rachel picked up, Sehr's tone was curt and to the point. She explained what she'd learned, advising Rachel she was en route to Brussels.

Rachel didn't say anything to this. What she did say in a kind and calming tone was, 'Are you all right, Sehr? Did anything happen in France?'

Sehr swallowed a fiery response. Esa's indifference couldn't be blamed on Rachel.

Then it occurred to her she'd never asked him if there was someone else. He was so warm with Rachel, so close to her – why hadn't she noticed this before? And why hadn't he told her as much, if her suspicions were true? Maybe he thought nothing would stop what he'd once called her reckless pursuit. Or maybe he preferred to keep his secrets to himself.

'Sehr?' Rachel prodded. 'Are you there?'

Miserable at her own thoughts, Sehr pulled herself together. 'I'm here, Rachel, I'm sorry. Do you have any leads for me to follow up in Brussels?'

Rachel summarized their findings in Izmir. She was in a car headed to the Syrian border. Just the thought of it made Sehr worry.

'How close to the border, Rachel? What are you chasing that's worth the risk?'

She heard Rachel ask Ali a question along these lines.

'Not that close. We won't get snatched across the border. But the boss wants me to ask if you found out anything about the storage receipt or about the name CIJA?'

Sehr ascended into fury. 'Tell him to ask me himself!'

She hung up without another word.

Then she reconsidered. She knew what CIJA was – the name had come up during her research. She'd been distracted by Audrey's trip to Brussels, but wasn't the storage facility more significant? She considered Delft's location, pulling up a map on her phone. She moved the map around until her suspicions were confirmed.

She had a good idea what the storage facility contained.

And she knew why Audrey had made the trip to Delft.

31

Camp Apaydin
Hatay, Turkey

THE GATED ENTRANCE TO CAMP Apaydin was guarded by a pair of Turkish soldiers in camouflage gear and matching caps. They were lounging under a makeshift shelter, but when the van pulled up to their gates, they jumped to their feet, demanding papers.

Rachel looked out through the passenger window. They'd approached via a downslope that offered a broad view of the camp – rows of white tents neatly laid out, stamped with the logo of the Turkish Red Crescent. Rachel had done some reading: the camp housed four thousand residents. Nearly all were military officers who'd deserted the Syrian army; the rest were members of their families. Apaydin was under the jurisdiction of the prime minister's Disasters and Emergencies Directorate, a division known as AFAD. Well maintained and strictly patrolled, the camp was bordered with a perimeter of corrugated tin topped by rolls of barbed wire, while the camp itself was on the grid. Transmission towers were staged throughout the camp.

Rachel could see children playing on the ground on the other side of the fixed red gate. There was a blue gate house behind the gate, a pair of trash cans in front. They could see the interior of the camp, but they couldn't reach it without permission. Rachel wondered if its inhabitants were under guard.

She stayed in the van with Ali, whose face was pale with fear. Did he think he'd be turned over to the Turkish authorities to join the camp's inhabitants? Their papers had been checked in Cesme, where they'd disembarked from the ferry. Roux's credentials had stood the boy in good stead there; he'd been waved through with the rest of their party.

She searched the camp for signs of what was troubling Ali – apart from the guard at the entrance, there were no overt signs of military activity. Gazing south-east into the barren distance, she wondered if she was viewing the Syrian border.

The distance to the border could be measured in a handful of miles. And on the other side of the line was misery that couldn't be quantified, poorly understood in other parts of the world.

Eleven million people displaced.

Rachel's mind couldn't grapple with the scale of Syria's destruction. Khattak engaged the guards in conversation. His papers were held up for inspection. If Khattak called for her assistance, Rachel would join him, but he seemed to have the situation well under control. The guards were professional; they weren't attempting to intimidate him. Nor did they search the van. They did, however, ask Khattak to accompany them inside the gate house. The screening area was unlocked to allow Khattak to be processed through.

'This is it,' Ali muttered. His hand reached for the door of the van. Rachel turned to look at him, staying the movement of his hand.

'What do you think you're doing?'

'I should go take a look. This might be my only chance. They've left the gate open.'

'It could be electrified,' Rachel pointed out.

'It isn't.'

'Why do you want to get in there? Do you know someone in the camp – or do you think Israa is in there?'

His slight hesitation told her that whatever he said, it wasn't going to be the truth.

She kept the door firmly shut. 'You can't break into a camp

under the Turkish government's authority. Either we get invited in or we don't.'

'I need to see,' he insisted. 'Israa might be there.'

Rachel couldn't fathom a scenario in which that might be possible. 'Why would Israa return to the border? Why would she leave her little sister?'

The boy's face was tinged with green. His voice shaking, he said, 'She wouldn't. She wouldn't.'

Rachel placed a hand on his shoulder and squeezed. 'Look,' she said, her voice gruff. 'I know you've been through hell. We're doing the best we can to find Audrey – when we do, don't you think she'll have better answers than you could dig up here? Unless you have some other reason for wanting to get into that camp. You've been here before. Do you know what Audrey wanted in the camp?'

He set his jaw. 'Israa,' he said stubbornly. 'We both want Israa.' Rachel thought of the bodies that washed up on the beaches. Surely Israa had been in the boat that had accompanied Ali's. It was possible she'd drowned, and the tides had carried her body to a different shore. Still, she thought Ali was lying.

She jumped when Khattak rapped at the window. She wound the window down. 'Any luck, sir?'

He shook his head, his hair falling across his forehead. He was casually dressed for the humidity – the sleeves of his white shirt rolled up, a knotted kerchief at his neck to protect it from the blowing sand. He was wearing his sunglasses against the glare.

'Despite the call Inspecteur Roux put through to Ankara, I'm not able to obtain clearance. I'm afraid we're not gaining entry to Apaydin.'

A moment later, one of the soldiers who'd been guarding the gate sauntered up to the van. He shrugged an apology at their group, peering into the van for a better look at Rachel.

She smiled at him, and he nodded. Then he stuck his head in the window. Rachel tried to shield Ali, but the guard's face broke out in a smile.

'Hey, it's my friend.' His English was casually colloquial. 'Did you bring cigarettes this time?' His grin encompassed Rachel. 'You have all the luck, man. Another pretty lady you've been keeping to yourself.'

'Charmer.' Rachel tried some flattery of her own. She read the name tag on his shirt and addressed him by his first name. 'Are you talking about my friend here, Emre?' She pulled up a photograph of Audrey on her phone.

He squinted at her phone, nodding.

'When's the last time you saw her, do you remember?'

Emre shrugged. 'Ali could tell you, he was with her. Ten days ago, maybe two weeks?'

'She hasn't been back? You've been here the whole time?'

He showed her his flashy watch. 'I have to pay for this life. I don't have anywhere else to be.' He saw the concern on Rachel's face and added, 'I'm sorry, I haven't seen her. She came here asking questions about the officers...' His words trailed off. He cast a quick look back at the gate house, suddenly conscious that Khattak was paying close attention to his words. 'Shouldn't have said that.' He pinched his lips shut. 'I talk too much.'

Ali spoke up from the back of the van. 'Emre, man, please. I'll bring you cigarettes next time. Did Audrey come back after I came with her?'

'No,' he said quickly. 'She spooked a lot of people in the camp, so the boss said no more visitors. They don't even let local politicians in.' He mimed hefting a rocket launcher onto his shoulder. 'In case they get footage of jihadists-in-training.' He laughed. 'I'm kidding. That's what everyone says about Apaydin, but the Russians started that rumor.'

Rachel didn't know whether to believe him.

He took advantage of Rachel's interest to lean farther into the van. His breath was hot in her ear. 'You know why this camp is under guard, don't you?'

'Generals,' Rachel said bluntly, keeping her voice low.

'Syrian defectors. High-value targets.'

Emre moved too close; she gave him a quick shove back. His smile was unrepentant. 'Sorry, miss. Yes. We're protecting these bastards from the people who fled them. At least, I think that's what we're doing.'

He didn't have more to offer; as his partner joined him at the gate, he stepped away from the van with a cheeky salute and a wink.

'She hasn't been back,' Khattak said to Rachel. 'At least that's one thing we can cross off the list, one less place for us to search. I'd like to have seen the camp for myself, though.'

As he opened the door, Rachel's cell phone rang. It was another call from Sehr, who spoke without preamble.

'I've figured out what CIJA is. And I know what's in Delft.' She dictated an address to Rachel, then in a firm, no-nonsense voice, she added, 'Tell Esa to meet me there.'

When they were back on the dusty track to Izmir, Rachel looked over at Ali.

'Why did you come to the camp? Why did you go there in the first place? You were nervous the whole time, especially when Emre recognized you.'

She thought about the fact that Amélie Roux hadn't seen fit to accompany them to Apaydin. If Roux was keeping track of their investigation, why had she abandoned them in Izmir? She'd placed a call on their behalf, but maybe she'd known ahead of time that Camp Apaydin wouldn't yield any answers. Or maybe the call she'd placed had been to instruct the Turkish guards to refuse them entry to the camp.

Which begged the question of what Roux was trying to hide.

Ali knotted his hands in his lap. His curls shielded his face; Rachel couldn't read his expression.

'I don't know what you were doing there,' she said to him. 'But I know it wasn't about Israa.'

32

THEY DIDN'T SPEAK TO EACH other during the cab ride to the storage facility. Sehr looked out the window feeling wretched, wondering how she'd gotten to this place. She'd taken the blame on her shoulders for too long – yet how could she blame Esa for not seeing in her the things she'd found in him? The only way to handle it was to do what he was doing, retreat into professionalism, and speak to him with a stilted politeness without quite meeting his eyes.

She'd called Rachel back, explained her discoveries. Rachel had told Esa, who'd texted Sehr a time and place to meet. She'd agreed to meet him because the clock was running out on Audrey. And to prove to him that no matter what else he thought of her, she didn't lack the courage to face unpalatable truths.

The cab stopped in the shadow of the Oude Kerk, a Gothic Protestant cathedral known for its leaning tower. At any other time, Sehr would have chosen to do some sightseeing. She'd been to Holland but not to Delft; the Old Church's fine timber vaulting and pyramid-shaped roof stirred her interest. From the reading she'd done to distract herself, she knew the painter Jan Vermeer was buried at the church.

They ended up on the west bank of the canal, where cars were parked on one side, and bicycles on the other. Colorful shop fronts lined the canal, the tower casting its reflection in the water. She walked along beside Esa, not saying anything, conscious of a buried sadness at the widening gulf between them.

He held the door for her once they reached the storage unit. It was in a small office building, attached to others in a row of housing, and from its entryway, it didn't seem as though there was room for much storage of anything. Where in this facility would Audrey's boxes be hidden? She thought she knew what the boxes contained. She was waiting for confirmation so she didn't look like a fool.

A pleasant young man with an air of competence took Esa's police identification in his stride. He read the letter Inspecteur Roux had provided on Interpol letterhead. If he raised the issue of a warrant, Sehr had her arguments ready. He didn't. He produced a pass card from a locked drawer and led them through sliding glass doors to a second set of doors.

The main storage area was behind these doors. Banks of cabinets with digital displays ran along the walls. He cast a look around for the one assigned to Audrey Clare: Unit 601. He nodded to himself, hesitating for a moment before he keyed in an override password.

'I'll leave you to it, shall I? If you need anything else, please don't hesitate to call me.' He pointed to an intercom button on the wall.

Sehr stepped back so Esa could search the unit. The boxes it contained were wide and flat, not much bigger than shoeboxes. Sehr estimated each box could hold fifty pages of paper. They were stacked in numerical order.

Esa reached for box 1 and placed it on a table in the center of the room. She watched Esa's face as he read through its contents. She saw the sick pallor of his skin, the lowered line of his brows as he made sense of what he was reading. These were numbered documents with prefixes and codes attached, the documents embossed with the emblem of a tiny gold hawk. They were signed in green ink and accompanied by photographs.

Esa drew in a breath, turning the photographs over before Sehr could take a look. Gently, she eased them out from underneath his hand.

'Sehr,' he said. 'Don't look.' But he didn't stop her by placing his hand on hers.

She ignored his warning, steadying herself. She'd seen worse things in her work.

'It *was* about Camp Apaydin. It comes back to Assad in the end.' She pointed to the panels attached to each photograph. 'Look at this – 215,' she said. 'Every bit of this is crystal clear.'

'I'm not following.'

Esa's face was so pale that Sehr wondered if she should urge him to a seat. Instead, he braced his hands on the table, briefly closing his eyes.

'Why these boxes are here in Delft, what CIJA means, who Sami al-Nuri was – what those burns on his body were – why he was killed. It's all here in this box.'

Esa turned his head. For a moment, they simply looked at each other. Then Sehr switched into her mode as prosecutor.

'We're twenty minutes from The Hague, from the International Criminal Court. That's why Audrey brought these boxes here. She was planning to hand them over.'

'What about CIJA?' Esa asked.

'It's the Commission for International Justice and Accountability. Those calls we couldn't trace must have been to her liaison at CIJA. She was trying to arrange a pickup.'

'Why to CIJA? Why not to the International Criminal Court?'

'CIJA is the first independent agency to conduct a war crimes investigation. They have the funding to investigate, but no mandate to prosecute crimes. Ordinarily, war crimes would be referred to the ICC by the UN Security Council, but given Russia's presence on the council, any attempt to do so would be vetoed. My guess is we won't be hearing of prosecutions until the war is over. In the meantime, CIJA is collecting and preserving the evidence. You must have heard the name Bill Wiley.'

NO PLACE OF REFUGE

CIJA had been founded by Bill Wiley, a Canadian war crimes investigator who'd pioneered the effort to collect evidence of Syrian war crimes. Activists on the ground had collected evidence of the regime's crackdown that was ultimately unhelpful in furthering prosecutions. It had been Wiley's idea to redirect these efforts to document a wider range of abuses. CIJA had received funding from the UN, and from several different nations, including Canada, to train Syrians on procedures for collecting evidence – and on the kind of evidence required to corroborate prosecutions.

'For the past fifteen months, activists have been smuggling evidence out of Syria. The Syrian people are building the war crimes case, at great personal risk to themselves.' Sehr looked down at the coded photographs. 'CIJA has interviewed two hundred and fifty witnesses, some at Apaydin, in an attempt to secure pattern evidence.'

'I'm not familiar with the term.'

Sehr knew they were speaking to each other in this manner to obscure the horror on the table. She hastened to explain, glad there was, after all, something of value she could offer.

'To build a war crimes prosecution, you need proof that crimes have been perpetrated in a systematic manner. You need to show the impact of government policy on individual citizens.'

She gestured at the photographs. 'That's what this is, Esa. It's the evidence. Documents with the embossed hawk emblem are directly from the Central Crisis Management Cell.'

She explained the significance of Audrey's collection. Shortly after the uprising in 2011, the Central Crisis Management Cell had held a meeting at the Baath Party Regional Command. The Baath Party was Syria's governing party; it was ruled by Bashar al-Assad.

When the Syrian uprising had spread to other parts of the country, the CMC blamed itself for not coordinating the response of Syria's security services. A new set of commands was issued at that meeting: the security branches were authorized to launch daily raids against protesters, security agents were to coordinate with neighborhood militias to keep the opposition out of protest hotspots, a joint investigation was to be launched that would incorporate representatives from all the security services. Their purpose was to interrogate detainees who would give up fresh targets for the security branches to detain.

The CMC sent these orders down multiple chains of command. In a stunning coup in 2014, CIJA had acquired proof of these orders. The Baath Party had instructed its organs to crush the protests. Those orders were clear. What CIJA required in addition was proof that the orders had been executed, protesters detained, tortured, or killed.

The Crisis Cell had insisted its branches provide lists of detainees. The security branches confirmed that orders were carried out.

We did that a long time ago.

So thorough was the evidence demonstrating command responsibility that the US ambassador at large had said: 'When the day of justice arrives, we'll have much better evidence than we've had anywhere since Nuremberg.'

The photographs on the table were examples. Each body in the photographs was assigned a reference number from the security branch responsible for the death. If a corpse was taken to a military hospital, it was given another number to falsely document that the death had occurred in hospital – presumably while the victim had been undergoing treatment. The deaths of detainees were routinely attributed to heart attack or respiratory failure.

The case had been broken open by a defector known as Caesar, an official forensic photographer with the military police. In January 2014, overwhelmed by his burden of documenting death, Caesar had smuggled out fifty thousand images of murders carried out by the Mukhabarat, with evidence of systematic torture.

Caesar had made a chilling statement: 'The regime documents everything so it will forget nothing.'

He'd given the images to the Syrian National Movement. Members of that group had formed the Syrian Association for Missing and Conscience Detainees. They took custody of the files, which were transferred to Human Rights Watch. The files contained evidence of twenty-seven detention centers that served as factories for torture.

'These images are new,' Sehr said. 'They're recent – from this year. They're not part of the cache authenticated by CIJA. The Caesar photographs were made available through the news source Zaman al-Wasl, then picked up by various Facebook groups.'

'Why?' Esa demanded. 'These photographs are appalling. Why would anyone make them public?'

Sehr understood there was a possibility she'd faced darker things than Esa had. They were both officers of the law, but her transition to refugee law had opened up a world in chaos.

'It's very simple, Esa.' She kept her tone neutral. 'So their families can identify the dead.'

Esa's hand came down on the table. 'But *these* photographs – the horrors they show –?'

'There's no other way to know. It may be a terrible answer, but it *is* an answer.'

Esa studied the photographs. 'How many?' he asked.

'Eleven thousand.' She quoted from the report published on the basis of the Caesar files. 'Documented industrial-scale killing; systematic, pervasive torture.' Weighed down by her own words, she added, 'But the Caesar photographs represent only a fraction of the dead. They cover a two-year period. The photographs are from the al-Khatib branch of the security services in north-east Damascus. So as damning as they are, they're deficient in terms of giving us the whole picture.'

'Meaning?'

'The Caesar photographs are the ones Caesar had access to. It's a fraction of the actual number of those who died in detention. There must be other records to document the rest. I think that's where Sami came in.'

Esa nodded his agreement, his voice dispassionate and cool. 'You think he was a defector. Kept safe at Apaydin until he found Audrey and passed these files on to her. There's at least a thousand pages here. He couldn't have smuggled them out on his body. And if Sami was a defector, why was he tortured so badly?'

Sehr looked down at her hands. The things she'd had to learn were things she wanted to forget.

'When the memorandum came down from the Crisis Cell, protesters were detained for the purpose of obtaining confessions. They served a purpose. Assad orchestrated the illusion of a conspiracy against the state: the confessions justified that illusion. Guards at detention centers were pressured to make prisoners confess to treason. If agents weren't enthusiastic about obtaining those confessions, they too, would disappear.'

She realized her hands were trembling and that Esa had noticed. She clasped them behind her back.

'Sami al-Nuri may have been someone with access, who'd fallen afoul of the Mukhabarat. Maybe that's how he knew to get out – but why he was killed on Lesvos, I can't say.'

At the troubled expression on her face, Esa reached for her hands. He held them in his own, despite her attempt to retreat.

'I didn't want you involved in this. I'm sorry you've had to face this...'

Sehr freed herself from his grip. She couldn't bear what he was doing – telling her to stay away, then crossing these boundaries anew.

Her words careful and measured, she said, 'You're not responsible for my choices. I'm doing the job I was asked to do by Nate. Paid to do, in fact. I don't need your protection.'

He looked stung. 'Sehr...'

'Esa.' She adjusted the strap of her briefcase. 'Don't do this to me. Since you're stuck with me for the moment, treat me like a colleague.' She tried to suppress the emotion in her voice. 'I'm not breakable,' she said. 'I'm not Samina – though I know in your mind Samina is infallible. I realize you don't hold me to that standard, but I *am* capable of operating on my own – I'm not someone who needs my hand held.'

She waited for his admonition, the weight of it bowing her shoulders.

He would say it now again – *Don't ever speak about my wife...*

It was hard to look at him, but she did. She had to face this, so it was finished.

Irreparably broken, as he wanted.

She felt oppressed by the closeness of the room, locked into a situation she'd never wanted. Esa had taken her in his arms on his return from Iran: she'd misread his intent. He'd been thanking her for her help, nothing more. But his tenderness was unexpected, uncharacteristic for a man who treated women with the reserve of his faith; she'd thought he was ready to move forward. He'd urged her close, then refused a deeper intimacy.

She was wrenched by his reversals, ragged and worn inside. She repeated to herself like a mantra, *With hardship comes ease. Lo, with hardship there will be ease.*

Esa shifted away from the table. He took a step closer to Sehr then stopped, not knowing what she'd seen in his face to cause her to look so panicked. She hadn't been sleeping well, there were shadows under her eyes. Her hair had unraveled from its knot, falling in soft waves around her shoulders.

He'd never noticed the little gold chips in her eyes, or the tints in her hair. Or her defenseless expression. His words on the terrace had been cruel, spoken from a place of pain, but this he didn't want – this severance, this parting of ways. He was trying to come to terms with the thought that though he'd insisted on distance, perhaps he no longer wanted it.

Had Sehr been right to accuse him? Did he blame himself for Samina's death? Would Samina blame him for getting on with his life? His thoughts had never strayed to Sehr during the years of his marriage, though Samina had asked him to help with the task of finding Sehr a partner. Sehr hadn't responded, and Khattak's only interest had been in the wife he adored.

Samina *hadn't* been infallible – she would have been the first to deny Sehr's claim.

But perhaps Sehr's conclusions were closer to the truth than Esa was willing to admit, his memories of Samina acquiring a patina of perfection over time.

Looking at Sehr's tense expression, he realized his determined indifference had made their relationship more hazardous, not less. She'd been right to call him a coward. And to ask him why he kept her at the periphery of his life, expecting comfort without commitment, or affection without reciprocity.

Ashamed of himself, he said, 'Forgive me, Sehr. I shouldn't have said those things in Athens. Please know how sorry I am.'

She gave a defeated shrug. 'This proximity won't last. You'll find Audrey and I'll be able to get on with my work.'

Sehr's emotions were transparent. She wore them so close to the surface, he knew when he'd hurt her, he knew he *could* hurt her. It was wrong of him to take advantage, but it gave him the courage to speak.

'Samina was right. You commit yourself completely to any cause you endorse.'

A stinging color slashed her cheeks. 'You spoke of me with Samina?'

He wondered why that disturbed her. 'You were her closest friend. She talked about you often.'

Her hand reached for the edge of the table. When she stumbled and he tried to assist her, she snatched her hand away.

'Don't!' she said sharply. 'Please don't touch me.' She swung around and buzzed the intercom. 'Can you finish up here on your own?'

'Sehr.' Esa tried to calm her by keeping his voice even. 'What are you afraid of? You told me to own up to this... to whatever our relationship is.'

Sehr whirled back to face him. He was dismayed to see tears in her eyes.

'Did she know?' Sehr demanded. 'Did Samina know that I –?' A wild gesture of her hand finished the sentence for her.

Esa couldn't answer. He was stunned by her admission.

Had Sehr loved him all this time? Since the day he'd married Samina?

He didn't know how to respond. If Samina *had* known, she wouldn't have spoken of Sehr so lightly. She would have created distance between her husband and her friend. Her tact and sympathy would have been intolerable to Sehr.

His voice low, Esa said, 'No, Samina didn't know.'

Then he said the worst thing he could say in the circumstances. 'It was a chance infatuation, Sehr. You were so young when we met.'

Sehr sucked in a breath. Her eyes became opaque.

'I'm sure you're right.' She spoke in a careful voice. 'I don't think we need to discuss this further. This isn't the place for it – not with the horrors we've just witnessed.' She shifted her briefcase in her hands. 'I'll figure out what to do about these boxes.'

His thoughts tumultuous and confused, Esa didn't answer. He passed a hand over his face. Seeing him do so, Sehr stabbed the intercom again. When the glass doors slid open, she hurried down the hall.

Esa looked at the photographs he'd spread out on the table without seeing them. He didn't want to look back; he didn't want Sehr's confession to color a past he cherished.

He couldn't accept anything that would change the way he'd loved his wife.

But were his memories vulnerable to suggestion? It was possible Samina had kept Sehr's secret in order to spare her feelings – or to protect their friendship, perhaps fearing he would ask her to disengage Sehr from their lives.

It was a terrible thought.

He'd been ruptured by loss since the death of his wife, but the love between them was the bedrock of his life. He wanted to talk to someone – he needed reassurance. His feelings for Sehr were changing with a suddenness that shifted the ground. They'd said things they hadn't said before. And she'd rebuffed him in a way that was new, asserting her rights against him. He felt shaken by the change – that he could *be* shaken told him there was something at stake that he'd been unable to acknowledge.

Unwilling to face these truths, he turned his attention to the box.

Sehr made several calls, seeking out friends in legal practice who could find her a contact at CIJA. When none proved forthcoming, she called Rachel.

'Where are you now?' Rachel asked her.

Sehr explained their presence in Delft with an overview of their discoveries. She listened as Rachel pondered the links between Camp Apaydin, Sami al-Nuri, and CIJA. Rachel's theory developed quickly; as she shared it, Sehr could see she was right.

'Sami made contact with Audrey and Audrey tried to get his files into the hands of CIJA. Why not straight to the ICC?'

Sehr went over her reasoning again, digging into CIJA's background a little more.

'Hang on,' Rachel said. 'There is something I can check. Let me have a look at Audrey's phone records for the dates she was in Delft. She wouldn't have put the papers in storage unless she had to. Maybe there was a delay before she could get them to CIJA. If she was called back to Lesvos, for example. By the way, I think I can answer another question for you. She was running her printers at Woman to Woman, night and day. Shukri Danner complained about Audrey's extravagance with resources. Say Sami got out some kind of record – evidence on Assad's prisons. A thumb drive or a few CDs, and Audrey printed up the material for The Hague.'

'Where is the drive itself, then?' Sehr asked, fiddling with the snaps of her briefcase. A little nervous distraction helped her to focus her thoughts. 'What about the fact that some of the documents are originals?'

'Maybe a few *were* smuggled out. I've been wondering about these trips between Turkey and Greece, and the fact that Ali tagged along – hard enough for him to transit once, why did Audrey allow him to make such a dangerous crossing again? Was he helping her search for Israa? Or was he involved in something else? Something connected to CIJA?'

Sehr tried to puzzle this through. The quickest way to find answers would be to locate Audrey's contact at CIJA. There was still no sign of Esa, so she pulled out her laptop and began a search.

Despite her efforts, she couldn't find a website for CIJA. She looked for phone numbers, contacts, names. None were provided, even as an offshoot under the UN, the EU, or the International Criminal Court. Strange. It puzzled her because it made her wonder how those in a position to report on Assad's crimes could make their information safely known to CIJA.

She encountered a small amount of press coverage devoted to the Caesar photographs and to the key players at CIJA: Bill Wiley, Stephen Rapp, a man named Charles Engel. She'd already read the Human Rights Watch report; now she remembered the Caesar profile in the *New Yorker*. She skimmed it quickly then backtracked.

The reporter had understated one of his observations: the location of CIJA's headquarters wasn't publicly disclosed; neither were the identities of their Syrian volunteers. The reasons for this were evident. It was to ensure a safe conduit for the delivery of documentation like the Caesar cache. And for the couriers of the evidence.

She opened a file on her laptop and began to make notes, her expression thoughtful as she collected the facts: there was a chancy nature to CIJA's work. It was dangerous for the Syrians involved. Sami al-Nuri had been shot at close range – did she need further proof?

Perhaps this was also the reason for Audrey's itinerant activity, and the absolute absence of written communication as to what she'd been pursuing. If Audrey was acting as a courier for CIJA, she must have had a contact at CIJA. Whoever that contact was, they needed to hand over the boxes. Sehr frowned, a delicate knitting of her eyebrows.

That still didn't explain Audrey's trip to Calais or her detour to Brussels. How could Sehr find the links between the stops on Audrey's route? Like the answer to a prayer, her phone rang. It was Rachel. She had two numbers for Sehr that she'd pulled from the records collected by Paul Gaffney in Toronto. Though the numbers were unattributed, both were local to Delft.

Sehr decided not to wait for Esa. Whatever was taking him so long in the vault, she was grateful for the reprieve. She called the first of the two numbers and heard a busy signal. The second number rang through, to be answered by a young man.

'I'm calling on behalf of Audrey Clare,' Sehr said. 'I think I have something you want.'

There was a pause on the line. 'I don't know what you mean,' the man said.

Sehr decided to take the risk. 'I'm calling about Caesar.'

A longer pause this time.

Then the man said, 'I think you're looking for my boss.'

33

Delft, the Netherlands

THE PHOTOGRAPHS ON THE TABLE were terrible to study. Esa felt a surge of wretchedness at this evidence of Assad's crimes. The nightmare reality he'd plumbed during his case in Iran was exponentially worse in Syria. How many thousands of Syrians had been processed through these centers to face these unspeakable acts? These violations had taken place at the instigation of the four main intelligence agencies that made up the Mukhabarat: the Department of Military Intelligence, the Political Security Directorate, the General Intelligence Directorate, and the Air Force Intelligence Directorate. The Crisis Management Cell coordinated these four bodies, reporting directly to Assad. Each of the four agencies had a central branch in Damascus, as well as regional and municipal branches with separate detention facilities. Once a detention center became too crowded, prisoners would be transferred to new locations, while retaining their original affiliation.

In Arabic, the transferees were called *ida*, a word that meant 'deposits.' The majority of these cases represented enforced disappearances, a process whereby agents of the state detained ordinary citizens on trumped-up charges of sedition or terrorism or threats to national security, and then refused to acknowledge the detention or the detainee's location. Nothing could change their fates – not the extortionate bribes demanded for information, not highly placed connections within the regime, not the offer of cooperation or collusion.

He remembered Ahmed Fakhri's desperate offer.

I can give you all of their names.

Fakhri had fallen back on lessons he must have learned in detention – his terror at being questioned now fully explained. He'd assumed that Khattak had wanted him to inform on other Syrians – anyone who disagreed with Assad's butchery – and he'd snatched at an imaginary list – his cellmates? his friends? – to stave off the further possibility of torture.

The war crimes trials would come too late to deliver those in Assad's hands. Khattak forced himself to look at the photographs, to observe the forensic details. Each photograph had three numbers assigned, but Esa couldn't tell what the numbers meant. Going back through the documentation didn't make it clearer. Which meant that the need to get these photographs into the hands of experts was exigent: they urgently required a thorough forensic analysis.

Paging through the evidence, he realized he'd seen at least some of these numbers before. When Suha Obeidi had shown him Sami al-Nuri's application in Toronto, a list of numbers had been appended that weren't connected to Sanctuary Syria's protocols.

A sick feeling in his stomach, Khattak realized the numbers referred to detention centers: 215, 216, 220, 227, 235, 248. The numbers linked Sami al-Nuri to Syria's detention system, his tortured corpse *prima facie* evidence. Audrey had stumbled onto something terrible, something she'd never discussed with Nate. And he didn't think she'd told Ruksh either, though when he was done in this room, he would call his sister to find out.

The pictures provided testimony of the methods the Mukhabarat had used to kill, a design of overarching evil, a word Khattak used advisedly. The pictures were of boys and young men. Their emaciated bodies had sharply defined pelvic bones and ribcages; their faces were deeply sunken. There was ample evidence of trauma, suffocation, starvation, gunshot wounds to the head, open head wounds, dried blood in body cavities, and other forms of torture.

Khattak turned to the accompanying report. He read the description of the most common types of torture used in detention: beatings with an object, electrocution, *shabeh, dulab, falaqa, basat al-reeh*. He didn't require a translation of the Arabic: each term was accompanied by a drawing.

Shabeh: to be hung from the ceiling by the wrists and beaten to force a confession, beatings that continued for hours. *Dulab*: to have the head, back, and legs forced inside a tire and be beaten with batons and whips. *Falaqa*: to be beaten on the soles of the feet with whips and batons until the feet were swollen, making it impossible to stand. The *basat al-reeh* or 'flying carpet': to be tied to a board with the head suspended, hands and feet bound, and be beaten with a braided cable. Esa forced himself to keep reading. To read horrors as debased as these was the least one human soul could commit to another, the record an act of witness.

Phrases stained his mind, corrupting what little of his innocence remained.

There are places that God never visits.

My death was near me all the time.

There were no questions, just accusations.

But I didn't do anything.

Except I screamed.

Because I couldn't bear the pain.

They put electric prongs on my teeth… they kicked me with their boots… every time I called for help, they laughed… my body was blue from the beatings… they made me suck my blood from the floor… they tied me to a metal chair… they used electrodes… they wrapped wires around my genitals…they raped me… they raped me, four, five men at a time…

I died. I never came back to life.

Esa took several deep breaths. He closed the file, seeking a moment of respite.

His thoughts turned to the refugee crisis. The destruction of Syria and the grave suffering of its people were ignored as the root causes of the crisis, absent from the broader political discussion, absent from the news. Would things have been different if instead of printing the word MIGRANT, the headlines had screamed of torture? He didn't have much faith that they would.

From the starting point of a refugee's journey to the end, there wasn't much kindness on offer. There was the reporter who'd kicked a child at the Hungarian border. Smugglers who robbed and raped along the route. Counterfeit life jackets that pulled bodies into the sea. The raid by Golden Dawn, with blocks of stone pelted from the hills. The detention centers in countries around the world, the makeshift, unsanitary camps. The burning of the Calais Jungle. The fences, the checkpoints, the border controls, despite the promise of safety to those at risk of harm.

These records documented another vein of suffering, the persecution of a people within their own borders, where home was no longer a place of refuge. Would greater knowledge of the atrocities authorized by Assad make a difference to public perceptions?

Widespread, systematic torture. Industrial-scale killing.

Regrettably, he knew the answer. Assad's politicide had been conducted over a period of years. Chemical warfare, the bombing of civilians, hadn't altered perceptions at all.

To Esa, there was no question of what Syrians were fleeing. But he'd heard the range of responses: *Why don't they have any papers? Why don't they wait their turn? Why don't they stay and fight?*

But he wondered how civilians could fight against explosives dropped by jets, or chemical weapons deployed by their own government. If they took up arms, they were branded jihadists; their neighborhoods suffered the punishment. Over time, jihadist groups *had* infiltrated the war, adding to the share of killing and destruction, until the Arab Spring was no more than a memory.

He replaced the photographs, wondering how CIJA's operatives achieved distance from these realities. Or how the prosecutors did. His fingers rested on a page that had become separated from the others. He glanced down at it. Someone had typed up a translation of two paragraphs in Arabic, a description of a session at Branch 215. He skimmed it, sweat forming on his brow. He tried to avoid the details but his attention was caught by the final sentences, by how well he understood them.

My cellmate couldn't last. He screamed for his mother. When that didn't help, he cried for the Prophet Muhammad. So the guards brought the Muhammad stick, and then they beat him with that.

The Muhammad stick.

Named for the messenger of peace. Used in the name of terror. His face gray, his mouth pinched with horror, he put his head in his hands and wept.

34

Delft, the Netherlands

THEY MET AUDREY'S CONTACT FROM CIJA at the Stads-Koffyhuis, a charming street-side café whose windows were framed in the blue-and-white palette of Delftware. A green arboreal border strung with pinecones and tiny lights hung above the patio. Lise Cloutier, a French-Canadian attorney, had insisted they meet inside and wait in an inconspicuous corner.

As they waited for Cloutier to arrive, Esa and Sehr sat across from each other in silence. Esa watched as Sehr perused the menu, but in the end all she ordered was coffee. He chose to wait for Lise Cloutier; when she came, he viewed her arrival with relief, taking her briefcase and pulling out her chair.

When their orders had been placed, he took a moment to study her. He was struck at once by the fierce intelligence in her eyes. He knew not to underestimate her in any case; she was a former prosecutor who'd worked as a special advisor to the high commissioner for human rights at the United Nations. She was one of CIJA's secret weapons, heavily involved in the training of volunteers, and in collating records smuggled out of Syria.

She offered them nothing until Esa handed over his police ID and showed her a copy of his authorization. Even then, she took out her phone and verified his name and background through Community Policing's website. She studied the photograph on the website, compared it to the man sitting across from her, and nodded. Then she frowned at Sehr.

'And you, mademoiselle? What is your stake in this investigation?' A touch defensively, Sehr explained her position. Lise Cloutier flicked through her phone again, this time confirming that Sehr had worked as a prosecutor in Ontario. Her eyebrows rose as she skimmed Sehr's background. Sehr didn't interrupt, a subtle color rising under her skin.

Cloutier's résumé and reputation were exceedingly distinguished. She'd diagnosed the reasons for Sehr's career transition in moments.

'Is this some kind of personal redemption for you? Is that why you've accompanied Inspector Khattak?'

Khattak stayed quiet, knowing his intervention would be unwelcome.

Sehr gave the older woman a steady glance.

'I was hired by Nathan Clare to assist in the search for his sister. I'm Woman to Woman's counsel. And Audrey Clare is a friend.'

'I see.' Lise Cloutier transferred her gaze to Khattak. 'So then? What do you have for me? Why did you want to see me?'

'We have files that were smuggled out of Syria. We're here to turn them over.'

Lise Cloutier's eyes widened. 'Where?'

Khattak nodded at the window. 'On the street, in the trunk of that parked car. Twenty-five boxes' worth. Audrey stored them here in Delft. I presume it's you she came here to meet.'

'Just a moment.' Lise Cloutier made a call on her phone, speaking rapidly in French. Khattak, who'd followed the general sense of her words, offered, 'We'd be glad to drive these boxes to your headquarters.'

Cloutier made a sharp gesture of negation. 'That won't be necessary, Inspector Khattak. We've been waiting for these boxes for weeks. We didn't know Audrey was missing until you called us.'

Khattak had thought about his questions for Cloutier in some detail, and now he asked them, deciding not to wait for

Sehr's input. Whatever had happened between them, they had to remember Audrey was their reason for being here.

Cloutier gave them a rapid summary of her meetings with Audrey. The purpose of the meetings was as Khattak had surmised. A defector known to CIJA had been in touch with Audrey – his name was Sami al-Nuri. Audrey had used her contacts to channel his message to CIJA. She'd made a visit to Delft to discuss CIJA's needs in terms of documentation, then returned to Greece to assist Sami with the channeling of that information through contacts at Camp Apaydin. Sehr didn't know what had delayed Audrey's delivery of the documents – she'd come to Delft especially for the purpose of the meeting. An unavoidable delay on Cloutier's part in communicating a rendezvous point had altered things. Audrey had made an abrupt return to Lesvos, but Cloutier didn't know the reason for Audrey's sudden change in plans. Nor had Audrey had time to wait to transfer over the documents.

Khattak observed that it had taken courage for Audrey to embark on her mission, a mission she'd kept a secret.

'That was at our request. We asked her to assist our courier,' Cloutier said. Reflecting on his words, she added, 'I'm assuming you looked at what was in those boxes. You must have seen the photographs.'

Khattak agreed that he had. He'd kept his reaction to his discoveries from Sehr, trying to assume the appearance of neutrality, but he wasn't finding it easy.

'You're giving credit to the wrong person. If you saw the men in the photographs, you must know what Sami was risking. This is a Syrian story. It belongs to the Syrian people.'

Khattak was silent. It was difficult for him to accept that from the moment he'd landed on Lesvos, even with his experience of the camps, he'd seen the case through the lens of his worry for Audrey. To Esa and Rachel both, Audrey had been the priority. She still was.

In answer to his thoughts, Cloutier said, 'Audrey is your

responsibility, I understand. I was speaking about CIJA: we've taken none of the risks, we've suffered none of the losses. I was sorry to hear your news of Sami. He was dedicated to this cause. Without him, we wouldn't have singled out the torturers at Camp Apaydin.'

The look of sorrow on her face deepened as she told them, 'We promised to help resettle him in Canada, but Sami kept delaying. He believed he could do more.'

'You spoke to him?' Khattak asked, a memory ticking over in his mind.

'Many times on the phone. He was exceptionally bright – kind, decent, deeply caring about the plight of his fellow Syrians – he was the brave one, Inspector. Not that Mademoiselle Clare wasn't helpful, but she didn't share his risks.'

Audrey's disappearance may have suggested otherwise, but Khattak didn't demur. He felt like a schoolboy who'd been chastised by a teacher. His coffee had grown cold and he signaled for another, including his companions. He looked over to find Sehr watching him as if she knew what he'd been thinking, and he was struck by how easily she seemed to read his mood. She asked Cloutier a question.

'Can you think of anyone who had reason to harm Sami? Was the Interpol agent Aude Bertin tied into CIJA's work? Perhaps that's the reason they were targets.'

Cloutier looked at Sehr with dawning interest. 'Agent Bertin was not affiliated with CIJA, I have no idea why she was killed. As for your other question, many people had reason to wish Sami al-Nuri dead. He was an enemy to those who run Assad's detention centers, he was an enemy to some at Apaydin. From my conversations with him, I can tell you one thing. He wasn't about to give up on Apaydin, any more than he intended to give up his search for Israa.'

Khattak's hands jerked together. He looked at Sehr in shock. Sehr shook her head, indicating he should ask.

'Sami was searching for a girl named Israa?'

Cloutier was surprised. She waved a hand over her coffee cup. 'Of course. It was why he kept returning to Turkey. He thought the more valuable he was to us – as an interpreter or informer, call him what you like – the more likely it was that we'd be able to assist in resettling his friends. Legally, the Fakhris weren't eligible to sponsor Sami's friends; their safe resettlement in Canada was the condition Sami imposed.'

His nerves on edge, Khattak took out his phone. He found Rachel's photographs from the morgue. He showed the picture of Aude Bertin to Cloutier. Her mouth folded up in sympathy.

Then he pulled up the photograph of Sami's abused body.

'They were shot together at close range. Aude Bertin may have been killed trying to defend Sami.'

Cloutier gripped the phone. 'What do you mean?' she asked.

'That *isn't* Sami al-Nuri.'

Leaving Sehr to wrap up their meeting, Khattak stepped out into the street to call Rachel. He wandered down to the canal, where he breathed in the scent of freshly budded trees hanging over the river. He passed an unexpected little grove of elms, then found a quiet place to make his call under a thicket of trees bearing their branches to the ground.

'It's *not* Sami al-Nuri?' Rachel repeated, incredulous. 'Then who the hell is it?'

'Think back to our interview with the Fakhris. What did Dania say when we showed her the photograph of Sami?'

Wherever Rachel was, it was noisy. She asked him to repeat himself, and he did.

'Ah, I've got you now, sir. I think we *told* her the boy in the photograph was Sami, and she asked if we were certain he was dead.'

Khattak remembered now. That was exactly what Dania had said.

'Sir.' There was a doubting note in Rachel's voice. 'She knew he wasn't Sami al-Nuri. She knew he wasn't a relation of hers, because remember she said, "*This* boy didn't contact us. *He* isn't our family."'

As usual, Rachel was right. Though Dania hadn't placed quite that emphasis on the words. But he'd thought he'd glimpsed a strange relief in her eyes.

'Rachel.' He wanted her to follow his line of thought to see if it took her to the same conclusions. 'Lise Cloutier doesn't know who the young man in the morgue is. She just knows it's not Sami al-Nuri. But she did say that the Sami she spoke to was looking for a girl named Israa – he wouldn't turn his documents over to CIJA until he received a guarantee that his friends would also be resettled.'

Rachel didn't point out that this resembled a bribe – that was hardly the point.

'I'll be on Lesvos in half an hour, sir. Commander Benemerito is taking me across. You should get back here, pronto.'

'Why is that, Rachel?'

She sounded resolute. 'We need to talk to Ali.'

Back in the café, Esa asked Cloutier if she knew the name Ali Maydani.

'He's a friend of Sami's. He brought us testimony from Military Intelligence in Aleppo, *and* from Hospital 601, where he was later transferred.'

Khattak frowned in concentration. Audrey had stored her records in a unit of that number. And in Sami's application, 601 was a number on Audrey's list.

'A hospital?' Khattak studied Cloutier's shuttered expression. 'What kind of testimony comes from a hospital?'

Cloutier shook her head. 'That's none of your business.'

Sehr intervened. 'Given the prime minister's backing, and the sensitive nature of your work, I think we can agree that anything that helps us find Audrey is relevant both to your investigation and ours. I've read the 2015 report, but it would save us time if you tell us what you know.' Politely, she asked Esa, 'We're headed back to Lesvos, aren't we?'

Because she sounded as though she wasn't certain of her role, Esa nodded. To Lise Cloutier he said, 'If we find your courier, this Sami al-Nuri, what will happen to his request for asylum now that we've turned in his files?'

Cloutier's response was brisk. 'Sami is a priority for us, we'll make sure he lands on his feet. We need to protect his identity so he can testify once we go to trial.'

'How long will that take?' Sehr asked.

Cloutier mimed a gesture of dismissal. 'You're a bright young woman, mademoiselle. I'm sure you understand as well as I do the lack of political will. Maybe one day, they'll send Assad to The Hague. At any rate, we'll be ready.'

Esa could see that Sehr didn't require further explanation. And he wondered if he could speak to her comfortably, at least about the case.

'What about Israa and Aya?'

Cloutier looked back at Sehr, her composure unruffled, her certainty intact. 'You've handed over Sami's leverage.'

At the ready distress that sprang to Sehr's eyes, she added, 'Inspector Khattak *does* have a direct line to Ambassador Mansur.'

It shouldn't have surprised him that Cloutier knew more about him than she'd disclosed, or that she knew the players involved in orchestrating Syrian resettlement in Canada. It was tied in to her work, and though she was working at CIJA in an independent capacity, she was still a Canadian national.

She was getting ready to depart, so Khattak repeated his question. 'Hospital 601. What can you tell us about it?'

'Any number of horrifying things that would rob you of your sleep.' She cut off Khattak's protest. 'You might have seen a little in those boxes, but if you haven't seen the Caesar files, you've barely scratched the surface. Hospital 601 sits at the base of Mount Mezzeh. The presidential palace is perched at the top, which should give you some idea of how closely the regime is tied to the Mukhabarat's atrocities. Detainees are brought to the hospital – they think for treatment for the brutality they've endured. At the hospital, they're assigned numbers instead of names. Hospital 601 is a slaughter house.'

A young man arrived to collect Cloutier. Khattak handed over the keys to their car, to allow for the transfer of boxes.

Appalled, Sehr asked Cloutier, 'How do you make sense of it all? How do you count the dead?'

Her face severe, Cloutier answered, 'I'll count each one at The Hague.'

35

'SHOULD I GO ON TO Brussels?' Sehr asked.

If Audrey had gone on to Brussels, it might be necessary to follow her trail to Belgium. But Sehr had no contact name and no specific idea of what Audrey had been doing there. At the camp in Calais, Matthieu Arnaud hadn't been able to clear this up. She'd be visiting the mission with no idea of what she was searching for. She would have been grateful for the distance from Esa, but Audrey's disappearance was her priority as well.

Esa took out a note case from the inside of his jacket. He scanned a typewritten list before he passed it to Sehr.

'I think we've cleared up the question of what brought Audrey to the Netherlands.' He didn't smile at her, but his voice was a little warmer as he offered, 'You did excellent work on CIJA. You would have made a fine detective.'

A young couple walking hand in hand passed them on the narrow street, causing Esa to move closer. Sehr took a step back. Esa's face tightened. With impatience or anger, she couldn't tell. She pushed past the moment. 'We're each doing what we can.'

He nodded at the list. 'I was wondering if instead of returning with me, you could make sure we haven't missed anything. Those are the numbers Audrey called while she was in Delft, as connected to locations she visited. I did a cursory check: the storage unit wasn't her only stop.'

'The others could be places where she met Cloutier. One of them could be CIJA headquarters.'

'Cloutier wasn't forthcoming, but we shouldn't ignore other leads.' Esa's eyes narrowed against the sun. He brushed away a leaf that had landed on his shoulder.

Sehr looked away from his face, focusing on the list. She knew he was pushing her away – this time she didn't mind. There was a new look on his face, a fragility behind his eyes. He wasn't going to share what was bothering him, unless it was with Rachel. He was heading back to Lesvos because he wanted to talk to Rachel.

Pretending to be absorbed in the list, she said, 'I'll be glad to rule out these leads. Should I drive you to the airport first?'

'I'll take a cab, you keep the car. And take these as well, they might open a few doors.' He passed over the letters of introduction from Roux and from Ambassador Mansur. 'Sehr –'

She looked up. He was watching her with an unusual intensity. 'When you come back to Lesvos, I'll meet you at the airport. We need time to talk without the pressure of what's been happening.' Though her pulse had begun to race, Sehr tried not to read too much into his words. She nodded, not knowing he'd read the hope in her face, or that he'd taken heart from it. It wasn't a victory he'd earned or one she would have wanted him to have.

When she'd gone, he made a call to Ambassador Mansur, a call she answered on the first ring, the warmth in her voice fading to horror as he told her about the connection to CIJA.

'What do you think has happened to Audrey? Was this the reason she was taken? Did she make herself a target in the eyes of someone at Camp Apaydin?'

He could hear the worry behind the questions, the shadow it would cast over Canada's efforts at easing the refugee crisis if Apaydin became seen as an escape route for Assad's men.

'I don't know,' he told her frankly. 'I haven't looked at the politics of this, only at the crisis. The situation on the islands is bleak; now that the borders have closed, we're effectively talking about detention in these camps.'

Camille Mansur's voice softened. 'You are new to this, *habibi,* or you'd know that's what all these places are. Think of Zaatari in Jordan. It's an end in itself. There's no going forward for hundreds of thousands of people.'

Esa didn't want to hear this. He didn't want to confront the reality of it, though he'd seen it in Souda, Kara Tepe... Moria. He discussed his suspicions for a few minutes more; at the end of the call, Ambassador Mansur promised to convey his concerns to the prime minister.

'You'll be careful, yes? You have too much experience not to know where to draw the line.'

He reassured her the best he could, though he knew he couldn't have said where that line was, or where he wanted it to be.

Mytilene, Lesvos

In the bar, Rachel was surrounded by a group of men who joked with each other loudly, though she suspected their banter covered their feelings of despair.

Two-thirds of those who'd made the crossing the previous night had drowned. The Greek Coast Guard and the Hellenic Rescue Team were still fishing bodies out of the water. Whether the bodies would be identified, whether their families would ever learn what had happened to them, Rachel wished she knew. She didn't ask – she could see that her new friends were drinking to forget.

Peter Conroy's pale skin had flushed red with his consumption of too many beers. He'd become verbose and was regaling Vincenzo with stories about the Top End, a region of Australia Rachel was fairly certain Conroy had never seen. Vincenzo egged him on – the outlandish size of crocodiles in the north grew bigger with each telling.

The door opened and though Rachel was expecting Khattak, it was Eleni Latsoudi and Shukri Danner who entered. Eleni was still dressed in her rescue gear, and Shukri was wearing a warm coat because she'd been at Eftalou Beach. Her head covering was drenched at the ends.

Rachel shifted to another table and beckoned the women to join her.

They'd spent part of the night together, scouting for boats. They'd all been present when the dead had reached their shores.

Their table was near the fire, and as Eleni stripped off her helmet to shake out her blond hair, several of the men turned to look. Illario Benemerito wasn't one of them. He'd bought Rachel a beer, and now he tipped his glass at her.

Rachel ordered Shukri a non-alcoholic cider, surprised to learn the bar kept a variety of non-alcoholic drinks available for their new contingent of customers. Vincenzo, as drunk as Conroy, gestured rudely at Shukri.

'What's she doing here? We don't need her kind in here, they're everywhere as it is.'

A sharp rebuke from Benemerito silenced him.

Shukri ignored the commotion. She huddled close to the fire, and unlike the men, the three women talked over the night's activities. Both Eleni and Shukri asked after Khattak; Rachel responded with a sigh.

'His flight has landed. He should be here any minute.'

Rachel had been waiting for this moment. She placed a folder on the table between the two women. She asked a pointed question. 'When the shots were fired at Kara Tepe, did either of you visit the crime scene?'

Both women shook their heads, clearly surprised.

'And you, Ms Danner, when you were summoned to Athens by the police, were you shown pictures of the victims? Were you taken to the morgue?'

Sipping at her cider, Shukri answered no.

Rachel opened the folder. She showed them the photograph of Aude Bertin. Another one of the dead to add to the weight of what they'd witnessed.

'Ah, God rest her,' Eleni said.

Rachel showed them the photograph of the boy in the morgue. Shukri set down her glass with a thump. The three women ignored the shouts of laughter from the next table.

She muttered a formula that Rachel recognized as one she'd heard from Khattak. *From God we come, to God we return.*

Except that Shukri chanted it more like a spell, a warding off of evil.

Eleni's eyes widened. 'What happened to this poor boy?'

'You don't recognize him?' Rachel asked, watching their faces. Shukri looked up. 'Of course I do. But the police said Sami al-Nuri was killed.'

'Alongside Agent Bertin, you mean.'

'Yes.' Shukri nodded vigorously. 'This doesn't make sense.'

'Why?' Rachel asked, a keen light in her eyes.

'Because this isn't Sami al-Nuri.'

Lowering her voice, Shukri told them the boy's real name. Rachel caught her breath, her suspicions confirmed. She slid the photograph back into the folder.

'Who identified this body as Sami's?'

Bemused, Shukri spread her hands. Eleni took another swallow of her beer.

'Was it the French Interpol agent?' Eleni and Shukri exchanged a glance before Eleni spoke. 'I think it was. Inspecteur Roux is her name.'

'You met her?' Rachel asked sharply.

'She conducted interviews with everyone who'd spoken to Agent Bertin.'

'She's not on the island now.' Rachel had done some investigating of her own. 'The Greek police told me she caught a flight off-island earlier today. Did either of you know that?'

A trail of steam was rising from Eleni's gear. She patted down her arms with a napkin. Illario stopped by their table.

'Can I help in any way?' he asked. 'You look worried.'

The door to the bar opened. Rachel looked up with relief. 'No,' she said. 'Thank you. Inspector Khattak is here.'

36

Kara Tepe, Lesvos

THEY TOOK A TAXI UP the road to Kara Tepe. They moved between the row of tents, past the Woman to Woman headquarters, which was still marked off as a crime scene. They moved down opposite lanes, looking for signs of the boy.

A stone skidded past Rachel on the path. It was nearly midnight but Aya wasn't asleep. She waved at them from her tent.

Rachel whistled at Khattak. He followed her lead to the tent. It wasn't raining, but the night air was cold. Aya ran up to Rachel and hugged her. Khattak ducked into the tent. There were two sleeping bags on one side of the tent; Ali rested on one, the other side was occupied by an elderly man and his grandchildren. Ali sat up on his elbows and waved.

'What is it?' His voice was husky. 'Is it Israa? Did you find her?'

Khattak shook his head. 'Come outside.'

Rachel gathered Aya up in her arms. They commandeered a set of plastic chairs.

'We found Ali Maydani,' Khattak said.

The boy rocketed to his feet. 'What are you talking about?' he demanded. '*I'm* Ali Maydani.'

'But you're not, are you?' Khattak said. 'Your real name is Sami al-Nuri.'

There was no moon to ride the slow, hypnotic pitch of the waves. Rachel and Khattak used their flashlights, making their way along the shore, the boy they now knew as Sami walking ahead, Aya skipping behind, fresh and full of excitement.

'Tell us,' Khattak said to the boy. 'You can trust me, I won't let any harm come to you.'

And Rachel remembered when Khattak had said as much to her in a town called Waverley. A knot formed in her throat. She believed Khattak's promises.

The boy seemed to be weighing Khattak as an adversary. In a voice warm with empathy, Khattak said, 'I prayed at your side in Izmir. I view that as a trust.'

Sami kicked at stones on the beach, ducking his head to hide the tears in his eyes. 'I know you do,' he said. 'But I once thought a Syrian would never kill another Syrian.'

They let him have a moment, the waves bleeding into silence at his feet.

At last, Khattak asked, 'Were you in the tent when the shots were fired? Were you the one who fired them?'

The boy brushed the tears from his face with both hands. 'No. But it was my fault.'

Aya ran up to Rachel and clutched her hand, sensing the oppression of the moment. Rachel gave her an encouraging squeeze.

'Why do you say that?'

'Agent Bertin asked to meet me at Woman to Woman. She said she had news about Israa. A boat was coming in and I wanted to wait and see if Israa was on the boat, so I told Ali to go ahead without me. We had almost made it back to camp when I heard the gunshots.'

'You knew they came from Woman to Woman?'

'Yes.' He swallowed. 'You could tell. So I ran the rest of the way.'

'Did you get there before the police did?'

He nodded. 'I didn't touch anything other than his papers. I just looked to see if I could help.' He began to cry. 'I couldn't.

They were already dead.' His eyes wide and haunted, he said, 'I've seen the dead, so I knew.'

When Rachel would have gathered up Aya and left Khattak with Sami, he waved a hand at her. 'Aya has seen the dead, too. You don't need to protect her.'

'Did you see who shot Agent Bertin and Ali Maydani?'

Sami shivered in the night air, though Khattak had bought him a thicker coat in Izmir. It was the shiver of a boy who felt the presence of ghosts at his heels.

'There was so much noise and confusion. Everyone who'd been on the beach seemed to be rushing to camp. Peter, Shukri, Vincenzo. Even Octavio, the owner of the bar.'

'Peter Conroy was on the beach?' Rachel interrupted to ask. He shouldn't have been. He should have been on Chios. Yet, just as he was tonight, Peter was here on Lesvos with his same group of friends.

'He was the first person to reach me on the hill. He didn't see me at the tent. I don't think anyone did.'

'And of course, you didn't confess you'd been there,' Rachel said.

'How could I? If I ended up in detention, what would happen to Aya?'

'Shukri knew the boy who was killed wasn't Sami al-Nuri. She told us his name is Ali Maydani. She must know who you are, as well.'

'She does, because she helped me register when we landed. But I've stayed out of sight since Ali was killed, so she doesn't know about the mix-up.'

Khattak cut in. 'Then who identified the body in the morgue as yours?'

The boy's lips trembled. 'I put my identification on the body. I have documents in Arabic that don't have a photograph attached. And I took Ali's papers for myself.'

'But everyone here has been calling you Ali. And you've known at least some of them for some time... Commander Benemerito, Vincenzo. Perhaps Peter Conroy.'

'Except for when we registered with Shukri, I told everyone I *was* Ali. I did it to keep him safe.'

They had come to the edge of the stony beach that bled into a boardwalk with a ledge. Rachel set Aya down on the ledge and sat down beside her. Sami came to a halt, his throat working as he tried to tell them the rest. Khattak placed an arm around his shoulders.

'It's all right,' he said. 'Whatever it is, we'll handle it together.' He held on to the boy, offering his protection.

Sami struggled to continue.

'You know the things I told you at Camp Apaydin? The reason we went there, the reason Audrey took us there?'

Khattak nodded. Rachel could see from the resolve in his face that he'd already guessed the answer.

'Ali was able to point out the defectors who shouldn't have been offered refuge at the camp. They were torturers, murderers. They committed terrible crimes.' He shuddered. 'They committed those crimes against *Ali*. The Turkish authorities didn't know. Or maybe they did, and were bribed to look the other way. Maybe the camp is guarded so people like me don't ask questions.'

'That explains the injuries on Ali's body. Was he a protester? Is that why he was tortured?'

Sami shook his head. 'Worse, much worse,' he whispered. 'Ali was a member of the Syria Civil Defense in Aleppo. He was captured by Assad's troops when he was wounded in a bombing. He was transferred into the hands of the Mukhabarat.'

And when they looked at him, confused, he explained, 'Ali was a White Helmet.'

Shocked, Rachel found herself whispering as well, 'The White Helmets? The ambulance service that rescues people from the bombs? Ali was just a boy.'

Sami shrugged. 'Maybe you can't tell from the body at the

morgue, but Ali was twenty-two. There are younger volunteers who work with the Civil Defense. We don't have much choice, because we are all we have.'

The blue-black tones of the night lent a poignancy to Sami's words. Khattak cleared a constriction in his throat.

'How did Ali escape the Mukhabarat? His body is covered in the signs of their work.'

'He was transferred to Damascus because of his value as a prop. His family is well placed so they were able to arrange what they thought was his rescue by paying an enormous bribe. He was sent to Military Hospital 601.'

Khattak's head snapped up. He'd explained his findings to Rachel on their walk up to Kara Tepe, speaking with an unfeigned distress that told her more than he knew.

'Military Hospital 601 is an extension of the detention system.'

Sami's hands balled into fists. A profound relief lit his eyes. 'You *know*,' he said. 'Finally, someone knows.'

'It was in the boxes,' Rachel explained. 'The boxes Audrey took to Delft.'

Khattak cut across her words, his own question urgent. 'How could Ali have escaped from Hospital 601?'

Sami crammed his fist into his mouth. He was on the verge of hyperventilating.

Khattak eased his hand away, murmuring in an undertone. 'Trust me,' he said to the boy. 'Tell me so I can help.'

'I was an assistant at the hospital. I helped the military photographer photograph the bodies, and I delivered the bodies to the transfer vans for burial. Ali was nearly dead when he arrived at 601. Before they could do anything more to him, I took him to the loading bay. One of the drivers was my cousin. He let me ride in the van and dropped us both at my house. The transfers take place in the dark. I smuggled Ali into our house. Israa took over his care, and I went back to work. I needed to alter the records so no one would know. I deleted his photograph from hospital records.'

'Why?' Rachel asked, shocked by the risks the boy had taken. 'Why save Ali instead of someone else?'

'I was planning to leave Damascus within the next few days. And I thought – I thought I should take someone with me. It was a place of death – the stink of death was in every breath I took. I was sent to Ali's hospital room and I saw – I saw...'

'What did you see?' Khattak asked gently. 'Tell me. Get it out of your mind.'

'He was lying on his bed with his eyes closed but he was holding up one finger.' Sami showed them the gesture, raising his right index finger, the others tightly furled. 'He was reciting the *shahadah*. I took that for a sign.'

It was the fourth body Sami had taken to the hospital from Branch 215, the branch they called 'the branch of death.' Over the course of ten days, Sami had transported forty bodies from the prison whose inhumane conditions were merely a respite from torture. The prisoners lived in filthy surroundings, sometimes for months and years, subject to slow starvation, drinking from toilets, their clothes disintegrating in the heat, suffering from a range of diseases, the least of which was mental breakdown. If they survived the shabeh *and the* basat al-reeh, *they were tortured by other means.*

He was down to his final death of the day, transporting the body from the hospital to the garage, the morgue too full to receive it. He waited while the forensic doctor assigned the body a number and wrote up his brief report. The body was photographed – this one bearing unspeakable deformities. When the photographer was finished, the doctor ordered Sami to wrap the body in plastic. He caught a glimpse of the cause of death: heart failure. Only two verdicts were recorded: heart or respiratory failure, neither an accurate reflection of the actual cause of death.

The morgue was out of plastic sheeting because the week had been busier than usual. The prisoners who'd been transferred from

Aleppo to Damascus were members of the Civil Defense. As far as Sami knew, no White Helmet had lived to speak of his heroism. He knew their commitment to the wounded was entrenched; he wished he was working with them.

The guard he was partnered with gave him a blanket to cover the body. He wrote the name of the body on a card, along with the ID number the doctor had assigned. The card was tucked inside the prisoner's underwear. Sami carried the body to the entrance of the garage for removal. The processing session was over. He looked at the man's face – he always looked at the faces. And he tallied up the deaths for the week, his heart a stone in his chest. He knew he was less than human. He was so tired he didn't care.

His partner went for a cigarette break.

Deciding in an instant to do it, Sami raced back to the morgue. The photographs were stored on the morgue's computer. He hid in a doorway, waiting for the photographer to finish up his work. He had a minute, maybe two, before his partner returned. When the photographer left, he slipped into the morgue. He downloaded the week's cache of information onto the drive in his pocket. Sweating with fear, he wedged the drive into the toe of his boot.

By the time his partner returned, Sami was leaning against the outer wall. Basil dropped him off at night: it was the regime's way of monitoring his actions. But Basil was too lazy to be vigilant. Most nights, he had a wife he was eager to get home to.

Sami wanted to ask Basil's wife if she knew how many bodies her husband's hands had disposed of, but he'd have to ask the same question of himself.

Basil was holding a blanket. 'There's another one. They don't think he'll make it, poor bastard.'

He called all the dead 'poor bastards.'

Though Sami's heart clenched in his chest, he nodded. 'Let's go.'

Basil tossed him the blanket. 'You go, I'm meeting friends.'

Sami made a token protest. He knew it was his partner's night to gamble. Basil was watching him. 'You'll get yourself home when you're done?'

'I've got nowhere else to go.'

There was nowhere he could go if he didn't want to join the bodies in the morgue. He was conscious of the thumb drive in his shoe. He'd been expecting to go straight home, where he would have hidden the drive until the end of the next week's shift. He had to be careful not to lose it. If anyone saw the photographs, they'd match the numbers on the bodies to his shift. Then he'd be sent to 215, if he wasn't shot at first sight.

Basil pointed him to a room. 'There's a jihadi in there. If he's not already dead, it won't be too long now.'

When Basil left, Sami crept into the room. A nurse in a mask nodded at him as she left the room. Sami looked over at the bed. The young man lying on it had a battered face. He didn't look like a trained jihadi – he was weak, probably starved, he didn't have an overgrown beard. He wasn't hooked up to any of the monitors. He wasn't being treated; he was being watched.

When Sami made a careless sound, the young man's eyes flickered open. He whispered something to Sami. Sami looked down at his hand. The prisoner's finger was moving. He was praying, preparing for death. He was so small and slight, so certain of his fate, meeting it with more grace than Sami would ever possess.

He made his decision in a heartbeat.

He threw the blanket over the prisoner, carrying him out into the hallway. He passed the nurse, who seemed to be expecting it, and made for the garage. He was taking a terrible risk, but what was the point of going on if he didn't? Everything hinged on his cousin showing up as the driver of the van. The prisoner would probably die either way.

The risk was worth it to Sami.

Khattak cradled the sobbing boy to his chest, looking at Rachel over his head. She'd missed the significance of Sami's words, but he understood why a boy who believed he was at the end of his life would want to leave the world with the *shahadah* on his lips – testifying to the oneness of God, to Muhammad as His messenger. It was the submission of a believer.

Torture was meant to rend the individual from himself, to divorce him from reality as he was stricken of every hope. In his darkest hour, Ali had clung to a cornerstone of his faith.

The perverse degradation of the Muhammad stick touched Khattak's thoughts again, firing his mind with outrage.

How could You? rang the helpless echo of his thoughts. *How could You let this happen?*

He held the boy until he was calm, then asked the question he'd picked out from the summary of Ali's ordeal.

'*You* were CIJA's courier, weren't you? That's why you returned to the border, why you and Ali risked that visit to Camp Apaydin. *Ali* was the third passenger on that bus ride, not Aya. You were collecting documents smuggled out of Damascus. You asked Audrey to get them to The Hague.'

Sami sank down on the ledge beside Rachel. Aya climbed into his lap and linked her arms around his neck, trying to console him.

He gave Khattak a searching look. 'Both of us were at risk. I might have been recognized as a defector from 601, though they couldn't have known I smuggled out the photographs. Or that there were other defectors in Apaydin who had passed me physical records – orders from the CMC. And Ali might have been recognized as a member of the Civil Defense. We thought, between the two of us, his was the more dangerous identity, because military intelligence had had him for so long. So I took on his name, he took on mine, in case we were being followed.'

'By a member of the Mukhabarat who slipped into the camp?'

'We saw faces we recognized at Apaydin. They may have recognized us, too. We didn't know who'd made it to the islands. If they knew we could identify them – they may have meant to kill Ali.' His hand stroked over Aya's curls. 'Or I might have been the target, and Agent Bertin was in the way.'

It seemed possible, even plausible, to Khattak.

Two people murdered to protect the identity of someone who'd done much worse. He'd felt the creeping dread of Apaydin, the suspicion on all sides, though he knew the camp's inhabitants were mainly those who'd refused to prosecute Assad's war.

He was left with the question of whether Audrey had witnessed the shooting; she might have been in hiding from someone at Apaydin. Which made him consider whether Agent Bertin was involved in the transmission of files to CIJA. War crimes and crimes against humanity fell under Interpol's ambit.

'Was Agent Bertin helping you? Was that her connection to Audrey?'

'Audrey was helping me. I didn't know anyone else.' Sami's young face looked anxious. Khattak decided to push him harder. 'Did you see Audrey that night at the tent?'

Sami twisted his hands together.

'I can't help you unless you tell me everything.'

Aya spoke up in a soft, sweet voice. 'Miss Audrey was there. She ran from the tent to the beach. We chased her.'

Sami's face went pale. 'No, we didn't,' he said to Aya. 'You weren't with me.'

Aya's head bobbed. 'Yes, I was. I followed you, you didn't see me.' Khattak pinned Sami with a razor-sharp glance. 'So Audrey *was* there that night. Did you follow her to the beach?'

The words he'd held back now tumbled from Sami's lips. 'I saw her run from the tent. She took a different path down to the beach. Someone was chasing her – I couldn't see who it was – it was just a shadow. When Audrey reached the road, there was a van waiting with its lights off. The person who was chasing her hit me on the head. I heard a cry, I heard the van drive away. When I got to the road, she was gone.'

'Did you recognize the van? Could you see a license plate?'

'It looked like a tourist van, it was white with big black windows.'

'Can you tell us anything else about it?'

The boy's chest heaved with a sob. 'I couldn't *see* anything else. The van was old. It was dirty with mud from the road.'

Rachel patted his shoulder. 'Why didn't you tell anyone what you'd seen? The police have been looking for Audrey – this information could have helped them.'

Khattak knew the answer, even if Rachel didn't.

Sami hadn't known who to trust.

37

The Hague, the Netherlands

SEHR'S FEET WERE ACHING. SHE'D been to every address associated with a credit card purchase on the list Esa had given her, and she hadn't turned up anything more than cafés, restaurants, and a whimsical antique store.

She'd saved the address in The Hague for last because she thought it was most likely connected to the role Audrey had been playing as a courier for CIJA. On her first day in the Netherlands, Audrey had taken a train from Schiphol Airport in Amsterdam to The Hague Central Station. Sehr mapped the location on her phone and drove herself to the station. She parked her car, strolling over to Hague Central to take a look around.

The blue glass construction was a recently renovated paean to modernism – it loomed over the square like a butcher's block edged in steel. The signage was clear inside, and directions to the numerous platforms were relatively easy to follow. Audrey had purchased a tram ticket from the station; Sehr spent a few minutes orienting herself until she found the track for Tram 1. She purchased a ticket for herself, boarded the tram, and a few minutes later, she exited at the World Forum, a gleaming convention center in the heart of the city that hosted regular trade fair business. She didn't enter the building because she couldn't see why Audrey would have come here. There was a directory in the middle of the giant outdoor park, close to a pond fronted by small green shrubs. She parsed it carefully. Audrey had made no other purchases that would narrow down her destination: there were several hotels, a museum, an opera center, the World Forum itself – and then, to one side, the International Criminal Tribunal for the former Yugoslavia.

She hadn't forgotten the Drayton inquiry that Rachel and Esa had been embroiled in – but she couldn't see how the tribunal would be relevant to Audrey's disappearance. She was about to give up and find a bench so she could call Esa for clarification when from the corner of her vision she caught sight of three concrete buildings sheeted in glass, arranged like a series of blocks. From a distance, they seemed ominous and impressive. She was in the international zone – was it possible the buildings represented the United Nations? Flags lined the pathway that led to the first of the concrete blocks.

Sehr checked the directory for further elucidation. She checked again to be sure.

She followed the trail of flags, her pounding heart telling her she was on the right trail. She cast a glance over her shoulder, not certain why she was nervous. The day was bright and warm; the people around her were a mix of bureaucrats and tourists.

Hastening her pace, she found herself in front of the complex and saw that the three blocks were attached to a central base. A royal blue flag with a circle of yellow stars looked familiar. More familiar was the sign bearing the building's name.

She'd discovered Europol's headquarters.

When she tried to obtain admission through the visitors' entrance, she was told very pleasantly she required written permission that could be obtained through the website. She asked to speak to someone in authority, showing the gatekeeper her letters of introduction. Phone calls were made and quiet conferences were held between sober-faced, immaculately uniformed personnel.

Sehr fidgeted with the strap of her computer bag, which had scorched a trail of fire down her shoulder. Her nervous fidgeting drew the staff's attention. A man in his forties with white-blond hair directed her to place her bag and purse on the security belt. Her possessions were searched, her passport and driver's license scrutinized, but she was treated with excessive courtesy. She walked through a security gate to be wanded by a woman who bore a passing resemblance to Audrey. After these rituals were completed, she was led to a windowless room, halfway down a corridor. She wished now that she'd texted Esa about her discoveries, or her present location. She could see her phone and laptop were not likely to be returned in time for her to do so.

On the other hand, no one had confiscated them for forensic analysis. When she was asked to state her business, she wiped a sticky strand of hair from her forehead and said, 'I'm inquiring about Audrey Clare, a Canadian citizen who is missing in Greece. I'd like to know who she met with at Europol. It would help us in our search.'

The man with white-blond hair and nearly transparent eyes nodded once. He left the room, taking Sehr's purse and computer, and shutting the door behind him.

She glanced around the room. It was the kind of office that might be loaned to visiting colleagues, bland and impersonal with its metal filing cabinets and sleek glass desk. Her mind was sorting through her memories of Europol's mandate. It was clearly distinct from Interpol's, yet there was a leather note case on the desk bearing the Interpol logo.

She picked up the case and opened it. A pad of lined paper was covered with writing in French. Sehr's French was adequate; she made a quick survey of the page, frowning when she caught sight of Audrey Clare's name followed by the words *trafiquants d'être humains*. She was startled to see her own name linked with Esa's.

She didn't have her phone to photograph the page, but if she acted quickly, she could rip out the page and take it, assuming she wasn't detained.

She didn't have long to think it over. She'd just raised her hand to tear out the sheet when the door opened and a woman's voice said, 'I wouldn't do that if I were you.'

Slowly, Sehr turned around. She recognized the woman because they had met in Athens, after the murders on Lesvos. She was the French liaison with Interpol.

Her name was Amélie Roux.

'So you found me,' Roux said. She took the seat across from Sehr. Confused, Sehr said, 'Weren't you just in Turkey with Inspector Khattak?'

'He mentioned you were heading to Delft, so I knew you were getting close.'

'Close to what?' Sehr knew better than to mention CIJA until the other woman confirmed her suspicions. Was it Inspecteur Roux who'd gotten Audrey involved as a courier for CIJA? But war crimes didn't fall under Europol's mandate. Europol was the EU's criminal intelligence agency. So what had brought Audrey here? Had she come to meet Inspecteur Roux?

'You're not investigating Agent Bertin's murder, are you?'

'On the contrary, I assure you I am. Agent Bertin was a member of a Europol Joint Investigations Team – she involved me because she used to work for me.'

That didn't clear anything up for Sehr. 'Why is Interpol involved?'

'Because Europol is a criminal intelligence agency that does not operate outside of Europe, and Turkey is not a member of the European Union, despite existing cooperation agreements.'

Sehr was lost, trying to put the pieces together. 'Do you think Audrey killed your friend? Is that your connection to this case?'

'No, mademoiselle. You completely misunderstand. Audrey Clare came to us. She asked us for our help. We would have found our way to Lesvos eventually because it was tangential to our investigation.'

Sehr puzzled this through. Knowing she shouldn't be the first to put it in words, she did anyway. 'Did Audrey ask you to assist her in getting proof of war crimes to CIJA? Were you waiting for a courier in Apaydin?'

'What? No.' Roux gave an impatient toss of her head. 'This isn't about war crimes. Europol has nothing to do with the Turkey-Syria border.'

Sehr stared at the other woman. 'Then why did Audrey come to see you?'

'It's very simple, mademoiselle. She came because of Israa.'

The uniformed guard knocked on the door. He was carrying a tray of coffee that he set down on the table. A thousand questions crowded Sehr's mind. It was evident now that Roux was investigating more than the death of her colleague. Her presence at Europol confirmed this. Her knowledge of Audrey's activities was proof of the same. But she seemed to be suggesting a different track than the one Esa and Sehr had pursued. She wondered if they'd finally reached the point where Roux would tell them the truth. She ventured a tentative question.

'Are you saying Audrey wasn't acting as a courier for CIJA? I've seen the documents myself.'

Roux was unflustered by Sehr's keen appraisal. 'I know you have. That's why I'm here. We've worked at cross-purposes too long.'

Sehr choked back a protest at the injustice of this remark. It was Amélie Roux who had kept them in the dark, Roux who could have put them on the right track from the start. Guessing at her thoughts, Roux said, 'I had no reason to trust a costly and sensitive operation to your discretion. I didn't know you, I didn't know what your government's role was, or where your loyalties lay. So I waited to see what you would do.'

Sehr sat back in her chair, making her face a blank. 'And now? Did something change your mind? Is that why you came here to meet me?'

Roux tipped her head to one side. 'You left me no choice. I couldn't have you blundering into the path of our operation. You've learned all you can on your own. It's time we worked together.'

Sehr understood the nuances Roux chose not to make explicit. By surrendering the documents in Audrey's locker to CIJA, she and Esa had proven themselves to Roux. Their loyalty to Audrey hadn't served as an excuse to obstruct justice.

Getting to the point, Sehr said, 'You said this was about Israa. Was Israa the courier? Was she Audrey's contact?'

Roux looked at her with a faintly pitying expression. 'Audrey never met Israa. Nor did she disclose anything beyond what was necessary about her work with CIJA. She assisted their courier, nothing more. But in the course of that work, she came to realize she was hearing stories about disappearances.'

Sehr nodded. 'As a function of Syria's prison system.'

Inspecteur Roux offered Sehr an espresso, taking a long sip of hers. Her fingers tapped impatiently on the table.

'No, mademoiselle. I refer to disappearances along the refugee route. Unaccompanied minors are missing from the route – we suspect in the thousands. You haven't read the report Europol released in January?'

Dumbfounded, Sehr shook her head. 'But then – are you talking about human *trafficking*? Is that why Audrey came to you?'

'Yes,' Roux said. 'I told you. She came about the girl, Israa.'

'I thought Israa drowned at sea.'

'Not true, mademoiselle. Miss Clare paid a great deal of money to find out what happened to the girl. Israa didn't drown – she was kidnapped.'

'Audrey told you this?'

'She didn't need to. The Joint Investigations Team has been investigating traffickers for years. Agent Bertin's team was composed of members of different EU nations – law enforcement, prosecutors, judges. I'm involved because France is the lead nation coordinating the operation. Agent Bertin's team accumulated substantial evidence that unaccompanied children were falling prey to exploitation. Criminal gangs have taken advantage of the refugee flow. I did try to suggest as much to your colleagues in Izmir.' She broke off to mull this over, managing to convey her disappointment. 'The efforts of these gangs have intensified in the past eighteen months. They're cooperating with each other: there are those who smuggle refugees into Europe, and those who exploit the vulnerable for slavery or sex or both. Israa was *held back* from her boat in Turkey. Aya was luckier than her sister.'

Sehr sipped her coffee, gripped by Roux's revelations. She listened as Roux laid out the JIT's case. The number of unaccompanied minors had been estimated at 27 percent of the previous year's arrivals in Europe. Of the staggering number of 270,000 children in transit, Europol had *conservatively* estimated that 10,000 children were unaccounted for.

'Children have gone missing in Italy, Sweden, and the UK. But a disproportionate number of minors are missing from the Turkish coast. If they're snatched before they're registered in Europe, they simply disappear. If they register a destination such as the UK and don't arrive, there's no way to track where they've ended up. We don't have the systems in place, we don't have personnel or resources.'

Of all the terrible permutations of the refugee crisis, this was one Sehr hadn't considered. She'd been distracted by the discovery of the documents in Delft. But Audrey had begun in Izmir – her thoughts cleared in an instant.

'The counterfeit life jackets made Audrey think about the factories. From the news reports on the police operation, she knew Syrian children had been conscripted to work there – is that when she began to suspect the smugglers had widened their operations? She thought they were targeting children?'

Inspecteur Roux looked at her with satisfaction. 'You're

very bright. From her inquiries, Audrey learned of other disappearances. So she began to track them.'

'Is Israa lost, then?'

Her face hardening, Roux said, 'There is a massive team working on this. Israa is not irrecoverable. Neither are the others.'

Sehr tried another tack. 'So you don't think Audrey vanished out of choice?'

'I think she was taken as a means of silencing her.'

'And killed?' Sehr asked. 'Or trafficked?'

Roux's response was frank. 'Audrey called to tell us she was on the cusp of confirming the identity of the ringleaders of the gang operating in Greece and Turkey. She was afraid to share her suspicions without proof, so we sent Agent Bertin to assist her. Agent Bertin knew the full parameters of the JIT operation in Europe; we knew she'd be able to connect the dots in Greece. Whatever else Audrey was in the middle of, she made it back to Lesvos for that meeting. She prioritized it. It's evident someone found out about that meeting, someone with a reason to prevent it. It's possible they killed Audrey, but if her body had been found with the others, this would be a different investigation. Your government's involvement would put a spotlight on the traffickers.' She sighed. 'Disappearing Audrey was safer than leaving her body to be found.'

Roux's purpose on Lesvos was becoming clear to Sehr. 'You're not looking for Audrey. You're looking for the leaders of the ring.'

'Bon,' Roux said. 'That has been the focus of Agent Bertin's work since the beginning of the refugee crisis; we are not about to abandon it. And now you know enough to help us.'

Sehr swallowed the urge to scream. So much time had been wasted in the search for Audrey because of a Europol investigation they'd known nothing about. She didn't intend to waste another minute.

'Why did Audrey go to Calais? Why the trip to Brussels?'

'She was tracking the smuggling route, confirming her

suspicions to herself. Children from the Calais Jungle are also unaccounted for. But Brussels, mademoiselle, don't you know what took her to Brussels?'

Sehr bristled at the censure. She'd pieced together as much as she had in the face of Roux's calculated silence.

'I *don't* know and I don't want to guess.'

Roux's tight smile acknowledged Sehr's anger. She handed over Sehr's bag. 'Missing Children Europe is the organization that highlights these issues: their headquarters is in Brussels. Audrey went to Brussels so she could sound the alarm. Missing Children referred her to me. That's how this all began.'

38

SHOWERED AND RESTING FROM THE detour of the past two days, Rachel was at the Sirena guesthouse. Sehr had called her from Amsterdam to pass on a long list of facts that made Rachel curl up her hands, her nails biting into her palms. Sehr was furious at Roux. Rachel tried not to be distracted by a similar sense of outrage. What a waste of time it had been. Roux hadn't needed to accompany them to Apaydin because she'd been ahead of them. She'd known the reason for Audrey's visit to Apaydin – she'd had an outline to work with.

Rachel sat down with her notebook and a pencil whose eraser she'd chewed off, working out what they now knew about Audrey's activities. Audrey had been working on two parallel tracks, tracks that didn't overlap, as far as Rachel could tell. Of greatest importance: she'd been assisting Ali – or Sami, as she must now remember to call him – with his search for Israa. Sami was the key to Audrey's actions. Everything Audrey had done sprang from her relationship with Sami. Sami was the one who'd directed her course, who'd driven her actions forward. He'd trusted her to help him find Israa, he'd trusted her to aid his precarious work as a courier. But Audrey had trusted no one, crushed by her responsibilities and by the weight of her secrets.

She'd tried to help a boy she'd grown to care for, only to find herself floundering in the depths, swept up by dangerous currents.

She could have told Nate why she'd needed more money, but she must have been afraid of tipping someone off; she'd kept her network closed because she'd gotten in over her head. She could have asked for help, she *should* have asked for help. But maybe she was more like Ruksh than Rachel had guessed, determined to prove something to her brother.

Either of the tracks Sami had persuaded her to pursue could be the reason for the murders and her disappearance.

Ali might have been the target; Aude Bertin would have been in the way.

Or Agent Bertin had been the target, and Ali had been a collateral kill – in the wrong place at the wrong time.

Rachel thought she knew which scenario was more likely. If a defector had escaped Apaydin, he wouldn't have lingered on Lesvos. He would have moved on to the European continent and disappeared.

The first time she'd visited Moria, Rachel had overheard the conversation of a pair of volunteers. What they'd said tracked with the information Sehr had just supplied.

They'd warned the Afghan father not to leave his daughters unattended. Boiled down to its essence, they'd warned him against bad men.

Rachel had assumed they'd meant residents of the camp.

But Sehr had said traffickers were picking off kids from both sides of the crossing. So the unaccompanied minors in the camps on Lesvos and Chios were vulnerable.

But who could pass in and out of the camps without drawing attention to their actions? She considered the possibilities. Volunteers who worked for the various NGOs. Members of the militant group Golden Dawn, who'd raided the Souda camp. The men who'd been watching Khattak from their table at the fish restaurant. The Greeks who ran the guesthouses near the camps.

Rachel remembered something. The proprietor of the hotel she'd stayed at on Chios – Nikos Papadakis – had approached the camp after the Golden Dawn raid. He'd made a list of names, offering rooms to women and children.

A benevolent gesture, or a means of marking off targets?

She should get back to Chios and check if there were new reports of missing persons. There *had* to be a way for her to confirm who was involved. If Audrey had inadvertently stumbled onto an answer, Rachel would get there faster. Her thoughts raced back through her encounters on the islands, through bits of information she'd gleaned first-hand or through peripheral knowledge – faces, places, dates, leaping from point to point, searching for correlations.

She found them.

Her face and her neck flushed red. She snapped her pencil in half. She had to find the volunteers at Moria. Because they'd spoken of a *witness*.

Of a girl who'd escaped.

She'd made another assumption, thinking the volunteers had been speaking of a sexual assault. What if they hadn't been? What if they'd meant a *kidnapping*?

What if the same van had been used? And the witness had seen the van?

She shoved her chair back from the table, making for the door.

Just as she reached for the handle, Nate entered the lobby. He looked relieved to see her, a smile breaking over his face. She could see from the shattered look in his eyes that he was losing hope – the search was getting to him.

Rachel swallowed hard. She didn't want to tell him what she'd learned. Whatever he was fearing, his fears would be amplified to the point of terror. She couldn't hurt him like that.

'You've found something?' He seemed to read the tension in her face. 'Have a drink with me?'

He didn't need to look for his host. At his entry, the manager brought over two glasses of beer on a tray covered by a doily. It was a simple place, but the manager had done his best to echo Nate's air of careless prestige. He set the tray down at a table in the lounge area, and told them to ring if they wanted anything more.

'I was about to check out a lead.'

'On Audrey?'

She nodded. He tugged her over to a sofa. Rachel took a seat with some reluctance, picking up her glass and cradling it in her hand.

'Tell me,' he said. 'This waiting is worse than anything.'

Rachel took a fortifying sip of her drink. In a low tone, she sketched out what she knew of Audrey's role acting as a courier for CIJA. Then she hurried over Sehr's discoveries at Europol. Nate took the news badly.

He rubbed his eyes with his fists. Then he grasped Rachel's shoulders, forcing her to face him.

'How long have you known this? How long has Esa?'

'Ten minutes,' Rachel said.

The quiet words defused his anger. He released his bruising grip with an apology. When he looked at her again, his eyes were wet with tears.

'So she's gone,' he said in a hollow voice. 'She's dead, or she's taken – I don't know which is worse.'

Rachel wanted to console him without falling into the trap of offering him false hope. Since she couldn't think of a way to do that, she scrambled to her feet. 'We can try to get answers,' she said. 'Then we can take it from there.'

Nate looked around the lounge as if his eyes were having trouble focusing. 'Where's Esa?'

'He's waiting for Sehr at the airport.'

'And Inspecteur Roux? Christ, she could have told me this the day I landed. How much time has she cost us?'

Rachel was able to consider this with more objectivity than Nate. She hadn't known that his pain would resonate so personally, or that her feelings had deepened to this extent. She had suffered the agony of Zach's disappearance – she couldn't bear what was happening to Nate.

He wanted Esa, she could see. He wanted reassurance from his closest friend because he knew Esa would offer hope. So she tried to act in Esa's stead.

'Listen,' she said. 'They've been searching for Audrey longer than we have, with first-hand knowledge of her actions. That time isn't lost. Our actions support theirs – not the other way around.'

She grabbed his hands and held them in her own. His amber eyes focused on her face. After a moment, he nodded.

'You've got to hold it together. Audrey needs you to *think*.' She worked up the nerve to say a little more. 'You're not alone,' she mumbled, amazed at herself for taking the risk. 'I won't leave you alone.'

His expression softened. He shifted his hands so they were holding Rachel's. For a moment, she felt weightless, hopeful and expectant.

'There are so many things about you, Rachel. So many things that I –' He broke off. 'Where were you going?'

Encouraged by this beginning, she responded, 'I'll explain on the way.'

She had a hazy memory of the volunteers in Moria. A Danish girl named Freja with blond hair, and a young man who was a translator. She stopped at each NGO and described them. No one seemed to know them, but she was directed to the service tents near the toilets.

The stench assailed her nostrils, but Nate didn't seem to notice. There was a zeal in his eyes that disturbed her because it was so familiar. So many times she'd thought she had the answer to Zachary's disappearance. Each time she'd been wrong.

When she'd met Khattak three years ago, she'd been going

through the motions, angry at everyone, angriest at herself. She prayed the same thing wouldn't happen to Nate.

She thought of Audrey's teasing e-mail to Ruksh. *I hope Nate doesn't blow this thing with Rachel.*

She was trying not to look at the truth, trying not to accept it. Whatever this was between her and Nate – and she wasn't sure what she wanted it to be – part of her knew it was over. She would always be tied to the outcome of this case, and to its prospects for grief.

She knew what Zach's disappearance had done to her parents.

She couldn't bear to be the reminder of someone's tragedy again. They found Freja at the tent that dispensed hot chocolate.

She didn't remember Rachel, but she took Rachel's ID as evidence of her right to ask questions. She snatched a tray of hot chocolates and led them to a less crowded corner. Rachel's gaze skipped from one of the children's faces to another, though she didn't know what she was searching for. Perhaps she was making her own record.

She was still staggered by the figure Sehr had quoted her: ten thousand missing children. And she wondered how hard it would have been to record their photographs and names.

Rachel asked after the translator. Freja told them he'd left the camp. Rachel kept her face impassive; she didn't want Nate to view his absence as a setback.

'You mentioned a girl who fought off an attack in the camp. You said she'd scratched her assailant. Is that girl still here?'

Freja shook her head. 'She moved on to Athens a few days after the incident. I have no idea where she is now.'

'Was she alone?' Rachel asked. In her peripheral vision, a group of children were playing with a set of cardboard shapes in a game of their own invention.

'No, she had parents and younger brothers. She had taken a walk to the beach by herself – you know where the road meets the beach?'

That allowed for the possibility of the van. She pressed ahead. 'Was it a physical assault?'

Freja looked uncertain. 'She says the man was tall and very strong. She couldn't see his face, but he was trying to get her in the van.'

Nate gripped the lapels of his jacket. 'You were right,' he said in a tight voice.

Rachel cautioned him. Their knowledge about the trafficking ring had to be kept to themselves until they were given the all clear from Roux. There was also the possibility that the van had been used to take the girl to another location for the purpose of sexual assault.

'Did she see the van? Could she describe it?'

Freja nodded, her ponytail bouncing with her desire to be of use. 'She gave us the license plate. You can use it to crack the case.'

Rachel took a breath to calm herself. 'Do you still have that number?'

The girl beamed with pride. She pulled out her phone: she'd kept a record for herself.

'Did you report the incident to the police?'

'Of course! But I don't know if they followed up. No one got back to us, but we've been keeping an eye on the kids.'

'Freja –' Rachel hesitated. She had to ask her next question with utmost care. 'Why did you warn that father about bad men? You said "men," not "man." Was there a reason why?'

Bemused, the girl answered, 'Did I? I don't remember that. But you hear things, you know. All around the island. Men coming in after the boats arrive, strangers in the camp who aren't volunteers. Sometimes kids come for meals several days in a row, then we don't see them again. If we check back with the authorities, they say they can't keep track. The intake process is a sieve. So we worry about these kids, though there's nothing we can do without better institutional support.'

She was confirming Rachel's suspicions. 'You said the men in the camp were strangers?'

When Freja nodded, Rachel described the men she'd seen on Chios. She also described Papadakis at the Athena.

'But those men are Greeks! I'm sorry, the strangers in the camp weren't Greeks.'

Freja was describing volunteers like herself.

39

ESA WAITED FOR SEHR TO join him in the lounge. He'd had a brief conversation with Rachel, who was on her way back from interviewing a witness. She was stopping off at the local police station, and she and Nate had split up the car rental agencies on the island in the hopes of tracking down a van that might be the same one Sami had spotted. He hoped Sehr would hurry so they'd have a chance to speak about more than just the case.

She'd been tired when he picked her up at the airport, but she'd put her mind to Audrey's disappearance on the drive back to the guesthouse. She'd left Amélie Roux in Athens. Esa guessed Roux was coordinating her team's operation on the ground, advising the Greek police. He'd been strictly warned through Sehr not to jeopardize their work.

He didn't see how he could. He was no closer to finding Audrey than the day he'd arrived on Lesvos. Rachel had warned him of Nate's increasing agitation at their lack of progress. He intended to speak to Nate as soon as he returned.

When Sehr came down from her room, the manager suggested they take their tea in the garden. Esa agreed, holding the door for Sehr, disturbed when her body brushed his.

They chose to walk along the wall that separated the terrace from the rambling descent to the sea. The waves brushed the shore in a sinuous rhythm. The light was beginning to die, a vast expanse of gold flung over igneous blues. Looking at the sea now, he couldn't imagine the crossing as other than a voyage of grace.

It had been a warm day. The stone wall retained that warmth as Esa leaned against it. He studied Sehr's face. She had changed into a flame-colored dress and wore a silk pashmina. Her hair was brushed into shining waves; her skin was smooth and glowing.

She had dressed for him, he thought, and knew a surge of longing that shocked him.

They hadn't spoken of personal things; he'd made no admissions to himself. To sort out his tangled emotions with Audrey still missing was something he wasn't prepared for. Yet Sehr was here with him now, and her presence was illuminating his ability to deceive himself about things he urgently desired. Her comfort, her support, the warmth of her respect, the sense she knew the things about him that mattered, and that she understood.

He turned at her side to face the sea, his arm touching hers, conscious of a fraught new awareness. He wanted something he wasn't entitled to. He didn't know how to ask for it.

She looked up into his face and said, 'Do you still want me out of your life?'

She'd given him the opening he needed. Quickly he answered, 'No.' The faltering breath she drew was painful for him to hear. He'd been arrogant and self-involved. He had some sense now of how he'd hurt her, of how he was still thinking of himself. Of what Sehr could give him, instead of the things she was due.

She looked back at the sea, and instantly he missed the intimacy of her glance. She was following the path of fishing boats sailing in to shore. A child raced madly down the hill; his laughter reached the terrace as the sun burned down to the sea.

Sehr's shawl slipped from her shoulder. He caught its folds and draped it at her neck, his fingers touching her collarbone. She freed herself from his touch, a mutinous spark in her eyes.

'Don't you want this?'

Her mouth firmed, she raised her chin. 'What makes you think I would?'

312

'Sehr.' He said her name and waited for her to look at him. When she did, he pushed past his misgivings. How often must Sehr have experienced the same self-doubt in his presence.

'Don't you?'

Tears flooded her eyes. 'Damn you for doing this to me. You've never given me anything. I doubt you ever will.'

His face tightened at her reproach, the pain of it striking hard because of how deeply it was warranted.

'I haven't been honest with myself.'

When everything he was coming to want was poised at the edge of loss, he knew each word he spoke to her mattered.

He didn't mention Samina – he didn't dare to. With her quickness of mind, Sehr unraveled the nature of his struggle – his sudden, sharp sense of fear. There was a softening in her face, a willingness to offer him things he hadn't earned. Where did her generosity spring from? He couldn't meet her on her ground, so he did what his instincts were telling him to do.

He took Sehr in his arms.

He could smell the jasmine on her skin. He curved a hand under her hair to turn her face up to his. He kissed her deeply, taking his time, a slow warmth flooding his senses. When he raised his head again, her hands had come up to rest beneath his shoulders.

In a voice darkened by desire, he asked, 'Do you want me to apologize for that?'

'Do you want to?' she countered.

'No.' Impatiently, he kissed her again.

She wound her arms about his neck, drawing him close to her heart. The gate banged with unnecessary force. Rachel was standing there, a startled expression on her face. He shifted to draw Sehr away, but he kept his hand at her waist.

In a gruff voice, Rachel said, 'Ruksh is trying to reach you. She called me when she couldn't get through.'

She held up her phone in her hand. The moment was weighted

in ways Khattak couldn't decipher; he only knew he couldn't hurt Sehr again.

He pressed a kiss to the corner of her mouth, making his longing clear.

'I'm sorry,' he said under his breath. 'For the interruption.' And in a louder voice so Rachel could hear, 'I'll have to take this. You know how persistent Ruksh is.'

Sehr gave him a shaky smile; the fist that squeezed his heart unclenched. She hadn't given up on him. He could still afford to hope.

He took Rachel's phone with a word of thanks, leaving the two women alone.

Rachel cursed herself for the awkwardness of her timing. She was a detective, for God's sake, but not for a moment had she guessed at Khattak's feelings. She could see the radiance in Sehr's eyes, and something about it hurt her.

'I'm sorry, Rachel,' Sehr said.

Rachel flushed to the roots of her hair. She had no idea why Sehr was apologizing – she didn't want to find out. Her normal wisecracking abilities deserted her; she opted for clarity instead.

'*I'm* sorry. I try not to blunder into other people's business.'

Seeing her embarrassment, Sehr asked after Nate.

'He's checking out a car rental. He should be back any minute.'

'Where is Sami al-Nuri? I'd like to talk to him myself.'

Rachel didn't ask why. She didn't want to be in Sehr's company, prey to the kinds of confidences she imagined women unlike herself might share, but she had to wait for Khattak. She was relieved from her discomfort by his reappearance.

'Anything urgent, sir?'

He smiled at her. 'Ruksh could have told you as easily, but she wanted to hear my voice.'

Rachel tipped her head and waited, knowing the news would be welcome to Khattak – a conciliatory act on Ruksh's part after such prolonged discord.

'She remembered something.' He held out a hand to bring Sehr to his side. 'Audrey mentioned a meeting with someone on the island, Ruksh said it sounded important. She thinks the person's name was Lenny. I'll have a look at her e-mails to see if we missed it before.'

Rachel was swamped by a wave of panic. 'I don't remember someone named Lenny in the e-mails.'

Khattak didn't hear her. He was reading the e-mails on his phone. Rachel cast a glance at Sehr, needing help she couldn't ask for. Though Khattak took his time scrolling through the list, Rachel's thought processes had stalled, absorbed by what she'd interrupted. She knew the moment he found the e-mail because he put his phone away, the light in his eyes growing dark.

'You're right,' he said. 'There's no mention of Lenny.'

'Esa, what's wrong?' Sehr caught it too; unlike Rachel, she had the right to reach for him to console him. She curled her fingers around his wrist, a careful gesture of comfort.

Nate banged through the gate before Esa could answer.

'Rachel!' His breath was coming fast. He must have run up the hill.

'You found the car?'

He nodded vigorously, taking a moment to catch his breath.

'Esa, Rachel – listen. It's not from a car rental. But the clerk at the agency knows who owns it because he doubles as a mechanic at the garage. He knew the plate, the description, everything.'

He looked round the circle of three expectant faces, a desperate hope in his eyes.

'It belongs to a member of the Hellenic Rescue Team. Her name is Eleni Latsoudi.'

40

THEY LEFT SEHR AND NATE at the guesthouse, speaking with the rapid-fire familiarity that was second nature to them as partners. Khattak hailed a cab to take them to Eleni Latsoudi's little house on the hill. It was dark out; all the lights were looped around the harbor, the sky a purple-veiled dome. He focused on making sense of Eleni's connection to the van.

Eleni was Lenny.

As a member of the Hellenic Rescue Team, could she be behind Israa's disappearance? She was in an ideal position to identify the vulnerable, out on the seas every day. But that didn't fit with the woman he'd met, the woman who'd told him, *The water will break your heart.*

Had his skills and insight so failed him that he'd missed seeing the rot at the core of Eleni's charade? Was it no different than the way he'd missed his sister's deepening rancor? Thoughts of Ruksh overshadowed the fragile happiness he was struggling to protect.

Eleni wasn't on duty. She welcomed them in, her shoulders wrapped in a hand-knitted blanket, a book and a glass of wine on the table near her sofa. She invited them to sit, dropping the blanket to the sofa, using her fingers to comb out her hair. They remained on their feet, their eyes searching the house.

Khattak now noticed the covered portico at the back of the little house, visible from the patio. He nodded at Rachel. The van

316

wasn't there, but the little station wagon Eleni had driven to the beach the other night was parked in a space big enough for two cars. Its tires were mud-spattered; it hadn't been washed.

'Is that your only car, Eleni?'

'No,' she said, turning to follow his gaze. Picking up on the seriousness of his manner, she added, 'Why? Is something wrong?'

'Where's your other car? You live alone, don't you? Why do you need two cars?'

A frown on her face, she led them out to inspect the portico. 'The other is a van,' she said. 'Someone must have borrowed it.'

A pair of olive trees was growing to the side of the portico. They skirted these to reach the empty space.

'How could they do that without your knowledge?'

'I leave it unlocked. The keys are always inside.'

'Why would you do that?' A hard note entered his voice. Her explanation was unconvincing. 'It might get stolen.'

Eleni shivered in the breeze that swept the hill. Confused, she said, 'On Lesvos? We don't lock our houses. I leave my van unlocked because volunteers use it to ferry passengers from the beach to the camps.'

Khattak considered her gravely. 'Do you know the license plate number of your van?'

She told them. Khattak's gaze flicked to Rachel, who looked as tense as he felt.

'Do you keep a record of who borrows it?'

'Why would I need to?' Perplexed, she said, 'Esa, Rachel. Why are you asking about my van? What's going on?'

'Eleni.' Rachel said her name, drawing out the syllables. 'Does anyone call you Lenny? Maybe it's your nickname?'

'What? Of course not. Everyone calls me Eleni.'

'Did Audrey ask to meet with you the day she disappeared?' Bewildered, Eleni admitted that she had.

Watching for signs of deception, Khattak said, 'You didn't tell me this the other night.'

He caught it – the telltale glance away, the hand that rubbed her shoulder.

'There's nothing to tell. One of the volunteers told me Audrey was looking for me. I was at a training session on Chios. I didn't see Audrey. In fact, I stayed in Chios because I had another meeting.'

'Where did you stay?' asked Rachel.

'The Hotel Athena.'

Khattak made the connection. 'Can anyone prove this?'

Eleni nodded. 'There were twenty trainees at the session. And I suppose Nikos could confirm it as well – he runs the Athena.' Nervous now, she asked, 'Why are you treating me like a suspect? What is it you think I've done?'

'Your van was seen the night Audrey disappeared. She was forced into it and driven off.'

Eleni clutched one of the pillars. 'My van was here when I returned from Chios. The next night it was borrowed again.'

'Who borrowed it?'

'They all do. It's impossible to keep track. Shukri, Freja, Hans. Even Peter did once, and Vincenzo when he's helping out.'

Khattak seized on the name. Was it possible Ruksh had heard 'Vinny,' not 'Lenny'?

'Vincenzo's often here on Lesvos. He's with the Guardia Costiera.'

Urgently, Khattak asked, 'Did he borrow your van tonight?'

Her fingers pressed to her lips, Eleni said, 'He may have. It was gone when I got home.'

'Where would he have taken it?'

She sank down on the sofa. 'To Eftalou Beach, where else?'

'Eleni.' She looked up at Khattak, trying to collect herself. 'Can you think of anywhere on the island, anywhere near the beach, where someone could be hidden without attracting notice – if they screamed for help, for example, or were able to bang on the walls?'

Her face white, Eleni said, 'You think Audrey is still on the island?'

'Please,' he said. 'Is there anywhere that you know of?'

She shook her head.

'Sir,' Rachel interrupted, 'let's get down to Eftalou. Let's get on this right away.'

'Call the local police, Rachel. Have them meet us there.'

He turned back to Eleni. 'Don't tell anyone we were here, don't tell anyone we asked these questions. It's critical to your safety. And please – lock your doors and windows.'

'What's happening?' she asked in the same bewildered tone. 'What's happening on this island?'

He shook his head. 'I can't tell you yet.'

They were at the door when Eleni's voice followed after them. She had chased them to the drive.

'Wait,' she said. 'There's nothing near the beaches. But up in the hills, the farmers have sheds they use when the nights are cold and livestock have gone missing. They're storage sheds. There's no proper road by which they can be reached, the tracks get muddy in the rain.'

But traversable for a vehicle with four-wheel drive.

'Which ones are near the beach road?'

Eleni shook her head. 'I don't know. I'm sorry, I wish I could help.' The police knew the local roads better than they did, but Khattak was dismayed to find Sehr and Nate at the station. Nate drove his own car; he couldn't be dissuaded from joining in the search. Captain Nicolaides, Sehr's contact with the IPCD, had already invited Sehr into his car. When Khattak objected, Nicolaides advised him that Sehr had been on the islands for weeks: she'd been the one running point on the search.

Rachel slid into the backseat with Sehr. 'Let's go, sir. We're losing time.'

She'd looked over at Nate to see if he wanted her company, torn between her duty as Khattak's partner and her concern for

Nate – her longing to be needed. He didn't sense her concern or notice her glance, he was laser-focused on the search.

Nate followed the second police car in the opposite direction. Nicolaides drove in the direction of the village of Xidera, where several store houses were located. Khattak didn't attempt to dissuade Sehr again, but Rachel could see he wasn't happy.

They'd been assured there were no hiding places near the beach that weren't subject to the daily traffic of fishermen loading and stowing gear, but that three or four store houses were dotted above the olive groves on the hill. Nicolaides explained that these storehouses were locked for the winter. Most of the farming on Lesvos was done by hobby farmers who kept a few sheep or a handful of goats. Grazing practices had changed over the years, the land becoming more arid. Milk and cheeses were produced locally, to be sold in the villages.

Rachel paid no attention to this, though Khattak asked questions at intervals. She was following their progress up the hill. Most of the landscape was bare, but now and again she saw stone-wall enclosures that served to mark off grazing areas, or boulders that had fallen from the top of the hill. At one point, they passed a flock of sheep herded under a clump of Valonia oaks. There were no other cars on the road. Rachel questioned how effective Nate's private investigators had been if they hadn't uncovered the van or thought to search the storage sheds on the hills.

Then she reminded herself she'd only learned about the van through Aya's direct confession. Sami hadn't trusted them enough to tell them until they'd made their own roundabout discoveries.

Rachel didn't have to imagine Sami's anguish at Israa's disappearance: she knew it first-hand. She'd thought Israa had been abandoned until Sehr made it clear that Roux's focus was on the children who were slipping through the cracks of the crisis.

She spied the flash of moonlight on tin and called a warning to the others. The car came to a halt. Rachel scrambled up the hill. What she found was a cobbled-together tin shack, partially demolished by the weather, corroded sheets of tin listing in the wind. The smell of dried manure rose from the other side of a ramshackle wooden fence.

The shed was open to their view. There were no signs of recent occupation. They climbed back into the police car as a call came through from Nicolaides's partner. Rachel held her breath. Nicolaides frowned – there was no news of Audrey.

Rachel looked at Nicolaides's map. The island was bigger than she'd realized – too large for their search party to cover. It was cross-hatched by pastures, though Nicolaides assured them the villages were no more than twenty minutes from the beach. It seemed reasonable to begin by searching the area closest to Kara Tepe.

They drove a little longer, occasionally stopping to question villagers. After a while, Rachel leaned forward to tap Khattak's shoulder.

'Sir,' she said, 'we're not going to have any luck like this. We need to coordinate a search-and-rescue team. What say we head back to the pub and get our hands on Vincenzo?'

Khattak turned in his seat. 'Let's give it some time. Someone will spot the van – it's the best lead we have.'

The radio squawked at them and Nicolaides picked it up, speaking into the transmitter.

A flurry of remarks were exchanged at high volume, then Nicolaides locked the car into a three-point turn, reversing at speed down the road.

'We have something.'

'The van?' Rachel asked with a sense of premonition.

'There's a lead in Xidera. The villagers say they've seen the van go up the road behind their village. There's a store house there, an old one. It hasn't been in use for years, no one from the village goes up there. I think it's worth checking out.'

They completed the drive in silence, the road increasingly rugged as it climbed the north face of the mountain. A vehicle approached from the rear. Rachel urged Nicolaides to allow the other car to pass, but her warning came too late. The vehicle hit them broadside, then accelerated and drove past. She caught a fleeting glimpse of the taillights of a van before the police car flew over a massive piece of stone that tore through the car's undercarriage. It spun on the slippery road, careened off the path, and plunged wildly down the hill.

It came to a halt fifty feet from the road, at an angle facing the sea. Rachel hadn't been wearing her seat belt. Her head received a thump against the partition between the front seat and the rear. Sehr had been more responsible. She unsnapped her belt and staggered out of the car to the driver's side door, unharmed like Esa, who she'd checked on first.

Nicolaides was unconscious in the driver's seat. Sehr tried to tug him loose.

Khattak helped Rachel from the car, then gently pushed Sehr aside. Rachel hurried to help, though her vision felt impaired.

'I can manage,' he said. 'Sit down, Rachel, before you fall.' Rachel fell back, feeling sick. She stumbled over to the oak tree she had missed, leaving Khattak to extricate Nicolaides from the car she now recognized was steaming.

'Sir!' she shouted. 'Get away from the car!'

She scrambled back to it, diving into the front seat to yank out the portable radio.

Nicolaides was almost loose. Khattak pulled his body from the car to the road, then adjusted his weight over his shoulder and carried him to the nearest tree.

Freed from their weight, the car dipped toward the sea. It skidded close to Sehr. Khattak yanked her out of the way. He lost control, shouting at Sehr. 'You could have gotten yourself killed!'

'Sir!' Rachel interrupted, diverting them both. 'Look there!'

She'd moved to the opposite side of the road, and just above the ridge, the outline of the store house was visible. It was bigger than she'd expected – a gray stone shed edged with broken terracotta tiles. The window to the side of a solid wooden door was blacked out.

Rachel had seen something more. A white glint of steel around the corner – the back of a van. Was it the van that had clipped them?

'We need to get up there.' She glanced over at Sehr, puzzled by her stillness. 'Radio in for help.' She'd grabbed the map with the radio, and now she passed them both to Sehr.

'Rachel.' Sehr was looking at Khattak. A red stain marred the front of his shirt. He put his hand to it, surprised. It came away damp and discolored.

'Christ.'

Rachel stumbled to his side, her head aching from the blow she'd sustained in the crash.

'It's not deep,' he said. 'It's nothing.'

Rachel didn't respond. She stripped away his shirt, checking the wound herself. He was right, it wasn't deep, but it was bleeding freely. She ripped a sleeve from his shirt, trying not to react to the sight of the scar that bisected his torso.

'Sehr. Come hold this.'

Rachel ran to the car. Smoke was escaping from the back.

'Rachel, don't!' Khattak's voice was urgent with fear.

Rachel didn't listen. She had a minute, maybe two. She wrested the trunk open and grabbed for the first-aid kit. The car gave a mighty jerk, nearly ripping her arm from its socket. She braced herself, holding on. The bumper slipped out of her grasp. The car jerked down the hill, meeting its inevitable fate. Flames licked up its side in an orange fury. But by the time the car caught fire, Rachel had the kit in her hand.

'Sorry, sir.' She hurried over to Khattak. 'You know I don't follow orders all that well.' She flashed him a reassuring smile.

Sehr was applying pressure to the wound, using Khattak's sleeve as a bandage. She gave him a tremulous smile. If it was meant to be encouraging, she wasn't doing it right. Rachel found the disinfectant and managed a passable field dressing. She didn't mention the scar, though the sight of it shocked her. How on earth had Khattak gotten a scar like that?

'You radio in, sir. We need backup and Nicolaides needs attention. I'll head up to the shed.' She jerked her head in the direction the van had gone.

'No!' Khattak said sharply. 'Not alone, Rachel. You can't risk it on your own.'

'Sir, I think we were run off the road. Audrey could be in that shed. If she is, we have to get to her before that van comes back. Someone tipped them off.'

'Then I'm coming with you. Sehr can stay with Nicolaides.'

Esa tried to rise but couldn't. He sank to the ground with a muffled curse, his back against the tree. Rachel didn't wait.

'Stay with him,' she said to Sehr. 'I don't know how bad that wound is. Get him something to wear.'

She didn't stick around to listen to more from Khattak.

Sehr gave him Nicolaides's jacket and radioed in to Mytilene. She hunched beside Esa on the ground. He opened his eyes to find her watching him.

'I'm fine, Sehr.'

'Esa.' She touched a hand to his scar in horror, her touch lingering on his skin.

'Don't,' he said, placing his hand over hers. 'I'm not hurt, I've just lost a little blood. Did you radio in?'

She nodded. 'They're on their way. But I don't know how far away they are.'

'Sehr,' he said. 'Help me up. I have to go after Rachel.'

'Absolutely not!'

'I have to. If the van is there, she's at risk. I can't let anything happen to her.'

'So you'd risk your life for Rachel?' Sehr sounded angry. As angry as he'd been earlier.

'Just as she would for me. You saw her grab the kit.'

Sehr didn't answer this. 'Are you sure it's not worse than you're telling me? The scar –'

He leaned his head against the tree, his eyes closing. 'It's from the accident with Samina. You remember the surgery.'

He was seeing it again. The car spinning into flames, Samina trapped inside. He'd been helpless to save his wife, his throat ravaged by her name.

His side was burning, but he knew Rachel's bandage would hold.

There were so many things Rachel did well, he wondered if anyone had ever told her. She didn't panic in a crisis. She became more certain, more utterly reliable. She had trained herself to be all things to Zachary. And as he'd learned in Algonquin, she was guided by a moral imperative of her own. He needed to go after her *now*.

He looked over at Nicolaides. The crash might have been deliberate. For the traffickers to be operating from Lesvos, many different players would have to be involved. Nicolaides could have been trying to delay and simply miscalculated the risk. He didn't know Rachel's determination like Esa did. Rachel wouldn't let anything derail her quest to find Audrey.

Sehr's head turned. She thought she'd heard a siren. But when she looked down the road, no vehicles were in sight. What if the police couldn't find them? What if she'd given the wrong directions?

Esa tried to rise again. Sehr pushed him back, studying the path Rachel had taken up the hill.

'Fine.' She placed the radio in Esa's hand. 'Wait for the police. I'll go after Rachel.'

'No!' His eyes flew open. 'I won't allow it, Sehr.'

She leaned forward and kissed him on the mouth, surprised by her own boldness. In the extremity of the situation, it was warranted. She could have lost him, and the knife-edge certainty of what that would have meant diminished her resentment.

'You're in no condition to stop me,' she warned him. 'And even if you weren't, I don't take kindly to being bossed around. Not even by you, Esa Khattak.'

She gave him a quick smile, infusing more confidence into her voice than she felt. Grabbing the flashlight from the first-aid kit, she followed Rachel up the hill.

The landscape near the store house was bare, save for a pair of ancient oaks whose branches spread over the door. A gravel path led around the side of the shed. Rachel checked the van first, peering through the tinted windshield. She couldn't see past the empty front seat. She tested a door handle: it was locked.

Stealthily, she moved around the side of the shed to the small, square window. She had to stretch to her tiptoes for a look inside. She'd been right in her guess. This window was blacked out, too. She'd check the other side of the building, and as a last resort, the door.

She could hear a kind of grunting inside – was something being dragged? As quietly as she could, she felt her way around the building, trying not to scatter gravel as she moved. There was another window on the far side. She stretched to her full height. This one wasn't completely covered; she could see through a strip at the bottom. She pressed her face against the glass, her eyes attempting to penetrate the gloom.

There was someone inside the shed. A hand was chained to a rusted pipe, the body wrapped in a plastic tarp, the head hooded in black. It wasn't moving. Rachel tried to clean the glass with her hand. She couldn't see anything else. A shadow moved across the window. She heard a muffled noise.

And then, more loudly, footsteps. The shadow froze.

A knocking on the door was followed by a voice. It was Sehr calling for Rachel.

The door of the shed was thrown open. Rachel heard a cry of surprise, then another body was dragged into the store house. Sehr was struggling with a figure dressed in black. Rachel thought she recognized something. It moved out of the light too quickly for her to be sure.

She had to get into the shed before something happened to Sehr. She weighed her options. What if she broke into the van? And sounded the horn – it could serve as a distraction. Or she could break the window and draw Sehr's assailant outside. Her hand slipped on the outer frame. Suddenly she noticed there was no movement in the shed, no sound. The night was eerily quiet. She heard a faint rustling and froze. Was it the wind through the oaks?

She had made up her mind to act, when a rough hand seized her by the waist. She felt a heavy, hot breath against her neck. When she turned her head, she caught a flash of orange in her vision.

From the uniform of the Guardia Costiera.

A hand over her mouth, she was swung around and set on her feet without a sound.

She looked up into a face she knew, a face she should have guessed at. Vincenzo was holding a gun.

41

Lesvos, Greece

'STAY QUIET,' HE SAID, SPEAKING in her ear. 'I don't have to shoot you, but I will.'

The gun nudging her ribs, Rachel followed his lead. She expected to be taken to the shed, where the door now stood half-open, sounds issuing from within. A scream from Sehr, a violent oath, a shocking slap.

Rachel was shepherded to the van. Its cargo doors were open, the interior bare of passenger seats, the space cleared out for cargo. It wasn't empty. There was a body wrapped in plastic at the back.

Vincenzo's hand was feeling around at her waist.

'Do you have a gun?'

Sweating with fear, Rachel nodded. A frantic pulse pounded in her ears. She was waiting for an opening, trying to clear her thoughts. Praying Sehr was still alive. No shots had been fired because whoever was in the shed couldn't afford the noise. But Rachel had seen two bodies, so these men were prepared to kill.

Vincenzo felt for her gun, his own buried deep in her ribs.

'Get in,' he said. She obeyed. She thought of slamming the door into his head by swinging it outward, but he was too quick for her.

He looked into her face, closing one of the doors.

Then to her astonishment, he handed over her gun.

'You'll only get one chance. When we load the bodies into the van, you have to take the shot. Do you understand me?'

She didn't, but Rachel nodded anyway. When she moved to raise her gun in his face, in an anguished voice he said, 'Please, I need your help.'

She lowered her gun. There was something in his misery she trusted. He slammed a cargo door shut. Rachel waited, praying she was doing the right thing. She was playing with Sehr's life. And she didn't hear sirens on the hill.

She knew Khattak was passionately involved – his anger on the hillside was the anger of a man who feared losing what he loved. If Vincenzo killed Sehr, Khattak would never forgive her. She was racked with the fear of how much that mattered.

The door to the store house banged open; she heard two men conferring in low voices. They came closer, carrying Sehr's body. She struggled until one of the men slapped her. He cursed Vincenzo when he saw the cargo door was closed. He let go of his grip on Sehr, yanking on the door.

Rachel crashed her gun down on his head.

He staggered back but didn't fall, gathering himself to charge her. Rachel's gun went flying. She could hear sounds of a scuffle – had Sehr tackled Vincenzo? She couldn't think, couldn't see, her body thrown like a child's into the back of the van, where it slipped over the tarp. A low cry sounded from under the covering. Rachel's thoughts froze but the man was on her, straddling her body, his strong hands at her throat.

She kneed him in the stomach and gained herself an inch of space, tearing at his arms, ripping at his sleeves, adding the fury of her nails to the scratches that ran up his forearms. He grunted, leaning closer. He pressed his elbow to her windpipe. She knew at that moment there was nothing she could do to save herself.

There was a scrambling sound beyond the van.

'No!' a voice cried, followed by a thump.

The man's body went slack over Rachel's. She looked up into Khattak's pale face. He'd smashed his gun down on the back of the man's head. His own wound bleeding, he dragged the man's body off Rachel and shoved it out of the van.

It sprawled into the glare of the flashlight quivering in Sehr's hand.

Breathing harshly, Rachel stumbled out of the van. Vincenzo was semiconscious on the ground beside the other man.

Rachel sank to her knees and stripped off the other man's mask, expecting to see Peter Conroy.

But the man who faced her with bold, unblinking eyes wasn't Peter Conroy.

It was the commander of the Coast Guard, Illario Benemerito.

He spat at Rachel and missed, his lips curled back in a grimace. 'Don't!' Vincenzo cried. 'You have to stop now, Benny.'

Stunned, Rachel said, 'Illario? What are you doing here?' Her hands and voice were shaking.

Too weak to struggle to his feet, Benemerito turned his face away. Rachel touched his arm. 'Illario –'

His head swiveled round, his dark eyes impenetrable.

Without expression, he said, 'You have nothing you can use against me. And I'm not saying a word.'

In the noise and confusion that followed, Sehr sat unmoving at Vincenzo's side, watching police and paramedics gather around Esa and Rachel. One of the medics had stitched up Esa's wound, and the ambulance had been dispatched down the hill to take Philip Nicolaides to the hospital.

A second ambulance was stationed under the oaks, its red and blue lights blinking against the dark, showering the sky with sparks. The steady pulse of the lights caused a throbbing behind Sehr's temples.

Nate was pacing outside the store house, his face streaked with tears, his fists clenched at his sides, waiting for police to secure the scene. Two officers were inside, attending to the body in the shed.

When Amélie Roux arrived, Nate was granted permission to enter the store house.

Sehr kept her eyes on Esa, who hadn't looked around for her. He was leaning into the ambulance, Rachel at his side, something inside capturing his attention.

Sehr didn't feel anything. She was replaying the last fifteen minutes in her mind.

Esa had found her locked in Vincenzo's grip, just as Benemerito had launched himself at Rachel. She didn't know what Esa had witnessed during those frenzied moments. She couldn't guess at how he'd arrived at his difficult decision. Or if it *had* been difficult.

He'd left Sehr to Vincenzo, flying to Rachel's rescue, careless of his wound in his desperation.

And even the sight of Audrey, small and shivering in the circle of Nate's arms, couldn't thaw the cold at the center of Sehr's perceptions. She'd trusted Esa. She'd risked herself for him.

And Esa had made his choice.

As always, his choice was Rachel.

'What's your name?' Esa asked the girl in the ambulance. His voice was very gentle, but when he saw he'd frightened her, he motioned Rachel closer and Rachel said, 'Sami and Aya are looking for you. They'll be so, so happy.'

He heard the raw emotion in Rachel's voice and knew she was thinking of Zachary. It was why she'd bonded so strongly with Sami: she understood his unwavering commitment when everyone had told him Israa was dead, never to be recovered.

The girl's eyelids flickered before she said, 'My name is Israa.' Then she began to cry.

There was a commotion outside the ambulance. Another car had pulled up. Sami had hitched a ride to the scene with one of the volunteers. He called Khattak's name, his voice throbbing with fear.

Khattak found him in the glow of a police car's lights. He called Sami over, urging him to the doors of the ambulance. He squeezed Sami's arm, telling him, 'She's here. She's safe.'

Sobbing openly, Sami peered inside the ambulance. Rachel moved out of the way. Israa raised her head from her pillow. A soft smile fluttered to her lips.

'Sami.' His name was a whisper of joy.

'*Ya Allah,*' he cried in disbelief. '*Ya Allah, ya Rub, ya rasul.*'

He climbed into the ambulance and gathered Israa up.

Khattak left them with Rachel. Nate was calling his name.

At the door of the shed, he was holding Audrey in his arms. Khattak's steps faltered. Not from the moment he'd landed in Athens had he hoped for such a conclusion. His thoughts full of wonder, he found his way to his friends. Audrey threw her arms around his neck and kissed him soundly on the lips.

'You found me,' she said, whispering the words into his neck.

Esa hugged her close. 'It was Nate,' he told Audrey over the lump in his throat. 'Nate would never let you go.'

But in his heart he was saying, *All glory belongs to God.*

Mytilene, Lesvos

In the early morning, a series of interviews were conducted jointly by Amélie Roux and Philip Nicolaides, who'd suffered a concussion but was otherwise unhurt. Esa and Rachel were not asked to participate; Sehr had insisted on being present for Audrey's debriefing.

At the end of it, Audrey was released to Nate's care and given permission to leave the island. She would be required to testify in the case against the trafficking ring, and this she promised to do with a fervor that spoke of the agony of her ordeal. During that period, she'd been expecting Benemerito to kill her. Roux hadn't been as shocked to find Audrey and Israa alive. Girls were the most valuable of all commodities to traffickers, fetching high prices and generating revenue well into the future. In Audrey's case, there was the additional possibility of ransom. Esa tried not to think of what could have happened if their luck had broken differently. There were missing who were never recovered.

He was at the hospital with Rachel and Sami, waiting for an update on Israa's general health. Roux had told them up front that though Israa was suffering from malnutrition, she hadn't been abused. She was worth more to the traffickers untouched. Roux had promised to tell them more at a meeting later in the evening.

As Rachel kept Aya occupied with a game, Esa brought Sami up to date.

Mournfully, Sami said, 'Illario was my friend. He took me to Turkey to search for Israa. He solved the problems related to my papers.'

Esa sighed. This was easily the worst part of what he had to share.

'He was separating you from Aya, waiting for an opportunity to snatch her from the camp. He wasn't going to the beaches to help pull in the boats. He was marking out unaccompanied children, looking for those who wouldn't be missed. When he took you back to Turkey, he was making contact with the smugglers on the other side. And he was keeping an eye on your discoveries, seeing how far you'd get.'

'I know I should believe you,' Sami said. He knuckled his eyes like a child. 'I thought I'd seen the worst of what we do to each other in Syria, but this is just as ugly. What would have happened to Israa?'

Esa put his arm around Sami's shoulders. He wouldn't darken the boy's thoughts with the sordid truths he'd learned.

'She would have disappeared. We don't know anything beyond that.'

'Why was she still on Lesvos? Why didn't they sell her, if that's what they had planned?'

There was no scenario Sami hadn't envisioned for himself.

'Because of you, Sami. You notified Audrey the second Israa went missing, and once Audrey was involved, there was a spotlight on the operation. Interpol, Europol, the Greek police – look at what you started. Benemerito had to lie low until the traffickers could get Israa to the continent. She made the crossing from Izmir, she just didn't reach safety.'

Sami avoided his eyes. 'They had her for weeks. Did they –?'

'No,' Esa said at once. 'Israa wasn't harmed. She's going to be all right. And all of that is thanks to you. You were brave. More than that, you were unshakable in your faith.'

Sami swallowed noisily, leaning into Esa's shoulder, perhaps thinking of his brothers. Esa let him cry. When he'd composed himself, Sami asked, 'What will happen to us now? We're in the same position, except worse. The borders to Europe are closed. We'll have to return to Turkey.'

Esa smiled. 'You don't know Audrey if that's what you think will happen. You and Israa will be asked to testify against Benemerito. In exchange, Audrey will ensure that all three of you are granted asylum.'

Sami shot him a startled glance. 'In Germany?'

'No,' Khattak said. 'Where your sister is, Sami, in Canada. I think I understand why Dania said she didn't know you.'

Sami's eyelids lowered, as if he was debating what to say. In a toneless voice, he answered, 'She doesn't trust the authorities. She sold everything to secure Ahmed's release from Sednaya. He was nearly dead when they gave him back to her. When the Mukhabarat returned, Dania and Ahmed had already escaped. She had good reason to think they were hunting members of our family. If she admitted who I was, she thought she'd be passing a death sentence on me or on my brothers. She doesn't know I'm the only one left.'

Khattak had seen soul-wrenching ugliness over the course of his work. There was no scale by which to measure the depths of Sami's loss.

Damascus, the city of jasmine. Damascus, the city of ruin.

More to himself than Sami, he whispered, 'Israa is safe. So is your sister.'

They let a little time pass in silence. Then Sami asked, 'So this wasn't about the papers we smuggled out for CIJA? No one at Camp Apaydin was involved?'

Khattak shook his head, his dark hair falling across his brow. A pretty nurse with a startlingly voluptuous figure passed them in the hall. She turned and looked back at Khattak to give him a sexy wink. Sami laughed. It was the first time Khattak had heard the boy laugh.

'That must happen to you all the time,' he said.

Esa's smile was mischievous. 'It would be insufferable of me to agree.'

He considered the question about CIJA, thinking of how Amélie Roux had held the upper hand. 'This wasn't about CIJA, no. But for however long it takes to process your application for status in Canada, you're not going near the Turkish border. You have one job now, and that's to take care of Israa.'

Aya gave him a happy wave from the end of the hall. He waved back at her.

'And Aya,' he amended. He rose to his feet, looking at a boy whose suffering and loss he couldn't quantify. He wanted to find the right words, words of fellowship, of brotherhood, of sojourners on a common journey – he couldn't. No matter how he strove for empathy, this was a chasm he couldn't cross – a suffering he couldn't claim. So he said, 'Don't look back. There's nothing left for you in Syria.'

It was advice he couldn't have followed. A homeland was a place of the heart, a place of memory and belonging. To lose it, to leave, to watch it dissolve into agony, to be coerced into exile – it was a severing of self.

But wasn't he dissembling to say this to the boy? All these years, what had he been doing, except looking back? Looking away from the woman at his side, the woman who'd loved him all this time.

He nodded at Rachel, letting her know it was time to return to their hotel.

He needed to tell Sehr the truth, plainly and boldly.

He'd been hiding from himself.

42

Mytilene, Lesvos

IT WAS NATE AND AUDREY's last night on Lesvos. Rachel and Khattak were staying a few extra days to assist Amélie Roux. They were waiting for Roux now. Esa walked over to the hotel desk to make their arrangements. Rachel sat with Nate in front of the fire, absently tracking Khattak's conversation. Audrey was resting in her room.

Nate studied the bruising on Rachel's throat.

'I should have gone with you, I could have stopped Benemerito, but I was convinced that *I* would be the one to find Audrey.'

Something in his voice, in his way of holding himself apart, told Rachel the conversation wouldn't turn out the way she hoped. Though Audrey was safe, something had altered between them, and it wasn't because of something she'd done.

'Would you be willing to wait, Rachel?'

The elevator pinged. Audrey stepped out, looking fragile. Nate's demeanor changed – focused, bright, alert. Rachel felt like an obstacle to be dealt with, conscious of a dullness inside.

She was a fool. She'd put herself in this position, believing in something that would always be out of reach. She forced herself to face the truth: she'd wanted to try with Nate, she'd thought she'd found a way to ease her loneliness. To have someone see all the things she was. And not be able to endure without her.

His eyes on his sister, Nate said, 'We'll be caught up in this for months. The Greek police, CIJA, figuring out what to do about

337

our NGO – Audrey can't handle that alone. She's at risk until she testifies. So I hope you'll give me some time.'

Rachel couldn't fault him for what he'd said. She tried to ignore the warning that she was opening herself up to pain. Testing the waters, she said, 'I could help you, Nate. I'd be willing to take that on.'

She registered his impatience, knew he'd missed the significance of her words.

'You know how it is with family, Rachel. We're used to relying on ourselves.'

Rachel conceded the point. Where it mattered most, he couldn't see her as a part of his life. But how could she protest, given how she'd dealt with Zachary?

Lost in her painful thoughts, she let her gaze stray over to Khattak. He'd slept for eight hours straight, and now he seemed recovered.

Nate noticed her abstraction. Alarmed, he said, 'Rachel, I'm only asking for a little time. Please don't write me off.'

But she could see what it would be like. She was trying to alter course, to assert the worth of her presence. To deny her importance to someone else wasn't a pattern she intended to repeat. All her life, she'd accepted her mother's devotion to Zachary, the way she'd pushed Rachel aside. She knew what Nate was asking of her, she wouldn't do it again. She couldn't live on the margins of his life. She'd have time to think it through once she was back in Toronto. Right now, she needed to escape.

Watching her face, Nate sighed. 'It's Esa, isn't it? He's the one you want. I can't say I blame you.'

She heard the bitterness beneath the words – the echo of an estrangement that had nothing to do with her. She could see why he'd misunderstood. Her relationship with Khattak was complex, they hadn't unraveled its complexities themselves; she doubted others would understand what bound them.

But she hadn't fallen prey to Khattak's attraction, as she'd worried. In his dark shirt, with his *tasbih* wrapped over his wrist, he looked handsomer than ever. Rachel had ceased to notice. She'd come to understand the nature of her feelings. She was close to Khattak because of the way he'd treated her when she'd sought refuge from her boss's harassment. Khattak had delivered her from MacInerney by putting her on his team.

She hadn't known then that he'd asked for her, chosen her... *valued* her.

He'd treated her with kindness and continual respect. So she'd struggled with the idea that maybe his actions added up to love.

The part of herself that she hid from the world – the girl who'd grown up bullied by Don Getty, whose mother had loved her brother instead of her – that girl knew it did. And only because Esa had been so careful was she able to see that for herself.

She wasn't in love with Khattak. She didn't want to be his lover. What she wanted was what he'd given her: the sense that she belonged, that she was good and brave and valuable. That she mattered to someone like him.

Tears blurred Rachel's vision. There was no way on God's green earth she could say any of this to Nate. He wanted her to wait, but they'd never be at this place again, reaching for each other, trying to soldier through.

'Esa is a good person.' She used his name without constraint, wiping a hand across her eyes. 'I haven't had much of that, you know? That's really all it is.'

To Rachel that was everything.

Amélie Roux joined them in the garden. Only Khattak and Sehr abstained from taking a glass of ouzo as they gathered together around an outdoor brazier that lent a shimmering warmth to the night. Audrey was at the center of the group, triangular shadows under her eyes and in the hollows of her temples. She gave them the briefest summary of her ordeal, though Khattak guessed that she and Ruksh would speak of it for days and weeks to come.

He asked the question on everyone's minds. 'What happened that night in the tent?'

Audrey shrank down in her chair. Nate took her hand and held it. When she'd gained a measure of calm, Audrey began to speak.

'I'd spoken to the girl in the camp – the girl Benny tried to grab, the one who got away. From her description, I thought it was Benny, but I'd begun to suspect him long before. There was something about his reaction when I mentioned the counterfeit life vests. All I did was pass on a tip, but he seemed to suspect me of more. He was watching me. And then I began to wonder why a commander of the Italian Coast Guard was on the Greek islands so often. At the beach would have made sense, but why was he in the camps?' She took a moment to collect her thoughts, guilt shadowing her voice. 'I told Inspecteur Roux I was close to confirming the identity of the ringleaders of the gang, but I needed to be sure. She sent Agent Bertin to Lesvos to help me. Aude wanted to meet Sami but he was waiting for a boat, just in case Israa was on it. He sent Ali with me instead. Benny must have gotten wind of Aude Bertin's arrival.' Tears filled her eyes. 'He followed us, he must have eavesdropped on us. When he threatened Agent Bertin, I pulled out my gun.' She shook her head sorrowfully. 'I couldn't bring myself to use it. He got the gun away from me. The rest I think you know.'

She confirmed Khattak's guess that Aude Bertin had tried to protect Ali. And that Audrey had escaped, to be chased and captured at the beach. Since then, she'd been in the store house, where she'd also found Israa. Benemerito had delayed moving them until he was out of options. Roux's appearance on Lesvos had triggered his need to act. He'd been following Khattak, ascertaining his actions. He'd used the attack on Souda to break into the Woman to Woman tent and steal the life vests.

'There are many, many men involved in this operation,' Roux told them. 'On the Turkish side, in Greece. And throughout the continent – Germany, France, the UK. If we break Benemerito, we'll make significant progress in shutting down this ring.'

'He hasn't confessed?' Khattak asked.

He knew Roux was thinking of Aude Bertin when she promised, 'He will.'

When Benemerito had spat at Rachel, rage had swamped Khattak's thoughts. And knowing Benemerito had struck Sehr – he had some sense of what Amélie was feeling.

Roux summoned the waiter for another glass of ouzo. She took a sip before she turned to Sehr.

'The trouble you experienced, the obstruction on the islands and in Athens.'

Sehr raised her eyebrows and waited.

'Yannis Andreadis, Nikos Papadakis at the Athena, the German medic, Hans. The Golden Dawn ringleaders who raided Souda camp. They're all members of the ring. We think Benemerito was the one in charge, though we can't say for sure.'

'What about Captain Nicolaides? Or Peter Conroy? Or Eleni?' Khattak had wondered about each one.

Roux shook her head. 'They have been vetted. They are not involved.'

'And Vincenzo?' Rachel asked Audrey. 'What part did he play in all this? Did he get cold feet at the end?'

Wonderingly, Audrey shook her head. 'He's a member of the Coast Guard. Benny acting outside his purview made Vincenzo suspicious. When he confronted Benny, Benny threatened his family. Vincenzo came to me because he could see I was figuring it out. He told me we had to catch Benny in the act, or the members of the ring would go to ground. He knew Benny was watching him. He also knew he wouldn't get another chance. Last night was his moment.'

She didn't discuss the toll the waiting had taken on her, and Khattak knew better than to ask.

'I want to see Sami,' Audrey said. 'I want to see Sami *and* Israa.'

'*I'm* here, Audrey,' Sehr promised. 'I won't leave Lesvos without them.'

Esa glanced over at her. He hadn't known Sehr was planning to stay on Lesvos.

When their party broke up, Esa asked Sehr to remain, conscious of her remoteness. Why she'd withdrawn, he didn't know. It could have been the things he'd said to her on the hill, or his reference, obliquely, to Samina. Maybe she felt excluded from his thoughts. He couldn't blame her if she did.

Gently, he said, 'I'm sorry about what happened yesterday. How are you feeling now?'

The left side of her face was bruised. Ignoring the question, she asked, 'Which part?'

He hesitated, wondering if she was angry at his insistence that she remain behind. She couldn't know what he'd thought when the car had come so close to clipping her. Or when he'd heard the sounds of her struggle in the shed. He never wanted to feel that kind of terror again.

He could see the car burn. He could see his wife dying inside it. To face that with Sehr –

Unsure of himself now, he said, 'I don't know what you mean.'

She looked away from him, her profile pensive. 'Which part are you sorry for, Esa? That I didn't leave you on your own, or that I got in the way of your attempt to save Rachel?' She shook her head to herself. 'I didn't get in the way, though. You knew what mattered to you.'

It took him a minute to understand. Then he was swamped by a sense of relief that opened his eyes to the truth. She didn't know what she meant to him because he'd been too cowardly to speak. He rose to his feet, pulling her into his arms. She stood there without moving, without reaching for him in turn, resistance etched into her limbs.

'Is that what you thought?' he asked. 'That I wouldn't choose you, if I had a choice to make? I overheard Vincenzo's plan, I

342

knew he wasn't going to hurt you. That's why I went after Rachel.'

'Why should I believe you? You've never thought of me.'

He muttered a protest against things he couldn't deny – knowledge that had come too late.

'God knows that's been true, Sehr. It isn't anymore. It won't be from this day forward.'

'What you said to me about Samina, what you *did* – I can't face that over Rachel.' The words were quiet, masking the effort it took to say them.

But he knew what he'd done – he grasped the distance that stretched from Samina's grave to this garden. He'd been given this moment to speak. He wouldn't be granted another.

Now he didn't hesitate, starkly aware of his need.

'I won't deny that I care about Rachel, but she isn't who I want, Sehr. I'm done pretending now.'

Carefully, he traced her cheek. His fingers strayed to her lips. The brilliant light in her eyes pierced him all the way through. Did he imagine the call to prayer? Or was he simply reverent, grateful for this unforeseen moment? And for what they might one day be.

'What were you pretending?' she asked.

'Not to love you,' he answered.

Author's Note

Though this is a novel that focuses on the Syrian refugee crisis, the crisis cannot be properly understood without situating it in the context of the ongoing war in Syria, begun in 2011. The war is often described as a complex conflict whose origins are unclear and whose peaceful resolution is unlikely in the near future. At the time of writing in fall 2017, the death toll of the war in Syria was 465,000, with 11 million Syrians displaced as a consequence of the war (5 million as refugees, another 6 million internally displaced). The refugee crisis is ongoing, with the Syrian diaspora mainly dispersed across the Middle East and Europe.

The conflict has been driven by a specific set of social and political conditions, beginning with the Arab Spring revolutions of 2011 in Tunisia and Egypt. The Arab Spring reignited the aspirations of the Syrian people for political freedom and socioeconomic well-being. Until that moment, the House of Assad had ruled Syria with an iron fist for forty-one years: a rule synonymous with widespread political repression, crony capitalism and corruption, flagrant human rights violations, periods of mass killing and destruction, and a prison system comparable to the Russian gulags.

A small spark lit the blaze in Syria: schoolboys in Daraa (Deraa) scrawled graffiti in support of the Arab Spring, and were arrested and tortured for doing so. Peaceful protests broke out in response, demanding the release of the boys, one of whom was killed in detention. The government responded to the unrest with force, killing and detaining hundreds, triggering nationwide protests calling for reform and the freeing of political prisoners. As the government's repression increased, so did the demands of the protesters, leading to a call for the resignation of Syrian president Bashar al-Assad.

During the first year of the uprising, protests were overwhelmingly non-violent and non-sectarian in nature. One year later, all of the major human rights organizations – including Human Rights Watch, Amnesty International, and the UN Special Commission of Inquiry on Syria – had charged the Assad regime with war crimes and crimes against humanity. The door to mass violence had been opened. When the conflict entered its second year, it became militarized and then increasingly radicalized as hundreds of rebel groups formed to fight the Assad regime. Many of these groups were backed by regional powers, each with an agenda of its own. Saudi Arabia and its allies were on one side of the conflict supporting various groups, while Iran and its allies backed the Syrian regime.

As the level of violence in Syria intensified, culminating in the use of chemical weapons, extremist rebel groups affiliated with Al-Qaeda emerged, becoming key players in the conflict. It is in this context that ISIS, the so-called Islamic State of Iraq and Syria, first evolved. Initially, ISIS fighters broke away from the major Al-Qaeda faction in Syria and established links with the remnants of Al-Qaeda in Iraq. In time, they became a separate group that rapidly expanded its area of influence and control in eastern Syria, establishing a de facto capital in the city of Raqqa. One of the defining characteristics of ISIS has been its extreme brutality toward its perceived enemies, among them foreign journalists and aid workers. Especially heinous is ISIS's treatment of Shia Muslims, Yazidis, Christians, ethnic minorities, and women. The ultimate goal of the group is the establishment of an ISIS-defined caliphate throughout the Islamic world. The rise of ISIS is a by-product of the war in Syria and has reinforced Assad's narrative that the choice in Syria is between the continuation of his rule or that of radical extremist groups like ISIS.

There is also an international dimension to the conflict, with the United States and Europe on one side, and Russia and China on the other. As a result of divisions among the international community, the United Nations Security Council has been paralyzed in terms of an effective response to the mass violence against civilians in Syria. Russia's role has been significant. From 2011 to 2017, Russia cast its veto on the UN Security Council ten times to block an international resolution of the crisis. Then in 2015, Russia's military directly intervened in the conflict, tilting the balance of power in Assad's favor and deepening the humanitarian crisis on an unprecedented scale, as embodied by the destruction of Aleppo, Syria's second-largest city.

When the conflict began, President Obama called for Assad to step down; yet American policy has been largely non-interventionist, ceding Russia and Iran effective control of the war in Syria. With a new administration in the United States, there has been no change in US policy on Syria: the focus remains on defeating ISIS, without attempting to address the roots of the Syrian crisis or the war crimes and crimes against humanity perpetrated by the Assad regime.

While there is no disputing that all parties have committed atrocities in Syria, in terms of scale and proportion, it is the Assad regime that is overwhelmingly responsible for crimes against civilians. According to the Violations Documentations Center in Syria, between March 2011 and September 2016, the Syrian government was responsible for 90 percent of civilian deaths during the conflict. Aided by Russia, the Syrian government has targeted hospitals, clinics, schools, and civilian population centers with a wide range of weaponry: barrel bombs, cluster munitions, mortars and artillery, and chemical weapons that have included chlorine and sarin gas. Beyond this, the opaque and labyrinthine prison system overseen by the Assad regime has been cited as carrying out killing and torture on an industrial scale that amounts to extermination. In Saydnaya (Sednaya), a prison near Damascus, thirteen thousand political detainees were executed in the period between 2011 and 2015.

With the conflict in its seventh year, the tide of the war has turned in Assad's favor. Some international players see this as a development that could lead to peace and stability in Syria. But in light of the regime's devastating human rights record, Assad cannot be seen as a guarantor of the hopes and aspirations of the Syrian people for dignity and political freedom.

Recommended Reading

For background on the Syrian conflict, I recommend the following works: *Syria* by Samer N Abboud, *Burning Country: Syrians in Revolution and War* by Robin Yassin-Kassab and Leila Al-Shami, *The Syrian Jihad: Al-Qaeda, the Islamic State and the Evolution of an Insurgency* by Charles Lister, and *The Impossible Revolution: Making Sense of the Syrian Tragedy* by Yassin al-Haj Saleh.

For more personal works, I suggest *The Home That Was Our Country: A Memoir of Syria* by Alia Malek; *We Crossed a Bridge and It Trembled: Voices from Syria* by Wendy Pearlman; *Syria Speaks: Art and Culture from the Frontline,* edited by Malu Halasa, Zaher Omareen, and Nawara Mahfoud; and *The Morning They Came for Us* by Janine di Giovanni.

Human rights reports on the Syrian conflict are also widely available. Independent International Commission of Inquiry on the Syrian Arab Republic:

www.ohchr.org/EN/HRBodies/HRC/IICISyria/Pages/IndependentInternationalCommission.aspx

Violations Documentation Center in Syria: http://vdc-sy.net/en/

Amnesty International, 2017. *Human Slaughterhouse: Mass hangings and extermination at Saydnaya Prison, Syria*:

https://www.amnestyusa.org/files/human_slaughterhouse.pdf

Human Rights Watch, 2015. *If the Dead Could Speak: Mass Deaths and Torture in Syria's Detention Facilities*:

https://www.hrw.org/report/2015/12/16/if-dead-could-speak/mass-deaths-and-torture-syrias-detention-facilities

Human Rights Watch, 2012. *Torture Archipelago: Arbitrary Arrests, Torture and Enforced Disappearances in Syria's Underground Prisons Since March 2011*:

https://www.hrw.org/report/2012/07/03/torture-archipelago/arbitrary-arrests-torture-and-enforced-disappearances-syrias

Human Rights Watch, 2011. *By All Means Necessary: Individual and Command Responsibility for Crimes Against Humanity in Syria*:

https://www.hrw.org/sites/default/files/reports/syria1211webwcover_0.pdf

For updates on the Syrian refugee crisis, please visit the UNHCR's Syria homepage at: http://www.unhcr.org/sy/.

Acknowledgments

In many ways, this book is a continuation of the themes of *Among the Ruins,* the previous book in the Esa Khattak/Rachel Getty series. Both books examine the impact of authoritarian rule on civil society and both interrogate the plight of political detainees, though the crisis in Syria is by every measure worse. To fully appreciate how, I interviewed people concerned with several different aspects of it: refugees from the war, government and NGO employees, resettlement workers, sponsorship agreement holders, Middle East analysts, journalists and lawyers, and those who traveled to the Greek islands to volunteer. Many of the people I consulted must remain fully or partially anonymous, but they have my unceasing gratitude for contributing so much to my understanding of the war and the critical plight of refugees.

This was a difficult book to write. I couldn't have written it without their support, and without their willingness to speak about deeply painful issues. To the people of Syria, may the lost and beloved country be restored, and may there be an accounting one day.

To Rawan and AbdelKader, for your immense bravery and generosity in speaking to me about your family's journey to Canada, my deepest gratitude. Your thoughts are the heart of this book, and I pray for your family's safety.

To Brenda H – how can I begin to express my admiration of the work that you and your group of women do? I'm so grateful for the time you spared me, and so moved by the compassion and commitment of your example.

To my wonderful new friends, Rim-Sarah Alouane and Emilie Gascon-Léger, thank you so much for help with the French language and French names, and for your encouragement with the writing of this book. To Dr Terri Sands, thank you for your very kind help with Greek customs and the Greek language, and for answering my questions. Thank you to my dear friend Farah Bukhari for facilitating this discussion for me. Thank you to the brilliant Negin Sobhani for educating me about the work of volunteers on the islands, and for your own commitment.

To my very old friend Yara Masri, who knows the pain of impassable borders far better than I do; thank you for your help with Syrian names and with the Arabic language.

Thank you to one of the most amazing women I know, Dr Nozhat Choudry, for arranging such an important interview for me, and for your endless compassion. Thank you to my beloved Summer for sitting in on the discussion and taking it to heart.

Thank you to my dear friends Uzma Jalaluddin and Sajidah Kutty, for talking over the many agonies of this book with me, and for helping me steer Esa in the right direction. You truly are my sisterhood of the pen.

Thank you to my lion-hearted husband, Nader, for those long discussions about Syria, for all that you contributed to this book – and for everything you do, always. Your courage helps me find a little of my own.

Thank you to my incomparable family and friends for your continual encouragement and support. I don't know what I'd do without you. And thank you to a truly amazing and selfless community of writers and readers with whom I've found a home. I wish I could name you all, but I do most sincerely thank you.

To the many wonderful people at Minotaur Books and the Nelson Literary Agency, thank you for everything you do to support my books and bring them into the world. To Hector and Kristin, especially, thank you so much for being there. And thank you so much to Catherine Richards and Nettie Finn for joining me on this journey.

To all my friends at No Exit Press/Oldcastle Books who have taken Esa and Rachel to their hearts – Geoff, Ion, Katherine, Claire, and especially the brilliant and lovely Clare Quinlivan – thank you for everything you do for me and these books, and for your hospitality. Thank you also to all the wonderful booksellers, bloggers, readers, and writers in the UK for an exceptional book tour, especially to Sue and Katherine.

To the beautiful and boundlessly talented Danielle, for the many ways you helped me write this book, for your unceasing patience with a year of difficult questions, and for how often you reassured me when I couldn't find my way – my gratitude is endless.

And finally, to Elizabeth, to whom I owe more than I'm able to express. Thank you for being such a gifted and luminous editor, and for being the kindest, wisest partner I could have asked for on this journey. Thank you for valuing Esa's voice and mine.